Gingerly, Gabria picked up the gem and held it up to the light from the hall's entrance. The jewel tingled between her fingers. She looked into the gem's brilliant, scintillating interior and wondered if this strange pulse was caused by magic. The gem had come from Medb, so it was possible that he had put a spell on it.

The thought of Medb's magic frightened her. She was about to drop the jewel back on the fur when suddenly an image began to form in the center of the stone. Gabria watched, horrified, as the image wavered, then coalesced into an eye.

Not a simple human eye, but a dark orb of piercing intensity that stared into the distance with malicious intelligence. Gabria shuddered. The eye's pupil was dilated. Looking into its center felt like falling into a bottomless hole.

"Put the stone down!" a voice cried.

Gabria leaped back, startled out of her wits. The image vanished. The gem fell out of her hands, bounced off the stone step, and rolled to Savaric's feet.

The chieftain had just entered the hall, and it was he who had shouted at Gabria. The gem, a present to him from Lord Medb, was very valuable; a member of his werod had no business examining it without his permission. Without another word, Savaric bent over to pick it up.

"No," Gabria cried abruptly. "Don't touch it."

Other  **Books**

Dark Horse

Mary H. Herbert

Cover Art
FRED FIELDS

TSR, Inc.

DARK HORSE

This book is protected under the copyright laws of the United States of America. Any reproduction or other unauthorized use of the material or artwork contained herein is prohibited without the express written permission of TSR, Inc.

Distributed to the book trade in the United States by Random House, Inc. and in Canada by Random House of Canada, Ltd.

Distributed in the United Kingdom by TSR UK Ltd.

Distributed to the toy and hobby trade by regional distributors.

DRAGONLANCE is a registered trademark owned by TSR, Inc. FORGOTTEN REALMS is a trademark owned by TSR, Inc. TM designates other trademarks owned by TSR, Inc.

First Printing, January, 1990
Printed in the United States of America.
Library of Congress Catalog Card Number: 89-52091

9 8 7 6 5 4 3 2 1

ISBN: 0-88038-916-8
All characters in this book are fictitious. Any resemblance to actual persons, living or dead, is purely coincidental.

TSR, Inc.   TSR Ltd.
P.O. Box 756   120 Church End, Cherry Hinton
Lake Geneva, WI 53147   Cambridge CB1 3LB
U.S.A.   United Kingdom

For Keith. You really earned this!

Dark Horse Plains

Murjik Treld

Amnok
Treld

Five
Kingdoms

Geldring Treld

Citadel of Krath

Corin Treld

Bahedin Treld

Ab-Chakan

Pra Desh

Calah

Dangari Treld

Reidhar
Treld

Sea

Darkhorn Mtns.

Himachal Mtns.

Wolfeared Pass

Isin River

Jehanan
Treld

of

Tannis

Goldrine River

Tir Samod

Marakor

Khulinin Treld

Marshes

Wylfling Treld

Shadedron Treld

Turic Lands

Altai River

Ferganan Treld

1

abria paused and leaned wearily against her walking staff. She could not go on much longer like this. Her ankle ached from a bad fall and her shoulders were rubbed raw by the unaccustomed pack. The wind, which blew cold from the icy passes of the mountains, cut through her woolen cloak and chilled her to the bone. She had not eaten since fleeing from her home at Corin Treld two days before.

The girl sat down on a rock and threw her pack to the ground. There was some dried meat and trail bread in the old pack, but Gabria had no idea how much longer she would have to walk and food was difficult to find on the plains this early in the spring. It was better to save her rations until she was desperate. At any rate, she had no desire for food now. Her body was too numb with grief and despair.

Gabria wearily examined her boots. The soles were almost worn through from the sharp shale she had struggled over. Ragged boots, the sign of an exile. Her breath suddenly caught in her throat and, for a moment, she nearly surrendered to the anguish that tore at her resolve like starving vultures. No! she cried silently. I cannot weep. Not yet.

Gabria pounded her knee with her fist while her other hand convulsively gripped the short sword at her belt. Her body trembled violently as she fought to regain control of her despair. There was no time for grief now. Nor did she have the strength to waste on self-pity. Her family and her clan had been massacred at their winter camp at Corin Treld. She was the only one left to claim their weir-geld, recompense for the blood of her family that stained the grass of their home. She would seek her revenge and then she could weep.

Gabria closed her mind to all but her grim resolve. It was the only way she could survive. It gave her a strength and a purpose in the face of a debilitating loneliness and fear. She was an exile now and therefore dead to her people unless another clan accepted her. She was a wanderer and an untouchable. Somehow, she had to find a clan that would take her in. Somehow, she would claim her vengeance.

Slowly her trembling eased and the emotions that threatened to devour her were forced into a deep prison. She remembered that her father had once told her that strong emotions were a power to be harnessed and used like a weapon. She stood up and smiled a feral grimace, like the snarl of a wolf. To the north, the direction from which she had come, a line of clouds lay along the horizon. It seemed to her that a pall of smoke still hung over her home.

"My grief for you will be used, Father," Gabria said aloud. "Our enemy will die."

Out of habit, she reached up to brush a strand of flaxen hair out of her face, only to touch the rough-cut stubble on her head. The girl sighed, remembering the pain she had felt when she had cut her hair and burned it with the bodies of her four brothers, including her twin, Gabran. Her brothers had been so proud of her long, thick hair. But she gave it to them as a gift of mourning and in return she took her twin's identity. His clothes now covered her body and his weapons were in her hand. She would no longer be a girl. For the sake of survival, she would become a boy, Gabran.

It was clan law that no woman could claim weir-geld alone; she had to be championed by a male member of her family. To make matters worse for Gabria, the clans usually did not accept an exiled woman unless she was of exceptional beauty or talent. Gabria knew she had little chance of being accepted on her own merits. On the other hand, she was slim and strong and had been raised with four boisterous boys who often forgot she was only a girl. With luck and careful attention, she thought she could pass well enough as a boy. The deception could bring her death, but it could also give her a greater chance for survival and revenge.

Ignoring the jab of pain in her ankle, Gabria shouldered her pack once more and limped southward across the hillside. She was in the Hornguard, the low, barren foothills that lay like a crumpled robe at the foot of the Darkhorn Mountains. Somewhere in one of the sheltered valleys to the south, she hoped to find the Khulinin, her mother's clan, led by Lord Savaric. She hoped her kinship with the Khulinin would overcome the stigma of exile. Gabria prayed it would, for even driven by the strength of her desire for revenge, she knew she would not be able to go far. The Khulinin were still many days distant and either her twisted ankle or her food would fail long before she could find another clan.

Gabria hurried on, forcing her legs to move. It was almost twilight and she wanted to find shelter before dark.

Then, above the wind, she heard the howling of wolves. Hungry and insistent, the cries sang through the dusk like wild music. Gabria shuddered and gripped her staff tighter as the feral hunting calls sounded again. The wolves were not after her, she realized. They were upwind of her and deeper in the hills. Still, that was too close. Alone and virtually defenseless against a pack, Gabria had no desire to meet the vicious marauders. She stopped and listened, following the progress of the hunt.

The howling continued for several minutes. The animals were moving south, running parallel to her. Then the cries grew louder, for whatever the wolves were chasing seemed to be trying to reach the open ground of the plains. Gabria tensed and her eyes searched the hills for the approaching pack. But the howling stopped abruptly, and the wolves broke into yowls of glee and triumph. The girl sighed with relief. The wolves had caught their prey and would not hunt again for a while.

She was about to move on when she heard another sound that froze her heart: the enraged squeal of an embattled horse. "Oh, Mother of All," she breathed. "No!"

Before she could consider her choices, she limped toward the sound even as the echoes faded. The howling burst out, sharp

with rage and frustration. Gabria ran faster, forcing her sore
legs to navigate the rugged, brush-covered hillsides, while the
pain stabbed through her ankle and the heavy pack slammed
against her back. She knew it was utterly stupid to think of
challenging a pack of killers for their chosen prey, but this prey
was different. Horses were special to her, to all her people.
They were the very existence of the clans, the chosen of the
goddess, Amara, and the children of the plains. No clansman
ever turned his back on a horse, no matter what the danger.

The yowling abruptly increased and the horse's screams took
on a note of fury and desperation. Gabria pushed on until her
breath came in ragged gasps and her legs were heavy with pain.
For a moment, she despaired reaching the stricken horse before
it was brought down. The sounds became louder, but the distance seemed so much greater than she had expected. She
dropped her pack, then pulled off her cloak and wrapped it
around her arm as she ran.

Suddenly the sounds ceased. Gabria faltered when she lost
the guidance of the cries. She stopped and listened again, trying to locate the attack. The wind whistled around her, carrying the smell of an old winter as the hills dimmed in the
approaching night. Beyond the grasslands, the full moon was
rising.

"Oh, Mother," Gabria gasped. "Where are they?"

As if in answer to her plea, another furious squeal came out
of the growing darkness and the howling rose in response. This
time, the sounds were quite close, perhaps in the next valley.

Breathing a silent prayer of thanks, Gabria broke into a run.
She topped one hill, plunged into a valley, and toiled up the
next slope. At the crest she stopped and peered down the hill.
The land at her feet sheered off into a deep gully between three
hills, where several run-offs emptied into a bowl-like depression. After the last thaw, melted snow had gathered in the center, creating a pool of mud and standing water rimmed with
ice.

In the midst of the pool, now churned to a filthy mire, stood
a huge horse, very angry and very much alive. Gabria's eyes
widened in astonishment and excitement when she recognized

the animal. It was a Hunnuli, the greatest of all the horse breeds. They were the legendary steeds of the ancient magic-wielders, and, even though their masters had been destroyed by hate and jealousy, the horses themselves were revered above all others. Their numbers were few and wild, and when they deigned to be ridden, they only accepted the men of the clans. It was said that the first Hunnuli was sired by a storm on the first mare of the world; a streak of lightning was left indelibly printed on their descendants' shoulders to prove it.

Gabria had never seen one of these magnificent animals before, but there was no mistaking this was a Hunnuli. Even in the twilight, Gabria could see the jagged white streak that marked the black hide at its shoulder. She simply could not believe one of those horses had been brought to bay by eight or nine wolves.

She moved behind a scrub pine to where she could see without being detected. The wolves were still there, slinking around the edge of the mire and keeping their distance from the wicked teeth of the horse. The horse itself was obviously exhausted, and steam rose from its heaving flanks.

Suddenly the Hunnuli lunged, squealing in fury as it tried to lash out at a sneaking wolf. The girl knew then why the horse had not run, for it was trapped in the clinging mud. Its back legs were sunk to the haunches in the freezing mire and its front legs pawed desperately for purchase on the slippery edge of the pool. It could only use its teeth to fight the wolves for fear of sinking deeper into the mud.

The horse settled back warily and snorted. Two wolves then made a feint for the horse's head to draw its attention while a third leaped from behind to slash at the unprotected tendons in the horse's back legs.

Gabria screamed and the horse whipped its head around and slammed the leaping wolf into the mire. Like a snake, the Hunnuli flung back and snapped viciously at the other two beasts. One wolf screeched in agony and fell back with its leg hanging in bloody splinters. The second was more successful. It caught the horse by the neck and left a gaping slash dangerously close to the jugular. The other wolves yipped and snarled.

Gabria's mouth went dry and her legs were shaking. She wished fervently for her bow and some arrows to bring down the wolves, but the bow lay in the ashes of her tent, and she did not trust her skill with the sword that hung by her side. All she had was her staff. She hefted it and swallowed hard. If she waited to think any longer, all would be lost. The horse was weakening rapidly and the wolves were growing bolder.

With a wild yell, the girl sprinted down the slope, lurching on her injured ankle. The wolves whirled in surprise to face this new threat and the horse neighed another challenge. Before the hunters realized their danger, Gabria was upon them, swinging her staff like a scythe. The wolves snapped and lunged at her, and she fought them back with a strength born of desperation. One wolf fell, its back broken. Another lay whimpering with smashed ribs. A third leaped away and was caught by the teeth of the great horse, which flung it high in the air. Using her cloak as a guard for her arm and her staff like a double-edged sword, Gabria drove the wolves away from the pool. At the foot of the enclosing hills, they broke and ran.

Gabria watched them disappear over the rim of the hill, then she turned to gaze with some surprise at the bodies lying in the gully. Something seemed to snap inside her and she sagged on her staff, feeling utterly exhausted and aching from head to toe. She stood there for a while, panting for breath, sweating and trembling with dizziness.

The girl glanced blearily at the wild horse and wondered what to do next. The big animal stood immobile and watched her quietly. She was relieved to see its ears were swiveled toward her rather than flattened on its head. The horse seemed to realize she was not an enemy.

The evening had dimmed to night and the full moon swelled above the plains; its silver light flooded into the gully and gleamed on the standing water. Gabria limped to the edge of the mudhole and sat down to rest while she studied the horse. Even mired in the mud, she could see the animal was enormous. It probably stood about eighteen hands at the shoulder, and Gabria mentally cringed at the thought of moving such a massive animal out of its trap. Yet she obviously could not leave the Hunnuli. The wolves could return and the horse was in no condition to free itself. Somehow she would have to devise a way to free it. But how? She had no tools, no rope, and very little strength. Of course, its size gave the Hunnuli incredible power, but if it struggled too much against the heavy mud it would wear itself into deadly exhaustion.

The girl shook her head. At least the horse did not appear to be sinking deeper. Gabria hoped that meant the ground was frozen below the mud and would support the horse through the night. There was nothing more she could do now. She was too weary, beyond thought and beyond effort, to do anything else that night.

Gabria stood up, feeling slightly better, and walked slowly around the pool. She stared at the horse, her face wrinkled in a frown. There was something odd about this horse that she could not quite discern in the moonlight. Its glossy black hide was filthy with muck, and blood oozed from the gash on its neck, making a slick rivulet down its withers. But the blood was not the problem. There was something else . . . something unusual for a seemingly healthy horse. Then she realized what it was.

Oh, no, Gabria thought. So that is why the Hunnuli was trapped so easily. She is a mare and heavy with foal.

There was no alternative now. Gabria knew she would have to extricate the Hunnuli or die trying. She glanced up at the horse's head and saw the mare staring intently at her. Their eyes met and the meeting was so intense Gabria was rocked back on her heels. Never had she seen such eyes in any creature. They were like orbs of illuminated night, sparkling with starlight and brimming with incredible intelligence. They were gazing at her with a mixture of surprise, suspicion, and an almost human glint of impatience.

"How did *you* get caught like this?" Gabria breathed softly, her voice mingled with awe.

The mare snorted in disgust.

"I'm sorry, it was unfair of me to ask. I'm going to find firewood. I'll return."

It was normal for her to talk to a horse like another human

being, but this time the girl had the oddest feeling the mare
understood.

Gabria put her cloak around her shoulders, for the air was
turning bitterly cold, and went to find her pack. She found a
dead tree on her way back and broke off enough wood to last
the night. As an afterthought, she dragged the dead wolves
out of the gully and left them downwind of her camp.

She lit a small fire in the shelter of the cliff wall, where the
horse could see her, and set most of the fuel aside for an emer-
gency. There was only stale bread and dried meat for a meal,
but Gabria ate it gratefully. For the first time since she fled the
devastation at Corin Treld, she was hungry.

She sat silently for a while, staring at the horse. In the darkness, it loomed as an even darker obscurity on the edge of the
firelight. Every now and then it would shift slightly and the
flames would reflect in its eyes. Gabria shuddered. The blackness in her mind began to creep insidiously over her thoughts.
Fires licked in her memory and the phantoms of things remembered grew out of the shadows. The flames rose and fell and
ran with blood. There was blood everywhere. Her hands, her
clothes, and even her scarlet cloak was stained with blood and
reeked of death.

The girl stared at her hands, at the stains she could not remove. Her hands would never be clean. She frantically wiped
her palms on her leggings and moaned like a wounded animal.
The tears burned in her head, but her eyes remained dry as she
stared glassily at the ground. Her shoulders shook with silent
sobs.

"Father, I'm sorry," she cried. Above her, the moon followed its unseeing path and a damp, chill wind swept through
the hills. Beyond the gully came the sounds of bickering wolves
from where they were tearing at the bodies of their dead.

After a long while, the fire died down and the phantoms
faded from Gabria's mind. Moving like an old woman, she
stoked the fire, then curled up in her cloak. She fell asleep,
borne under by the weight of utter exhaustion.

*   *   *   *   *

A horse neighed, strident and demanding, above the hoof-beats that thundered over the frozen ground. Half-seen forms of mounted men careened past to set their torches to the felt tents. Swords flashed in the rising flames as the attackers cut down the people, and scream after scream reverberated in the mist, until they blended into one agonized wail.

Gabria started awake, her heart pounding as the cry died on her lips. She clutched her cloak tighter and shivered at the dream that still clouded her thoughts. A horse neighed again, angrily. The unexpected sound dispelled the nightmare and brought the girl fully awake. This sound was no dream. She stiffly sat up and blinked at the Hunnuli. The mare was watching her with obvious impatience. Gabria realized the sun was already riding above the plains, though its warming light had not yet dipped into the gully. The chill of the night still clung to shadows, and frost flowered everywhere, even on the mud-encrusted mane of the trapped mare.

Gabria sighed, grateful the night was gone and the wolves had not attacked again. With infinite care, she eased to her feet, convinced she would shatter at any moment. Every muscle felt as if it were petrified.

"I'm sorry," she said to the horse. "I did not mean to sleep so long. But I feel better." She gently stretched to work out the kinks in her joints. "Perhaps I can help you now."

The mare whinnied as if to say "I should think so," and a wisp of a smile drifted over the girl's face. For a moment the smile lit her pale green eyes, then it was gone and the pain that had dulled her expression for three days returned.

Sitting by a newly built fire, Gabria emptied her pack onto the ground. There was very little in it that would help her to dig a gigantic horse out of the mud trap: only a bag of food, a few pots of salve, a dagger of fine steel that had been her father's prized possession, an extra tunic, and a few odds and ends she had salvaged from her family's burned tent. At the moment, she would have traded it all for a stout length of rope and a digging tool.

She sat for a time, totally at a loss over what to do next. Finally, she walked around the pool and considered every possibility, while the mare kept a cautious eye on her. In the daylight, Gabria could see the mare had none of the fine-boned grace of the Harachan horses Gabria was accustomed to. The Hunnuli's head was small in comparison to her immense neck, which curved down regally to a wide back. Her chest was broad and muscular and her shoulders were an image of power. There was granite in her bones, steel in her muscles, and fire in her blood.

"Well," said Gabria at last, hands on hips. "There's only one thing I can think of now. Food."

She laid the contents of her pack on her cloak, rolled it up, and set it aside. Then, with her knife and empty pack, she went in search of grass. On the hilltop she paused to watch the sun climb the flawless sky. It was going to be a lovely day despite the early season. The wind had died, and a fresh smell of new growth rose from the warming land. A few patches of stubborn snow clung to the sheltered hillsides, but most of the winter's snowfall was gone.

Before her the foothills fell away into the valley of the Hornguard, a broad, lush river valley and the favorite wintering place of her rival clan, the Geldring. The land rose again beyond the river's domain into the Himachal Mountains. The small range of rugged peaks sat like an afterthought in the midst of the grasslands. From their feet the vast steppeland of Ramtharin flowed for leagues to the seas of the eastern kings. This was the land of the twelve clans of Valorian and the realm of the Harachan horses, the fleet, smaller cousins of the Hunnuli. The steppes were hot in the summer, cold in the winter, dry most of the year, and merciless to those who did not respect them. They offered little to a people beyond the wind and the immense solitude of their rolling hills, but their grass was rich and the polished dome of the sky was a greater treasure to the clans than all the palaces of the east.

Behind Gabria, the mountains of Darkhorn marched south, then bent away to the west. Somewhere beyond the curve was the valley of the Goldrine River and the Khulinin clan's winter encampment. She looked southward, hoping to see something that would encourage her, but the landmarks she knew were lost in the purple haze. She bit her lip, thinking of the miles she still had to travel, and bent to her task.

Gabria soon had a pack full of dried grass for the mare and a few half-frozen winterberries for herself. Although the fare was meager for a horse of that size, the old prairie grass was well cured by last year's summer sun and was rich enough. The Hunnuli would survive for a while.

The horse was watching intently for the girl to return and greeted Gabria with a resounding neigh.

"This is all I have for now," Gabria told her. "I will bring more later." Cautiously she laid the grass within reach of the horse. The mare tore voraciously at the proffered food, bobbing her head in her efforts to swallow quickly.

Meanwhile, Gabria tried to decide what to do next. She examined every possibility that came to mind no matter how ridiculous, but there seemed to be only one hopeful course—and the very idea of that nearly defeated her. She would have to dig the mare out.

Fortunately, the standing water had run off during the night, leaving only the deep, thick mire. The properties that made the mud so treacherous might help her in its removal. It was so thick, it stuck everywhere. Nevertheless, if the Hunnuli thrashed about or tried to fight her off, it would be impossible to get close enough to do anything.

Gabria shrugged and picked up her empty pack. She could only hope the mare would understand her attempts to help. She walked up one of the eroded stream beds that ran into the gully and soon found what she needed. There was an abundance of loose gravel and broken shale lying in bars along the dry bed. Quickly the girl filled her pack and returned to the pool. After several trips, she had a large pile of rock close to the mudhole.

Next, she went to collect broken branches, fallen logs, twigs, dead scrub, and anything that would suit her plan. In a nearby stand of pine, she cut boughs of springy needles and hauled them to the growing heap. Finally, she was ready.

Panting slightly, she spoke to the mare. "I know I have not earned the privilege to be your friend," she said. "But you

must trust me. I am going to dig you out and I cannot spend
my time avoiding your teeth."

The Hunnuli dipped her head and snorted. Taking that as a
positive sign, Gabria eased to the mare's front legs and
watched the ears that flicked toward her. The mare remained
still; her ears stayed perked.

Gabria knelt in front of the horse. With a long, flat rock, she
began scraping the mud away from the mare's legs. The muck
was not deep by the edge and Gabria was able to reach frozen
earth in several places.

"I'm going to make a ramp here for you," she said to the
horse. "So you can stand without slipping." The Hunnuli remained still, apparently waiting.

By late morning, Gabria was drenched with sweat, and mud
covered her like a second layer of clothes. She stood up, wiped
her hands on her tunic, and surveyed her work. She felt a moment of pride. The mare's front quarters were free of the clinging mud and her front hooves rested on a short ramp of logs
embedded in the mud and banked on either side with rock and
dead brush. The horse's belly and hindquarters were still
firmly mired, but Gabria felt a little relief and a twinge of
hope.

The girl ate a quick meal and returned to work. First, she
laid a narrow platform in the mud around the horse so she
could work without fighting the mire herself. Scraping and
digging with her rock shovel and her bare hands, she cleared
away the mud from the Hunnuli's sides, then packed in hand-
fuls of gravel and shale to keep the walls from slipping in. It
was agonizing work. Gabria's back was soon a band of pain and
her hands were sore and blistered. The mare watched her constantly, remaining motionless except for the occasional swing
of her head. Only her tail twitching in the mud betrayed her
controlled impatience.

The first stars were glimmering in the darkening sky when
Gabria stopped digging. She looked at the trapped mare in
dismay and said, "I'm sorry, it will be another day before I can
get you out." She groaned and staggered to her feet. "The digging's going so much slower than I expected."

In the long afternoon's work, she had only cleared away a distressingly small area of mud surrounding the huge horse. At the pace she was going, it might be several days before the mare was free. Weary and depressed, Gabria collected more grass for the horse and rubbed down her front legs to stave off swelling. She was rewarded with a soft nicker.

She looked at the Hunnuli in wonder. The mare returned her gaze calmly, her eyes glowing like black pearls. Impulsively, Gabria leaned over and buried her face in the Hunnuli's thick mane. It did not seem possible she could feel something after the destruction of her home and family. She thought every emotion had withered within her when she looked on the mutilated bodies of her brothers. Only revenge had remained to hold her together and fill her heart. Yet, this trapped horse awoke a feeling of kinship in her, and the battered remnants of her old self reached out desperately for comfort. Perhaps, she thought with a frantic yearning, this great horse would accept her as a friend. If so, that friendship was worth a lifetime of labor.

But after a while she stood up and rubbed her face, chiding herself for her fantasies. Hunnuli only accepted warriors and old sorcerers, not exiled girls. It was ridiculous to even imagine. She cleaned herself off as best she could and rekindled her fire. She ate some bread and was asleep before the flames died to embers.

The next morning came with a dismal dawn and a brief but heavy snow. The mountains were veiled behind a raiment of gray and silver clouds, and the wind gusted through the valleys. Gabria woke with a groan. She was badly chilled and so sore she could barely move without pain stabbing somewhere in her body. Her shoulders and back ached and her arms felt petrified from her exertions of the day before. Closer inspection showed her ankle was still swollen. She moaned irritably and pulled her boot back on. Much more of this, she thought, shaking the snow off her cloak, and the wolves will have two meals. She decided to wrap her ankle for better support and hoped the rest of her abused body would gradually lose its kinks.

The Hunnuli was watching her as she ate her meal, showing

none of the impatience of the previous day. The snowfall had patterned the horse's black coat like a bank of stars in a midnight sky, yet she did not bother to shake it off. Gabria glanced at her worriedly and wondered if something was wrong. The wild horse seemed abnormally subdued.

The girl became more alarmed when the Hunnuli ignored a fresh armload of grass. The horse's eyes were withdrawn and dull, as if the light of their glance was turned inward.

"Please, tell me it's not true," Gabria said, sick at the realization that dawned on her. The mare moved restlessly in the mire and turned to nose at her belly. It was difficult to tell under all the mud, but some of the signs were apparent. If Gabria was right, the mare would foal soon. The trauma of the attack and the two days in the mudhole had probably triggered the labor prematurely. Gabria looked at the mare's bulging sides and wondered how far along she actually was.

Desperately, Gabria went to work. The digging she thought she could do in two days now had to be finished in one. Some of the mud had slipped back during the night, but most of the walls had held. Extending these deeper, Gabria dug along the mare's stomach and down her haunches. She could see how the foal had dropped, and she hoped it would be an easy labor. The mare was stiff and weakened from her imprisonment and was in no condition to fight a difficult birth.

The morning passed slowly, broken by intermittent snow and moments of warm sun. Gabria stopped several times to collect more shale and brush, then continued on as fast as her complaining body allowed. Once, she had to stop to wrap the bleeding blisters and lacerations on her hands.

By late afternoon, Gabria was nearing the end of her strength. Only her intense desire to free the mare and the unborn foal gave her the energy to keep digging. Her movements became automatic: scoop out the mud, throw it aside, and pack in the rock. The aches in her arms and back united into one massive hurt, then faded as she pushed herself to the edges of endurance. After a time, it became easy to ignore the melting snow that trickled through her clothes. She only concentrated on fighting her growing lassitude.

The mare became agitated. Faint tremors rippled along her flanks, and she tossed her head in annoyance. Finally, in an effort to calm the horse and keep herself moving, Gabria began to talk aloud.

"I'm sorry, beautiful one, to be taking so long. I will have you out before your time, I promise. I just wasn't prepared for something like this." She laughed bitterly and flung a handful of mud behind her.

"Do you know how much is left when an encampment is burned? Very, very little. A few bits of charred rope, some blackened metal, and heaps and heaps of ashes. Many bodies, too . . . stabbed and slashed, or shot with arrows, or crushed by horses' hooves, or burned. But dead. All dead. Even the children. The horses and livestock are gone. There is nothing. Only death and emptiness and stench."

The Hunnuli quieted and was watching Gabria with an uncanny look of understanding and sympathy, but the girl was bent over her task and did not see the horse's eyes.

"It has never happened before, you know. Oh, we fight often. There is nothing a clansman likes more than a good fight. But not like this. Nothing like this. It was a massacre!" She fiercely wiped her eyes.

"I found my brothers together," Gabria continued dully. "They fought back to back and their enemies' blood flowed. I saw it. The murderers took their dead with them, but they left a great deal of blood behind. My brothers must have been too much for them, though. In the end, the cowards ran my brothers through with lances instead of fighting them like men. Father died before his hall and his hearthguard, his chosen warriors, defended him to the last man. There is no one else left."

For a time, Gabria was silent, and the ghosts of her dead clan haunted her memories. Even the pain of her body could not mask the aching loneliness that terrified her soul.

"I'm the only one," she snapped. "I was not there when they needed me. I ran off like a spoiled child because my father said I was to be married. When I came back to apologize for my heated words, he was dead. I am justly punished." She paused for a moment, then continued.

"I must earn the right to be a clansman now. I am neither man nor woman: I am an exile!" Gabria slammed a handful of gravel into the mud. "That is what is so ironic, Hunnuli. It was a band of exiles, renegades, that ambushed my clan. Exiles sent by that foul dung, Lord Medb.

"Oh, but he will pay the weir-geld for this, Hunnuli. He thinks no one is alive who knows. But I know, and I know, too, that Lord Medb will die. I, Gabria of Clan Corin, am going to take my weir-geld in his blood. He does not realize that I am still alive, but he will know soon. May his heart tremble at the thought of his treachery being shouted to the clans and the world."

Without warning, dizziness shook Gabria's head and she fell against the mare. The girl lay panting on the horse's warm back while her whole body trembled with rage and fatigue. "I must hold on." Her voice rasped in her throat.

The Hunnuli remained still, letting the girl rest until her muscles slowly relaxed and her violent trembling eased. At last, Gabria sat back on her heels. Her face held no expression except for the rigid line to her jaw, the only mark of her hard won control.

It was getting dark and another light snow was falling. Despite her own weariness, Gabria noticed the mare was getting more uncomfortable. Her worry increased, for if the mare went into labor now, she would not be able to pull herself out of the mud. It was time to get the Hunnuli out.

Her legs sore from kneeling, Gabria painfully worked her way off the log platform to the bank. The mare neighed irritably. Her eyes rolled in distress.

"Yes, I think I'm finished," Gabria said. "But I do wish I had some rope." She quickly threw more gravel on the ramp to give the mare added traction.

Much of the mud had been cleared away in a crude circle around the horse, but the heavy mire still clung tenaciously to her hind legs and a great mass lay under her belly. Gabria hoped with the log ramp beneath the Hunnuli's hooves, the horse could utilize her massive strength to pull herself out. There was nothing more Gabria could do.

"It's up to you now," she said to the horse.

The Hunnuli understood. She stilled and closed her eyes. Her muscles began to bulge as if she were concentrating all of her power into one gigantic upheaval. Her neck bowed and trembled in her effort. Her nostrils flared as her breath steamed like the vent of a volcano. Then, without warning, the mare lunged forward, her entire being straining against the confining mud. Her muscles bunched in cords of black along her neck and rump. Her sinews stretched until Gabria thought they would surely snap. Her huge hooves planted on the log ramp, the mare heaved upward, fighting for every inch of freedom.

Gabria sank to her knees, enthralled by the horse's struggle. She felt helpless just watching, but she knew she would only be in the way if she tried to help. There was no place for her puny efforts beside the colossal exertion of the black horse.

Slowly, the mud began to relinquish its hold. The mare's front legs jumped a step forward, driving the logs deeper into the earth. She pulled her back legs inch by inch toward the bank. Her stomach cleared the mire, clumps of mud clinging to her underbelly and to the distended milk bag. With one final effort, the mare threw herself upward. One hind leg lifted out and touched the ramp, then the other. She heaved out of the mudhole with a neigh of triumph that echoed through the gully. Gabria scrambled to her feet, crying with relief. They had done it! She threw her digging rock as far as she could and shouted again when she heard it hit the ground.

Immediately she went still. The Hunnuli was standing in front of her, her black form towering above Gabria's head and her neck arched proudly. Before Gabria knew what was happening, the horse reared. Despite her sluggish body and aching legs, the mare threw her head back and rose up on her hind legs in the Hunnuli's ancient obeisance of respect and honor. Then the mare leaped away and cantered out of the gully. Her hoofbeats faded in the darkness.

Gabria's head began to whirl. A Hunnuli had reared to her—a mere girl, an exile. No one could claim mastery over a Hunnuli; what they gave was freely given. That one would pay her such an honor was more than she could believe.

She stared numbly at the mire where the mud was slowly falling back in place. Her eyes dimmed and the hills swayed around her. Her muscles seemed to freeze, and, before she could stop herself, Gabria collapsed to the ground and emptiness closed her mind.

2

elp me! a voice cried in her dreams. *Help me, Gabria.*
She turned away from the insistent voice, wishing
it would go away. The voice was strange, almost inhu-
man, and some sense told her it was female, but she
did not care. Gabria just wanted to be left alone. She was so
cold, she did not want to know who it was. Something warm
nudged her cheek. She feebly pushed it away and wondered
vaguely why her arm was so unwieldy. Not that it mattered; it
was too much effort to find out. Sleep was more comfortable.

The thing shoved at her again with more force.

"Leave me alone," she mumbled.

Suddenly, something heavy slammed down beside her
head. The girl flinched and slowly pried her eyes open. The
moon had long set, and the sky was overcast. The darkness was
almost total. It was impossible to see more than a few feet beyond her outstretched hand. Groggy and chilled, Gabria
rolled over and tried to sit up. It was then that she saw a gigantic black shadow looming over her. Fear shocked through her.
She screamed, threw her arms up, and jerked away from the
terrifying apparition.

Help me, the voice came again, pleading in her mind.
Gabria crouched, staring about wildly. She had not heard a
sound other than her own pounding heart. Where had that
voice come from? The black shape had not moved, but stood,
looking at her, its eyes glimmering with a pale, spectral light. It
nickered softly, urgently.

Gabria's breath expelled in a loud gasp of relief. "Hunnuli?"
she asked.

She stood up, shivering uncontrollably, and stared at the horse in surprise. Something was terribly wrong. Gabria's fear for herself evaporated. She fumbled to the horse's side and was horrified to find the animal trembling violently and sweating despite the cold wind.

Gabria groped her way to her small camp and renewed her fire into a roaring blaze. The flames illuminated the Hunnuli and, in the unsteady firelight, Gabria saw her worst fears were confirmed. The mare was deep into labor; from the droop of her proud head and the tremors that rippled her mud-spattered coat, she had been for some time. Her hide was drenched in sweat and her ears wavered back in anxiety.

Slowly, so as not to startle her, Gabria stroked the horse's neck and carefully moved along her side to her tail. She had never delivered a foal alone, but she had helped her father with stricken mares and knew well enough what to look for. The horse stood immobile, panting hoarsely as Gabria examined her.

"Poor Hunnuli," said the girl. "What a time you've had. Your foal is so big. He may even be twisted inside." She prayed fervently it was not a breech birth. The mare's waters had broken some time before and her birth canal was painfully dry. If the foal was twisted inside, Gabria knew she did not have the strength to push the foal back against the natural contractions of the mare, straighten it, and pull it out again. She could only hope there was something else that was preventing an easy birth. She did not even know if the foal was alive, but something had to be done quickly if she was going to save it or the mare.

Rapidly, Gabria scraped some snow into her small water bag and set it near the fire. She sorted through her few possessions and picked out a pot of salve and her extra tunic. Then, working with all haste, she tore strips from the tunic and tied them with tiny knots into a soft rope with a noose fashioned at one end. As soon as the snow melted in the skin bag, she used the water to wash her hands and one arm clean. She took a liberal dab of creamy salve and rubbed it over her forearm and hand.

The girl picked up her rope, careful to keep it clean, and

moved to the mare's side. What she had to do next was going to be uncomfortable for the mare and herself, so she hoped the horse was too exhausted to complain. Using the utmost care, she eased her hand, holding the noose, into the mare's birth canal. The horse tossed her head, but she offered no resistance.

Gabria soon found the foal's front legs. She inched the noose around the tiny hooves and pulled it tight, then she pushed her arm deeper past the foal's knees, struggling against the mare's contractions, which squeezed her hand with crushing force. When she found the foal's head, she sighed with relief, for the baby was not breech. Only its head was twisted, jamming it tightly against the pelvic bone.

Gabria's relief was pushed away by a feeling of dread. As she edged her fingers down the foal's cheek, her heart sank. The body was very unyielding and had none of the wiggling, warm movements of a live foal. In despair, she straightened the head and withdrew her arm. The mare, as if sensing her release, lay down while Gabria took the rope. With each contraction the girl pulled steadily, softly talking to soothe the mare and hide her own fear.

At last the foal was born. It lay on the cold ground, its birthing sac wrapped around it, its eyes glazed in death. Gabria removed the sac and the afterbirth, and cleaned the foal's nostrils, although she knew her efforts were futile. The tiny horse had suffocated during the prolonged labor.

The girl sat down abruptly and stared at the dead foal. It was not fair, her heart cried. Why was she always too late? The baby was a stud colt of perfect proportions, with a streak of white on its black shoulder. Gabria's eyes filled with tears. If only she had not failed again, the colt would now be discovering its new life.

The mare lay motionless, half-dead with exhaustion. She made no move to examine her baby, as if she knew it was already beyond her help. Her eyes settled shut and her ragged breathing eased. Gabria sat with her arms on her knees and her head sunk in grief.

The fire slowly died to embers and its light was replaced by the glow of the rising sun. Night's gloom faded. A bird piped from a nearby clump of gorse. The clouds withdrew from the mountains, leaving the peaks in a dazzling coverlet of snow. On the steppes, the air was clean and brilliant.

It was the sun that finally roused Gabria. Its warmth seeped into her chilled limbs and nestled on the back of her neck until she raised her head. She took a deep breath of the passing breeze and stretched out the stiffness in her aching muscles.

The sun felt delicious. It was so good to just sit in its warmth. But the heat on her back reminded Gabria of a possible danger. The mountain snows would begin to melt soon in this heat and the water would fill every available stream and wash. The last thaw that had formed the mudhole in the gully had only touched the foothills. Should the mountain run-off come down the eroded valleys, the gully she and the mare were in could be flooded. The water would take a little time to gather, but she did not want to dawdle. She had spent too much time here as it was. Her food supply and her strength were dwindling rapidly.

Gabria picked up a pebble and flicked it away. Was it really worth the effort to leave? She was so tired. She knew that on foot it would take her perhaps fifteen days to reach Khulinin Treld and then only if she were in good condition. She shook her head. It was impossible. She had never walked that far in her life. Her feet were already blistered and her boots were worn just from the two-day journey from Corin Treld. Her ankle, which was still swollen and weak, would never heal under the strain of constant walking. Her muscles were already strained, her hands were badly lacerated, and her stomach was empty. She would trade almost anything for a warm bed and a hot breakfast.

Then Gabria sighed and stood up. It did not really matter how many problems she could list. She knew in her heart she was not going to give up. She was the last Corin and she would never give Lord Medb the satisfaction of her death in a muddy gully.

Gabria gazed at the dead foal and planned her next move. The colt would have to be buried, she decided. She could not bear the thought of its small body torn by wolves and kites.

The mare appeared to be sleeping, so Gabria lifted the colt and carried it to the hilltop. It was surprisingly light, even for a newborn foal, but its body was unwieldy and the hill was slippery with thawed mud. Gabria was limping badly by the time she reached the crest.

Sadly, she placed her burden at the foot of an outcropping of stone and there she built a cairn over the body. As she worked, she sang the death song she had sung when the flames devoured her brothers' bodies. When she was finished, she sat back and gave in to the desolation in her heart.

"Oh, Mother," she cried, "giver of all life, I am tired of this. Is this what I have come to? Burying everything that means something to me?"

Do not mourn for my son, a voice said.

Gabria jumped, startled out of her misery. It was the same voice she remembered from her dreams, a voice she could not hear. She gripped her arms, afraid to speak. The words had been spoken in her mind, and she knew of no mortal, except for the ancient sorcerers, who had telepathic ability.

The voice came again. *My son is dead, but perhaps he will return to me after another mating.*

"Who are you?" Gabria demanded, terrified by the invasion of her mind.

My true name is unpronounceable to your tongue. You may call me Nara.

In a flash of understanding, Gabria realized who was speaking to her. Dumbfounded, she closed her eyes and turned around. When she opened them, she saw the Hunnuli standing a few feet away.

"It *is* you!" she breathed.

Of course. The mare was filthy with muck and dried blood, her mane and tail were matted, yet her proud spirit had revived; her eyes glowed with a depth of wisdom that stunned Gabria. *We do not often communicate with humans. Only a chosen few.*

Gabria leaned against the outcropping for support. Her knees felt like melting wax. "Why?"

It is too difficult. Human minds are too confusing to us.

With some, though, it is worthwhile.

Gabria gestured weakly at herself. "No. Why me?"

I owe you a life. The voice became softer. *And you need my help.*

"Can you read my thoughts?"

No. I can only give you mine.

"If you could, you would know that I am unworthy of your help or even your offer. I am in exile."

The mare ducked her head and looked at the girl sideways with her full black eye. *I know what you are and what has happened. I understand much about you that you cannot see yet.* The mare snorted. *I am Nara. I am Hunnuli, daughter of the Storm Father. I choose whom I will.*

"I am not worthy of you."

You are stubborn. Forget worthy. You are my friend.

Gabria glanced away. Her green eyes brimmed with tears. "I could not save your foal."

My son was dead before I came to you. In my pride, I wished to bear my first-born alone, but I was too weak.

"I'm sorry," the girl said, feeling the inadequacy of the words.

There will be others. For now, I will go with you.

Gabria wanted to argue further. She was mortified that a Hunnuli, a creature of the legends she had grown up with, had offered her friendship. How could she accept it? She was an outcast with no clan to support her, no family to defend her, and no future. Her life was like a clay pot that someone had thrown carelessly away, so there was nothing left of the familiar, comforting shape but fragments and shards, and the memory of what it had been. What did she have to offer one such as the Hunnuli? Only fear, uncertainty, suspicion, and death.

No. No matter how she might wish for such a fantastic thing, she could not consent to Nara's offer.

Gabria's stomach felt leaden, and she shivered with a chill that was not caused by the wind. "Nara, I do not think there is anything left in me that can return your friendship. I am so empty."

If that were true, I would not have come back.

"I am seeking only revenge. After that . . ." Her voice failed. Gabria could not think beyond that goal. Although she did not care to admit it, she was terrified. Many had tried to kill Lord Medb, both in battle and duel, but he was a skilled and ferocious warrior. It was also said he was protected by forbidden magic. If that were true, and battle skilled men failed against him, how could she succeed? Her pride and grief would never free her from her duty, but she had no illusions about the future.

Nara dipped her nose until it was a hairsbreadth from Gabria's face. The mare inhaled deeply as a horse will do to acquaint itself with another creature. Gabria could smell the mare's warm, comforting scent that was a mixture of grass, sun, and the distinctive sweetness that was purely horse. The familiarity of the scent comforted her wounded spirit. Her objections faded to insignificance.

When Nara told her, *Let the days come as they will. I am going with you,* Gabria merely nodded, unable to speak.

In a daze, the girl limped down the hillside to her camp. She ate a quick meal and returned her belongings to her pack. Her torn tunic was useless and she threw it away. Her remaining tunic was as filthy as she was, and she thought how nice it would be for a bath. It might be the last one she would have in peace for a long time to come.

"Is there a stream or pool nearby?" she asked the mare, who was waiting patiently for her.

Yes. But farther from here are hot springs.

"Hot water?" Gabria breathed, unable to believe her luck. "What direction is it?"

Beneath the horned peak.

Gabria looked toward the line of peaks and smiled with relief. That had to be Wolfeared Pass, a strangely formed mountain with twin summits that stood to the south of the gully. She picked up her pack and her staff and threw her cloak over her shoulders.

"Lead on, Nara," she said, pointing with her staff.

The mare glanced at her with a glint of amusement in her brilliant eyes. *Do you not think it would be faster to ride me?*

Gabria's jaw dropped. "You would let me ride?" Her voice rose higher with each word.

You can ride, can you not?

"Of course, I just—"

I am not going to plod all day, waiting for you to keep pace. Besides—Her telepathic thought turned wistful—*I would like warm water, too.*

Gabria was stunned. She had never imagined this! "But Nara, women may not ride a Hunnuli."

The mare whickered in a way that surprised Gabria. It sounded much like laughter. *Could that be a tale spread by men who fear the ambitions of their women?*

The girl laughed and a great load of worry fell from her shoulders. She threw her walking staff away and climbed up a large rock. From that added height, she clambered onto Nara's broad back. Gabria was astonished by the heat of the Hunnuli's body; it was the vibrant, glowing warmth of a fire barely dampened. She reached out to touch the horse's ebony, arched neck and marveled at the power and intensity that flowed beneath the slick hide. It was as though the lightning bolt emblazoned on Nara's shoulder hid in reality within the horse's form.

Nara trotted out of the gully, and, once onto the treeless hills, she moved into an easy, mile-eating canter.

Gabria held onto a fistful of mane, not for support, but merely for something to do with her hands. She did not need to find her balance or even use her legs, as the mare moved with a surprising fluidity and grace for a horse so large. She felt herself mold into the movement of the horse as if they had been fused together by the heat of Nara's being. The girl settled back, letting the wind brush through her hair and the sunlight flow over her face. She began to relax in the delight of the ride.

They swept over the land as one, like the shadows of clouds pushed by the wind, until the gully in the Hornguard became a memory and the southern peaks of Darkhorn reared like sentinels in their path. Perhaps, Gabria thought for a fleeting moment, there was a little hope.

They made camp that night in a small valley of thermal pools and mineral springs. To Gabria, it was an eerie place of shifting vapors, strange smells, and pools that bubbled with odd colors and noises. But Nara, unperturbed by the strange landscape, found a water hole formed by the run-off of an erupting mineral spring. There they bathed and soaked away the aches of the past days. Before long, Gabria had forgotten her dislike of the valley in the bliss of the relaxing water.

They stayed in the valley for several days while their bodies mended. Gabria used her salve to dress Nara's neck wound from the wolf attack, as well as the other cuts and scrapes they both had. Nara, in return, gave the girl the rich, nourishing milk that had been meant for the foal. Gabria had heard stories of the effects of Hunnuli milk on humans, but her stomach had a stronger voice than the vague hints from old legends, so she drank the milk gratefully and attributed her fast recovery to the reviving waters of the spring.

When two days had passed, Nara sensed the coming of another spring storm. Reluctantly, Gabria packed her gear and mounted the mare for the final journey south. The Hunnuli and her rider cantered for three days through the foothills hugging the Darkhorn's towering ramparts. The country slowly changed as the air became warmer and more arid. The trees retreated up the mountain flanks, giving way to tougher shrubs and grasses. The hills, worn by wind and erosion, lost their sharp outlines until, to Gabria's eye, they looked like a soft, rumpled carpet. The Himachal Mountains on her left fell behind, and the eastern horizon flowed away on the endless rim of the steppes.

Sooner than Gabria imagined, the mountains began to veer west. She could hardly believe they had come so far in such a brief time. Visitors from Khulinin Treld to Corin Treld usually needed seven days on horseback, yet Nara had covered most of that distance in three.

On the evening of the third day, they came to Marakor, the Wind Watcher, the isolated, cone-shaped peak that guarded the northern entrance into the valley of the Goldrine River.

Behind Marakor, the mountains strode westward, then

swung around in a great arch to return to their southward trek into the desert wastelands. There, in the crescent valley where the Goldrine River spilled from its deep gorge, the Khulinin clan had its wintering camp. For generations, the Khulinin clan had roamed the steppes in the summer, pasturing their herds on the richest fields, and every winter they returned to the sanctuary of the valley. In the shelter of Marakor and Krindir, the twin peak to the south, they lived and danced and celebrated the Foaling as their fathers had done for countless years.

From where Gabria and Nara stood—on a crest just below Marakor—they could see black tents spread out like huge butterflies and the encampment's few permanent buildings. Gabria was stunned by the size of the treld. She had never seen all the Khulinin together in one place and, in spite of the dim tales she remembered her mother telling her, she was not prepared for the camp's sprawling size. Her clan had been small; they barely numbered a hundred. But this! There had to be many hundreds of people in the valley below.

She tore her fascinated gaze away from the encampment and looked at the pastures where the animals grazed. The number of horses and livestock was an indication of a clan's wealth, and Gabria could tell from the size of the herds that grazed along the river that the Khulinin were rich indeed.

As she made camp that night in a copse of trees, Gabria tried to recall every detail she knew of Savaric, chieftain of the Khulinin. There were not many. Although he was chief of her mother's clan, Gabria had only seen him a few times at the summer clan gatherings and she had been too busy then to notice very much. What she did remember was an image of a dark-haired, bearded man who constantly carried a falcon on his arm.

She knew her father had liked and respected Savaric. The two men had been close friends in boyhood, but Gabria did not know how far their friendship had extended or whether it would have any influence on Savaric's decision to accept her.

She wished she could learn more about Savaric before venturing into his domain. How was he going to react to the sole survivor of a massacred clan dropping the horrors and problems of her continuing existence at his feet? If he did not see through her disguise, would he accept her into his werod? He had ample food and wealth to support many warriors, even one as poor and inadequate as herself, but in all likelihood, he had as many warriors as he needed, Besides, Savaric probably would not want to risk taking such a dangerous exile into his clan.

Still, Gabria thought as she ate her evening meal, the fact that my mother was of Clan Khulinin, coupled with my father's friendship, might sway Savaric's mind. And of course, there was the Hunnuli. So few men rode the magnificent horses, Savaric would think twice before denying Gabria's plea and ignoring the honor Nara would bring to his people.

On the other hand, if he discovered her true sex, the question of her acceptance would be meaningless. Clan law strictly forbade any female from becoming a warrior. The chieftain would have to have Gabria killed immediately for masquerading as a boy and trying to join his werod.

She could only hope he would not find out, for she had no other chance for acceptance—and no chance of gaining her revenge against Lord Medb without the Khulinin's help. She would have to trust to luck and the guidance of the goddess, Amara, when she rode into Savaric's camp tomorrow. Until then, she decided to ignore her anxiety. Curling up under her cloak, she tried to rest, but it was a long while before she drifted off to sleep.

Gabria was awakened at dawn by the echoing, sonorous summons of a horn. The eastern stars were dimmed by a pale light that gleamed on the sharp ridges of the mountains. The horn sounded again, swelling through the valley with an urgent appeal to the sun. Gabria scrambled to her feet and walked to the rim of the hill.

Far below her, at the entrance to Khulinin Treld, an outrider of the dawn watch sat on a light-colored horse and lifted his horn to his lips for the third time. Darkness faded and the colors of day intensified. A red-gold sliver of fire pierced the dark horizon and painted the earth with its glow. The meager light of the stars was banished.

They do well to welcome the sun.

Gabria glanced at the mare standing beside her. "I went out on the dawn watch once with my twin brother, Gabran," she said slowly. "Father did not know or he would have whipped me for going with the outriders. But I begged and pleaded and Gabran finally let me come. We stood on the hill above the treld, and he blew such a blast of eagerness and joy, his horn burst. To me he looked like an image of our hero, Valorian, the Lord Chieftain, calling his people to war."

I know of Valorian. He taught the Hunnuli to speak.

Gabria nodded absently, her gaze lost in the memories of other mornings. In the valley, the outrider returned to the herds and the treld came alive with activity. The girl continued to stare where the rider had been, her face grim and her jaw clenched. A tear crept unheeded down her cheek.

Nara nudged Gabria's shoulder gently and broke her reverie. Gabria sniffed, then laughed. She wiped her cheeks with her sleeve and laid her fingers on the healing slash on the mare's neck.

"It is time to begin this game, Nara. You have brought me this far, but I do not expect you to go farther."

Nara snorted and dipped her head to give Gabria a sidelong look through her thick forelock. *This game began long ago. I would like to see how it is played.*

The girl laughed and, for a moment, she leaned gratefully against the mare's strong shoulder.

They returned to their camp, and Gabria added the final touch to her disguise. She had not washed her clothes, so they were still filthy with mud, sweat, and dried blood. She wrinkled her nose as she slipped on the black tunic. It smelled horrible and three days had not inured her nose to the stink. She rubbed dirt onto her face and hands and into her hair. If all went well, no one would look past the filth to realize she was not a boy. Later, she would have to devise another trick to hide her face until the clansmen became used to her. She did not want to remain filthy forever.

She fastened her short sword to the leather belt around her waist. Her father's dagger, with its silver hilt encrusted with garnets, was thrust into her boot. She picked up her pack, threw her cloak over her shoulder, and took a deep breath.

Nara sprang to the top of the ridge and neighed a bold, resounding call of greeting. The Hunnuli's call pealed through the pastures of Khulinin Treld and echoed from the far hills. Every horse below raised its head, and Nara's cry was greeted by the clarion neigh of a stallion.

The game had begun.

3

he stranger rode into the treld at morning, just as the horns were recalling the dawn watch. He was flanked by two outriders, who kept a wary and respectful distance from the Hunnuli mare which dwarfed the Harachan stallions they rode. The people froze, appalled, as he passed by, and they stared at his back in utter dismay. The news spread quickly through the tents. Men and women, whispering in fearful speculation, gathered behind the three riders and followed them up the main road through the encampment.

The stranger appeared to be a boy of fourteen or fifteen years with a lithe figure and features obscured by a mask of dirt. His light gold hair was chopped shorter than normal for a boy his age and was just as filthy as his face. He sat on the Hunnuli easily, his body relaxed, but his face was tense and he stared fixedly ahead, ignoring the crowd behind him. On his shoulders, like a blazon of fire and death, was a scarlet cloak.

The cloak was nothing unusual. Every clansman of the steppes wore one, but only one small clan, the Corin, wore cloaks of blood red. According to recent messengers, that clan had been completely massacred only twelve days before. Some said by sorcery.

Who was this strange boy who wore the cloak of a murdered clan? And to ride a Hunnuli! Not even in the tales told by the bards had anyone known of a boy taming a wild Hunnuli, especially one as magnificent as this mare. She shone like black lacquer overlayed on silver and walked with the tense, wary pride of a war horse. She wore no trappings and would tolerate none. The observers could not help but marvel how a boy, not even a warrior yet, had won the friendship of one such as she. That tale alone would be worth the listening.

By the time the three riders reached the circular gathering place before the werod hall, most of the clan had gathered and were waiting. The boy and his escort dismounted. No words were spoken and the silence was heavy. Then five men, their swords drawn and their golden cloaks rippling down their backs, appeared in the arched doorway of the hall and gestured to the boy. They took his sword and pack and, with a curt command, ordered him to attend the chieftain. The outriders followed.

The Hunnuli moved to stand by herself and snorted menacingly at the clanspeople. They understood well to leave her strictly alone. They settled into noisy, talking groups and waited patiently for the meeting's outcome.

Unlike many of the clans' wintering camps, Khulinin Treld had been established centuries ago. Generations of Khulinin had returned to the natural protection of the valley until it became instilled in the clan as the symbol of home. For the semi-nomadic people, the valley was their place of permanence and stability—a settlement they could return to year after year. Because of their pride in the ancient traditions of the treld, the Khulinin had built a permanent hall for clan gatherings, a building that would survive until the last hoofbeats dwindled from the valley.

The hall delved into the flank of a towering hill near the falls of the Goldrine River. From the massive arched entrance, the sentinels who stood on either side could look out over the open commons to the encampment that spread like a motionless landslide down to the valley floor. The Khulinin banners of gold swayed in the breeze above the door.

Inside, the main room of the hall ran deep into the hill. Wooden columns, hauled from the mountains, marched in two files down the long chamber. Torches burned from brackets on every column and golden lamps hung from the vaulted ceiling beams. A fire burned in a large stone pit in the center of the hall. Its flames danced in a vain attempt to follow the

smoke through the ventilation shafts. Trestle tables, a rarity in
an encampment, were piled against a wall in readiness for
feasts and celebrations, and several tapped casks of wine and
mead stood beside them. Tapestries and weapons taken in
battle hung on the whitewashed walls.

At the far end of the hall, the chieftain sat on a dais of dark
stone. He watched thoughtfully, his dark eyes veiled behind
half-drawn lids, as the stranger was brought before him. Behind him, in a semicircle, stood his personal retainers, the warriors of the hearthguard.

The men shifted uneasily as the boy walked toward them.
Savaric could feel their angered tenseness. It was little wonder
they were ill at ease, for they all had been disturbed by the
rumors of sorcery and the horrors of the massacre at Corin
Treld. Such a thing had never happened to the clans before.
The reverberations of this hideous deed might never end, and
the gods alone knew what aftershocks this boy was bringing.

Savaric masked his own concerns for the sake of the boy, but
he knew the others were openly wary. Even Savaric's son,
Athlone, who stood at the chief's right hand, was watching the
boy with unconcealed suspicion.

Four paces before the warrior-lord, the boy knelt and extended his left hand in a salute. "Hail, Lord Savaric. I bring
you greetings from my dead father." His voice was low and
forced.

Savaric frowned slightly and leaned forward. "Who is your
father, boy? Who greets me from the grave?"

"Dathlar, my lord, chieftain of the ghost clan of Corin."

"We have heard of the tragedy that befell that clan. But who
are you and how is it you have survived if you are indeed
Dathlar's son?"

Gabria felt a spasm of pain. She had expected the question
of her survival to be raised, but she still could not answer without guilt. She hung her head to hide her face, which burned
with her inner shame.

"Are you ill?" Savaric asked sharply.

"No, Lord," Gabria replied, keeping her eyes downcast.
"My eyes are not used to the shade of this hall." That part at

least was true. After the bright morning sun, the gloom of the hall made it difficult for her to see. "It is my greatest shame that I am alive. I am Gabran, youngest son of Dathlar. I was in the hills hunting eagles when I became lost in the fog."

"Fog?" Athlone broke in sardonically. Murmurs of astonishment and skepticism from the watching warriors echoed his disbelief.

Gabria glared at Athlone, seeing him clearly for the first time. He was different from the men around him, for he was taller, of heavier build, and fairer in skin. His brown hair was chopped short, and a thick mustache softened the hard lines of his mouth. There was a natural assumption of authority in Athlone's manner, and an unquestionable capability. Since he wore the belt of a wer-tain, a commander of the warriors, he could pose more of a threat to her than Savaric. Savaric was chieftain, but as wer-tain, Athlone was captain of the werod. If Gabria were accepted, she would be under his direct command. That thought unnerved her, for he came across as a man of power rather than charm, resolution rather than patience. He could be a formidable opponent.

Still, the way Athlone looked at Gabria irritated her. The man's brown eyes were narrowed in distrust, looking as cold as frozen earth. His hand was clenched on his belt, a hairsbreadth away from the hilt of a short sword.

"Yes, fog!" She snapped the word at Athlone, daring him to doubt the truth of it again. "You know we do not have fog in the afternoon of a cool spring day. But it came! Because of it, the outriders brought in the herds, and the women and children stayed in the tents." Except me, she thought bitterly. She had become lost in the fog on her way home and would never forget its dank smell.

"That fog was cold and thick, and when the attack came from every direction, there was no warning. They slaughtered everyone and combed the woods to ensure no one escaped. When they finished, they drove off the horses, scattered the livestock, and burned the tents." Gabria turned back to Savaric, her head tilted angrily. "It was well planned, Lord. It was an intentional massacre, done by men with no desire to plunder or steal. I know who is responsible. I am going to claim weir-geld."

"I see." Savaric sat back in his seat and drummed his fingers slowly on his knee. The chieftain was as handsome as Gabria remembered, of medium height with a dark, neatly trimmed beard and eyes as black and glitteringly dangerous as a hawk's. His face was weathered by years of sun and harsh wind and bore the marks of numerous battles. His right hand was missing the little finger.

He sat now, studying Gabria, waiting for a weakness or a slip of the tongue. He recognized a family resemblance in the boy, but oddly Gabran reminded him more of the mother, Samara, than his friend, Dathlar. Savaric was inclined to believe the boy's story, as incredible as it was. The chief's instincts told him that the boy was not treacherous and his instincts were always right. Still, he had to satisfy his warriors before he considered taking the boy into the clan.

"You have the red cloak of your clan, Gabran, and your story fits what little we know of the ambush. But I have no obvious proof that you are who you say you are."

Gabria bit back an angry retort. It was only to be expected that they would not accept her tale immediately. Rumors of war had been growing since last autumn, and, after the annihilation of an entire clan, every chieftain of the plains would be cautious.

She removed her cloak and swept it onto the floor before her. Its brilliant color drew every eye and held them like a spell. "My father was Dathlar of Clan Corin. He married Samara, a Khulinin, twenty-five years ago. They had four sons and one daughter." She spoke slowly as if repeating her history by rote.

"My mother was beautiful, as fair as you are dark. She could play the lyre and the pipes, and she wore a gold brooch of buttercups. She died ten years ago. My father was your friend. He told me of you many times. In token of that friendship, you gave him this." She pulled the silver dagger out of her boot and threw it on the cloak. It lay on the scarlet fabric, a silent messenger, its red gems glowing in the light like drops of blood.

Savaric stood up and reached out to pick up the dagger. "My guards are growing careless," he said quietly. He stared at the shining blade and turned it over in his hands. "If you are truly the son of Dathlar and he was slain in treachery, then I must also seek weir-geld for my blood brother."

Gabria was stunned. Blood brother! She had not expected this. If Savaric believed her and the garbled news he had received about the massacre, he was bound by his oath of friendship to Dathlar to settle the debt owed to Dathlar's family—what was left of it. Blood friendship was as binding as a blood relationship and carried the same responsibilities. The fact that Gabria was an exile was now irrelevant to Savaric. She had only to convince him that she was telling the truth and, most difficult of all, that she really did know who was responsible for the killing. Then he would do everything possible to help her.

"Lord Savaric," she said. "By the Hunnuli that bears me and the gods that nourish us, I am the child of Dathlar and I *know* who had my clan murdered." She spoke forcefully, her eyes matching Savaric's black gaze.

Savaric sat down again, still holding the dagger, examining it as if it bore a vestige of the man who had once carried it. "If nothing else, the Hunnuli is the strongest plea in your favor. She alone vouches for your character."

Athlone stepped to his father's side. "Hunnuli or no, there was sorcery at Corin Treld. We cannot accept this boy's word so easily." He leaned over and grasped the cloak. "Anyone with a little ingenuity could obtain a scarlet cloak and an interesting tale."

Gabria snatched the cloak out of his hands and held it tightly to her breast. Fury blazed in her eyes. "Yes, sorcery formed the fog at Corin Treld, sorcery spun by the hand of Lord Medb. Not I!"

It was the first time Lord Medb had been mentioned, and the significance of his name was not lost on the watching warriors. They muttered uneasily among themselves and no one looked surprised at her accusation. Athlone was not surprised either, and he made no attempt to hide his suspicions of Lord

Medb's rumored heresies.

"Perhaps not. But you could be a servant sent by Medb to spy on us. Certainly you could not have survived the massacre or obtained a Hunnuli mare without help," Athlone replied with deliberate derision.

"Certainly not," Gabria retorted. "Since you are convinced it cannot be done."

"I know it is not possible for a mere boy to earn a Hunnuli's respect. I ride a Hunnuli stallion and taming him was no task for a child."

"I can see why it was so difficult for you," Gabria noted with heavy sarcasm. "The Hunnuli are good judges of character."

Several of the guardsmen laughed. Savaric crossed his arms, watching the exchange with interest. The boy had pride and courage to stand up to a wer-tain. He certainly learned that from his father.

Athlone shrugged. "Then you accomplished it the simple way, with sorcery or coercion, knowing a Hunnuli could help you worm your way into our clan. How can we not think you are an impostor?"

"Why do you think that?" Savaric interrupted conversationally.

"Impostor!" Gabria nearly shrieked, cutting him off. She cringed at the high note her voice had hit and quickly lowered it again, hoping no one had noticed its feminine tone. She knew Athlone was deliberately baiting her, but she had had enough of him and his arrogant accusations. He did not realize how close he was to the truth. "You faceless, dirt-eating, dung shoveler . . ."

She continued on at length, richly describing Athlone's habits and character with every appellation she had heard her brothers use, until the men around her began to choke with ill-concealed laughter. Even Savaric was taken aback. Athlone's face began to turn red and his mouth hardened to a granite slash. Finally, before his son's temper exploded, Savaric cut Gabria off with a curt word.

"Now," he said to Athlone in the sudden silence. "I would like to know why you think this boy could be an impostor."

Athlone stood by the dais, his body rigid. There was something wrong about this boy—he could sense it. But he could not recognize what it was. Incredible as the boy's story sounded, it was plausible. Athlone knew full well that the Hunnuli could not be won by coercion or treachery. Yet a niggling little warning disturbed him. The boy was not telling the truth about something.

He stared hard at Gabria, at a loss to explain his suspicion. "Medb would like to have an informer in our camp. Why not a boy with a story of kinship to Dathlar?" He curled his lip. "Or maybe he is just a miserable exile using a stolen cloak to gain acceptance."

"I *am* an exile," Gabria cried. "Medb made me one. Because of him my clan no longer exists." A bitter sadness seeped into her heart, stifling her outrage. "I came to ask for a place in the Khulinin, to seek aid against Lord Medb, for he is too powerful for me alone. There was no magic in my coming to you, or treachery. Only blood ties. There was only pain and hard work in winning the Hunnuli." She held out her hands, palms up, and the men saw the raw cuts for the first time.

The cold left Athlone's eyes and his anger receded under the pain he saw in Gabria's face. He glanced at his father and briefly nodded.

Savaric stood up and the hearthguard moved to his side. "I would gladly accept you into this clan and do everything I can to help you attain your rightful blood debt. To my eyes, you are Dathlar's son, and to my heart, you are honest and very courageous. However, it is the clan that must sustain you. In this case, I will let them speak. Come."

He walked to the entrance, followed by Athlone, Gabria, and the others. Nara, seeing the girl surrounded by the guardsmen, firmly pushed between them and Gabria until the men drew off to a respectful distance. Gabria reached up and twined her fingers into the horse's glossy black mane.

You are well? Nara asked.

Gabria nodded, her face turned to the watching clansmen. The people were quiet as Savaric told them Gabria's tale and her reasons for seeking the Khulinin. They listened intently.

The men, in warm woolen jackets, baggy pants, and boots, stood to the front of the crowd. The women, dressed in long skirts and tunics of bright colors, stood as a brilliant backdrop behind their men. Many faces were expressionless, despite the fear that pervaded the encampment.

When Savaric was finished speaking, several men detached themselves from the crowd and conversed together for a few minutes. Gabria recognized them as the elders of the clan, Savaric's advisors. One wore the emblem of the herd-master, the head stockman, and one was a priest of Valorian. No one else from the throng offered a word. The decision, it seemed, rested on the elders.

The herd-master finally approached Savaric and said reluctantly, "Lord, we do not want to endanger our clan with the evil and taint of sorcery this boy brings, but there are too many sides to this tale to refuse him outright. He does ride a Hunnuli, and to turn the mare away might bring the gods' displeasure. If you agree, we feel it would be just to allow him a time of trial. If he serves you well and follows the laws of the clan, then let him be accepted. If he does not, then he is truly exiled."

Savaric nodded in satisfaction. "Gabran, you may stay with the clan. You and the Hunnuli are welcome . . . for now." He smiled at her as the clanspeople slowly dispersed. "Athlone will be your mentor," he said, ignoring Gabria's horrified look. "When you have washed and had some food, I would like to continue this conversation about Medb and how you won your Hunnuli."

Gabria leaned against Nara and said weakly, "Yes, Lord."

The dazed young girl was too drained to even react when Nara said in her mind, *The first contest is yours.*

4

ow can you be so certain it was Lord Medb who ordered the massacre," Lord Savaric asked as he leaned back on his fur-draped seat. "You have not given us sufficient proof to believe your accusation."

Gabria slumped in frustration. "I have told you everything I can."

"It is not enough. You are bringing serious charges against a clan chieftain. How can you know what happened at the encampment? Or that it was an exile band that slaughtered the clan? You say you were not there."

"No, I was not there during the killing, but I know! I can read the signs of battle and I know what led up to the massacre," she cried.

Gabria was sitting before the dais, facing Savaric, Athlone, and the clan's elders, who were seated in a semicircle before her. They had been interrogating her for several hours, and she had told them repeatedly everything she could remember of that awful day at Corin Treld and the days following. Still they were not satisfied.

Behind her, the men of the werod had gathered to hear her story. They clustered in silent groups around the fire pit. Gabria was very self-conscious sitting before this large crowd of men. It seemed as if any second, one of them would see through her disguise. They were so quiet and watchful. If she turned her head slightly she could see them, their dark, muscular faces regarding her with a mixture of surprise, disbelief, and speculation. A flagon of wine was being passed around, but few of the warriors were enjoying it.

The girl wished they would finish this inquisition. It was
night and getting quite late. During the day she had had a
chance to eat, clean off a little of the dirt, and rest. But now she
was getting tired. Gabria had refused to part with her cloak
and sat with it bunched up on her lap.

"Can't you understand?" she asked sadly. "Lord Medb
needed my father's cooperation. Our clan was small, but we
were the first he had attempted to win to his favor. The other
chieftains in the north respected Father. With his support,
Medb would have had some control in the northwest."

Savaric nodded to himself. He had been following Medb's
plots for some time, but even he was shocked by how far the
chieftain seemed willing to go. "And your father refused these
overtures of friendship?"

"Violently." She laughed bitterly, remembering her father's
exact words. "Medb only made one offer. When that was re-
jected, he resorted to coercion and threats and finally an ultimatum."

Athlone was sitting on a leather stool near his father. His
hand idly scratched the ears of a large deer hound as his eyes
watched Gabria and the reactions of the men around him.
"What sort of ultimatum?" he demanded.

Gabria spoke slowly, stressing each word. "Lord Medb made
it clear that he wants to be overlord of the clans. To that end, he
offered Father the lordship of all the northern lands. If Father
refused, our clan would die."

The men burst out in a loud clamor of outrage. Whispers of
Medb's bid for absolute power over all the clans had been
blown from one encampment to another all winter, but the
idea of a sole monarch was so far-fetched to the clansmen that
few people had paid close attention.

"No!" The herd-master's voice cut through the noise. "I
cannot believe this. No chieftain would have such audacity.
How can he offer power that is not his to give?"

"The power is not his yet," Gabria interjected. "But he
made good his threat to my father."

The master turned to Savaric, who was watching Gabria
thoughtfully. "Lord, how can you listen to this. Lord Medb's

clan is many days' ride from the Corin range. It would be senseless for him to look so far afield."

"Yet, you agree he is looking," Savaric replied.

The man shifted uneasily. "We have all heard the rumors of Medb's growing ambitions. But this is absurd."

Savaric stood up and paced in front of the dais. "Is it?" He posed the question to all the men. "Think about it. Medb needs allies to help him hold the vital regions of the grasslands. The Corin were a perfect choice. If Dathlar had agreed to his offer, Medb would have held a valuable hammer in the north, a hammer he could have used with his clan in the south to crush us in the middle. But," Savaric said as he gestured at Gabria, "when the Corin refused, Medb used them as an example to the other clans. He is proving he is deadly serious."

The warriors' voices quieted and even the herd-master looked pensive as the full impact of Savaric's words sank in. The chieftain stood by the stone seat, momentarily lost in his own thoughts.

Gabria closed her eyes and let her head droop. The chief seemed to understand after all, and if he did, that was all that mattered. She was too exhausted to worry about the others. Sleep was all she wanted now. The girl felt her body sag and her head seemed to grow heavier. She heard Athlone get to his feet and say something to his father.

Then someone dropped a cup on the floor, and the metal rang dully as it struck the hard-packed earth. The clang caught Gabria's attention like the distant clash of swords. She dragged open her eyes. Her glance fell into the fire burning in the center of the hearth. Everything was silent; she could feel the eyes of the men upon her, but she could not see them. She could only see the flames. The girl began to breathe faster and her heart raced.

In the back of her mind Gabria heard a faint thunder, like hoofbeats, that mingled with the crackle and roar of the fire. She tried to move as the sound grew louder, to escape the noise and the terror that came with it, but the thunder engulfed her and swept her into the light of the fire. The flames bounded high, burning away her self-awareness. The men, the hall, even the fire faded into obscurity while her consciousness fell helplessly through the lurid gloom and touched a dying link with Gabran, her twin brother. Born together, they had always shared a special bond, and now, like the touch of a dead hand, his presence coalesced out of the chaos and led her back to the paths of Corin Treld.

Her vision cleared and the familiar encampment lay before her, shrouded in a veil of thickening mist. "Fog," she mumbled. "Fog is coming in. Where did it come from?" Her voice changed and seemed to take on another personality.

Athlone tapped Savaric's arm and nodded at the girl. The chieftain suddenly frowned and stepped forward, motioning his men to keep silent.

Gabria swayed, her eyes pinned in the fire. "The herds are in. Everyone is here, but . . . wait. What is that noise? Taleon, get Father. I must find Gabria. There are horses coming. It sounds like a large troop." Her words came faster and her face drained like a pale corpse. The men about her watched in fascination.

"Oh, my gods, they are attacking us!" she shouted and stood up, gesturing wildly. "They are burning the tents. We must get to Father. Where is Gabria? Who are these men?"

Abruptly her voice went heavy with grief and rage. "No! Father is down. We must stand and fight. The women and children run, but it is too late. We are surrounded by horsemen. Fire everywhere. We cannot see in this smoke and fog.

"Oh, gods. I know that man with the scar. These men are exiles! Medb sent them. He swore to kill us and he has. The cowards, they are bringing lances. Oh, Gabria, be safe . . ."

The words rose to a cry of agony and instantly died into a silence of emptiness and despair. Gabria's link with her brother snapped and the vision was gone. She trembled violently, then crumpled to the floor. A sigh, like a suppressed breath, wavered through the listening men.

For a long moment, Savaric stood staring into the fire. Finally he said, "Take him to the healer. We have heard enough for tonight."

Without a word, Athlone and another man wrapped Gabria in the scarlet cloak and carried her from the hall.

* * * * *

The healer, a tall, wiry man in a pale rose robe, touched Gabria's forehead with a cool hand and glanced at Savaric. "Forgive me, Lord, but you pushed him too hard. The boy is exhausted."

"I know, Piers, but I had to find out what he would tell us."

"Couldn't it have waited?"

"Perhaps." Savaric gestured to the prostrate form, still wrapped in the red cloak, sleeping on a pallet. "The boy hid it well. He is strong. I did not realize how worn he was until it was too late."

The healer's mouth twisted into a smile. "An hour or two of questioning before the clan elders would tire a lion. You mentioned a vision?"

"Hmmm." Savaric poured wine into two horn cups and took a swallow from one before he answered. "He seemed to be reliving the massacre at his treld—through someone else's eyes. Is it possible he could have fabricated what he told us? Or did he truly see a vision of what happened at the encampment?"

Piers sat down on a low stool and picked up his wine cup. Savaric leaned against the center pole of the tent. "A terrible shock and exhaustion can do strange things," Piers said thoughtfully. "He may have been dreaming what he imagined happened, or . . ." The healer shrugged, his thin shoulders shifting slightly beneath his loose robe. "I do not know. Medb is a cruel man and his powers are strange. Maybe this tale was planted in the boy's mind to confuse us, or maybe he did have a vision. It's been known to happen before."

Savaric gave him a wry grin. "You are not much help." He looked at the healer curiously. "What makes you think Medb had anything to do with this?"

"Word spreads fast, Lord. Besides, only Medb has the capacity and the ambition to destroy an entire clan," Piers replied.

"You don't think it was a band of renegades or marauders?" asked Savaric.

"I doubt it. Raiders like that take women and plunder. This attack was total destruction. No, I think the boy was right, and if he is, then Medb is getting bolder."

Savaric nodded, the worry plain on his face. "And stronger. We have ignored Medb's ploys for power for too long, Piers. If we do not break him soon, he will become too strong for any of us."

Piers's mouth hardened. "You are talking war, you know. A war that could destroy the clans."

"Medb will destroy us if he becomes overlord. I would rather die a free chieftain than live as his underling."

Piers drained his cup and poured more of the light, fragrant wine he loved. He took a long swallow, then said, "They say Medb is reviving the black arts."

Savaric glanced at the sleeping form under the cloak, then back at Piers. "They say many things about him, but that fact I find hard to swallow. His clan would not tolerate their chief practicing magic. It would mean dishonor for all the Wylfling."

"Not if they were already under his thumb. Magic can be used for other things besides creating fog."

"So you heard about that already, too." Savaric chuckled. "Was there anything you missed?"

The healer stared at the tiny fire in his hearth for some time before he answered. "Have you had any word from Cantrell or Pazric?"

"No. I am not worried about Cantrell. The bard has been gathering information for me for a long time. He can take care of himself, even in Medb's camp. But Pazric should have been back from the south by now. It does not take this long to negotiate a trade with the Turic tribes."

Piers nodded. The men were quiet for a while, each wandering in his own thoughts. Their silence was companionable, born of a long friendship and respect.

Finally, Piers said, "That boy is an enigma. Perhaps he holds a key you can use to unlock Medb's doom."

Savaric shook his head and straightened. "That is very unlikely. Even grown men can't kill Medb." He walked to the entrance. "But take care of him, Piers, or you will have an angry Hunnuli trampling your tent."

"Did this mere lad truly rescue a Hunnuli?"

"He certainly did."

Piers raised his wine cup in a mock salute. "Then he shall be treated like a hero."

Savaric matched his salute and left the tent.

* * * * *

Gabria slept through the night and most of the next day, lying motionless beneath her cloak, too weak to move even in sleep. Piers watched her anxiously, and several times he checked her to be sure she was still breathing. Outside the healer's tent, Nara waited patiently. Savaric visited once to check the boy's progress, but Gabria made no sound and still lay as if lifeless.

In the late afternoon, Piers was giving Gabria a sip of mild tea between her slack lips when, without warning, she began writhing and lashing out at him. Her face was twisted in hatred and her breath rasped in her throat. "No!" she cried hoarsely. "You can't have me, too."

"Easy, boy, easy." The healer held Gabria down and soothed her until the dream passed. With its end came a slow awakening to consciousness. Gabria's body relaxed, her breathing eased, and her eyes crept open until she was staring into the healer's concerned face.

"I don't know you," she whispered.

Piers sat back on his heels at the edge of the pallet and allowed himself a rare smile. The boy was obviously on the way to recovery, for there was no fear or hesitancy in his voice.

"I am the healer of the Khulinin. Piers Arganosta."

"That is a strange name for a clansman," Gabria said. Her voice was stronger and color was returning to her skin.

Piers was relieved to see the boy was not withdrawn or dwelling on his grief. Savaric was right: the lad was very strong. "I am not a clansman," he explained. "I am from the city of Pra Desh."

"What are you doing on the plains?" she asked curiously.

"Amongst the barbarians?" he asked with a touch of irony. "The city lost favor with me."

Gabria bristled at the word "barbarian" until she realized
that Piers was not being insulting; he was merely repeating a
phrase he had heard too often. His face was rather pleasant,
she thought, if a little sad, and his pale eyes reminded her of
mica: smoky and opaque. There was nothing pretentious
about him, a characteristic she did not expect from a man from
Pra Desh, the greatest of the eastern cities. In fact, he seemed
to deliberately avoid drawing attention to himself. There was
little bright color about him, nothing to draw the eye. He was
pale with light skin and fair hair cut short.

His tent was plain and simply furnished with a portable
medicine chest, a few light pieces of furniture, and an undyed
carpet. Hangings of cream-colored wool hung on the walls of
the tent, and another curtain hid his sleeping area. The soft
rose of his healer's robe was the only extravagant color Gabria
could see.

"I have never been to Pra Desh," Gabria said as the man
stood up and fetched a bowl of soup from the small pot on his
hearth.

"Then you are very blessed."

Gabria was unexpectedly irritated. How dare he say something like that. He knew nothing about her. "I have not been
blessed," she snapped. "By anything."

"You are alive, boy. Enjoy that," Piers exclaimed.

"I have no right to be. My place was with my clan."

"Your place was where the gods chose to put you." He
handed her the bowl, but she ignored it and glared at the open
tent flap, where the afternoon sun was slanting through.

"You are a stranger. What can you know of our gods and
their ways?" she retorted.

"I do know self-recrimination is useless. It does not bring
back the dead, so do not waste your gift of life on guilt or lost
opportunities."

Gabria continued to stare outside. "May I get up now? It
must be late."

Piers sighed. Obviously, his advice was being ignored. "If
you feel like it. The Hunnuli is waiting for you, and I am sure
you can find food in the hall."

"Thank you, Piers," she said coolly.

"You are welcome, Gabran."

The girl flinched at the name he used and wondered if she would ever grow used to the pain that clung to it. She stiffly climbed to her feet. Immediately, she wished she had not. Her muscles trembled, her head whirled, and dizziness shook her like an ague. She took a few faltering steps, then her ears roared and her stomach threatened to rebel. Piers wordlessly handed her a stool. She sank down gratefully and rested her head on her hands before the nausea overcame her.

"What is wrong with me?" Gabria groaned.

"Do you expect to go through all you have and not pay for it? You have used your body beyond its limits. And you have hardly eaten a thing. Give yourself time to snap back." He gave her the soup. "Now, eat this."

She took the bowl and sipped the meaty broth. "Thank you," she said again, this time with more sincerity.

Piers stepped to the tent flap and summoned a passing warrior. "Tell Lord Savaric the boy is awake." The man hurried away and within minutes, Savaric entered the tent. He was caked with dust and sweat, and a large falcon gripped his padded shoulder where his golden cloak had been pushed aside.

"The hunting was fair today, Piers," the chieftain said, his eyes on Gabria.

She sat on her stool, staring into the distance. Lost in thought, she had forgotten her precarious disguise and did not rise to give her chieftain a warrior's salute of fealty. Just then Gabria realized the men were looking at her and she sprang to her feet, spilling the hot soup over her leg.

"Forgive me, Lord," she stammered.

Savaric waved off her apology. "Your forgetfulness hardly matters here. But do not lose your memory before my other warriors."

Gabria nodded and sat down, chagrined. Her face reddened with embarrassment. Piers gave her a rag to clean the spilled soup and refilled her bowl.

"Your newest warrior will soon be ready to assume his duties," the healer said to Savaric. "He will be tender for a day or two, but he will toughen."

"Good. The boy will need all the strength he can muster."

"I understand Athlone is to be Gabran's mentor," the healer said.

Savaric chuckled. "Of course. Athlone wished to personally handle the boy's training."

"Athlone can go jump in a swamp," Gabria muttered.

The chief turned to her, his expression hard. "What did you say, boy?"

Gabria winced. She had not meant to speak so freely. She had to remember she was no longer with her own family. Her face blushed even brighter, and she stared at the ground speechlessly.

"Keep a civil tongue, Gabran," Savaric ordered, hiding a smile as Piers winked at him. "Tomorrow, if you can ride, you will begin your duties."

"Yes, Lord," Gabria mumbled as Savaric strode out. She sagged on her stool and gripped her bowl to still her trembling hands.

I am an idiot! she thought to herself. *First I forget to salute the chief, and then I scorn the wer-tain in front of his father. Careless mistakes like those could draw unwanted attention and expose the weaknesses of my disguise. There were too many other things to remember about behaving like a boy to be caught in some dull-witted error. I have to be more careful!* Glancing sideways at Piers, Gabria stretched out her legs in a masculine manner and rested her elbows on her knees as she finished her soup.

"Your Hunnuli has been waiting. Perhaps you might walk out and reassure her," Piers suggested when Gabria returned the bowl.

The girl nodded and stood up, waiting for the dizziness that struck before. This time, the soup steadied her and she found she was able to walk without shaking. Nara was by the tent's entrance and nickered in delight when the girl came out.

I feared you might be ill.

"No, just weary," Gabria said. She wound her fingers through Nara's ebony mane. "Have you had any food?"

No, I have been waiting for you.

"Then let's go down by the river. I need to think."

They walked side by side through the encampment, ignoring the faces that turned to watch them and the fingers that pointed their way. No one greeted them or offered them hospitality, and no one came near. Gabria was relieved when she and Nara left the tents behind and reached the banks of the river. It was difficult to hide her weakness and walk like a Corin past the staring clansmen. Her legs were trembling again and she felt lightheaded by the time Nara found a secluded place by the water.

Gabria gratefully sat down in the long, lush grass of the treeless bank while Nara began to graze. The girl leaned back, letting the wind touch her face and tufts of grass tickle her neck as she listened to the rippling music of the river.

We are being watched.

Nara's thought was a rude awakening. The mare still grazed in apparent disregard, but she faced away from the girl toward a bare hillock, where a lone horse stood, its head turned toward them.

Gabria glared at the distant horse, then turned away in disgust. "I'm not surprised. Where is the rider?"

There is none. That is a Hunnuli stallion.

"Athlone, the wer-tain." Gabria pitched a pebble in the water and watched as the circles were overwhelmed by the flow of the stream. "He sent his Hunnuli to watch us so he could be sure we do not try to contact Medb—or do anything else suspicious," she said sarcastically.

The man is cautious and has a need to be, the mare pointed out with mild reproof. *He is to be trusted.*

"Trusted!" Gabria cried. "He would kill me if he ever found my secret. One mistake, one little slip of my disguise, and he will spear me as neatly as a jackal." She pulled her cloak closer and added, "Women are not permitted to be warriors among our people. But I must try to be one. Death is the only thing I can trust to receive from Athlone if I fail."

It is too bad you feel that way. He would be a powerful ally.

"You are the only ally I need. You, my sword, and the good will of the gods."

They remained by the river for a long time while Nara ate her fill of the rich grass and Gabria watched the meadowlarks dip above the grazing livestock. They both ignored the watching stallion.

But Gabria found that her peace had fled her. She could not relax or let her mind wander while the Hunnuli stallion guarded her every move. She was not accustomed to such distrust or being treated with dislike. In all of her seventeen years, she had never felt so alone, for Gabran, her family, and her clan had always been with her. Nothing had prepared her for the endless confusion and emptiness that had dogged her steps since the day of the massacre. She was not a Khulinin and she never would be, but she wished someone would accept her with open arms. She wanted to be warm and comfortable and welcome, not pushed out in the shadows like a thieving beggar.

The evening was growing cold when Gabria and the mare returned to the treld. Nara led the way to the healer's tent. Piers was gone when Gabria entered, yet she found another bowl of soup warming by the fire and her pack lying on the sleeping pallet. Everything in the bag had been cleaned and mended, and a new tunic of soft linen had been added. Sleepy again, Gabria finished the soup, curled up in her cloak, and sank into another motionless sleep.

*   *   *   *   *

Athlone came for Gabria at dawn, when the echoes of the morning horn were fading. Astride his towering stallion, he shouted at her to come, for her apprenticeship was about to begin. She barely had time to grab a warm bun from Piers's table, pin on her cloak, and dash out of the tent before the wer-tain was cantering off toward the meadows. Groggily, she clambered onto Nara's back and followed, her irritation wide awake.

"Come on, boy, your duties start at sunrise," Athlone said when Gabria had finally caught up with him. "And don't let me catch you shirking."

He led her to a practice field where several targets and makeshift figures were set up. "Before I can begin your training," he stated, sliding off his horse, "I need to know what you can do." His tone implied that he did not expect much. Then, his eyes hardened to stone. "Where are your sword and bow?"

Gabria felt her stomach fall to her knees. The day had barely begun and already she had made a careless error. No warrior left his tent without his weapons; she had not even brought her dagger. "Wer-tain, I'm sorry," she gasped. "I do not have a bow and I . . . left my sword . . . in the tent."

Athlone walked deliberately around the horses until he stood by Gabria's foot. The silence crackled. "You what?" he snarled with withering scorn. "If such carelessness is characteristic of your clan, it is little wonder they were wiped out."

Gabria stiffened as if he had struck her. Her face went livid and her hand flew to her empty belt.

Careful, Nara warned, sidling away. *Keep still.*

"Return with your sword," Athlone ordered. "If you know what one looks like."

Before Gabria could reply, Nara wheeled and cantered back to the treld. Once they were out of earshot, Gabria clenched her hands in the Hunnuli's black mane. "That dog!" she screamed. "Insufferable pig! He just insulted an entire clan and I can do nothing."

They came to Piers's tent. Gabria stormed in and retrieved her short sword, the one she had taken from Gabran's hand.

"Trust him, you said!" she raged as she flung herself back on the mare. "I'd sooner trust a viper."

Nara deigned to ignore her. She carried the fuming girl back to the field where Athlone waited impatiently. Gabria spent the next few hours keeping her misery and anger tightly leashed. Athlone worked her at swordplay and hand-to-hand fighting. They began on horseback, where Athlone's stallion, Boreas, could help Nara with complicated maneuvers. Then they moved to the ground. Athlone pressed Gabria to the limit of her strength and skill.

A thousand times Gabria blessed her brothers for teaching her the rudiments of their weapons. She was no match for the wer-tain, but she could keep her borrowed identity from suspicion as she fought Athlone through each of his testing exercises. No woman should have known the fighting skills Gabria used.

Athlone worked her hard, both mentally and physically, and he watched Gabria's every move, waiting for her to slip from anger or carelessness. He deliberately taunted her, shot orders at her, and gave her no rest. When he finally stopped, late in the morning, she fell to her knees, panting and drenched with sweat. He stood back and studied her. The nagging little warning in his head was ringing madly, yet he still could not put a reason to his suspicions. The boy could hold a sword and he knew most of the basic moves, but there were some important details he did not know about swordplay that he should have. There was also a hesitancy in his attacks that belied a normal boy's experience with weapons.

Athlone sheathed his sword and whistled to Boreas. Whatever the boy's secret was, it was obvious from the past few hours that he had a great deal of determination. That was something in his favor.

"Keep practicing the last three parries I showed you," the wer-tain ordered. "Remember to keep your weight balanced or you will find yourself in the dust. I will take you to the saddler later." He vaulted onto the stallion's back.

Gabria glared at him, too tired to move. Without thinking, she said, "What for? I do not need a saddle."

"No," Athlone replied sarcastically. "Nara will keep you mounted. But you will need the other trappings befitting a warrior."

Gabria bit her lip as the stallion cantered away. She had done it again. She had walked into that blunder like a child. This acting was much more difficult than she had anticipated. When she had thought of this scheme, Gabria had imagined herself drifting easily into the fringe of Savaric's clan and playing the part of a boy with little concentration and great ease until she found the right time to challenge Lord Medb. If she could handle a bow and a sword, she could pretend to be a boy for as long as necessary.

But Gabria had never fully appreciated the countless

differences between a male and a female, not only physically and mentally, but socially as well. A boy would never have questioned the wer-tain about the saddler, for a boy would have already learned what was intended. A woman, on the other hand, made her own leather goods. She had no need to visit the saddler, who was the warriors' craftsman for saddles, harnesses, and leather accoutrements—things a woman had little use for.

In the clans, a woman was expected to keep her place in the tent. She was protected by the men in her family or her husband's family, and in return, the men demanded obedience. Despite their restrictive lives, the clanswomen were intelligent, efficient, and often fierce, but they understood and believed in the social mores of the clans and followed them by habit. No woman was allowed into the werod, the council, or any of the important ranks of the clan. Only the priestess of Amara and the wife and daughters of the chief had any status and esteem.

As the daughter of Dathlar, Gabria had had status in her clan, and as the only girl in a family of five men, she had been raised with love, respect, and a measure of equality. Her family had given her more freedom and responsibility than many clanswomen had, and she had been happy and content. Before the massacre, Gabria would never have dreamed of pretending to be a boy, or joining a werod, or challenging a chieftain for weir-geld.

However, her life was drastically different now, and she was forced to make some radical decisions. Gabria had chosen this plan of deception because she thought she had enough self-confidence and a great enough understanding of males to pull it off. Now, she was not so sure. There were too many details to constantly remember and so many ramifications she had no experience with. It was so confusing!

Gabria was still deep in her musings when Nara came to her side and brushed the girl's cheek with a velvety nose. *Are you going to sit in the dirt all day?*

Gabria shook her head, smiled, and stood up, her sword hanging limply in her hand. The girl knew it was too late to alter her course now. She could imagine some impending difficulties with her disguise, and there would be other problems she could not expect, but she would just have to handle the pitfalls as they came and hope for a great deal of good fortune. Gabria rubbed Nara's neck affectionately, and together they went in search of a midday meal.

Later that afternoon, Athlone took Gabria to the saddler. The girl had to be completely outfitted with a shield, belt, boots, leather jerkin, helmet, and a quiver for arrows. The old craftsman promised to have the items finished within a few days and he gave Gabria a used, restrung bow he had no use for.

Gabria also found an old, wide-brimmed hat in a pile of scraps the saddler had planned to throw away. The old man laughingly gave it to her and threw in a leather thong to tie the hat down on her head. The girl pulled the brim down low over her eyes and tried to look casual as she leaned against a post and waited for Athlone.

Athlone was still speaking to the saddler when a boy arrived and gave him a message from Savaric. The wer-tain quickly ended the conversation and, without a word to Gabria, hurried her to the clan hall.

Savaric was waiting for them in the main room of the hall. He stood beside a tall perch, feeding tidbits to his falcon and talking to two of his warriors. The two men saluted as Athlone and Gabria approached, then the men quickly left the hall.

"I'm glad you could come now," the chieftain told Gabria and Athlone as he moved to the dais. "I have just received word that a messenger has arrived. I would like you both to stay and listen."

Gabria sat down on the stone rim of the fire pit and tried to be inconspicuous. She wondered if the news the messenger brought concerned her in some way. She had made no effort to hide her trail at Corin Treld, and it was possible that someone had realized there could have been a survivor and spread the word. Enough time had passed for the news to reach the farthest clans.

"Gabran," Savaric said, jolting her out of her thoughts. "Remove your cloak and keep it out of sight."

"Yes, Lord." She unpinned the red cloak, folded it into a cushion, and sat on it. She should have remembered it herself. Her anonymity would be lost if another clan learned of her presence with the Khulinin, and, without some cover to protect her until she was ready to challenge Medb, her life would not be worth a slave's wage.

While she waited, the girl watched the chieftain and the wer-tain as they talked quietly. She marveled at the rapport that existed between the two men. Both men were strong individuals with very different personalities and yet their respect and love for each other was unmistakable. Many chieftains would have feared an intelligent, strong-willed son like Athlone when the question of clan control came into contention, but as far as Gabria knew, that question had never been raised between these two men. They worked together to rule the large and powerful Khulinin.

In other circumstances, Gabria might have grown to like Athlone, as much as she liked the chief. Nara was right: the wer-tain would make a potent ally, but Gabria and the wer-tain clashed from the beginning and their relationship was slipping from bad to worse. He grated on her already battered confidence. His arrogance, his caustic contempt, and his probing suspicions made it impossible for her to accept him as only a man. He hung over her consciousness like a great storm cloud, blinding her to other dangers and overwhelming her with his potentially deadly vigilance. Around Athlone, Gabria was constantly on guard and afraid. It was little wonder she acted like a bungling fool whenever he was with her.

She was still staring at the two men when the messenger, wearing the green cloak of the Geldring clan, was escorted into Savaric's hall. Gabria, seeing the messenger's cloak, edged farther into the shadows of a pillar and hoped he would ignore her. The Corin argued frequently with the Geldring and there had been much interaction between the two clans. It was possible the man would recognize her if he had seen her or Gabran in the past.

But the messenger only gave her a cursory glance as he passed, for his mind was on the news he brought. He bowed before Savaric and offered his chieftain's greetings. "Lord Branth bids me tell you—"

Savaric straightened in amazement. "Branth! When did he become chieftain?"

"Just before the massacre at Corin Treld. Lord Justar died quite suddenly of a heart ailment", the messenger said.

"Did a dagger cause his 'heart ailment'?" Savaric asked dryly.

The messenger looked uncomfortable, as if that thought had occurred to him before. "I do not know, Lord Savaric. Only his wife and Branth were with him when he died and his body was prepared for the pyre by his wife's hands."

Athlone and Savaric exchanged glances of silent speculation. Gabria was relieved she had not tried to seek refuge with the Geldring. Lord Justar had respected her father, but Branth hated the Corin with a passion. If she had gone to him, he would have turned her over to Medb. It was well known he supported the Wylfling chief.

Savaric shrugged slightly. "All right. Continue."

"We found Corin Treld two days after the killing, and we spent some time reading the signs of the battle. We discovered there may be a survivor, but we do not know who or what that person was or where he went."

"How do you know this?" Athlone asked.

"There was a makeshift funeral pyre near the ruins and five bodies had been burned. One, by the shield and helmet, was Dathlar. No enemy who slaughtered the clan like that would have afforded the chief such honor. We also found foot tracks leading out of the treld. They went south, then we lost them in a storm. Lord Branth feels we should search the foothills and send word to every clan to seek this survivor."

"Absolutely," Savaric agreed with the right amount of enthusiasm. "This survivor could be the last Corin."

Athlone shot a quick look at Gabria, who was sitting motionless, as if carved from stone.

"The rest of the information was not clear either." The messenger hesitated as if unsure how to continue. "But it appears that a large band of exiles attacked the treld."

The reaction the Geldring was expecting did not come. Savaric merely raised an eyebrow and said, "Indeed."

"You may not believe me," the messenger replied stiffly, "but Lord Branth believes it to be true. The hoofprints were those of unshod horses, and we found several broken arrows with colorless feathers. The attackers took or burned their dead."

Savaric drummed his fingers on his knee and looked thoughtful. "Branth is a minion of Lord Medb's, is he not?" he asked casually.

The Geldring started at the unexpected question and his hand came to rest on his sword. "I do not know, Lord."

Savaric raised his hand to reassure the man. "Forgive me. That was not a fair question to you. I merely wished to know if there were other reasons besides my ignorance to warn me of the exiles' infamy."

"I only report what I am told." The Geldring paused. "But you are not surprised about the exiles banding together and carrying weapons? It could mean more death and pillage for us all."

"Did they pillage the treld?" Athlone inquired.

Surprise overcame the young man's face as the realization dawned on him. "No. No, they did not. They burned everything and drove off the animals."

"There were other motives for the attack besides the greed of a few brigands." Savaric suddenly looked tired. "If that is all your news, then please rest yourself and take Lord Branth my greetings."

The messenger bowed again and left. A silence dropped in the hall. In the doorway, the guards stood in the sunlight that streamed down from the west.

Finally, Savaric stirred and rose slowly to his feet. He looked as if his mind were still grappling with the meaning of the Geldring's news. "Gabran," he said at last.

Gabria glanced up at Savaric's face. For a moment he seemed so old, as though the growing flames of tragedy and deceit that burned among the clans were more than he wanted to deal with. Then the look passed, the weariness and defeat were gone, and his eyes glittered.

Unconsciously, Gabria straightened her shoulders. "Yes, Lord?"

"It seems that your story is falling into place. You were careless, though. Medb will soon know his bandits were not thorough."

"I expected he would find out one way or another, Lord."

The chieftain smiled humorlessly. "True. But we must be more circumspect. You will wear the Khulinin cloak from now on. I do not wish to startle any guests."

Gabria nodded. She wanted to keep her cloak with her. It was her only link to her past and the happiness she had known. Nevertheless, she understood that wearing it would be unsafe, as well as an insult to the Khulinin who had tentatively accepted her. She would obey. For now.

"Also," Savaric continued, "you have the choice of sleeping with the other bachelors in this hall or with Athlone in his tent. He has no woman, but it would be more comfortable than the hall."

Gabria did not even consider the choice. "I will sleep in the hall."

Savaric chuckled. It was Athlone's duty to care for his apprentice, but if the boy chose to be on his own, then so be it. The chieftain stretched his legs as he stepped off the dais. "You will ride with the evening outriders for now."

"Yes, Lord."

"And, boy, be careful. You *are* the last Corin."

5

he smells of cooking food for the evening meal were warming the treld when Athlone took Gabria to the leader of the clan's outriders and left her in his charge. The man, a pleasant-faced warrior of thirty some years, wore his black hair bound in an intricate knot and had several gold armbands on his right arm.

He gave Gabria a pleasant smile. "My name is Jorlan. I am pleased to have the Hunnuli with us. I hope she does not mind such menial tasks as guard duty."

Nara nickered her impression of laughter and rubbed her nose on Gabria's back.

With Athlone gone, Gabria relaxed a little and enjoyed the leader's unexpected friendliness. It made it easier to ignore the hostile glances of the other outriders and the blatant gestures they made to ward off evil.

"She does not mind at all. Besides, she has to do something to earn all the grass she eats," Gabria said.

Jorlan laughed. He sent his men to their tasks, then mounted his bay horse and gestured to the meadows where the clan's herds grazed. "You will be riding with the brood mares tonight. They are due to foal soon."

Gabrina was surprised. No wonder the outriders had been so hostile. The brood mares were the most coveted herd to guard and the duty was usually given to the favored warriors in the werod. She, as the newest warrior-in-training, should have been sent to the farthest fringes of the valley to stand sentry duty.

On the other hand, if she considered the leader's point of

view, it was excellent sense to put the Hunnuli mare and her rider with the valuable brood mares. Nara was the best possible protector, combining the speed, strength, and senses of several men and their mounts. The duty was not given as a reward but for expediency.

"Right now, I will take you to the meadows to meet the meara," Jorlan added.

They followed the well-worn track down the hill to the extensive meadows that filled the valley. To the north, where the fields were protected from the winter winds by the backbone of Marakor, the Harachan horses were divided into several herds, each led by a stallion or mare of high rank. The largest herd was the work horses, the second was the yearlings and young horses in training, and the third was the brood mares.

Over all reigned the meara, the greatest stallion in eminence and rank. Each clan had a meara, which was chosen from their herds for the finest blood and ability, and these stallions were the pride and heart of their clans. No man dared lay a hand on one, save the chieftain, and to kill a meara was a crime punishable by the most hideous death. In the summer, the meara fought for his rank against selected males. If he was victorious, he was honored for another year; if he failed, he was returned with gratitude to the goddess, Amara, and the new meara ruled the herds.

The Khulinin meara was named Vayer. He was standing on a small hillock near the river, a mounted outrider with him. Even from a distance, Gabria would have recognized the horse as the meara. She had never seen a Harachan stallion to compare with him in form, beauty, or strength. He was a large chestnut with a golden mane falling from his high arched neck, and the gleam of fire in his hide. Although the Harachan horses did not have the size or intelligence of the Hunnuli, this stallion was wise from years of experience, and he carried his nobility like he carried his tail, as boldly as a king's banner in battle.

When Jorlan and Gabria reached the hillock, Vayer neighed a greeting. As Jorlan spoke to him, Gabria looked closer and saw the horse's muzzle was hoary with age, and scars from many battles marred his red hide. Still, his muscles were solid and his regal courage blazed in his golden eyes.

Vayer gravely sniffed Nara and snorted. She neighed imperiously in answer. The stallion, obviously satisfied, nickered to the men and trotted away. The outriders watched him go.

Jorlan and the rider talked for a moment longer, while Gabria looked over the herd of young horses nearby. They were a strong and healthy group, and they had wintered well. Their long coats had not shed yet and were still thick and shaggy. It would be a few more weeks before their sleek beauty was revealed.

The colts reminded Gabria of the Corin's horses. She wondered what had become of the brood mares, the yearlings, and the stallions. Had the exiles stolen most of them, or had the horses wandered onto the steppes and been taken into wild herds? Perhaps some of them had found their way to other clans. One horse she would have liked to have back was the Corin meara, Balor. He had been her father's pride and joy.

"We had a good yearling herd this year," Jorlan commented to Gabria.

Gabria nodded absently, her mind still on the lost stallion. "Amara should bless you with another rich Foaling," she said.

Both warriors stared at her in angry astonishment. Men did not speak of Amara and the Foaling in the same breath for fear of incurring bad luck. Amara was a woman's deity.

"Your fortunes have been bad," Jorlan snapped. "Do not cast any of it on us."

Gabria winced at the reproof. It was well deserved, for she had spoken thoughtlessly.

I should keep my mouth shut, Gabria decided, but it was too easy for her to slip back into her old habits. To make matters worse, she had forgotten what Jorlan reminded her of: she still carried the stigma of exile and death. Most people would refuse to look beyond that, and if anything unfortunate happened, especially a poor Foaling, they would find some way to blame her. She was an easy scapegoat—particularly if the clan discovered she was not a boy.

Jorlan said no more to Gabria and, after bidding farewell to the outrider, guided her to the brood mare herd.

The mares were pastured in a small valley at the edge of the mountains, where a creek flowed out of the hills to join the Goldrine River. Cottonwood, willow, and birch shaded the creek banks, and grass, herbs, and shrubs grew thick on the valley floor.

Spring was not well advanced, but already the fodder was green and lush, and the trees were bursting with budding leaves. There was a delicate, almost tangible essence of anticipation in the valley, as if the rising life in the trees and grasses and the stream had combined with the sunlight to bless the mares and their unborn foals. Almost fifty horses grazed contentedly among the trees, while the lead mare, Halle, kept a close watch on them all.

Nara whinnied a greeting when Jorlan led them into the valley. Halle returned her call and every mare close by replied with a ringing cry of welcome. The mares trotted over to greet the Hunnuli. Their bellies were distended and they moved ponderously, yet their heads swung gracefully as they sniffed the Hunnuli and her rider.

Another rider hailed Jorlan from the creek and came splashing down the stream to meet them. "Ye gods, she is a beauty," he called. His mount bounded up the bank. "I heard there was a Hunnuli in the treld, but I could not believe it." He ignored Gabria and stared at the great black horse. He was a tall, deceptively languid man with muddy eyes and an unconscious curl in his lip.

Gabria disliked him immediately.

"Cor," Jorlan called over the heads of the mares. "This is Gabran. He and the Hunnuli will be riding with you tonight."

The young warrior's pleasure abruptly vanished and anger darkened his face. "No, Jorlan. That boy is an exile. He cannot ride with the mares or his evil will destroy the foals."

Gabria clenched her hands on her thighs and stared unhappily at the ground.

"As you so aptly noticed, the boy rides a Hunnuli. You know full well the mare would tolerate no evil near her," Jorlan replied. His voice was edged with sarcasm and irritation, and Gabria wondered if he, too, had doubts about her effect on the mares.

Cor shook his head forcefully. "I will not ride with him. Let me have the Hunnuli. I can handle her. But the exile must go."

"Cor, I appreciate your concern, but the boy and the Hunnuli will stay."

Cor pushed his horse closer to Jorlan's mount and shouted, "Why should that boy be allowed to ride guard on the mares just because he has a Hunnuli? Why can't he earn the duty like the rest of us?"

Jorlan's patience was at an end. "One more outburst from you," he said tightly, "and you will be relieved. Your disobedience and insolence are intolerable. I have warned you before about your behavior."

Cor's face paled and the muscles around his eyes tightened in anger. "Sir, the exile will blight the mares. It's not right!"

"He is a member of the clan, not an exile."

The outrider slammed his fist on the scabbard of his sword. He wanted to say more, but the look on Jorlan's face stopped him.

"Return to your duties," Jorlan snarled. His tone left no room for argument.

Something swirled in the silty depths of Cor's eyes like the flick of a pike's tail. He snapped a look of fury at Gabria, reined his horse away, and sullenly rode back up the valley.

"Sir . . . ," Gabria started to say.

"Gabran, you will learn that I will not tolerate such arrogance or questioning of my orders."

"You do not believe I will bring evil luck to the mares?"

"What I believe does not matter. Lord Savaric gave me his orders." Then Jorlan glanced at Gabria's face and his tone softened. "Do not be concerned about Cor. He has received several warnings about his vindictiveness and bad temper. If he gets warned again, he loses his duty as outrider. He is probably more worried about himself than the mares."

Gabria glanced at him in gratitude. It was a relief to know Cor's attitude was not entirely her fault.

Jorlan whistled sharply and two large hounds bounded through the undergrowth. He tossed them some meat scraps from a small bag at his belt.

"The Hunnuli can guard the herd better than our men, but stay close to these dogs. The hunters found signs of a lion in the hills nearby." Jorlan started to leave, then came back. "If you need help, there is a horn hanging in that tree by the creek. Your replacement will be here about midnight." Jorlan left, cantering his horse back toward the treld.

Gabria was relieved to be left alone with Nara and the mares for a while. She could relax in their undemanding company and enjoy the peace of the evening. The evening was a lovely one, clear and mild, and the twilight gently lingered into night. The wind was cool and the stars glittered overhead in glorious sprays. The night was full of sounds familiar to Gabria: the ripple of the creek, the rustle of the trees, and the sounds of contented horses. She hummed a tune to herself while she rode Nara along the creek and scouted the surrounding hills, keeping watch for a mare in trouble or a hunting predator. The hounds padded silently beside her.

She only saw Cor a few times in the course of their duty. He remained near the head of the little valley and stayed to himself.

The moon, now waning, rose near the end of Gabria's watch. She and Nara stood under the trees at the mouth of the valley with the mare, Halle. The night was quiet; the dogs sprawled on the ground, panting.

Suddenly, Nara tensed. Her head came up and her nostrils flared. *Gabria, there is trouble.*

A stray breeze wafted down from the hills, disturbing the mares. Halle stamped nervously and whinnied a warning. The dogs sprang to their feet. Gabria reached for the horn that hung close by.

All at once, a blood-chilling squeal tore through the night. The mares panicked. Like a storm breaking, Nara bolted up the creek, the dogs fast on her heels. Gabria hung on desperately to the Hunnuli and clutched the horn to her chest. Shouting and wild whinnying broke out ahead. Terrified mares galloped down the valley away from some horror. Nara had to swerve violently to avoid them.

The small valley narrowed, and trees crowded around the

stream, making it difficult for Nara to run. The dogs surged ahead. They scrabbled over a gravel bank, came around a curve, and leaped a fallen tree into a clearing. Cor was already there, on his feet, his sword drawn, watching a cave lion crouched over the body of a dead mare. Faint moonlight gleamed on the lion's fangs and on the white blaze on the dead horse's face.

The tableau seemed to freeze for a moment as Nara and the dogs burst into the clearing, then everything shattered into a chaos of noise and motion. The dogs leaped at the snarling cat from either side and Nara drove her front hooves into the lion's head. The cat was knocked off the dead horse into a tumbling pile of snapping dogs. Gabria lifted the horn and blew peal after peal of strident notes.

During the furor, Gabria forgot about Cor. He slunk back to the trees' shadows and watched the fight, making no move to help. He studied everything for a moment, then a calculating smile tightened his thin mouth. Without a word, he faded into the darkness.

Before long, the lion had had enough. It fought its way out from under the dogs and bolted into the underbrush with a squall of pain and rage. The dogs were about to follow when a whistle brought them to heel. Mounted men bearing torches and spears crowded into the clearing behind Jorlan. Their faces were grim as they looked over both the dead mare and the boy on his Hunnuli. Several men stooped over the body and studied the tracks of the lion, then they disappeared into the brush on the cat's trail.

Jorlan looked up at Gabria. "Report, Outrider."

Gabria explained as best she could what had happened. It was then she realized that Cor was gone. Her heart sank. It was horrible enough that this hideous killing had happened during her first night as an outrider, but without Cor to collaborate her story, the clansmen would heap the blame, undeserved or not, upon her. The lion had found the straying mare near Cor's position, and even Nara had not discovered its presence in time. But those were merely excuses. The Khulinin would never forgive her for the loss of the precious mare.

Gabria could see the men's faces in the flickering torchlight; it was obvious what they were thinking. Only Jorlan seemed puzzled. He had dismounted and was walking carefully around the clearing, scanning the ground.

Nara neighed as Cor walked out of the trees. He was leading his limping horse. His clothes were torn and dirty. He tried to look surprised and horrified as he saluted Jorlan.

"This was your guard position, Cor. Where were you?" the leader demanded.

"My horse bolted a while ago and fell into a gully north of here. He hurt his foreleg, as you can see. I had a rough time getting us out of there." Cor sounded unhappy, but he could not completely hide the smugness in his voice.

Nara snorted in contempt.

Jorlan crossed his arms and raked the man with a furious glare. "While you were so conveniently absent, the cat killed a daughter of Vayer."

Cor shook his fist at Gabria. "It is the exile! His curse has brought this down on us. I tried to warn you."

The other men looked at their leader uncertainly. All of them were unsure how to deal with this strange boy and the complicated twists of his destiny. It was easy to dump the blame for this tragedy at the Corin's feet, but the men knew Cor well and they sensed something was not quite right about his story.

Jorlan refused to respond to Cor's feigned anger. "The boy told me you were here before him, on foot, and that you made no effort to help."

"He lies!" Cor shouted.

"I don't believe so," Jorlan said. "I have seen your tracks."

Cor looked sideways at Gabria and realized he had made a serious mistake. He licked his lips. "The exile should not have been guarding the mares. It is his fault this happened." He paused, sensing he was losing his credibility. The other warriors were muttering among themselves, and Jorlan was staring at the dead mare. Gabria was watching Cor from the back of the Hunnuli, as if waiting for him to trip himself. Cor's anger and embarrassment suddenly overwhelmed his common sense and he threw his sword at the Hunnuli. It missed and landed at her feet.

"All right, I was here," he shouted furiously. "My horse threw me. But that sorcerer's servant was the cause of this. He drew the lion here and was going to leave me to be killed, too. We cannot let him stay in this clan! He will doom us, just like the Corin."

Jorlan strode forward, struck Cor to the ground, and stood over him. "You are a disgrace. You are relieved of all duties as an outrider and your behavior will be reported to the chieftain for further punishment." Jorlan's voice was cold with disgust.

Cor looked wildly around the dark clearing for some sign of support from the other warriors. When he saw only the disdain on their faces, he jumped to his feet and ran into the trees. No one moved to stop him.

Gabria spent the last hour of her duty in a blur. She was badly shaken by the lion's attack and by the hatred she had seen in Cor's eyes. It was all she could do to stop her hands from trembling while she helped the men bury the dead mare in the clearing. The women would come later to bless the mound and send the dead mare's spirit to Amara, but Gabria paused long enough to whisper a quiet prayer of peace. The familiar, comforting words in her head eased her own pain a little, and when her replacement came at midnight, Gabria was able to bid good-night to the remaining men and leave the valley with a straight back.

The ride across the fields to the treld was the last quiet moment she had for the rest of the night. News of the attack had spread rapidly through the encampment and the clan was in an uproar. A hunting party was being organized. Groups of men clustered around the tents, discussing the import of the news while the women wept for the mare and her unborn foal. Cor had stormed into the hall and, after gulping down a flask of wine, was cursing Gabria and Jorlan at the top of his lungs, protesting his own innocence. Jorlan and most of his outriders had already returned and reported to Savaric.

Gabria and Nara stopped at the edge of the treld and watched the activity for several minutes. Gabria slid off the horse, and the Hunnuli dipped her head and gently rubbed her nose along the girl's chest. Gabria scratched Nara's ears. The girl wished she could borrow some of the mare's vast energy to bolster her own flagging strength. She was exhausted now, but she would have to sleep in the hall tonight with the unmarried men. She doubted she would have much rest.

I am going to the meadow. If you need me, I will come.

Gabria nodded and gave the horse a final pat. When Nara trotted away, the girl pulled her new golden cloak tighter about her and walked wearily to the camp. The light from the torches and campfires danced around her. The black tents sat like noisy, humped creatures with their backs turned against her. The clanspeople were busy preparing to hunt the lion, and, to Gabria's relief, no one noticed her. She passed by, a sad shadow in all the hubbub, unseen by all but one.

Athlone stood in the darkened entrance of his tent and watched as Gabria came up the path. His handsome face was hooded in darkness, so she did not see him as she went by. He waited until she was past the guards at the hall before he turned to fetch his spear from his tent.

Something still bothered him about that boy. The nagging suspicion would not stop. Why? The Corin showed spirit and courage despite his grief, and his determination seemed unshakable. Jorlan had reported favorably about the boy and his actions during the lion attack. Neither these attributes nor his unmistakable love for the Hunnuli were the usual characteristics of an exile on the run or a spy for an ambitious chieftain.

The mare was another curious aspect of the boy. The Hunnuli had accepted him, and the horses of that breed were impeccable judges of character. Even Boreas liked the Corin, although the big horse found something humorous about the mare and her rider. If the boy was treacherous or wicked, no Hunnuli would come within smelling distance of him.

Athlone had heard very recently that Lord Medb had tried to win a Hunnuli by capturing it and keeping it penned in a box canyon. As he understood the story, the horse had nearly killed Medb before throwing itself over a cliff, preferring death to serving the lord of the Wylfling clan. Athlone did not know how true the rumors were of Medb's injuries, but he was greatly saddened and not at all surprised by the Hunnuli's death.

Nevertheless, Athlone could not reconcile himself to Gabran's presence. Something was not right with the boy. There were too many little details in speech and movement that did not fit. What was he?

For a fleeting second, Athlone remembered the Shape Changers, the sorcerers of ancient legend who had learned shape changing to avoid punishment for practicing magic. He shuddered. But that was long ago. The heretical magic was dead and its followers died with it. It did not matter, though. The boy was no magician, simply a clansman with a secret that might prove dangerous to all.

Athlone found his spear and walked out of his tent to join the hunt for the lion. He could only hope that he would discover what the boy's secret was before it proved fatal for someone in the clan.

* * * * *

The huge doors of the hall were still open when Gabria returned from the fields. She entered the hall reluctantly and stood blinking at the sudden light. A fire was burning low in the pit and a few lamps still glowed from the ceiling beams. As she became accustomed to the light, the girl saw her pack and the new bow lying by the nearest pillar. Looking up, she saw several men already asleep on blankets and furs along the right-hand wall, beneath the colorful tapestries of Valorian's adventures. The storerooms were closed and the heavy curtain was drawn over the entrance to Savaric's private quarters. Four other men were sitting on the opposite side of the fire at a trestle table. Two were playing chess, one was watching, and the fourth was slumped over a wine flask.

Every clansman was entitled to a tent of his own once he reached manhood. The huge, black felt tents were made by the man's family and presented to him at the initiation of his warrior status. However, the tents were difficult to maintain, and it was usually the women who kept the fires burning, patched the holes, and kept the tents neat and pleasant. Most bachelors, therefore, chose to sleep in the hall. It was warm, relatively comfortable, and did not have to be packed every time they moved. They could eat there and entertain themselves long into the night without disturbing the treld.

Yet, despite the freedom and convenience of the hall, most men did not stay there long. Marriage and the tents, even with their numerous problems, were preferable to the conditions of bachelorhood. A man needed a woman, his own hearth, and the privacy of the felt walls. The clans survived because of unity and cooperation, but they retained their identity because each man valued his own individuality and the strength drawn from his home, even one that was packed into a cart every summer.

Gabria certainly did not feel at home in the strange, pillared hall. She was nervous being with these men in such close and intimate quarters. She could see at least one of the sleeping men was wearing nothing beneath his blankets. With her own family that would not have bothered her, for she was used to seeing men in various stages of undress. But here she had no brothers to defend her, no chieftain's quarters for security, and no protection as the chief's daughter. She had nothing but a disguise—and a flimsy one at that.

Quietly, she slipped along to the right-hand wall to the gloomiest corner, away from the sleeping men. Gabria fervently hoped no one would notice her. If she could curl up in the blanket Piers had given her, perhaps they would not realize she was there.

"We have a new member in our illustrious ranks," a voice called out in a raucous tone. "Take note of him, men, a boy who has barely left his mother's breast and already he has lost his clan and killed our mares."

Gabria cringed at the words. Slowly she turned and stared at the speaker. It was Cor. He was sitting at the table, waving a wine cup in her direction. The other three men had previously ignored him, but now they watched in anticipation of some entertainment. Gabria turned her back on them and tried to disregard Cor's sniggers. Cor was swaying gently, but his voice was not broken or slurred.

"He sits on his great black horse and spits on us while he deafens the lords with his whining and pleas of innocence." Cor staggered toward the girl as the others watched in interest. Gabria listened apprehensively.

"But I know you. I can see what you keep hidden beneath your bold face."

Gabria stiffened and her eyes widened.

"You are a coward!" he hissed. He was so close to Gabria, his breath brushed her neck. "A spineless pile of sheep dung who fled his clan instead of standing and fighting. Or did you lead the attackers to the camp? You are so brave when you are sitting on that black horse, but how brave are you, worm, when you are low to the ground on two puny legs?" Viciously, Cor grabbed Gabria's shoulder and spun her around.

The girl stepped back against the wall, too terrified by the drunken rage that distorted Cor's features to run. The other warriors cheered them both and taunted Cor with bets and jibes. No one moved to help Gabria. Disgruntled yells came from the men who had been awakened. The shouts, jeers, and insults crashed together into an unnerving cacophony. Gabria threw her head back.

"Stop it!" she shouted. "Leave me alone."

"Leave me alone," Cor mocked. "Poor little worm is not so brave after all. He needs his mama. But she's dead and rotting with the other Corin." He rocked back and forth in front of Gabria, exuding wine fumes. His muscles seemed to bunch beneath his tunic.

Without warning, Cor slapped her. Gabria gazed at him speechlessly. "You brought the lion. It is your fault the mare died and I lost my duty. No one would listen to me . . . but you will. You are going to listen to me until you are crushed beneath my boot." He chuckled at himself. Getting no reaction from Gabria, Cor hit her again savagely. She tried to avoid it, but she was too late. The blow sent her reeling, and blood spattered her tunic from her split lip. The other men looked on, neither helping nor hindering. Cor came at her again.

"Stop it!" Gabria cried, stumbling away from him. "Go away."

"Go away," he sneered. "Not for a while, my little man, not until you crawl at my feet and plead for my forgiveness." He swung at her again and smashed her in the face. Gabria crashed into the wall and collapsed on the floor, her head ringing with pain, blood pouring from her nose.

"Crawl, worm," Cor shouted gleefully. He kicked her in the side. Waving to the others in victory, Cor stood over Gabria like a conqueror, gloating at his prize. He reached down for her again.

Gabria was lying still, panting in shock and fear. Then she saw Cor's hand coming. Deep within her emotional prisons, the frustration and anxiety she had suffered the past few days fused together in a furious surge of power. Unbeknownst to her, an aura began to glow faintly around her hands as the white-hot energy of her emotions burst outward to every muscle and nerve ending, overcoming her pain and weakness. The power ignited in her eyes. She screamed like a cat.

Without a conscious thought, Gabria reached behind her shoulder and grasped her new bow. The unseen aura in her hands flowed up the weapon. Before Cor could react, she rolled off the bow and, with both hands, swung it upward between his legs. The stave caught him neatly in the groin. Just for a second, there was a burst of pale blue sparks.

Cor howled in agony and doubled over. Gabria rolled away, stood up, and crouched, her bow held before her like an axe. But Cor could barely move. He slowly toppled to the ground and lay curled in a ball, moaning. As the warriors moved to him, Gabria backed into the corner, still gripping her bow and trembling with rage. Her green eyes glinted dangerously.

"Nicely swung, boy," one of the warriors said with a grin.

"Cor won't be riding for a day or two," added another man. "Especially the wenches." They all laughed uproariously.

Gabria stared at them speechlessly. The warriors shook their heads and left her alone while they picked up their whimpering companion and tossed him unceremoniously on his blanket. Then, the sleepers returned to sleep, the chess players continued their game, and a subdued quiet settled over the hall—all as if nothing had happened. Only Cor's soft moaning was out of place in the illusion of friendly peace.

Gabria stood in her corner without moving. Her anger and the pale blue aura that no one had noticed subsided, leaving her drained and empty. She dared not move for fear of disturbing the fragile peace.

Gabria knew fist fights and brawls happened constantly in the hall, often just for the fun of competition. But the violence and hatred of Cor's attack was not part of the camaraderie. He blamed his disgrace on her and wanted his revenge. Gabria glanced at Cor, as if he might jump on her again, but he remained curled like an infant, whimpering and weeping. She dreaded to think what Cor would do when he recovered. He did not have the manner of a man who forgave readily.

Gabria shuddered and sank to her knees. Maybe she should accept Athlone's tent. At least he would not beat her. No, she reminded herself sharply, he will kill me if I reveal my identity, and it will be much more difficult to hide in the confines of a tent. But is it safer here with more ears to listen and eyes to watch? Safer with Cor's dagger within easy reach of my heart? Oh, gods, what am I going to do? Either choice could mean death.

The girl clutched her blanket about her shoulders, thankful for its warm comfort, and huddled into the corner. Her face felt horrible—swollen and caked with blood—but she was not going to move from her corner. She was safe there, for the night at least. Perhaps she could decide what to do tomorrow. Cor might decide to leave her alone, although she doubted it, or perhaps her goddess would provide a way to protect her. Amara had always been with her. Gabria took solace in that, and, after a long while, when the fire had died down, she fell asleep.

Gabria awoke long before dawn. In the deepest hour of the night, she dreamed of a blue fire in the core of her mind. She tried to banish it, but it was a part of her and it would not be denied. It grew in intensity and surged outward from her hands, taking the form of a lightning bolt that seared a path through the surrounding darkness and burned with the vengeance of a dying star. Unerring, it struck a half-seen figure of a man and burst him into countless flaming fragments.

Gabria bolted awake in horror. She knew without question what that deadly flare had been. Sorcery. She cringed as she gazed at her hands in the dim light of the single lamp that still burned. She vaguely expected to see a glow of blue still on her fingers where the bolt had sprung.

How could it be? Why had she dreamed of magic? She knew nothing about the arcane except the half-truths of legends and the clan strictures that forbade its profane use. Sorcery had been eradicated generations ago and anyone guilty of trying to resurrect it was put to immediate death. So where had that dream sprung from? Gabria had never considered using such power, and she did not think wielding magic was an inherent ability.

Since birth, Gabria had been taught that sorcery was an evil heresy. The priests claimed sorcery was an abominable sham of the gods' power, an insult to the deities and the cause of hideous retribution upon anyone who tried to use it.

Gabria shuddered at the memory of her dream. It was impossible that she could create that blue fire herself. She did not have the knowledge or desire to do so. Yet why had she dreamed of that power now? She sat frozen in a crouch, musing over the fading images of her dream, very afraid of falling asleep and dreaming again.

When the horn of morning faintly echoed in the hall, Gabria was still awake. The warriors rose from sleep, laughing, yawning, and grumbling. They rolled their gear out of sight, into a storeroom behind a tapestry, and prepared themselves for another day. A serving girl brought cups of steaming wine and heaps of meat-stuffed rolls. Gabria remained still.

Athlone, back from the night's hunt, found her as she had been most of the night, hunched in the corner beneath her blanket, her eyes fixed on something in the distance. The wertain breezed into the room, smelling of morning dew and horse's sweat, and greeted the men. He saw Gabria in the corner and anger pulled at his mouth. Muttering a curse, he ripped off the blanket and yanked her to her feet.

"I warned you about shirking . . ." His voice trailed off as she slumped against him and he saw the bruises and dried blood on her battered face. She feebly pushed against him and tried to stand alone, but a searing pain melted her ankle. With a moan she could not stop, she fell to the floor. Sometime during the fight with Cor, she had wrenched her barely healed ankle again.

"What happened?" A look of pity intruded into Athlone's stony eyes.

"I fell down the steps last night," Gabria answered listlessly. She shoved against the wall and painfully levered herself to a standing position. She teetered on one foot, glaring at the wertain, daring him to gainsay her.

The pity faded and Athlone turned to the warriors who were watching as they ate. "What happened?" he repeated harshly.

One man jerked a thumb at Cor, who was still lying curled on his bed, apparently asleep. Athlone's brow lifted, and he strode over to the recumbent warrior. He leaned over to shake Cor's shoulder. At the first touch, his hand leaped back as if scorched.

"Good gods," Athlone said in astonishment. "This man is burning with fever. Tabran, call the healer quickly." Then he remembered Gabria standing in the corner with blood on her face, and his nagging suspicions turned to a noisy warning. But he still was not sure why.

"The rest of you men get to your duties," Athlone ordered. "Now."

The men glanced at each other uneasily, and fetching their weapons, filed out the door. Athlone stayed by Cor. The wertain's face was bleak and his body was tense with his unnamed suspicions.

"I am going to ask you again," he said without turning around. "What happened?"

Gabria heard the change in his voice immediately. He suspected something strange had happened between her and Cor. "I hit him with a bow," she snapped.

"Why?"

"I should think that is obvious, Wer-tain." Piers's voice came from the entrance. "Just look at him. The boy was being beaten."

Athlone and Gabria turned to the healer as he came into the hall. "I asked the boy," Athlone said, rankled by the man's immediate defense of Gabria. "I want to know what happened to Cor."

"I know what you meant." Piers's pale eyes were like the clouds of a winter storm as he helped Gabria to the fire pit and made her sit on the stone rim.

Gabria watched the two men surreptitiously. Even through her listlessness and pain, she could recognize the signs of a long-lived dislike between the healer and the wer-tain. Piers's movements were hurried and brusque. It was as if he could not wait to be away from Athlone's demanding presence. Athlone, on the other hand, seemed to be edgy and impatient dealing with the quiet foreigner. Gabria found Athlone's discomfort interesting, and she drew closer to Piers's supporting arm.

Athlone glared at them both, annoyed that the boy had found such a quick ally in the healer. "The boy will live. I called you here to see to Cor."

"If Gabran lives, it will not be because of your efforts. I asked you to go easy on him yesterday until he recovered, but you deliberately ran him into the ground." Piers squeezed Gabria's shoulder and went to examine the unconscious warrior. The healer's mouth opened slightly in surprise when he touched Cor. He quickly straightened out the man's body and checked him over carefully.

"How strange. I have never seen anything quite like this," Piers said worriedly. "What did you say happened to him?"

Athlone gestured to Gabria. "He hit him with a bow."

"Certainly a mere blow could not have caused this." Piers checked Cor again, and a small frown creased his forehead. "Hmmm. I wonder . . . have some men take him to my tent."

Athlone called the guard and gave his orders. He asked Piers, "What is wrong with him?"

"I am not sure. He has a high fever, among other things, but this is something quite unusual. Gabran, you had better come, too."

"He has work to do," Athlone said flatly.

The healer shook his head. "Not today. Not in his condition."

"Your defense of him is misplaced, Healer. He can obviously care for himself," Athlone stated as he picked up Gabria's fallen bow.

Gabria could not look at Cor. She stared at the floor, and the memory of her dream returned like a hidden shame. A pang of guilt made her shiver, but she could not believe it was possible that the dream held any truth. She had only hit Cor with a wooden bow, not magic. There was something else wrong with him, something very easy to explain.

"The healer is right, Athlone," a woman's voice came from the back of the hall.

"Good morning, Mother." Athlone smiled at the small, fair-haired woman standing by the curtain to the chieftain's quarters.

"Good morning, son, Piers, and you, Gabran. I am Tungoli, lady of Lord Savaric."

Gabria returned her greeting and, for the first time since she came to Khulinin Treld, she felt that she was meeting a friend. Tungoli's eyes were as open and as green as summer, and her expression was warm and smiling. She was a comely woman whose true age was hidden by a gentle beauty that grew old with grace and radiated from her contentment within. Her hair was braided and wound with a dark gold veil. Her hands were slender, yet strong and confident. She walked toward them with a loose-jointed stride that swirled her green skirt about her feet.

"The boy needs rest," Tungoli said to Athlone. "There is no sense having two warriors ill. But," she added soothingly, cutting off Athlone's next words, "if you insist he stay busy, I have a few things he can help me with." She slipped her arm through Athlone's and led him aside, continuing to talk to him all the while.

Piers sighed, an audible sound Gabria barely caught, and he shook his head. "Tungoli and Savaric are the only ones Athlone bows to," he said softly to Gabria. "Tread carefully around him."

Several men arrived then and helped Piers lift Cor's body onto a makeshift stretcher. The healer said, "Wait here, Gabran. I'll send them back for you."

In the corner of her eye, Gabria saw Athlone watching
them, and her pride dragged her to her feet. The pain sucked
the breath through her teeth. "No. I'll come now," she managed to gasp.

"Do not be long about it," Athlone demanded.

Tungoli lifted her eyes to her son in mild reproof. "Athlone,
your thoughtlessness is atrocious. Gabran, let them come for
you. When the healer is through with you, come to see me."

"Mother, you are interfering again."

"I know. But if I do not, who will? The entire treld is terrified of you," she said, laughter in her voice.

Gabria collapsed on the stone rim again and gazed at the
woman thankfully. Tungoli reminded Gabria of her own
mother, in a vague, comforting way, and it would be delightful
to spend some time with this lady and be out from under
Athlone's iron hand.

Piers nodded to Gabria and followed the stretcher bearers
out the door. Gabria did not respond, for she was too engrossed watching Tungoli and Athlone. The small woman
looked so incongruous standing up to the tall, muscular warrior, but Gabria was certain the mother won most of their battles. In her own gentle way, Tungoli was just as stubborn as
Athlone.

"All right, all right. The boy is yours for as long as you need
him. Just don't spoil him," Athlone exclaimed.

Tungoli crossed her arms and nodded. "Of course."

Gabria felt as if a great weight had been taken from her
shoulders. She was free from Athlone for a time and she was
free of Cor long enough to gather her wits. Gabria still had to
decide where she was going to sleep in the future, and she
wanted to consider her dream. Perhaps Piers could help her
understand. Being from Pra Desh, he would not have the horror of sorcery any clansman would. Maybe the healer would
talk to her and give her some reassurance that her dream had
been only a figment of her imagination.

Gabria still felt unreasonably guilty for Cor's sudden illness.
Although she was certain it was not her fault, she could not forget the flare of blue power that struck from her hands with

such deadly swiftness, or the nameless fear in her heart that there was a connection between the fight and her dream.

"Come on, boy." Athlone walked to her side. "I'll get you to the healer and back before my mother starts on another speech."

To Gabria's surprise, he slipped her arm over his shoulder and helped her up. Gabria was too stunned by his move to object. Speechless, she looked at Athlone from a few inches away. He met her eyes and, for the first time, his brown eyes did not clash with her green. The wer-tain gave her a sketchy smile, and they moved out the door.

6

ain was falling when Athlone and Gabria left the hall, a cold, steady drizzle that soaked through clothes in minutes and chilled everything into a lethargy. The low-slung clouds moved sluggishly over the mountains, as if they too were reluctant to hurry on. Gabria closed her eyes, not wanting to see the dismal dawn, and leaned wearily into Athlone.

His gesture of help surprised her. She would have expected him to urge her out with the flat of his sword rather than the strength of his arm.

"The healer was right. Cor beat you badly," Athlone said, looking at Gabria from only a headspan away.

The girl quickly turned her face away. If he was this close and watching her so intently, he could notice details she did not want him to see, like the smoothness of her cheek. There was no dirt to disguise her skin and not enough tan to hide the softness of her face at such a close range. The bruises helped, but the wer-tain was beginning to look puzzled.

Gabria deliberately stumbled and slammed into Athlone's calves as she fell. He lost his balance, tripped over a tent rope, and fell on top of her. Gabria froze in fright. His weight crushed her into the mud, but it was nothing compared to the fear of what he might discover as he lay on top of her. She had not meant to bring him down like this!

"I'm sorry, Wer-tain," she blurted from under a tangle of cloaks and swords. Athlone moved off her. Every bruise and ache in Gabria's body complained. It took all the willpower she had to control a cry of pain. The warrior stood up and offered a hand to her. Once again the wer-tain surprised her—he was laughing.

She staggered up and looked down at herself ruefully. Athlone would never cease to amaze her. Instead of berating her for her clumsiness, he was laughing like it was a joke. They were both covered with mud—at least she did not have to worry about her face for the moment—yet he was not angry. Thank the gods he had not put his hands in the wrong places.

"Keep this up, boy, and you will not live long enough to claim your weir-geld," Athlone said.

She smiled shakily at him and replied, "I will have my revenge if I have to crawl to Medb and stab him in the knees."

"No one has tried that yet." Athlone took her weight again and his humor disappeared. "You are the most stubborn whelp I have known. That trait is infuriating, but it can be a good advantage." He lapsed into silence, and they crossed the distance to Piers's tent in thoughtful quiet.

The healer's eyes widened as they came in, whether in surprise at Athlone's action or at their appearance, Gabria could not guess, for he only motioned to a water skin and bent back over his patient.

Gabria felt an unexpected warmth for the wer-tain at her side. It was the first sign of friendship he had offered since she had arrived, and the coldness in her heart retreated a pace as Athlone sat her down on the low stool, poured a bowl of water, and handed it to her with a rag.

Athlone paused at the tent flap before he left. A streak of mud creased his face and dyed half of his mustache. More mud was smeared on his gold cloak and down his legs. His soft boots were caked. "When you are through here, go to the Lady Tungoli. But do not expect to be coddled by her for long. I will be waiting for you." The wer-tain's voice turned glacial again. The veiled threats had returned.

Gabria stared after the warrior as the dark flap closed behind him. It was as if their moment of companionship had never happened. The wer-tain's suspicions closed around her again like a trap. The girl shivered. For just a moment, she had nourished a hope that he would leave her alone or maybe help her as Nara suggested. But his confusing manipulations leaped ahead of her and blocked her speculation like a granite cliff.

"The wer-tain is an interesting man," Piers said.

Gabria tore her gaze from the entrance and watched the healer as he worked swiftly over Cor. "Do you always know what I am thinking?"

"It does not take a mindreader to interpret that look on your face. You are overwhelmed by the good chieftain's son." He shook his head. "You are not the only one."

"I noticed you are not comfortable with him," Gabria noted dryly.

"No. Athlone has a strong presence. Savaric rules the clan, but Athlone is its mettle. Where he goes, the werod follows. Not even Pazric, the second wer-tain, wields the immediate obedience of the riders."

Gabria stretched her legs out to ease her ankle to a more comfortable position and dabbed half-heartedly at the mud on her face, considering Piers's words all the while. Cor was lying motionless on the mat she had slept on, his face still captured in pain. Piers was wrapping the warrior's body in warm blankets.

"Who is Pazric?" she asked when the silence had gone on too long.

"He is Athlone's second in command," Pier replied.

"I do not remember him."

"He is in the south, meeting with one of the Turic caravans."

"Does the werod always follow Athlone without question?" Gabria asked. She was trying to think of some way to lead the conversation around to her dream and Cor's condition. As repugnant as the answer might be, she had to know if there was any connection. The dream was such a strange coincidence, and only Piers would have the openness of mind to help her understand it.

"I realize you and Athlone do not approve of each other. It takes time to know him." Piers shrugged as he stood up. "Even that may not help. But don't ever go against his authority, or the entire werod will tear you to pieces." The healer removed some items from his chest of medicines and poured a small heap of dark gray grains into a mortar. As he ground the grains, a pungent smell filled the tent. It reminded Gabria of cloves, and she inhaled deeply.

Piers worked for several minutes before he spoke again. "What happened between Cor and you? May I assume he started it?"

"I don't know," Gabria muttered, feeling guilty again. "He wanted a fight with me, for what happened in the fields last night."

Piers added a few dried leaves to his powder and continued grinding, his robe swaying gently with his movements. "You are not accustomed to fighting, are you?"

Gabria stiffened. "What do you mean?" she asked carefully.

"It's obvious. You are beaten bloody and he does not have a mark on him. You won by luck . . . or something else." When Gabria did not answer, he laid the pestle down and turned to face her. His pale eyes were sad, but his face had a strange look of wariness. "Do you know what is wrong with this man?" His words were soft, but edged with steel.

Gabria felt as if her mind would shrivel into dust. A cold fear clenched her stomach and her breath failed even as she drew it. Piers obviously thought Cor's condition was not just a simple illness. All the terrors of her dream surged back in the face of his unspoken accusation. "No," she whispered. The word escaped her lips and leaped at his silence. "What have I done to him?" she cried, clenching her fists to her sides.

"So you admit this injury was caused by you."

Gabria stared at the healer miserably. "I don't know what I caused. I only hit him with a bow . . . but later I had a dream of a blue flame that sprang from my hands and struck a man. I don't know why I would dream of something like that. All I did was hit Cor to make him stop beating me." She suddenly stopped the flood of words, then took a deep breath and asked, "What is wrong with him?"

"I am not certain either," Piers said quietly. "I have a very good idea, if I can only believe it."

Gabria hunched over as if a pain stabbed her stomach. "What?"

"He has suffered a severe shock. He has a high fever and

rapid heart beat. Unusual symptoms for a mere blow to the groin."

"Will you just tell me?" Gabria cried.

"No." Piers strode over to her side and leaned over her, no longer hiding his anger. "You tell me, Gabran. You only hit him with a wooden bow, you say, but this man has been wounded by an arcane power called the Trymian Force. Where did it come from?" Abruptly, his hands dug into her shoulder, and he hauled her to her feet. She swayed, staring at him in dumb dismay. "That man may die, and I want to know why. Did your power come from Medb?"

The sound of that name galvanized Gabria like a shock. She wrenched away from the healer and grasped the center tent pole for support. "I received nothing from Lord Medb but death, and that is all he will receive from me," Gabria gasped, shaking with anger.

Piers eyed her dubiously, his arms crossed. He wanted to believe the boy was not an agent of Medb, yet the Wylfling lord was the only one rumored to be delving into sorcery and Gabran was the only one Piers knew of who had struck Cor in the past day. "Then how is it that Cor suffers from the Trymian Force?"

"I don't know! I don't even know what you are talking about." She leaned into the pole, her eyes beseeching him. "I didn't want to hurt him. I just wanted him to leave me alone."

Piers watched her expressions and was satisfied. The boy was telling the truth about this at least. After years at the court in Pra Desh, he had learned to recognize truth and deceit hidden in people's faces. The green eyes that met his were free of guile. Piers saw only bewilderment and a desperate plea to be believed.

The healer sighed as he stared into those eyes. Before, Piers could not have said what color they were; now he knew they were as green as the sea with the same subtle lights and the same feeling of power. He shook his head, surprised by the depth of Gabria's gaze. It seemed to the healer that even if the boy did not have a talent for magic, he certainly had the inner strength to wield it.

"All right, sit down," he ordered. He poured a cup of warm wine into which he added a small dose of poppy extract. "Here, drink this."

Gabria glared at him and did not move. "What is it, a truth drug?"

"No, boy. Now sit down. It will dull the pain so I can examine your ankle."

Gabria hesitantly accepted the cup and returned to the stool. Piers's attitude had changed. The suspicion was gone from his voice and had been replaced by a tone of resignation. She wondered what conclusion he had reached. It was difficult to read this city-bred man, for he kept himself behind an unbreakable facade—motionless features, still eyes, and a modest manner. He had none of the unrestrained character of the steppe clans. The endless, wild, easily given emotions of the clanspeople were alien to Piers's way of life. Nevertheless, the healer had abandoned his lifestyle and sought a new life on the plains. Whether he did this to forget his past or to find a new existence, Gabria did not know, but she wished she knew what had made him leave Pra Desh. The answer might explain much.

Gabria left her drink on the table for the moment and watched as Piers continued grinding the powder. Neither spoke. The healer seemed content to let the problem settle for a while and rationality return before taking the next leap. Gabria was relieved by his silence. The acknowledgment of the possibility of sorcery was made. But now that it was said, she was not sure she wanted to know if she was the source of that magic. It was enough to have to bear the weight of her grief and the need for revenge, without the fearsome burden of a heretical power she did not even want. No, she implored silently, gripping her hands. It had to be impossible. Sorcery was learned, not an inherent talent.

Piers laid aside the bowl and opened his medicine chest again. The large wooden chest, the only thing he had brought from Pra Desh, was filled with a myriad of drawers and trays. Gabria noticed each one was crammed with packets, bags, vials, bottles, boxes, wrapped bundles, and scraps of paper, all clearly labeled. The healer poked through several drawers, then, from one of the smaller trays, he drew out a smooth red stone the size of an eagle's egg. He juggled it several times before he spoke.

"Forty years ago, when I was an apprentice to the senior physician of the fon of Pra Desh, I met an old man in the market square. He claimed he was the son of a clansman and had been exiled because he accidentally murdered a cousin with sorcery. He had escaped death only by fleeing before anyone caught him."

Gabria stared at the stone in the healer's hand. "Why are you telling me this?"

"Because the man was a Corin."

She came alert. "You lie," the girl snapped, though she said it with more hope than conviction.

Piers shook his head. "My master was a fancier of magic and studied the history of its use. He thoroughly examined this man and confirmed the truth. The Corin, who had no training and had never witnessed a performance of sorcery, had been born with a talent to call the powers to his bidding."

Gabria felt numb. Whether she wanted it or not, the truth was coming out. Somewhere she would have to find the strength to face the awful possibility that she could be a sorceress. "What is the Trymian Force?" she asked. The fear in her voice threatened to spill into tears.

Piers saw the tense lines that altered the boy's face. There was a stubborn dimension to that face that showed his strength and will to survive. He had noticed it before, and now it was very apparent in the clenched jaw, the tight muscles around the mouth, and in the way the boy did not hide from the truth. It was good. Gabran would need every advantage to live to the next wintering. The healer knelt by Cor and stared at the warrior. A tremor moved beneath Cor's jaw where the blood raced under the skin, and the heat of his fever beaded into sweat on his forehead.

"The spell," Piers said slowly, as if remembering a long forgotten passage, "is the marshaling of the different flows of energy that constitute magic into one destructive force that can penetrate most defenses. It often appears as a blue flame. It is only as strong as the person who wields it, but if it is not controlled, it can appear as an automatic reflex in times of intense emotion."

"I do not understand. Do you believe this force came from me?" Gabria asked quietly.

"It's possible that it originated from someone else in the room, but that is unlikely," he replied.

"Piers, I know nothing about this sorcery. How could I have cast a spell of any kind?"

Piers looked straight at Gabria and said, "There are only two ways. If Medb did not give the ability to you, then your ancestors did."

"No, it cannot be," Gabria cried, her voice edged with fear.

Piers gripped the stone and rubbed his chin with his free hand. "I am a stubborn old man, Gabran. I see something I do not understand and I try to force an answer because I am afraid. You are the only answer I see. If you did not use the Trymian Force, even inadvertently, than the alternative is beyond my understanding. I am not certain there was sorcery. Only this can tell us." He held up the stone to the firelight and watched the warm glow of color spread over his hands like blood.

"My master told me once the steppe clans long ago produced the greatest sorcerers because they were empathetic to the primal forces that govern magic. He believed wholeheartedly that the ability to draw on that power was an inherited talent." He paused and then said, "Unfortunately, the legends of those years are hazy with time and prejudice. After the destruction of the city of Moy Tura and the persecution of the sorcerers, no one wanted to remember where the talent came from."

In Piers's hand, the large stone began to flare suddenly. For a moment, Gabria thought it was just the flicker of firelight reflected in the gem's opaque interior. But the radiance brightened, driving out the opacity until the stone shone with a scarlet luminosity and crowded out the light of day and fire. The entire tent filled with the ruddy gleam.

"Now we know. Fasten the tent flap," Piers ordered. He

held the stone gingerly over Cor's face as brilliant flashes flared out of the stone in radial bursts.

Gabria limped to obey and tied the fastenings tight with trembling fingers. She moved to the healer's side and watched in fearful awe. The rays of light from the stone seemed to probe into the warrior's head. "What does that stone do? What is it?" she whispered.

Piers answered slowly. "I do not know exactly what it is, only what it does." A weak smile touched his mouth. "I have never had to use it before."

"Will it help him?"

"I hope so. My old master gave it to me before he died. He said it was a healing stone that could only be activated by the presence of magic. The stone is supposed to remove all traces of magic from an injured person."

Piers laid the stone on Cor's forehead, and they watched in silence. The direction of the light beams focused into a downward spray that danced over Cor's face. Gabria noticed in amazement that the rays did not illuminate his skin, but sank into it like bright needles. She felt she ought to be horrified by this display of blatant heresy and leave before she was tainted further, but she held back and watched the light with an unacknowledged fascination.

The stone was beautiful and, if it could heal, it was a positive good—a denial of everything she had been led to believe about magic. Maybe sorcery was more complicated and multifaceted than she had imagined, with aspects both good and evil and every shade in between. Her mind boggled at such a revelation. Sorcery was supposed to be totally evil, a dark power that corrupted men into acts of hideous cruelty and depravity. It hardly seemed possible magic could also be helpful. She pushed the uncomfortable thoughts away and wondered instead how a healer could tell when the stone had finished its work.

As if to answer her question, a blue haze—the remnants of the Trymian Force in Cor's body—began to form around the warrior's head. The glow was pale at first, as indistinct as cold breath, then it brightened and thickened. The red stone blazed fiercely. The bloody light spread out over the blue haze and immobilized it in a prison of beams. Gradually, the red light began to recede into the stone's core, pulling the haze with it. The blue force seemed to struggle, bursting through its bonds with tiny blasts of purple. The red light grew stronger, and it finally dragged the last tendrils of the blue haze into the stone. There was a flash of violet and the light snapped out. The stone rested, dull and opaque, on Cor's forehead. His body shuddered and relaxed into sleep, and the grimace of pain on his face slackened into peace. Piers picked up the stone and gently wiped the sweat from his patient's skin.

"What happened?" Gabria breathed. She was shaken by the display. Until that moment, magic had been so vague to her, something obscure, something she could only guess at. Now, it was a tangible truth. Its power, whether good or evil, did exist.

"The stone seems to have worked," Piers replied. He could not hide his intense relief. "Cor is resting peacefully. His fever is down, too."

Gabria abruptly sat down on the stool. She could hardly believe what had just taken place. Her throat was dry, and, without thinking, she gulped down the contents of the wine cup on the table. In just a moment, a dull heat crept out of her stomach and slowly seeped into her limbs. She grew very sleepy. She had forgotten about the poppy extract.

The girl squinted woozily at Piers. "Will Cor be all right?" she asked thickly.

"He should recover. What he needs now is sleep." Piers returned the stone to its wrapping and placed it back in the chest. "I hope I never have to use that again." He did not look at Gabria, but gathered the contents of his mortar into a small bowl and added hot water to make a tea. He gently spooned the liquid down Cor's throat. When he was satisfied with the warrior's comfort, he opened his tent flap and turned to Gabria.

Piers was surprised to see her sitting on the stool again, leaning against the center tent pole. Her legs were thrust out in front of her and her eyes were dulled with drug and exhaustion. Without speaking, the healer eased the laces on her boot and carefully removed it. He tried not to jar the puffy flesh of her injured ankle. The joint was purple and red, and still tainted green from the original injury. He twisted it slowly, feeling the tendons and torn muscles beneath the soft skin.

Piers glanced up at his patient's face. The drug had relaxed Gabria's muscles, so her expression was slack and unwary. At that moment, the sun came out from behind the clouds, and the bright light poured through the open tent flap and illuminated her face.

Piers's hands froze; his body stiffened. Unbelieving, he wrenched his eyes from the face to the slim ankle in his hands, and the realization hit him like a blow. Gabria was gazing into the distance and did not see his horrified recognition. The medicine had dimmed her awareness and was carrying her to sleep. She did not even remember he was there.

Piers rocked back on his heels and wondered why he, of all people, had not seen it before. This enigmatic "boy" with the uncanny talent for magic and the companionship of a Hunnuli, was now even more inexplicable. A thousand questions hid her background, and Piers was only now beginning to understand a fraction of them. He thought back upon some of their previous conversations and the information he had heard from other clan members. He marveled at her skill in acting. It was a miracle of the gods' hands, if he cared to admit it, that this girl had survived so long undetected.

The healer considered telling Savaric, even though he knew the penalty for the girl's transgressions would be death. Gabran, or whatever her name was, had committed one of the most serious crimes in clan law by entering a werod in disguise, and, if the incident of sorcery were to be known, there would be no mercy. As a Pra Deshian, however, Piers did not share the clans' hatred for magic. Nevertheless, he had lived with the clans for ten years and their laws and customs were his. If he failed to reveal this girl's crimes, he would be just as guilty as she and would suffer the same punishment.

Piers began to move toward the tent flap. There would be warriors nearby who could fetch Savaric. In a few moments it would be over. With luck, Gabran would die before the poppy wore off. Then, the Corin would be gone, the Hunnuli would leave, and the magic would be ended. Piers's duty to his people would be fulfilled. The healer's hand felt for the opening.

"Father?" a weak voice whispered.

Piers stopped, and he realized with surprise that he was shaking.

"Father, don't go. I'm so afraid." The voice came again like a frightened child. A familiar echo of grief and despair woke memories Piers thought he had banished. Aching, he turned around, half expecting to see another girl with long blond hair and pale blue eyes, instead of a tall, dirty figure slumped on the stool. Gabria's eyes were closed and her head had fallen forward. Her cloak was on the floor, and her bare foot looked incongruous against the rest of her clothing. She was shivering.

"Father, what is all this blood?" she whimpered. Her fingers twitched as if she had touched something repulsive. "It is all over everything. Father, please don't leave me!"

Piers picked up the cloak and wrapped it around her shoulders. She cuddled into it and sighed. "I'm so cold. Where is Gabran?"

The healer listened sadly as she mumbled on about her family and the scenes she remembered of their murders. The images of their deaths mingled with his own memories of another painful death. Long ago he had run away from Pra Desh, carrying his unpurged grief and rage with him—and the guilt that he had failed his own daughter. He looked down at the girl, the last Corin in the clans, and wondered if he was being given a chance to atone for his failures. Ten years ago, he had been weak and had followed his lord's command, against his better judgment. As a result, his daughter had died, and he had done nothing to save her. Now he had a chance to save this girl.

He picked her up and laid her gently on his mat behind the curtains. He bound her ankle in cold cloths and went to heat water for a hot pack. Piers could understand why the Khulinin had accepted the exile, despite their reluctance. There were too many conflicting sides to the Corin's tale. Now, he added his own motives. The girl was an outcast, like himself, yet she had survived so much with courage and intelligence. She deserved a chance, not a betrayal. He would simply take his chances with Savaric's wrath if—no, *when*—the Khulinin discovered the girl's secret.

* * * * *

It was late in the afternoon when Gabria awoke. She lay on the warm bed, feeling more comfortable and peaceful than she had in many days.

Then she heard pots rattling, and she opened her eyes. Cream curtains met her startled gaze. The memories of the past days returned in a deluge. It was all true—the massacre, the search for the Khulinin, Nara, the death of the mare, and the fight with Cor were all painfully real. She sighed.

"Piers?" Gabria called.

The curtains were thrown back and the healer stood beside her. "Good afternoon, Gabran," Piers said, his face carefully masked.

Gabria's eyes widened. "Afternoon? How long have I slept?"

"Only a few hours."

"Oh, no. Lady Tungoli—"

"She is the one who ordered me to let you sleep as long as necessary. Athlone led another hunting party after the lion."

Gabria carefully sat up and gingerly moved her ankle. It was tightly bound, but the swelling was noticeably less and she could move it some without pain. Piers gave her a hand and she stood up. She hobbled to the stool. The healer gave her soup, bread, and cheese. The girl inhaled the rich smell of the soup and suddenly realized how hungry she was.

When Gabria was finished eating, she pushed the plates away and relaxed with a full stomach. She looked over to the pallet to see Cor still sleeping comfortably under the blankets. His face seemed free of pain, and there was no sign of the incredible magic that had invaded his body.

"How is Cor?" she finally asked.

Piers was cutting a slice of bread for himself and he glanced over at the warrior. "I am sure he will live, but he will never

take a wife." He felt pity for the young man. The blow from
Gabran's bow and the arcane force had probably ruined Cor's
sexual manhood. The man was an ill-tempered fool, but he
did not deserve the stigma of impotency.

Gabria stared at the ground for a long while. She had so
many thoughts and memories and emotions raging inside her
mind, she could not think. She had no idea what to do next.

After a time, Piers came over and sat on another stool by the
table. Gabria looked up at him. "What will you tell Savaric?"
she asked, trying to keep her voice level.

The healer's long hands played with a crust of bread. His
face looked old and tired. "I have been trying to think all afternoon of what I will say."

Gabria was pale, for she knew at this moment her life was in
the healer's hands. By law, Piers must accuse her of sorcery to the
clan chieftain and leave her fate to the chief and his elders. But if
he did so, Piers would risk himself, for he had used the magic in
the healing stone. It was a ticklish decision, and Gabria could
not even guess what the healer would do. "Have you thought of
something?" she inquired as calmly as possible.

"At the moment, I will simply tell him Cor was ill from
complications of his injury from the fight, but that he is recov-
ering now." Piers lifted an eyebrow. "Will that be sufficient?"

A faint sigh escaped Gabria's lips. She nodded quickly.
"Thank you."

Piers leaned forward, his hands on the table edge. "But we
still have to face the fact that Cor was struck by a magic power."

Gabria tensed. "I know!" she said. "I agree he was injured by
something more than my bow. But you have no proof I did it! I
do not know where the power came from and neither do you."

"I know, but—"

Gabria jumped up, knocking over the stool. Her fears and
emotions crowded in on her until she wanted to scream. She
had to get out of the tent, go somewhere and collect her wits.
She had to think. "No. Enough. Whatever happened, it will
never happen again."

Piers came around the table and grasped her arm. "You
don't know that," he exclaimed. "If you have this talent for

sorcery, it will not go away. It will always be there, waiting for some spark to set it off again."

"*If.* You only say *if*," Gabria shouted. "You do not know for certain. Even if I had this ability, what could I do about it?" She limped to the entrance, hoping to escape before the healer could say any more.

"Gabran," Piers said quietly.

Gabria cut him short. "Thank you for your help, Healer. I am grateful." Then she ducked out and fled.

The rain had stopped some time earlier, and the clouds were breaking into huge, fluffy islands. The sun poured through every rent and covered the hills with moving patches of light and shadow. A fresh breeze blew up to Gabria from the steppes beyond Khulinin Treld. She took a deep breath. The invigorating coolness relaxed her a little and helped her sort out her thoughts enough to know what she wanted to do that moment. She wanted to find Nara.

The girl pushed her shorn hair back and hobbled down the path between the big tents, toward the far pastures. Nara was probably out there, grazing, and Gabria wanted desperately to be near the comforting strength of the Hunnuli.

Most of the men were gone from the treld, hunting the lion, but many of the women were out of the tents, enjoying the bright sun. No one acknowledged Gabria as she passed, so she hurried on, trying not to feel the loneliness and self-pity that reared up inside of her.

By the time she reached the picket lines at the edge of the treld, she was limping badly again. She stopped to rest. In the fields before her, several men were training young horses. Another group of warriors was practicing archery. Gabria balked at the thought of crossing to the pastures, because she would need agility and speed to pass through all of the activity without getting in the way. At the moment, she had neither.

She watched the archers for a moment as they sent their mounts in a full gallop across the grass. As one, they roared a ferocious cry, wheeled their horses, fired a barrage of arrows over their backs at a target, and retreated, whooping with glee, to the starting point. Gabria watched the strange maneuver in surprise. It was a difficult one, requiring skill with horse and bow, and timing. The warriors had performed it flawlessly, and the target was riddled, witnessing to their accuracy.

"They are getting good," someone said behind her.

Gabria turned her head and saw Jorlan, the night commander of the outriders, standing beside the farrier's tent a few paces away. He was holding the halter of a snappish filly. The farrier, a burley man with huge hands, had the filly's foreleg clamped between his thighs and was trimming a hoof.

"Where did they learn to do that?" she asked.

"It is part of some new tactics Athlone is teaching. He learned it from the Turic raiders, who are masters of the hit and run," Jorlan replied.

Gabria glanced back at the archers who were lining up for another run. "Why should a clan this size have to worry about raiding tactics?"

Jorlan pursed his lips and patted the filly's neck. "Lord Medb is growing very powerful. He is pulling other clans to him or dealing with them as he did the Corin. We are not invincible. Before summer is out, I believe there will be war."

The farrier snorted, a sound not unlike his horses'. "Lord Medb is a fool. He cannot hope to control the entire grasslands or the clans. He will burn out soon."

"Maybe," Jorlan said thoughtfully. "As long as he does not scorch us in his passing."

The farrier laughed, startling the filly. "Stand still, you girl," he soothed. "You fret more than my wife."

"Have you seen the Hunnuli?" Gabria asked. She did not want to discuss Medb. The treld was closing in on her and she wanted to run.

Jorlan gestured to the river. "I think she is by the river. You did well last night. I am sorry about Cor," he added as an afterthought.

"So am I," Gabria shot back, irritated by the reminder of that incident. She did not want to think about last night until she was clear of the treld. She swung around, put her fingers to her lips, and gave a piercing whistle. She waited for a moment, wondering if Nara had heard.

Then came a thundering neigh in answer to her summons. The call reverberated through Khulinin Treld like the horns of a battle charge. Everyone in the treld paused in their tasks and listened again for the neigh of joy and pride. Movement ceased in the fields. Men and horses alike watched as Nara appeared on the crest of a distant hill. She neighed again, this time in greeting, and Gabria, feeling the mare's delight, laughed in pleasure.

The girl whistled once more. Nara leaped down the hill, her tail unfurled, and galloped toward the treld. Her mane whipped out like grass before a tornado; her hooves flashed as she flung her legs forward. Like a black comet, she burst onto the crowded field and swept through the men and horses. They parted before her power and grandeur. She thundered up the slope and skidded to a halt, inches away from Gabria. The mare snorted delicately.

Gabria laughed again, hearing the excited shouts of the men around her. She grabbed for the Hunnuli's mane and hauled herself up. "Go, please!" Nara spun around and ran to find the wind on the plains.

Jorlan watched them disappear and grinned. "I would give my best mares to do that."

The mare carried Gabria along the banks of the Goldrine River to the entrance of the valley, and swiftly passed between the two guardian peaks to the plains.

Beyond Marakor and its twin, the foothills fell away to the steppelands of Ramtharin. The semi-arid grasslands rolled out of the mountain's shadow and away into a dusky horizon. The plains were endless leagues of land that awed men by their sheer vastness and a subtle intensity, traits not found anywhere else in the land inhabited by the clans. The character of the high steppes was found in the ceaseless winds that shaped the rocks and bent the long grass, in the rough colors that blended in a myriad of shades, in the pungent aroma of the tough shrubs that grew in every gully, and in the bitterness of a winter blizzard or the heat of a summer drought. The steppes were an empty land that did not invite easy acceptance, yet the land suited the clans and their restless herds, and was beloved by them.

Nara galloped east, following the Goldrine River. She sensed something was worrying Gabria, but she kept her thoughts to herself and waited for her rider to speak of it.

When Marakor dwindled behind them and Gabria could no longer feel the eyes of the Khulinin watching her, she relaxed and settled down on Nara's broad back. The Hunnuli slowed to a walk, and they wandered quietly along the shallows of the broad river. The wind breezed by them, cool from the morning rain and heavy with the smell of wet land. Ducks paddled in the backwater and several antelope watched them curiously from a safe distance.

Gabria breathed a long sigh. "He accused me of sorcery, Nara," she said at last.

Who?

"The healer. He thinks I used some form of power to strike down Cor in a fight last night. The worst of it is, I do not know if Piers is right."

Why did the healer think you had used magic?

Gabria shook her head despairingly. "Cor was injured by this power called the Trymian Force. Piers says I was the only one who could have struck the man. He feels I have an inherited ability to use magic . . . but he has no proof." She was silent for a while, then added, "I did have a dream last night. It was horrible."

About sorcery?

"Yes. Oh, Nara, I have been told since I was born that magic was something foul and corrupting. But I am not like that. I can't be," Gabria flung her arms around the Hunnuli's neck and held on. The girl wanted to believe in herself, in the inherent good that was a part of her and her beloved family. If she did have a talent for sorcery, she hoped that her beliefs about magic were wrong, for she could never accept that she was evil.

Nara stopped. She swiveled her head so her lustrous black eyes were staring into Gabria's unhappy face. *How do you think the Hunnuli became as they are?*

Gabria's throat tightened. "They were created by the gods. Amara shaped the first mare, and Surgart, in the shape of a storm, bred her." She spoke hesitantly, as if uncertain.

*That part is true, but our creation goes farther. In the dawn
of the world, we and the Harachan horses were as one.*

Gabria took a deep breath. She felt as though she was standing on the edge of a crevasse. To her back lay her life, its basic
beliefs and morals unchanged. Before her lay new concepts
and strange truths, the strangest of which being the idea that
magic was not an evil power. All she had to do was jump the
crevasse and ask the Hunnuli the rest of the unspoken question. The girl already divined the gist of the answer, but the
unknown realms that the knowledge might lead her to frightened her more than anything she had ever faced. It could mean
a total disruption of her entire way of thinking and living. It
could mean that, for two hundred years, the clans had believed
in a lie.

Nara remained still, her gaze compassionate, while she waited
for Gabria to speak. Gabria slowly traced her finger along the
white lightning mark on Nara's shoulder and tried to find the
courage to even form the words of the question in her mind.

The jagged streak, she thought, was the mark of the gods on
an animal they, too, loved. The Harachan did not have the
lightning mark, yet Nara said they and the Hunnuli were born
from the same source. So why did the Hunnuli have the mark
of favor and the Harachan did not?

"What happened?" she whispered so softly even Nara
barely heard it.

But the Hunnuli understood the depth of the question. *In
your legends, you have a tale of Valorian in which he rescues
the crown of Amara from the demons of Sorh. In his escape he
was helped by a black stallion. The horse was badly wounded
by a bolt of fire, and, after Valorian returned the crown to the
goddess, he nursed the horse back to health. In gratitude for
his help, the goddess decreed the stallion would forever be Valorian's mount and that his offspring would always bear the
white scar to honor him. After that, Valorian taught the horse
to communicate and to protect him. He made the stallion in-
vulnerable to magic and to evil. With his sorcery, the hero gave
the Hunnuli a new existence.*

The chasm had been leaped. Gabria felt her body grow hot

and her hands began to shake. "Valorian was a sorcerer?"

There are many things your priests neglect to tell.

"Nara, I think I want to go back to the treld."

The Hunnuli nickered softly and complied. She trotted easily back to the encampment to give Gabria time to consider the information that was now shaking her belief. It would take days before the girl could fully accept the magic that was a part of her—Nara had known the truth from the first day she had seen Gabria—and many more days before she would understand the reality of her power. But it would happen. Gabria would have to break her bonds of prejudice and accept her talent to wield magic if she hoped to fight Lord Medb and survive.

On the edge of the treld, Gabria slid off and stood for a moment, fighting back the tears that balanced on her lids. She rubbed her fingers over the ebony hair on Nara's withers. "I have despised sorcery all my life." She paused and swallowed hard. "You tell me you are a creature of magic, but I can't hate you. You are my friend." Gabria clenched her jaw and marched up the hill to the hall. Nara watched her for a moment, then she neighed and returned to the quiet pastures on the outskirts of Khulinin Treld.

7

he rains of early spring fell heavy that year. The water filled the streams and rivers, and drowned the low valleys. The rain fell for days in a fitful downpour, until the tents began to rot and the animals sickened and tempers frayed. The Goldrine washed over its banks and threatened the brood mare herd in the valley, so the horses had to be moved to shelters within the encampment. The work fields became a quagmire, and the paths through the treld turned to treacherous gumbo.

Before long, the hall was the only dry place in Khulinin Treld and the floor was crowded with people seeking relief. Around the fires at night, the clansmen drained the last of the wine and whispered of Medb's heretical practice of sorcery. Could it be, they wondered, that Medb had grown so powerful he could control the weather? Did he hope to demoralize the clans by endangering their herds, ruining their tents, and spoiling their food? Was he trying to prove the strength of his power?

The whispers spread as far as the distant clans, whose chieftains were little concerned with Medb's plans for dominance. Medb's name was in every mind, and the influence of his deeds, real or rumored, spread like a thickening mist. The tale of the massacre at Corin Treld was passed from clan to clan. The first horror and outrage sparked by the news was eventually dampened with excuses. People listened, but no one wanted to accept the fact that the Corin had been slaughtered. Clan fighting was a normal pastime for entertainment, revenge, or profit. But for a clansman to deliberately annihilate an entire clan was inconceivable.

Yet the massacre was a reality, and the chieftains knew in their hearts that something like it could happen again. Unfortunately, no one was certain why the Corin had been murdered in the first place. It was common knowledge that Dathlar loathed Medb. Perhaps the Corin chieftain had angered the Wylfling lord once too often and had received the full force of Medb's wrath. Several chiefs thought that, if this were true, it would be wise to avoid Medb's displeasure. Secretly, they began to accept the Wylfling emissaries and to listen to the promises of wealth and power that could be theirs in exchange for alliance.

Lord Branth of the Geldring waited only until the period of mourning for Lord Justar was over before he married the dead chief's widow and swore allegiance to Lord Medb. Meanwhile, scores of exiles—banded together, well armed, and mounted—began to ride the steppes like marauders. No violence occurred, but often livestock was found slain or horses were missing after the band swept through a clan's territory. The clansmen were left furious and alarmed by the depredation, but the band was so large and moved so swiftly, there was little the individual clans could do against them. Only the council of lords who met at the clan gathering each summer would be able to instigate any united action against the exiles. Unfortunately, the council did not meet for another three months.

In his huge hall near the southern fringes of the steppes, Medb gathered the news from spies and messengers and watched with growing pleasure as the fruits of his plans began to fall into his lap. At night, he retired to a hidden chamber and pored over the fragile pages of an ancient tome he had bought from a beggar in Pra Desh. He was still shaken that the fabled *Book of Matrah* had fallen into his hands. Matrah, the greatest of the clan sorcerers, had died in the destruction of Moy Tura, but despite years of searching, no one had ever found his manuscript. His book held references to three hundred years of arcane study, and many men had coveted its priceless contents. Now, after all this time, the manuscript had been discovered by a ragged man poking through the ruins of

the sorcerer's city, and delivered to Medb as if by divine provi-
dence. The book could have so easily been destroyed or given
to another man. Instead, it had come to Medb. Now, he had
the means to overcome his crippling injuries—caused by an enraged Hunnuli— and the power to fulfill his dreams. No man
or army could stand against him while the forces of magic lay
within his grasp. An empire would be his.

To Medb's great amusement, the heavy rains were not of his
making, but they fell like another link in the chain of events
that was leading irrevocably to his victory. The destruction and
unrest caused by the weather further undermined the confidence of the clans, and the constant storms kept them separated while Medb strengthened his hand. Before long, he
would be ready to launch the next part of his plan.

*　*　*　*　*

In late spring, the rains finally ended. The Khulinin gratefully set to work repairing the rotted tents, clearing the flood
debris, gathering the first fresh food of the season, and caring
for the livestock. Many of the shaggy, long-legged goats had
sickened in the wet, and too many of the newborn kids died.
Days passed before the last goat recovered and the losses were
counted. The brood mares fared a little better and, as their valley dried out, they were released to graze on the verdant grass
that sprang from the mud like a carpet.

Cor recovered and returned to duty, although it was clear to
everyone that Gabria's blow had destroyed more than his
chances for fatherhood. He was surly and withdrawn and nursed
a hatred that ate at his soul. When the hills finally dried enough
to resume the hunt for the lion, he went out alone and after five
days returned with the lion's body slung across his saddle. He ignored the cheers and congratulations and Savaric's gifts of
thanks, and dumped the dead cat at Gabria's feet.

"Your servant," he snarled at her and stalked away.

Gabria did not need to look in his eyes to know this was not
the last word she would hear from him. She was only relieved
that Cor had moved his belongings out of the hall to his fa-

ther's tent and, for the time, was leaving her alone.

Life slowly returned to normal. The goats were sheared and new felt mats were made for new tents. The women spun and wove. The men and horses returned to training. There was too much for every person to do to worry about phantoms. Medb dwindled to a distant irritation and the thought of war was pushed aside by the demands of life.

The only blight in the pleasure of spring was Pazric's disappearance. The second wer-tain had not returned from the desert, and Savaric worried about his absence. It was not like Pazric to not send a message or be gone so long. Still, the clan had other things to worry about. The Foaling time was coming and all had to be prepared. Excitement grew with the length of the days. Many people silently prayed to the gods that the Corin's bad fortune would not affect the coming event.

Then, one night, Nara sensed the stirring among the mares. Gabria woke the clan, and by morning the first foal was born. Wet and clumsy, he struggled to his feet while the Khulinin watched in silent awe and thanksgiving. By all the signs, the Foaling would be good: the firstborn was a bay colt as strong as a lion.

As if to make up for the disastrous rains, the following days were gorgeously warm and dry. The brood mares responded eagerly and a night did not pass without the birth of a foal or two. In the burgeoning meadows, the babies capered by their dams' sides, little knowing they were the continuation of the clan's existence.

Gabria took little joy in the time of Foaling. Her heart was wrapped in her own thoughts and desires as she grappled with her changing belief in magic. The growth of the Khulinin herd meant little to her, except for the lessening animosity toward her. She was glad for Savaric's sake, because she had become fond of him, but the affairs of the clan seemed distant and unimportant to her at the time.

Athlone, still suspicious of the Corin, sensed her detachment and kept a close watch on her. Their training times grew longer and more strenuous as Athlone sought to break her guard. Gabria disliked him intensely, and it frustrated her endlessly that she could do nothing to avoid him.

In spite of Athlone's temper, Gabria had to admit that he taught her well. The wer-tain was quick to find fault, but he was highly skilled and fair in his judgment. The girl understood why he earned the unhesitating loyalty of the werod. Athlone was fiercely proud, courageous, and dedicated, and he received in full measure what he gave.

By the time early summer came, Gabria felt a grudging respect for the wer-tain. Because of his meticulous training, her muscles were tough, her balance and coordination were improved, and she could wield her sword like an extension of her arm. He gave her no mercy—and she knew Medb would have none—nor friendship. Rarely, Athlone would give her brief encouragement, urging her on to greater efforts. Gabria knew that she would never have attained such proficiency as a warrior without his help. If only he would forget his suspicions.

Gabria had little time for relaxation during the Foaling and even less as the Birthright approached. The Birthright was the celebration of thanks to the forces in the spiritual world that bestowed fertility on the clans and their herds. The predominating spirit of life was Amara, the mother goddess. It was for her that the Birthright was celebrated. She was the giver of life, the power that preserved it, and the guardian of the clans' continuance.

However, Amara was only half of a greater whole. While Amara was the positive side of life, her sister, the goddess Krath, was the dark side. Krath was the ruler of unbridled passion and secrecy, violence and jealousy. She had the power to destroy, not as her brothers, the two gods of man who commanded the forces of war, but in subtle ways that were slow and unnoticeable. Together Krath and Amara formed a whole that was embodied by the clanswomen.

Paradoxically, women were considered physically inferior to men. But because women had the ability to sustain life, they were endowed with potentially more spiritual power. The clansmen believed that a woman's smaller, weaker form was a compensating balance for the inner strength the life force gave her. Therefore, it was only natural that the women, the true beneficiaries of Amara's grace, should perform the ritual of thanksgiving in the Birthright.

Before the massacre, Gabria had enjoyed the Birthright. The secret rites of the fertility ceremony and the prayers for the herds were the first words she had learned, and the joyous celebrations that lasted through the night were the happiest times of her year. But this year she dared not even hum the chants. When the last foal was born and the procession of red-robed women gathered by the hall, Gabria hid in Piers's tent. She could not risk the slightest slip of the tongue this night.

While the women walked silently to the clan burial mounds, far from the treld, to perform the rituals in the presence of their ancestors, the men remained behind, waiting for the full moon to reach its zenith and the rituals to end. They were apprehensive of the mysteries of the Birthright, but they enjoyed the wild abandon of the celebrations after the rites. As long as the goddess blessed the clan, the women could do as they pleased this one night.

It was a beautiful evening for the Birthright. The moon hung like a pearl on the breast of night. The music of drums and pipes grew louder as the breeze died, and the torches danced around the distant mounds. A silence intense with expectation held the encampment. Even the animals were quiet. The horses watched the flickering flames warily, and the dogs stayed close to their masters.

In Piers's tent, Gabria heard the music crest the silence of the camp like the wind over the earth. It tugged at her mind, urging her to move, to sing the familiar words. The drumbeat lured her memories back to Corin's field, where she had drunk the wine of fertility and danced to please the goddess. The girl clasped her arms around her knees as the chants sang in her mind. It took every cord of her willpower to hold her body still and to stay seated at the fire like a disinterested boy. Piers was gone, but he could return at any time, and she would not betray herself now.

When the music reached its climax and the women shouted in triumph, Gabria sighed deeply. The final words of the ritual's benediction ran through her mind. It was over. Now the

women would return to bless the herds and the firstborn colt
would be sent to Amara with gratitude. Soon the clan would
celebrate.

Gabria could already hear the musicians warming their instruments and the excited talk of the waiting men. For a while
she considered joining them, but now she was as tired as if she
had just completed the ritual herself. She did not want to face
the boisterous gaiety. Instead, she curled up in a blanket and
stared at the flames of the dying fire in Piers's hearth. The girl
sensed rather than heard his coming. She was instantly alert.

"You are welcome to join us," Athlone said softly from the
entrance.

Gabria looked at his shadowy form standing on the edge of
the firelight. Like Nara, she thought with surprise, that night
in the gully. Even his eyes gleamed in the flickering light as he
watched her, wary but not threatening.

"I cannot," she said, hoping he would understand and
leave.

The wer-tain was quiet for a breath, then he said, "You have
served my father well these past days. Continue to do so." The
tent flap settled back and he was gone.

Gabria stared at the black wall long after he left.

* * * * *

By dawn the clan was asleep, tired and content with the
Birthright. Gabria woke early and slipped out of Piers's tent.
The healer had come in very late, reeking of wine, and had collapsed on his bed. She doubted he had seen her. The encampment was quiet for this hour of the morning, and Gabria was
relieved to see no sign of Athlone. The sun was barely above
the horizon, but already the heat was building and the flies
were starting to stir.

She decided to snatch the opportunity and spend some time
alone. Solitude was a rare gift in a large treld, and Gabria did
not want to lose this chance. She found Nara and they slipped
out of camp and cantered into the mountains. Only Nara was
aware that they were being followed.

High above Khulinin Treld, Nara found a stream that fell tumbling at her feet into the gorge and the Goldrine River. She started upstream. The mare forced her way through the heavy underbrush, following trails only she could see, past tiny marshes and through thickets of brambles and deer brush. Gradually, the low growth gave way to scattered trees and copses, and the water's voice was stronger as it fell over its rocky path. Nara climbed higher and deeper into the mountains as the sun warmed Gabria's back.

Finally, the mare was stopped by a steep rock wall over which the stream spilled in a cascading spray. Jutting rocks, cushioned with dark green moss, separated the falling water into thin streams veiled in mist and bejeweled by beams of sunlight. The water was collected in a deep, foaming pool before it continued down to meet the river. Moist gray-green lichen draped the pine and juniper that grew nearby. A thin undergrowth of grass, herbs, and wildflowers carpeted the sun-dappled ground. A squirrel chattered above them, and a dragonfly skimmed the water.

Gabria slid off the mare and dabbled her fingers in the cool water. "I am going for a swim," she said, looking at the pool happily.

Nara glanced back the way they had come. Her nostrils flickered in a gentle whicker. *Be careful. I will be back soon.*

Gabria started. "Wait. Where are . . ." But Nara was already gone. The girl was rather surprised by the Hunnuli's quick departure, but maybe the mare wanted to graze in a nearby meadow. Gabria shrugged. All that mattered now was the cold, glassy water that waited for her beneath the sparkling mist.

She tore off her clothes—the boy's pants, tunic, and the leather hat she had come to loathe—and dove naked into the pool. It was delicious. She swirled through the water like an otter. The bubbles tickled her skin, and the water flowed over her body like a sensuous massage, washing away tension and weariness. Gabria scrubbed off the dust and sweat, and combed her fingers through her hair, then she relaxed and basked in the mottled sunlight.

It was so good to forget about everything, to be herself without the guilt or the duplicity to encumber her. There were no eyes constantly watching her, no evil, no pretending, no remembering. She was a woman again. Gabria giggled as a water weed brushed her thigh, then she stretched luxuriously and swam to the waterfall.

Suddenly, over the noise of the fall, Gabria heard a Hunnuli neigh. Nara. Then another answered and her heart stopped. There was only one other Hunnuli . . .

"Oh, gods," she muttered and started to stand up.

"Hello, Gabran."

Fear jolted through Gabria's stomach. She fell back into the water and edged against the rock wall by the falls. Athlone stood on the bank by her clothes. Lazily, he nudged her sword with his foot and removed his own sword belt.

"How is the water?" he asked casually.

She only stared at him in wordless horror. He pulled off his tunic and unlaced his boots. "I followed you to be sure you did not have any trouble. These mountains can be treacherous." His pants joined the heap of clothes, and he stretched in the warm sunlight. His body was lean and muscular and traced with white scars. "A swim is an excellent idea. I think I will join you."

Gabria watched him dive into the pool and buried her face in the moss. "Oh, goddess," she pleaded. "Help me now."

While he swam toward her, the Corin bolted away toward the opposite bank in the vain hope that she could hide before the wer-tain saw her body. But the crystal water betrayed her. There was nothing to hide her curved hips or the swell of her breasts.

Athlone abruptly stopped dead in the water. He stared at her, and his eyes froze in astonishment and stunned realization.

Gabria stopped swimming, stood up in the shallow water, and faced him, her chin tilted up and the water running down her breasts. "Now what, Wer-tain?" she challenged.

Without warning, he lunged at her and his hands clamped her arms before she could move. Her eyes were pinned by his gaze of erupting fury. "By the gods," he snarled. He dropped her in the water, grabbed her hair with one hand and felt her breasts as if he could not believe his eyes. Gabria's skin crawled at his touch, and she closed her eyes. He shook her, nearly snapping her neck.

"A woman," he spat. "Are you Medb's little spy?" He pushed her underwater and held her, struggling, until her lungs burned, then he hauled her out like a gasping fish. "Who are you?" Athlone thrust her under again without waiting for an answer.

Gabria's fingers tore at his wrists, but she could not loosen his grip on her hair. She would have given almost anything for her sword at that moment. Inexplicably, she began to feel more anger than fear, and resentment surged through her.

Once more Athlone dragged her head out of the water. "Defiling pig!" he cried. "Who sent you to spread your lies in my father's treld?"

Gabria shrieked in fury and lashed out at his stomach. He dodged and shoved her under for the third time. She fought his merciless hold with frantic strength until her lungs were bursting and the blood pounded behind her eyes. Despite her training, she was no match for the wer-tain in unarmed combat. He was stronger, heavier, and more skilled. But maybe she could surprise him.

Unexpectedly, the girl went limp and let a few bubbles trail out of her mouth. Her head hurt horribly, but she concentrated on relaxing every muscle and floating as if dead. Athlone loosened his grip on her hair. As she felt his hands relax, Gabria drew her legs up, shoved violently against the bottom of the pool, and rammed her head into Athlone's stomach. He doubled over, cursing and gasping. Gabria fled for the bank. She scrambled over the damp rocks and moss as he came after her. The girl glanced back and saw the wer-tain plunging through the water like a furious stallion, his face twisted in rage and his eyes murderously dark. Frantically, Gabria ran for her clothes. Her fingers found her dagger, and she whirled to face Athlone as he lunged out of the pool.

"Keep away, Wer-tain," she cried, backing toward a tree.

Athlone paused for a moment, his eyes on her face. "Show your tooth, viper. Even Medb's snakes can be stepped on." He edged nearer.

Gabria's eyes flared with green fire, but she stayed with her back to the tree.

"Medb's whore," he taunted. "Is that how you survived the Corin's massacre? Did you spread your legs for him—and his exiles, too?"

A searing rage tore away Gabria's sensibilities and, like a catalyst, sparked the blue fire of her arcane power. "Curse you!" she stormed, unaware of the magic building within her. "You know nothing. You are as bad as Medb, rooting through corpses for a shred of self-esteem. You snap and snarl like a toothless dog."

Athlone laughed. "Far better to be an equal of Medb's than his whining cast-off. Will you grovel in the dirt to save your life again?"

Gabria leaped at the warrior like a cornered lioness. Her attack was so fast it took him by surprise and, when she stabbed at him, her dagger found the hollow of his left shoulder. The blade went deep, embedding in the muscle and ligaments. Even as the dagger sank in, the blue aura rose from Gabria's hand and raced down the jeweled hilt and silver blade into Athlone's body.

Her force was stronger this time and would have killed the wer-tain, except that the magic met a strange resistance. Instead of destroying Athlone, the attack only weakened him.

He gasped and went pale. He flung her violently away and stood rigid, staring stupified at the blood that trailed down his chest. The warrior hissed, "Sorceress! What have you done to me?" Then his strength failed and he collapsed unconscious.

Gabria stood for a long time, her body shuddering in the release of her rage. She closed her eyes and forcibly controlled her wild panting. The beast. He deserves to die, she thought triumphantly. How dare he call her Medb's whore. She leaned over and wrenched her dagger loose. The blood surged out of the wound and flowed down the wer-tain's side.

Gabria held the point of the weapon against the hollow of his throat, where life lay just below the skin. It would be so easy. One simple thrust. Then the wer-tain would be dead and his suspicions with him. It would be the first time she killed a man, but it would be wonderful to start with this one. She could still feel his hands pawing her body and hear his unspeakable insults. The knife dug into the skin as her anger rekindled. A bead of blood glistened on the dagger point.

Kill him, her mind said. He's dangerous. He will betray you if he lives. The blade eased deeper. More scarlet beads welled up. Red, Gabria mused as she watched the blood stain the tan of Athlone's neck. As red as the blood on the grass at Corin Treld.

In disgust, Gabria threw down the dagger and squatted on the grass beside him. She hated herself for her weakness, but she could not kill Athlone in cold blood. She had seen enough blood to last a lifetime, and, as her rage cooled, she realized that she did not really want the wer-tain's murder on her hands. Besides, he did not deserve to die like this. His wound was payment enough for his insults.

However, that still left the monumental problem of what Athlone would do to her if he recovered. Gabria had little doubt he would expose her disguise and have her killed immediately. But maybe, just maybe, he would wait long enough to talk to her. Perhaps she could convince the wer-tain to help her. Nara did tell her Athlone could be trusted. Gabria hoped the mare was right—it was Gabria's only chance.

The girl sighed irritably. If Athlone was going to live, she would have to bind his wound and take him to Piers quickly. But what would she tell Savaric? Unhappily, she dressed and cleaned the wer-tain's wound and bound it with strips from his own tunic.

Just as she finished clothing him, Nara and Boreas trotted through the trees to the pool. Gabria backed away, eyeing the huge stallion warily. She wondered if he would be angry at her for his master's injury.

Boreas sniffed Athlone and snorted softly. *I see you two have settled your differences.* His thoughts, lower and more masculine than Nara's, rang richly in her head. Gabria stared at him.

Nara nickered, obviously pleased. *We waited for this, Gabria. You need him.*

"I need him like a broken leg," she said vehemently. "Where were you two?"

Boreas nuzzled Nara's neck, and she nipped playfully at him. *We were occupied.*

"Why did you leave me alone?" Gabria demanded. "You knew Athlone would find me."

Of course, Nara told her.

Athlone is bleeding. We must take him to the healer. Boreas nudged Gabria.

The girl glared at them both, feeling furious, hurt, and annoyed. Nara had left her intentionally, knowing Athlone would come to the pool. Why? The mare knew that the wer-tain was dangerous. Although the Hunnuli accepted him, how could Nara risk leaving her rider to face Athlone alone and virtually defenseless? In his rage, Athlone had nearly killed Gabria, and it was only through luck she had escaped. Yet both Nara and Boreas had anticipated the outcome of the confrontation.

Hesitantly, Gabria picked up Athlone's gold belt and weighed the heavy metal in her hands. There must have been something that told the Hunnuli that Athlone would not or could not kill her at that time. Her hands tightened around the belt. Perhaps their intuition had something to do with the incident with Cor. Gabria had tried to forget the fight, her dream, and Piers's accusations, but the memories replayed in her mind time and again.

A sickening feeling grew in her stomach. This incident with the wer-tain was too horribly familiar. Oh, gods, she thought, looking at Athlone, what if I have done it again? Maybe the Hunnuli knew she had a hidden defense, one that could defeat even Athlone.

That idea was more than Gabria wanted to think about then, so, for the moment, she pushed aside the fears forming in her mind and wordlessly helped Nara lift the wer-tain onto Boreas's back. Gabria wrapped the golden cloak around Athlone's bare back and threw away the remains of his tunic.

They traveled slowly back down the mountain, Boreas stepping carefully to keep Athlone balanced. Gabria spent the time thinking of something to tell Savaric. She wondered if she should flee before Athlone regained consciousness. Even slow starvation would be better than the death Savaric would give her for impersonating a warrior and attacking a wer-tain. Her life could be over the moment Athlone recovered, and no power on earth could save her.

But where could she go? Gabria would be permanently exiled and marked for death. Any clansman who saw her would be obligated to kill her. She would have no clan, no honor, no hope to kill Medb. Yet if she stayed, she was risking her life on the insights of two Hunnuli. Somehow, Nara and Boreas had realized that Athlone was not a danger to her. Otherwise they would not let her return to the treld. Nara had said Athlone could be her best ally. Maybe it was true.

Perhaps if Nara and Boreas supported her, she could convince Athlone to help her. The wer-tain's willing skill and influence would be invaluable in the battle against Lord Medb. Gabria was beginning to realize that there was far more to killing a chieftain like Medb than a simple challenge and a duel. Athlone's help would greatly improve her chances. Unfortunately, she doubted she would be able to convince the wer-tain before he exposed her to Savaric. The wer-tain's rage would undoubtedly wake with him.

Give him time to think, Boreas told her, breaking her preoccupation.

Gabria started. She had the uncomfortable feeling that the Hunnuli could understand her thoughts, despite what Nara told her. "What?" she asked.

The man is not always impetuous. Give him time and he will understand.

"May I stake my life on that?" Gabria asked hopefully.

Yes. The stallion was adamant.

Gabria rubbed her hand down Nara's neck and sighed. "I hope you will move fast if Savaric orders me killed."

Nara shook her mane. *There will be no need.*

An outrider saw them as they walked down the hill, and he galloped back to the treld to find Piers. Gabria watched him disappear among the distant tents and steeled herself to meet Savaric. She would have to control her every movement and reaction for fear of the chieftain seeing through her feeble story. She just hoped he would not look too carefully at Athlone's wound beneath the makeshift bandages.

A crowd met them at the edge of the treld, and gentle hands lifted Athlone down and carried him to Piers's tent. Gabria did not try to hide her relief. But other clansmen watched her with open hostility. The hearthguard came and unobtrusively circled around her. Savaric stood before her with his arms crossed. His face was expressionless.

"How did this happen?" the chief demanded.

Gabria dismounted and met his gaze levelly. "Athlone followed me this morning when I went for a swim in the stream above the Goldrine. While Nara and Boreas were grazing, he climbed a rock wall by the pool and fell on a broken branch."

"Why?" The word was an accusation.

"I don't know," she said as innocently as possible. "Maybe the rocks were slippery. I only saw him fall."

"Why did he follow you?"

She glanced at Boreas and patted the horse's neck. Too many details could sound contrived, so she replied, "I guess he wanted to go riding."

The chieftain looked at the two Hunnuli standing protectively beside the girl and then considered her for an excruciating moment. She could feel the eyes of the other warriors boring into her back as everyone waited for Savaric to guide them. A minute passed and Gabria quelled the desire to bolt for Nara's back.

"Thank you for bringing him back," Savaric said at last

The ring of men visibly relaxed. The watching clansmen began to drift away, but Gabria still stood her ground. "It was my duty."

Savaric smiled, a knowing lift of his thin lips that held no humor. "Sometimes duty is not taken into account." He turned on his heel and left her, gesturing to his warriors to follow.

When she was alone with the horses, Gabria leaned back on Nara's shoulder and took a deep breath. "That is a dangerous man. Savaric sees many things people try to hide. Even Medb would do well to stay out of his way."

Savaric is no longer a match for the sorcerer, Nara told her.

"What?" Gabria was stunned. "That is impossible."

Medb has powers now even he does not understand. But he is learning fast.

Gabria ground her heel into the dirt and said, "I am such a fool to think I can kill him."

Boreas flicked an ear at her. *Yet you do not give up.*

"I cannot. By clan law, he owes me recompense." She looked at both horses. "I admit, though, I need help. Will you and Boreas support my plea to Athlone?"

Nara answered, *Of course. But we do not think you will need us.*

The two Hunnuli trotted off to the pastures, and Gabria walked up the path toward the hall. The encampment was swarming with activity as the women began the monumental task of packing and the men made preparations for the summer trek. All signs of the celebration were gone. The Birthright was over, gone with the rain and snow of the winter. Now the plains beckoned to the camp-weary clan and the sun burned hot on their backs. They would be leaving soon for the clan gathering at the Tir Samod, the meeting place of the Isin and the Goldrine rivers.

Lord Medb and the Wylfling clan would be there, as well as Lord Branth and his Geldring and the other clans who vacillated under Medb's increasing influence. Gabria thought that Medb would probably make a move at the council, when the chiefs of the clans were all together. One decisive attack could do irreparable damage to clan unity and reinforce his bid for supreme rule. But Gabria hoped to ruin his plan, whatever it might be, by challenging the chief to a duel. A duel to the death was her right under the rules of the weir-geld. Even if she could not kill Medb, maybe she could spoil his plots before he plunged the clans into war.

"Gabran!" Piers's voice stopped her cold. She saw him standing by his tent and her heart lurched. His face was grim, his hand gripped the tent pole like a crutch, and his pale eyes spoke to her as clearly as his words.

Wordlessly, she followed him into the tent. Piers said quietly, "This is the second time."

He moved aside and she saw Athlone lying unconscious on

the pallet. His wound had not been tended yet, and the bloody bandages lay like dark stains on his skin. She started to say something when she noticed the healing stone resting on the wer-tain's forehead. A stray gleam of purple still flickered in the core.

"Oh, Piers," she breathed.

"Athlone has been struck with the Trymian Force," Piers said with controlled calm. "And this time you were the only one with him."

"You still cannot prove that. How do you know I did not find him like this?" Gabria demanded. She was grasping at straws and they both knew it.

"You said you were with him."

"Not the entire time."

"You were not there?" Piers picked up the red stone from Athlone's forehead and put it back in its wrappings.

Gabria shifted nervously. "I brought him home."

The healer returned the stone to its tray and slammed the chest door shut, then turned back to Gabria. "Granted. But should I tell Savaric the injury in his son's shoulder is a knife wound?"

Gabria stared at the healer in alarm. She had forgotten that Piers would recognize the cause of the wer-tain's injury. If the healer told Savaric the truth, no one would believe it was only self-defense. Savaric would kill her. Of course, if Athlone's rage recovered with him, her fate would be the same.

"Tell me the truth, Gabran," Piers prompted. "I think you did this, however unintentionally."

"It was a misunderstanding," she mumbled.

"And the Trymian Force?"

Suddenly, Athlone's last words began to pound in Gabria's head. "Sorceress, what have you done to me?" He had felt it! Somehow he had realized that she had struck him with something more than a dagger. Her fear and confusion closed in as the truth came crashing down around her.

"But I don't know how to cast a spell," she cried.

"You have to face the truth, Gabran," Piers demanded. "You have the power and Athlone nearly died of it. The next time, you might kill someone."

"You are wrong. I am not a sorceress!" She flung the last word
at him and fled from the tent. She ran furiously through the
treld, dodging dogs and children, but the word followed her like
a curse. Sorceress. A creature despised. It could not be true. She
had never felt this arcane power and, the gods knew, she did not
want it. Piers has to be wrong, Gabria concluded desperately.
He's only a foreigner and knows nothing about me.

Gabria nearly slammed into an old woman carrying an armload of newly dyed wool before she regained her composure.
With a quick apology, she helped the woman with the heavy
wool, then she walked tiredly to the hall. Sorceress or not, it
would hardly matter if Piers or Athlone revealed the truth. Her
punishment for any one of her crimes would be irrevocable.

The cool gloom of the hall was comforting, and, luckily, the
long room was empty. Gabria poured a cup of wine and sat in a
corner by the main door to wait. There was nowhere else to go.

8

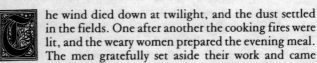he wind died down at twilight, and the dust settled in the fields. One after another the cooking fires were lit, and the weary women prepared the evening meal. The men gratefully set aside their work and came home, until all but the outriders were comfortably settled by their hearths. In the hall, Lady Tungoli and her women lit the lamps and torches, then served the bachelors from a pot of simmering stew.

Through the noise and activity of hungry, raucous men, Gabria sat in her corner in stony silence. She ignored their questions and offers of food, and stared at the entrance, waiting for one man to walk through and accuse her. But Savaric never came. His place at the table remained empty. After a while, the others forgot her and she was left alone in her self-imposed solitude. The fire was allowed to burn low in the central hearth since the weather was warm. Most of the warriors wandered outside to take advantage of the pleasant evening. Gabria still sat in tense expectation, wondering how Savaric would feel to learn the truth about Dathlar's "son."

Moonlight was flooding through the open doors when a young warrior slipped into the hall. Many of the men had returned for the night, and he squinted at the sleeping forms as if looking for someone. Finally he moved next to Gabria.

"Gabran," he whispered loudly.

Gabria stood up stiffly. So, Savaric had sent a messenger. The girl was surprised he had not come himself or sent the hearthguard, but perhaps he felt she did not deserve the honor.

The warrior waved her over. "Come on, hurry up. The wertain wants to see you."

She paused in surprise. Athlone. Not Savaric? "The wertain?" she repeated.

"Yes, now. He woke up a while ago and moved back to his own tent," the warrior said impatiently.

He led Gabria down the paths to Athlone's tent and left her by the entrance. Her knees felt weak and, for a moment, she had to stop. The night air was cool and refreshing, and the sounds of the camp were pleasantly familiar. If she closed her eyes, she could feel the similarity to Corin Treld, even to the smell of wood smoke and the barking of a dog. The thought gave her comfort, just as the memories of her clan gave her strength. Gabria leaned on that strength now as she pushed the tent flat aside. She wondered why Athlone had requested her presence, but she realized that he probably just wanted her there when he revealed her lies to his father.

Resolutely, she stepped inside. The only light in the large tent was from a lamp burning on the center tent pole. On the edge of its glow, she could see Athlone lying on a low bed. The sleeping curtain was pulled back and he was watching her in the flickering shadows. To her astonishment, they were alone and his sword was propped against a chest, too far away to be easily reached. She stayed by the tent flap, keeping the light between them, and stared at him through the flame. They stayed silent and eyed each other like two wolves on a narrow path.

Athlone gingerly sat up. He waved to a stool, then poured two cups of wine. "Sit down," he ordered. He tasted his wine and set the other cup on the floor for her.

Her heart in her throat, Gabria obeyed. She took a quick swallow of wine to ease the dryness in her mouth and let the liquid warm her stomach before she spoke. "You have not told Savaric."

He grunted. He was still very weak and any movement was an effort. "Not yet. I have some questions I want answered."

"Why haven't you?"

With an ironic grimace, he pointed to the cut on his throat.

"First you tried to kill me, then you changed your mind and brought me back. Why?"

"Nara said I should trust you," Gabria replied.

"She puts much faith in me."

"Too much."

Athlone cocked an eyebrow much like his father. "Yet you did not kill me, even though I could sentence you to death."

Gabria looked away and her fingers tightened around the cup. "It was a chance I had to take. I need your help."

"Blunt. After nearly killing me, you ask for my aid." He took a drink and considered her. "Remove your hat."

Surprised, Gabria pulled off the leather hat and shook her head. Her hair had grown out a little since she cut it at Corin Treld, and it curled in uneven waves around her neck.

"Who are you?" Athlone muttered as if debating the answer himself. His eyes were no longer suspicious, only puzzled, and he leaned toward her, ignoring the pain in his wounded shoulder.

"Gabran's twin sister," she said, her voice hesitant. "I am Gabria."

He snorted. "Gabria? Doesn't your name mean buttercup? What an ill-matched name for a lioness. At least you are a child of Dathlar, that is obvious. You have his stubbornness." He paused. "How did you escape?"

Gabria bit her lip. It still shamed her to remember that disgraceful argument with her father, but she was not going to lie about it now. "I had a disagreement with Father and I ran away to be alone."

Athlone refilled his cup. "What about?"

"Marriage," she said angrily. She took another gulp of wine to hide the flush that burned on her cheek.

The wer-tain laughed outright and nearly spilled his wine. It was the first time Gabria had seen Athlone laugh, and she was amazed by the pleasant change. The hard lines of his face relaxed and his eyes warmed to a rich, dark amber.

"I am sorry," Athlone finally apologized. "I just cannot imagine any man taming you. You are much like your Hunnuli."

Gabria was relieved by his compliment, however unde-served, and her hope grew. Perhaps Athlone would keep her secret. His rage from their earlier confrontation seemed to be cooled, and, if he could laugh at her and apologize, he was not planning to have her head removed immediately.

"Why did you come to us?" the wer-tain asked, returning to seriousness.

"For the reasons I told your father," Gabria answered.

"To claim weir-geld against Lord Medb?" He shook his head. "You don't have a chance. The man is a chieftain and a reputed sorcerer." Suddenly Athlone stumbled over his words and stared at Gabria as if something had jogged his memory.

The girl slammed her cup down and said too quickly, "Yes, I want weir-geld. I am the only Corin left to claim it, and man or woman, I am entitled to revenge. That chieftain—" She spat the word contemptuously. "—is responsible for the murder of an entire clan!"

"And for your revenge, you want Medb's death?" Athlone asked slowly. He was taken aback by this girl's vehemence and was uncertain how to deal with her incredible behavior. And yet, she fascinated him like nothing he had ever known.

"Of course."

"Even if you break clan law to obtain your revenge."

Gabria's face hardened. "I will do what I must to see Lord Medb dead."

"He will destroy you."

She nodded. "Maybe. But I have to try. And, Wer-tain, I will use any means or any person to attain my vengeance. Even you."

For a long moment Athlone was silent, and, as he stared into the flame of the lamp, his eyes seemed to soften and his body sagged back on the pallet. The last of his indignation and hesi-tation vanished. "Warning accepted," he said at last. "Despite my earlier temper, I have not told Savaric yet that a woman is a warrior in his werod. You intrigue me. Your will and persist-ence go a long way to balancing your deceits."

"Will you tell him?" Gabria asked.

"You didn't leave me in the mountains to die. I owe you

that at least. I won't tell him, but know also I will do nothing to save you if he discovers your secret from someone else."

Gabria nodded. That was fair. She was beginning to understand why Nara and Boreas trusted Athlone. He was a man of honor and, as long as one stayed within his boundaries, he would do everything to keep his word. She only hoped he had forgotten any suspicions of sorcery he might have. Gabria had seen the glint of speculation in his eyes when he mentioned sorcerers. The gods only knew what fantastic ideas he might have about her connection with it.

"If I'm not to be executed," she said, "what now?"

"You are still in training. If you insist on fighting Medb, you'll have to know more than the simple tactics of the practice field. Your dagger attack was atrocious."

Gabria nodded and replaced her hat. She stood up and saluted him with boundless relief. "Thank you, Wer-tain," she said gratefully.

He smiled wearily. "I hate Medb almost as much as you do. Perhaps between the two of us we can at least discomfort him." Gabria had turned to go when he added, "You have been courting disaster sleeping in the hall. Move to either my tent or Piers's."

Gabria was jolted by the mention of the healer. "Piers. He knows I stabbed you."

Athlone lay back and laughed softly. "He knows more than that. He has kept your secret for some time."

"What?" she gasped. "How could he have known?"

"A healer learns many things. You should ask him why he did not expose you."

She walked dazedly to the tent door. "Good night, Wertain. Nara was right."

As the flap closed behind her, Athlone sighed and murmured, "So was Boreas."

*   *   *   *   *

Piers was drying herbs when Gabria stalked into his tent and dropped her belongings on the floor. She stood in the middle of the pile and crossed her arms as if daring him to challenge her presence there. The felt tent was steeped with earthy smells of mint, hazel, and wild rose. Piles of freshly cut plants lay on the wooden table.

At the sound of the weapons and bundles hitting the carpeted floor, Piers glanced over his shoulder. "Good evening, Gabran. There is a pallet for you over there." He pointed to the sleeping area and turned back to his work.

Gabria saw another cream curtain already dividing the sleeping room in half and a wool-stuffed mat and several furs and blankets waiting for her. After the heated words of the afternoon, Gabria was not certain Piers would want her as a guest, but he had obviously already thought of it. Nevertheless, the girl did not want him to feel pressured into being a reluctant host. She wanted the arrangement to be acceptable to him as well.

"You were expecting me?" Gabria asked, surprised.

Piers hung another bundle of herbs on his drying rack. "It is safer for you to move out of the hall; I am the older of two bad choices." Gabria still had not moved, and the healer smiled briefly when he turned and saw her standing in her heap of clothes and weapons. "You are most welcome to stay," he added gently. "I had a long talk with the wer-tain this afternoon. We thought you would choose my tent." He paused, then added, "In case you were wondering, Athlone does not remember much about the stabbing except that you did it."

Gabria was relieved to hear that news. She studied the healer for a moment and thought about their earlier argument on magic. She was relieved that she could move out of the hall, but living with Athlone was out of the question. Staying with the healer who called her a sorceress was almost as objectionable. On the other hand, Piers had not betrayed her. Gabria's curiosity prompted her to give him a chance.

"How long have you known about my disguise?" she asked.

Piers chuckled and came over to help pick up her belongings. "From the day I bound your ankle."

"Then why didn't you tell Savaric?"

His brief humor faded and was replaced by an abiding

sorrow. "I will just say you reminded me of someone."

"That is quite an excuse for risking your life for a stranger."

Piers picked up the girl's blanket and cloak. "It was enough." He helped her pack her clothes in a small leather chest ornamented with brass. She hung her weapons on the tent supports.

As they worked silently, Gabria wondered if this someone the healer mentioned was responsible for him leaving Pra Desh. A sadness was still in his face, and his mind seemed to be years away.

"Did this person resemble me or just pretend to be a boy?" Gabria asked the question lightly to draw him back to the present.

Piers did not answer at first. He stored his fresh herbs in a damp cloth, then poured a cup of wine and sat staring into its depths for a long while. Gabria had decided he was not going to answer when he said, "I drink too much of this. Before she died, I never touched wine."

"She?" Gabria prompted. There was a bitterness and grief in Piers that echoed her own. This shared pain, whatever had caused it, began to dispel her anger toward him.

He continued as if he had not heard her. "You resemble her in a vague way: fair hair, young. But you are stronger. She was pretty and delicate like silk. When she married the fon's youngest son, I did nothing to stop her."

"Who was she? What happened to her?"

Piers stood up. His reverie was reaching into places he wanted to forget. "It doesn't matter now," he said curtly. "She is dead. But I want to keep you alive, so get some rest." He went to his own pallet and drew the curtain.

Gabria sighed and sat down. She had not meant to push him so hard. Whoever this girl was, she must have been very close to Piers to kindle such a response. The mysterious girl's influence was still quite strong if she were the only reason for Piers not telling Savaric of Gabria's disguise. Maybe later the healer would reveal the rest of his tale. Until then, she would accept Piers's hospitality, whatever his motives were.

After a while, Gabria blew out the lamps and sat in the darkness of the tent, considering the day. With the stroke of an ill-aimed dagger she had found two allies, three if she could add Boreas, and by her reckoning she was no longer an exile.

By clan law, an exile was a man or woman who committed a criminal offense or who, for some unusual reason, was totally separated from a clan. Until that person was accepted by another clan, he or she was considered an untouchable, an outcast. Gabria had been accepted temporarily by the Khulinin, but she knew that they had agreed only on the merit of her disguise and the Hunnuli. Therefore, in her own mind, she was still an exile.

Tonight, though, Piers and Athlone had acknowledged her for herself and, by their acceptance, erased the stigma of rejection in her mind. Piers, by his own admission, had become her protector, and Athlone was her mentor. With the help of these two men, Gabria knew she would survive, at least until the clan gathering.

Only Piers's accusation of sorcery bothered her. Gabria still could not completely accept the idea that she had an inherent talent for sorcery. Cor's injury and the dream, Nara's revelations and now Athlone's collapse were not enough to overcome all of Gabria's prejudices. A part of her still hoped the growing evidence was nothing more than strange coincidence. So far, she only had a single dream and Piers's word for proof that she was the source of the magic involved. It was possible the dream was only a part of her imagination and Piers was wrong. Gabria hoped that nothing else would occur and she could put the whole ugly problem aside like a bad dream.

Gabria yawned and realized the night was getting late. She had been chasing her thoughts around for too long. The girl made her way to her sleeping area, removed her pants and boots, and sat down on the comfortable pallet. After living with the constant noise in the hall at night, Gabria was relieved to hear only Piers's soft snoring. Before long she was lulled to sleep.

But like any ugly problems, the question of sorcery refused to be ignored. Deep in the night, when Gabria was asleep, she dreamed of a blue fire that rose from her being and grew in

strength like a storm. It fed on her emotions, drawing its power
from her until it burned in every vein. Then the fire flared in
her hands and exploded outward as a bolt of lightning. Again
it struck and burned a half-seen figure of a man, only this time
the man wore a golden belt.

Gabria jolted awake and lay shivering in the darkness. It was
another coincidence, she told herself. It had to be. She
dreamed of the blue force because she had argued with Piers
about it that day. That was the only reason. For the rest of the
night Gabria tried to convince herself that the dream was not
important and she needed sleep, but when the horn sounded
at dawn, she was still wide awake.

* * * * *

To Savaric's amazement, he learned the next morning that
Gabran had moved out of the hall and into Piers's tent. The
healer had been alone for so long that the chieftain found it
difficult to believe the man had asked the boy to share his tent.
On the other hand, they shared a bond of two uprooted people, and perhaps they were drawn together by similar needs. If
that was the case, Savaric was pleased. He was fond of them
both and felt they deserved friendship.

Savaric received another surprise after the morning meal,
when he rode past the practice fields and found his son teaching Gabran dueling exercises with the short sword. Dueling
was a frequently practiced method of ending blood feuds, set-
tling arguments, or claiming weir-geld. The rules were strict
and rigidly adhered to, and, because it was fought solely with
swords, dueling was restricted to skilled, initiated warriors of a
werod. With no mail or shield for protection, a man needed
every advantage to survive. Boys Gabran's age could not hope
to best an older warrior in personal combat, so Savaric saw no
reason for Athlone's training.

But when he questioned the wer-tain, Athlone merely
shrugged and replied that the boy was determined to challenge
Medb and there was no harm in humoring him. Savaric eyed
them both doubtfully, but he trusted his son, so the chief only

shook his head and cantered off with his men to hunt.

Meanwhile, Athlone turned back to Gabria. His arm was in a sling and his face was strained from weakness, but he held his sword as if it were a feather and watched Gabria's efforts with a sharp eye.

"One thing puzzles me," he said during a rest. "Where did you learn to use a sword?"

Gabria smiled. Since Athlone's acceptance of her true sex, she felt like a wasting illness had suddenly vanished from her mind. He still distrusted her, and Gabria noted that the vestiges of his anger and resentment would probably never disappear—at least as long as she wore pants and carried a sword—but his suspicions were gone. She found it easier to assume her role as a boy and to keep her mind concentrated on the details of survival.

"My brothers liked to pretend I was a boy," she answered with some humor.

Athlone examined her critically from head to toe. "If you looked then as you do now, your brothers did not have to pretend very hard."

Unconsciously, her hand crept to her short hair beneath the ever-present leather hat. "If I had been pretty, I would be lying in a cold grave now instead of keeping warm with light work," she said mildly.

"Light work! Impudent wench, I'll show you work." Athlone lifted his sword, and their blades clashed. He fought her hard, showing her tricks with the flick of the wrist or the turn of the blade. The short sword, generally used in melees on horseback, had a flat, broad blade that was better suited to slashing and hacking. Gabria had difficulty adjusting to the more polished form of swordplay used in dueling. But Athlone was a master swordsman and, by the end of the morning, Gabria was beginning to understand this new method of fighting.

"Remember," Athlone told her, "in dueling, the sword is the only protection you have. It must be your shield as well as your weapon."

He would have continued the training, but by noon the

strenuous work had caught up with him. Athlone was exhausted. His skin was gray and blood stained the bandage on
his shoulder. He returned to his tent for the rest of the day,
promising to continue Gabria's lessons the next morning.

Gabria was left to her own devices. She went in search of
Lady Tungoli. She found the chieftain's wife in one of the
hall's storerooms, supervising the distribution of the remaining foodstuffs for the trek to the clan gathering.

Stacks of cheeses and cloth bags of dried fruit lay in heaps
around Tungoli's feet, and huge earthen jars of grain were being emptied by other women into sacks for easier transporta-
tion. The Khulinin produced most of their own food through
their herds, hunting, and some gardening. Many things, however, were traded for at the gathering with other clans and merchants from the south and east. Delicacies such as figs, fruit,
honey, or dried fish, as well as necessities such as salt and grain,
were taken in exchange for furs, goats, woven rugs, cloth, felt,
saddles, and occasionally horses. To the competitive clansmen,
the bartering was half the fun.

When Gabria walked into the storeroom, Tungoli gave her a
smile and gestured to the piles of food. "If you would like to
help, you are just in time."

Gabria was quickly put to work lifting the filled grain sacks
into a pile by the main entrance, where several strong boys carried them to various families. After months of Athlone's training, Gabria was pleased to find the sacks easy to move. The last
time she had done a task like this her brothers had had to help.

People bustled in and out of the storeroom, shouting, talking, and calling questions, while the stores slowly disappeared.
Tungoli stood in the middle of the chaos and hummed softly as
she sorted the bags and bundles. The women worked for several hours in companionable chatter until the room was nearly
empty. Gabria was happy to work quietly, listening to the
voices and relishing in the company.

At last only Tungoli remained, along with the final stores.
The busy crowd had moved on to other jobs, leaving Gabria
and Tungoli in the storeroom in a backwash of peace. There
was still one jar left to empty when Tungoli was called to an-

other task; she left Gabria to finish the last bags. By that time, the girl was pleased to be alone in the cool, quiet storeroom. The tapestry over the doorway was pulled back to admit the afternoon light, and she could hear other people passing back and forth in the main hall. Gabria worked unhurriedly and became lost in her own thoughts. She didn't notice when everyone left the hall and two men entered.

Gabria was scooping the last grains into the leather bag when she heard a horribly familiar voice. Her body froze. The jar, balanced on her hip, slipped from her fingers and dropped to the floor. Its fall was muffled by the filled bag and Gabria managed to grab the jar's edge before it struck the ground. She shakily sat the jar upright and leaned against the wall, trying to regain her breath. Like her heart, her lungs seemed to have stopped at the sound of that voice: the voice with the slight lisp that came from the throat of Medb's most trusted emissary.

The last time she had heard that hateful voice had been in her father's tent when the Wylfling delivered Medb's ultimatum. Now he was here, soliciting Lord Savaric's aid. She realized that the chieftain and the envoy did not know she was in the storeroom. Gabria thanked all the gods that she had been out of sight when the Wylfling arrived, for he had seen her several times at Corin Treld and could have recognized her.

Gabria slipped quietly to the door and flattened against the wall in the shadows, where she could see the two men. Savaric was seated on his chair, watching the short, brown-cloaked man who was standing before him. The Wylfling had his back to Gabria, but she knew the figure immediately, and in her mind she saw his face. The emissary's face was not easy to forget: it was hollow like a wind-eroded rock, and its clean-shaven skin was as immobile and as pallid as limestone. The envoy reminded her of a statue.

She wondered what message he had for Savaric. It was difficult to read the chief's reactions. Surely the emissary was not offering Savaric the same bribes and threats that Medb had offered her father. That would be a mistake with a clan this big. Perhaps the Wylfling had been here before.

"The Khulinin is a powerful clan," the man was saying.

"And a large one. It is well known your tents lap the edges of the valley and your herds overgraze the meadows before you leave each summer. Soon your young men will be pressing for tents of their own and there will be nowhere to go. You need more land, perhaps new valleys, to begin holdings for another encampment before the Khulinin burst apart."

"I was not aware the Wylfling were paying so much attention to our problems. I am honored. I suppose you have a solution?" Savaric asked with barely concealed sarcasm.

"Oh, not I, Lord," the emissary purred. "But Lord Medb. He feels the lands to the south of Marakor should be relinquished to you and your heirs for a second, even a third holding. He would be willing to endorse your petition to the council for the formation of another holding."

"That is most generous of him, but I doubt the tribes of Turic would appreciate my claims to their holy land."

The emissary waved aside the notion. "You would have nothing to fear from that rabble. They will come to heel when they see the combined swords of Wylfling and Khulinin."

"Combined?" Savaric asked, his eyes glittering.

"Of course. After all, our clan holdings border the Turic's land as well. They would be trapped between two enemies. My Lord Medb is so pleased with the idea he is willing to aid you in your claim on the southern hills."

"In return for what?"

The man shrugged eloquently. "A small tribute—once a year, perhaps—to help feed our growing werod. We, too, are pushing the limits of our winter holdings."

"I see." Savaric raised an eyebrow and asked thoughtfully, "Why does Medb concern himself with the welfare of other clans? If he wants use of the Turic lands, he could take them himself."

"It is no secret that Lord Medb's ambitions exceed the position of chieftain. He needs strong, loyal allies, and he is willing to pay well for them. His generosity can be endless."

"With lands and favors that are not his to give," Savaric said with deceptive mildness.

The emissary's manner shifted subtly from ingratiating to a

self-confident superiority, the arrogance of a man assured of his future position. "The lands will be his soon. Lord Medb's hand is growing stronger and if you do not accept his proffered friendship . . ."

"We will end our days in smoking ruins like the Corin," Savaric finished for him.

The man's eyes narrowed. "Possibly."

"May I have time to consider this generous offer?"

Gabria smiled to herself and regretted her father had not taken the same tact. Perhaps if Dathlar had controlled his temper and not thrown the emissary out, they would have had time to escape Medb's wrath.

The emissary was taken aback. He had not expected any co-operation from the obstinate Khulinin; he assumed even the vain hope of gaining the rich grasslands to the south would not sway them to Medb's rank. Perhaps the Corin massacre had affected the clans more than the Wylfling imagined.

The emissary hid his surprise and smiled coolly. "Of course. You may tell Lord Medb in person at the gathering." The man hoped that would discomfit the chieftain, since it was very difficult to say no to Medb's face.

Savaric only leaned back and nodded. "Fine. I will do that. Was there anything else?"

"Yes, Lord. My master asked that I give you this as a small token of his esteem." The emissary drew a small bag out of his belt and dropped something onto his palm. Gabria craned her neck around the door to see what it was as the man handed the object to Savaric. The chief held the thing up to the light, and Gabria gasped when a flash lanced through the hall with brilliant beams of color. It was a gem called a fallen star, a rare and very precious stone once loved by the sorcerers.

"The stone is a flawless blue taken from one of Lord Medb's mines in the hills. He wants you to have it as a reminder," the man said blandly.

Savaric's brows rose together. "Indeed. This is quite a reminder." He sat back in his seat and nodded toward the door. "Tell your master I will think about his offer."

The emissary accepted Savaric's abrupt dismissal with ill-concealed irritation. He bowed and left. The chieftain sat for a moment, juggling the gem in his hand as he stared at the floor.

Gabria wondered what Savaric was thinking. She knew the chief well enough to know that he was not seriously considering Medb's offer, but she did not understand why he had accepted the stone. Medb's gifts were always double-edged.

The girl was about to return to her work when Lady Tungoli called to Savaric from their private chambers. The chief tucked the jewel under his cloak, which was lying on the dais, and went to talk to his wife, drawing the tapestry closed behind him. The hall was empty. Gabria knew she should not pry into the chieftain's business, but her curiosity got the better of her. She waited a full minute, listening for voices or footsteps, then she slipped to the dais and pulled aside the gold fabric. The gem was set in a cloak brooch of finely woven gold, and it glittered on the dark fur of the seat like its namesake, the star. It was an unusual gift to give a chief such as Savaric. The offer of land was a far better bribe to the lord of the Khulinin. Why had Medb sent it? He had offered no gifts like this to her father, and Gabria could not believe that Medb was giving a fallen star to Savaric out of the generosity of his heart.

Gabria picked up the gem. A strange tingling touched her fingers. Surprised, she dropped the brooch and the tingling stopped. What's this, she thought. She gently touched the gem and the sensation happened again, like the distant vibration of a faint pulse of power. Gabria was inexplicably reminded of Piers's healing stone. She had not touched the red stone, but she sensed intuitively that this gem and Piers's stone would have the same feeling of power.

Gingerly, Gabria picked up the gem again and held it up to the light from the hall's entrance. The jewel tingled between her fingers. She looked into the gem's brilliant, scintillating interior and wondered if this strange pulse was caused by magic. The gem had come from Medb, so it was possible he had put a spell on it.

The thought of Medb's magic frightened her. She was about to drop the jewel back on the fur when suddenly an image began to form in the center of the stone. She watched horrified as the image wavered, then coalesced into an eye.

Not a simple human eye, but a dark orb of piercing intensity that stared into the distance with malicious intelligence. Gabria shuddered. The eye's pupil was dilated. Looking into its center felt like falling into a bottomless hole.

"Gabran! What are you doing?"

Gabria leaped back, startled out of her wits. The image vanished. The gem fell out of her hands, bounced off the stone step, and rolled to Savaric's feet. He leaned over to pick it up.

"No," she cried abruptly. "Don't touch it."

Savaric's hand halted in midair, and he glared at her, his black eyes menacing. "Why not, boy?"

Gabria stumbled over her words and her face flushed with guilt. She backed away from the dais, still shaken by the memory of the eye in the stone.

Savaric straightened, and the gem sparkled by his foot. "Why not?" he repeated harshly.

"It came from Medb. It's dangerous," she mumbled.

"How do you know where it came from?" the chief demanded.

She glanced back at the storeroom, then down at the floor. "I overheard the Wylfling emissary."

"I see. And why do you think this gift is dangerous?"

Gabria swallowed. Her throat was very dry. What could she say? That she had felt the power embedded in the stone and saw the image of an eye in its center? She could hardly believe that herself. But she was certain of the danger the gem posed and the damage it could do if Savaric was not warned.

"I, uh . . . it is not exactly dangerous," Gabria replied, stumbling over her words. "But it is . . . I have heard Medb is learning sorcery. I thought he may have tampered with the gem. It feels strange when you touch it."

"I noticed nothing strange about the gem." Savaric crossed his arms and stared at the girl. His face was dark with anger. "But you felt free to see for yourself."

"I am sorry, Lord. I should not have touched your gift, but . . ." She paused and from somewhere in her memory, she remembered an old story her father liked to tell about a jealous sorcerer and a seeing stone. "Father told me a tale sometimes," she said, looking up at Savaric, "about a sorcerer who kept watch on his wife through a jewel with a spell on it. It was a spell of surveillance, and it enabled the man to see and hear everything the lady was doing."

The anger on Savaric's face cleared a little. "I have heard that tale, too," he said thoughtfully. "What made you think Medb may have done something similar to this brooch?"

Gabria clasped her hands behind her back to hide their shaking. "The Khulinin are dangerous. Medb needs to keep close watch on you and a spy would be too obvious. This gift just seemed overly generous."

Savaric picked up the gem and turned it over in his hands. He slowly relaxed and, when he finally spoke, his voice was no longer caustic. "I thought there was a hook in this gift, but I never imagined something like a seeing spell." The chief gestured toward the door. "Did you know the Wylfling?"

Gabria sighed with relief, for it seemed Savaric had accepted her explanation. She considered the lord's question and her lip curled. "He delivered several messages to Father. Has he been here before?"

Savaric was about to answer when something occurred to him. With a deft motion he folded his cloak and wrapped the jewel in the thick material. "If you are right about this," he said, tucking the bundle under his arm, "we don't need to announce your presence to Medb."

Gabria drew a long breath. She had not even thought of that. "What will you do with the jewel?" she asked.

"Since I have chosen to trust you, I would like to see if your suspicion is right. The gods knew where you got this idea, but if it is true, perhaps we can use the gem to our advantage. I might try a little test. It would brighten Medb's day if he thought the Khulinin would accept his offer."

"He would be most pleased," Gabria said with a small smile.

"For a while. He will have a rude awakening at the gathering." He stopped and studied her intently. "Do you seriously intend to claim weir-geld by challenging Medb to a duel?"

"Yes. It must be a Corin who takes the payment."

"It may not be possible."

Gabria stiffened and her eyes met Savaric's stern gaze. The chief was not going to dissuade her from challenging Medb. She had trained her body and prepared her mind for battle against her clan's killer and no man, no matter how close in kinship or strict in lordship, was going to divert her. She would fight the Wylfling lord against her chief's direct order if need be. "I will make it so," she stated flatly.

Savaric walked to Gabria's side and put his hands on her shoulders. His dark eyes glittered like jet, but beneath the cold glints was a warmth of sympathy. "I know you have your will set to fight Medb alone, and I will honor that as best I may. But there are other factors you do not know about that may influence your decision. When the council is held, remember who is your chief."

Gabria nodded. She was relieved that Savaric seemed to accept her resolution and her obsession for vengeance. What bothered her, though, was his reference to "other factors." There could be nothing that would stand between Gabria and her vengeance on Medb.

Savaric's hand dropped and amusement eased the hardness in his face. "The emissary will be here for another day or two, presumably to rest before he returns to Wylfling Treld. I will see if Athlone is fit enough to argue with his father over the rule of the clan. Medb would be fascinated to think a rift was developing in the Khulinin."

Gabria smiled. "And will you wear your new cloak brooch, my lord?"

Savaric chuckled. "Of course. You had better stay out of sight." He shifted the folded cloak to a more casual position and walked purposefully out of the hall.

Gabria watched him go and noted with a pang of familiarity the way his stride lengthened and his body tensed as he prepared for some important activity. Her brother, Gabran, used to radiate that kind of energy, a concentration of thought and power that boded ill for anyone who tried to thwart him. It was a calculating, tightly controlled strength that had helped him defeat many opponents in chess or swordplay. She had seen the same energy in Savaric before.

Gabria knew now that Savaric was concentrating on the jewel and his plan to test her warning about the seeing spell. If all went well, Medb would fall for Savaric's ruse and reveal his hand. Gabria knew the gem had been tampered with, and she was certain of the purpose of the spell. But how had she known? Savaric had not noticed anything strange about the gem. Only she had felt the power in the stone and saw the image of the eye. After the incident with Athlone the day before and her second dream, this encounter with sorcery was too coincidental to be ignored.

Something was happening to her, and she did not like it. Medb was a sorcerer, not she. Yet she was the one who was accused of striking two men with an ancient arcane power. She was the one who recognized the spell on the brooch. If what Piers said were true, then she was the same as Medb: a profaning heretic.

Footsteps sounded lightly behind the girl, breaking her distraction, and she whirled in alarm to come face to face with Tungoli. The lady's arms were full of rugs. "Gabran, I am sorry to startle you. Jorlan is looking for you."

Gabria's eyes flew to the doors where the evening sun was setting beyond the rim of the plain. "Oh! I didn't know it was so late." She dashed to the entrance, thankfully leaving her thoughts behind. "Thank you, Lady," she called and was gone.

9

abria rode guard duty that night and, after she had bid good-night to Nara, trudged to Piers's tent for some welcome sleep. Savaric visited them briefly and told her that the "argument" had gone as planned, with Athlone playing the impatient, disgruntled heir. The next morning passed uneventfully while the clan continued to pack for their summer trek. Savaric acted the congenial host to Medb's emissary, and Gabria stayed out of sight in Piers's tent. The chieftain made no mention of the mock disagreement with his son to anyone to be sure that Medb could have only learned of it through the stone—providing Gabria was right about the spell.

At nightfall, Gabria left for her duties. When she returned, Piers told her that Athlone had requested her for another game in his tent. She went with a curious foreboding in her heart and a chill in her fingers. She found Athlone and Savaric both waiting for her. From the quiet triumph on their faces, she knew she had been right.

"Come in, boy," Savaric said. "You have not only proved to me that Medb is resurrecting sorcery, but your quick wits have saved us much grief."

Gabria sat down heavily on a stool and hugged her knees. She was horribly afraid her wits had nothing to do with it.

Athlone removed the sling from his arm and paced back and forth across the deep carpets. He grinned. "Medb heard our fight, every last word of it, and he went for it like a weasel after a mouse."

"Good," Gabria said, trying to sound enthusiastic. "Is he

trying to unseat you?"

Her question was to Savaric, and he answered with a dry laugh. "He offered the world to Athlone in return for my death and the loyalty of the second most powerful clan." He lapsed into silence and stared at the floor.

Gabria realized that Savaric had moved into a deeper concentration. He was absorbed in his thoughts and his muscles wasted no effort in pacing or excess motion. Only a part of his mind was answering her, while the greater part wrestled with the problems posed by Medb.

"The world is a large order, even for Medb. Will Athlone be able to control that much holding?" Gabria asked with mild sarcasm.

"Medb plans not, I am sure," Athlone replied. "We are too close to Wylfling Treld for Medb's comfort. He will probably try to dispatch both Father and me. Then, with Pazric missing, Medb could put a man of his own over the Khulinin. Only then will his back be safe."

The three of them fell silent, busy with their own thoughts. Savaric sat on his stool like a priest in contemplation, while Athlone paced noiselessly and Gabria twisted the light fabric of her pants between her fingers and imagined Medb in his tent, congratulating himself for putting a wedge into the all-powerful Khulinin.

Gabria shook her head. This feigned division of father and son was the only leverage they had at the moment, and it was a poor one, for it would only last until Medb put pressure on the Khulinin to accept his rule or he discovered Savaric's deception. Gabria had found the secret of the jewel, and the gem might help them mislead Medb for a while to gain time, but it would not tell Savaric and Athlone how the other clans received Medb's ploys or how strong the Wylfling werod was—or how powerful Medb's arcane skills had grown. The stone would not help Savaric many days hence when the Khulinin were given their ultimatum and had their backs to a cliff.

Gabria knew, as surely as Savaric must, that the clans were being swept into war. Like a game master, Medb had leashed each clan and was drawing them into a confrontation that would tear them apart. If Medb forged his empire, the clans as they had endured for centuries would cease to exist. Instead of autonomous entities of a similar tradition and ancestry, they would become scattered pieces of a monarchy, ruled by one man and bound by one man's desires.

Yet, even if the clans defeated Medb, Gabria realized that the clanspeople would still lose a great deal. In a war between brothers, complacency dies fast, fury burns hot and the flames take longer to cool. The girl couldn't imagine how the clans would survive the conflagration of this war or what their lives would be like when peace fell on the steppes. She sighed softly, regretting the changes that were coming.

Savaric heard Gabria's almost soundless breath and raised his gaze to her face. Their eyes met and locked in understanding. Like Piers before him, Savaric recognized the strength behind Gabria's look. Until that moment, he had only considered his friend's child to be a stubborn boy, who, like any young, hot-tempered adolescent, demanded to fight for his clan's revenge because of an overdeveloped sense of outrage. But as he looked into those green eyes, Savaric suddenly understood that Gabria's determination went far beyond adolescent eagerness, to a calculated, controlled obsession. He knew without a doubt that "Gabran" would do anything to bring down Lord Medb. Inexplicably, the thought frightened him. He was not certain what a boy could do against a chieftain and a professed sorcerer, yet it occurred to him with a great deal of surprise that "Gabran" might succeed. Savaric remembered Piers's words the night the boy rode into camp and set the clan back on its ear. The healer said that the boy might be the key to unlocking Medb's doom. Maybe he was right.

"Well, Father," Athlone said, startling both the girl and the chieftain. "Now, at least, we know the rumors of Medb's heresies are true." He glanced oddly at Gabria, but continued. "What do we do now that we have him on the wrong trail?"

Savaric broke off his stare and looked at his son. "Keep him there for as long as we can. It will not hurt us to let him think the Khulinin will fall into his grasp."

"What did he offer you, Wer-tain?" Gabria asked. She was

feeling very tired and wanted to return to Piers's tent, but she wondered what the Khulinin were worth to Medb.

"That crow of an agent came to see me this evening." Athlone paused and looked thoughtful. "I would like to know how Medb contacted him so fast. Maybe he has a seeing stone, too. He offered me, in Medb's name, men, gold, land, and the chieftainship in return for obedience and my father's head."

Savaric chuckled. "I hope you will not be too free with either."

"Nothing is worth that price."

Gabria listened to the brief exchange with a little envy. Despite their differences, the two men were devoted as a father and son and even closer as friends. Only her brother, Gabran, had been that close to Gabria, and his death left a void that would never be filled. Nara helped heal some of the wounds in her soul, but there were a few hollows no one would ever find, hollows still filled with unshed tears. Gabria closed her eyes and turned away. It was still too soon to cry.

Savaric noticed her movement and said, "Daylight will be here soon and we have much to do."

They said good-night, and the chieftain walked with Gabria as far as Piers's tent. He hesitated as if he were going to speak, then he changed his mind, nodded, and left. Gabria watched Savaric until he disappeared between the tents. She felt closer to him that night than ever before, and she had the impression something had altered his thoughts about her. The way he looked at her in Athlone's tent—it was as if he had stripped away everything but her basic strengths and weaknesses and had accepted what he found. She was pleased by his understanding and relieved, too. She had no living family left, and she was beginning to appreciate how much Savaric and his family meant to her. Gabria closed the tent flap behind her. With a prayer to Amara, she fell asleep.

*   *   *   *   *

Like huge butterflies, the black tents of the treld began to fold their wings and disappear. Wrapped around their poles and ropes, the tents were bundled onto large, brightly painted wagons pulled by oxen or horses. Each family's possessions were packed beneath the tents and protected by carpets. After generations of practice, a clan could often dismantle their treld in a few days and their trail camp in a few hours. Packing the encampment was a fine art, and the women prided themselves on their expertise and speed.

The morning the Khulinin left their treld, the day dawned cloudless and hot. The faint dew quickly dried in the breeze and dust billowed everywhere. The first breaking of camp always took longer than usual, so the clan rose before sunrise to bring down the remaining tents, close the hall, saddle the horses, and bid farewell to those few who elected to remain behind. When the horn sounded at dawn, the caravan was already forming in the work field as each family took its position. The old people, the sick, and those who remained to care for the empty treld watched sadly and helped as best they could to send the clan on its way. The bachelors of the werod gathered the livestock. The three Harachan herds were mingled into one since mating would begin soon, and those horses that were not being ridden or worked were moved to the entrance of the valley. The mares, foals, and yearlings trotted about excitedly, but the stallion, Vayer, stood at the foot of Marakor and sniffed the wind that blew from the steppes and listened quietly for the signal of the horns.

Savaric himself closed the great doors of his hall and took down the golden banner. He passed it on to Athlone, who held it high and galloped Boreas down the path to the fields where the caravan waited. A shout of joy rose from every throat and echoed through the valley. Horses neighed in reply; the dogs barked frantically in excitement. The chaos of people and animals slowly shifted into a vague pattern of order. Forgotten items were retrieved, last minute good-byes were said, wandering children were found, and the ropes on the carts and pack animals were checked and rechecked.

Finally, when all was ready, two outriders carrying horns rode to the mouth of the valley. A silence of anticipation fell over the caravan. Then, in unison, each horn bearer lifted his horn to his lips and blew a great note of music that soared out over the empty plains like a cry of triumph and welcome. The clans-people roared their approval. Savaric, riding beneath the huge golden banner, lifted his sword to the sky as Vayer neighed.

Like a giant snake, the caravan crawled forward. Gabria sat on Nara's back and watched with awe-tinged respect as the Khulinin moved out of their valley. It was a sight she would always remember.

From the moment Valorian taught the first clansman the joy of mounting a horse, the clans had been nomads with the wind of the steppes in their faces and the dust of the trail on their clothes. Although the clans had slowed down over many generations and were unknowingly growing roots in the places they had chosen for winter camps, they were still nomads at heart. Wintering was fine for the cold months when the blizzards froze the land, but when the freshness of spring gave way to summer, the clans returned to the old ways and left the trelds behind.

For Gabria and her clan, the packing and preparations for the trek had always been simple. With only twenty-five families, the Corin had been able to move often and with little fuss. They had been more nomadic than the Khulinin and sometimes never bothered to winter in their treld. But this trek fascinated Gabria. The Khulinin, with their numerous families, huge herds, and powerful werod, moved ponderously out of the treld in a wondrously noisy cavalcade.

At the head of the caravan rode the hearthguard and the chieftain. Behind them was the main body of the clan in a procession of wagons, carts, pack animals, people on horseback or on foot, and a vociferous crowd of excited dogs and children. The livestock came next, and in the rear was another troop of warriors. The werod was spread out along the flanks of the caravan, and five outriders kept the horse herd off to the side to prevent mishaps. Gabria marveled at the organization that kept each man in his place and prevented tempers from exploding, but she could not help but wonder how the tremendous caravan traveled very far in a day. At the rate they were moving now, the gathering would be long over before the Khulinin arrived.

To her surprise, the caravan slowly increased its momentum until it was moving at a fair pace along the banks of the river. Before long, the rich green foliage of the foothills' brush and trees was left behind. Instead, deep-rooted herbs and grasses, already maturing to a golden green, stretched to the horizon. Old, thickly matted growth cushioned the travelers' steps as the caravan wove across the grasslands. Beside them, the Goldrine River grew from a foaming, bouncing headstream to a staid, contemplative river that meandered through gravel bars and basked silently in the sun. Ahead of the clan, several outriders rode the point to keep watch for marauders or game. Raiders rarely bothered a clan the size of the Khulinin, but this year Savaric took no chances.

Medb's emissary rode with them, having blandly explained that the Wylfling were already on their way to the gathering; he would meet them just as fast as if he traveled with Savaric's clan. Both Athlone and Savaric knew the real reason the agent stayed, and they made a point of waging frequent arguments while Savaric wore the star brooch. Because of the man's presence, Gabria was forced to ride with the outriders in the caravan's rearguard.

The days passed quickly under the open skies as the clan traveled east to the gathering at the Tir Samod, the holy meeting of the Goldrine and the Isin rivers. Breaking camp became a habit again and muscles adapted to walking and riding. The heavy winter cloaks were exchanged for lighter, linen cloaks with long hoods that were worn as the occasion demanded: either draped around the head for protection against the sun and wind, or drawn across the face for battle. Clouds rarely marred the boundless expanse of the sky, except for an occasional afternoon thunderstorm.

The summer heat increased and with it, as the time to the gathering shortened, the tensions in the clan grew heavier. Savaric's eyes constantly roved the horizon as if he were expecting a yelling horde to sweep over his caravan. Arguments flared among the warriors, and even Medb's emissary lost his aplomb at times and was snappish to the men he was supposed to charm. Messengers, who were usually numerous as the clans

grew closer together, were strangely absent this year. No word
came from anyone.

Athlone had Gabria relieved of her duties and spent the
warm evenings sharpening her skills with the sword, out of sight
of the clan. Most of the warriors ignored Athlone's curious attention to the outsider, but Cor still nursed his hatred for Gabria.
Before the trek, he had been too busy to deal with her as he
wanted. Now, he followed her constantly, looking for excuses to
report her to Jorlan or humiliating and insulting her before
other clansmen. He pulled petty tricks on her and dogged her
like a jackal waiting for a meal. He avoided her when Athlone
was near, but the wer-tain was constantly occupied during the
day and Gabria was too proud to tell him of the wretched man's
tormenting. She began to detest the sight of Cor.

Gabria tried to reconcile herself to Cor's hateful presence
since she could not avoid him, but his murky eyes and his
twisted sneer grated on her and his jibes cut with increasing irritation. There was nowhere she could go during the day to escape him. At night she dreamed of his rude laugh. She slipped
around the camp, looking over her shoulder and wincing every
time someone laughed. Even with Athlone, she was distracted
and nervous. She could only hope to ignore Cor until they
reached the gathering. Then, everyone would have more on
their minds than petty vendettas.

As the day approached when she would meet Lord Medb
face to face, Gabria was beginning to understand more of the
ramifications of her demand for weir-geld. One night she was
sitting with Athlone in Piers's tent, listening to the two men
discuss the coming council meeting. The healer and the wer-
tain had found a common ground in their shared knowledge of
Gabria's secret and had become tentative friends. It dawned
on Gabria, as she considered their words, that her claim to
Medb was only a small portion of the charges against him. Although she was the only survivor of her clan and could give evidence of Medb's complicity in the massacre, the other
chieftains would probably not allow her to fight him. They had
too many other matters to settle with him besides her desires
for revenge. Even the destruction of an entire clan paled in the

light of Medb's revival of the forbidden arts of sorcery. She doubted even Savaric would have an influence over the council's decisions.

The thought that her struggles would be worthless was almost more than Gabria could bear. She was so close, yet Medb could still slip through her fingers. A specter rose unbidden in her mind of the smoking, charred ruins of Corin Treld, and a small moan escaped her. The men's voices stopped. She glanced up, her eyes bright with unshed tears, and saw Piers and Athlone looking at her strangely. Without a word, she bolted from the tent. Gabria ran blindly through the tents and wagons, pursued by the black phantoms of her memory.

All at once a figure leaped out of a shadow, grabbed Gabria's arm, and whirled her around. She caught the smell of old leather and wine when the man began to shake her violently.

"It is the wer-tain's favorite," Cor's voice hissed. "And where are you going in such a rush, my pretty little boy?"

Gabria twisted fiercely in his grasp, but his fingers crushed into her elbows.

"Not so fast, Corin. You and I have things to talk about." Cor dragged Gabria into the shadow of a tent and pushed his face close to hers. His breath reeked of liquor.

"I have nothing to say to you," Gabria snapped. Her tears were threatening to spill over. She fought him, frantic to escape.

Cor grinned wickedly. "Now, now. Is that any way to treat a friend? I know someone who might be interested in meeting you."

The mocking triumph in his voice chilled her and she stopped struggling. "What do you mean?" she whispered.

"That's better. You'll like this man. I heard he was a close friend of your father."

Gabria stared at him in growing alarm. There was only one man in this camp Cor would be pleased to take her to and that was the one man she desperately wanted to avoid. "No. Let me go, Cor. I'm busy."

"Busy," he sneered. "Running errands for your precious wer-tain? This will only take a minute."

Suddenly, Gabria was furious. With a curse, she wrenched

away from Cor and swung her fist into his stomach. Then she
bolted into the darkness, leaving him doubled over and swear-
ing in futile pain.

She wove through the camp like a fleeing animal, to the
dark fields and the comfort of the Hunnuli. Nara came before
she whistled. Together they walked along the banks of the river
until long after the moon rose. But even the company of the
mare did not ease Gabria's fear and depression. Voices and
memories came to haunt her, and Cor's rude laugh echoed in
her mind. She was still frustrated and angry when she went
back to camp, her tears unshed. To her surprise, Athlone was
waiting for her.

He fell into step beside her as she walked past his tent. "I do
not want you disappearing like that," he said.

Gabria glanced up at him irritably and was amazed to see his
face showed worry. "Surely you were not concerned about me. My
loss would hardly be noticed." Her voice was full of bitterness.

"Oh, I don't know," he said dryly. "Cor would be so bored
without you."

She came to a stop. "You know about him?"

"He is one of my men." Athlone leaned back against a tent
pole and watched her in the dim moonlight. Somewhere
nearby, a woman was playing a lap harp and singing softly. Her
music filled the darkness around them like a distant lullaby.
"Why didn't you tell me?" he asked softly.

"Cor is my problem."

"He is a self-serving, weak bully who is harassing and distracting one of my warriors from training. That makes him my
problem," Athlone replied tightly.

Gabria crossed her arms and said, "I am not one of your
warriors."

"While I train you, you are."

Unexpectedly, Gabria laughed. "Do you realize what a
strange remark that is to say to me?"

Athlone was about to say more, but he changed his mind
and laughed with her. "I never believed I would be telling a
girl this, but you are getting quite good with your sword."

Gabria laughed again, this time with resentment and anger.

"Little good it will do me, Wer-tain. I will not be able to fight Medb. The chieftains will not let me near him. There will be too long a line."

"Perhaps you're right. But watch and wait. Your opportunity may come when you least expect it. Just continue your training."

"May I practice on Cor?" Gabria asked irritably.

Athlone glanced at her, a strange, thoughtful look in his eyes. "Maybe you already have."

Her fingers clenched at her sides and she took a deep breath. What did he know? She searched his face for any indication of his thoughts, but his features were impassive and his dark eyes glimmered without guile.

Athlone returned her look. He was intrigued by the play of shadows on her face. Fascinated, he reached out and pulled off her leather hat. The shadows vanished, and her visage was bathed in moonlight. He wished he had not done that, for the moon stole the colors from her face and transformed her into a pale ghost. There was nothing to show the deep feelings and desires that moved beneath the surface of that pallid flesh. Her skin looked so cold in the silver gleam, he wanted to touch her cheek to see if it was soft. His hand twitched, but he held it out of sight.

This girl was unreal to him. She had more determination and courage than many of his warriors and a way of meeting one's eyes that was disconcerting. She did not meekly submit to the laws governing women, nor did she bow to the devastating events that changed her life. Although Athlone did not admit it aloud, he was glad she was not submissive. Her stubbornness and strength of character made her unique.

Briefly, Athlone tried to imagine her as his lover. He did not remember very much of their fight at the pool, yet he did recall her body was too shapely to be called boyish. Nevertheless, he could not reconcile the image of a warm, passionate woman with this stiff-backed, sword-wielding, fierce-eyed girl. He decided that she would probably never make any man a good wife—if she lived long enough for any man to offer.

Unexpectedly, the thought of Gabria dead made Athlone

queasy. He had grown to like her, despite her strange behavior, and he was horrified when he fully recognized what the consequences of her actions would probably be. Even if the council refused her challenge to Medb, the Wylfling lord would mark her for death. If she fought him, the end would be the same, for Gabria had no chance to kill Medb in a fair duel.

Bitterly, Athlone tossed her hat to the ground. If the girl chose to revenge the murder of her clan, then so be it; he honored that choice. But that did not mean he had to like the price of her decision. He brushed past her without another word and went back to his tent.

Gabria stared at her crumpled hat in dismay. Something had upset Athlone. She thought back over their conversation to see if she had said something to anger him. She picked up the cap. It could have been her remark about practicing on Cor. Maybe Piers had told Athlone of Cor's injury and the healing powers of the red stone. Maybe Athlone, too, thought she was a sorceress and was trying to dissuade himself. Or perhaps he just did not appreciate her remark.

She hoped that was all it was. Gabria desperately needed the wer-tain to continue her training and further her cause at the council. She also didn't know if Cor was serious about taking her to the Wylfling emissary, but she would take no chances. She would tell Savaric about Cor's threat in the morning so the chief could keep the emissary distracted with other matters.

Gabria crumpled her hat in her hand and moved slowly back to Piers's tent. For the first time in her life, she prayed to Surgart, the warriors' deity, to guard her and give her strength for the challenges that lay ahead.

*   *   *   *   *

Five days later, the Khulinin reached the junction of the two rivers. By this time, the Goldrine had widened into a broad waterway. It wound through a wide, level valley and converged with the Isin, which flowed down from the north. An arrow-shaped island, named the Tir Samod, had formed long ago at the junction of the two rivers. On the island, in a circle of standing stones, was the only sacred shrine dedicated to all four of the immortal deities. It was a holy place, filled with the magic of spirits and the powers of the gods who protected it. Even in the years of heavy rains or snowfall, the shrine had never been flooded. Only priests and priestesses were allowed to set foot within the circle of stones. But on the last night of the gathering, every man, woman, and child came to the island to worship in a ceremony of thanksgiving to all the gods.

Around the island, on the banks of both rivers, gathered the clans. The gathering was the only place and time in the span of the seasons when all the clans were together. In that short time, the business of many thousands of people was dealt with.

The clans as a whole had no leader. Each clan was led by an independent ruler who was accustomed to being a law unto himself. These men did not easily yield to a greater authority, save tradition and the laws of the gods. But the clans liked to maintain their ties and traditions, and so once a year the chieftains met in council. The council had the power to alter laws, punish certain criminals, settle arguments or feuds between clans, establish new holdings, accept new chiefs, and continue the traditions handed down from their fathers.

Clan gatherings were also a time to reestablish old acquaintances, see relatives from other clans, and exchange gossip, stories, and songs that would enliven many cold winter nights to follow. Young people, unable to find mates within their own clans, vied for each other's attentions. Games and contests were held, horses compared, and races run every day on the flat stretch of the valley.

Merchants from the five kingdoms to the east and the desert tribes to the south arrived early and quickly set up shop to trade with the enthusiastic clanspeople. A huge bazaar sprang up even before the last clan arrived. There, people could barter for anything their hearts desired: rich wines from Pra Desh, fruits, nuts, grain, salt, honey, sweets, figs, jewelry, perfumes, silks from the south, salted fish, pearls, metals of all grades, medicines, livestock, and rare spices. Besides the foreign merchants, each clan fostered its own group of artisans who specialized in particular crafts and always displayed their work at the gathering. The foreign merchants had a ready market for the clan wares and bartered hotly for everything they could get.

When the Khulinin arrived at the Tir Samod late in the afternoon, four clans—the Geldring, the Dangari, the Amnok, and the Jehanan—had already encamped along the rivers. After countless gatherings, the clans had unwritten rights to their preferred areas. These grounds were blessed with the clan's particular tokens and were considered inviolate. The Khulinin's place was on the west bank of the Goldrine, not far from the site of the giant council tent.

But this year, as the head of the Khulinin caravan crested the ridge that overlooked the valley, Savaric saw the green banner of the Geldring floating above Lord Branth's tent in the place where Savaric's tent should be. Savagely, he reined his horse to a halt and stared down at the offending clan in astonished fury. The hearthguard and several outriders gathered about him, their outrage plain on their faces. The caravan ground to a halt. No one behind Savaric could see over the hill, but word of the Geldring's insult flew down the line of wagons until the warriors in the rear began to edge toward the hilltop.

Gabria watched Athlone gallop Boreas to Savaric's side and, even from her distant position, she could see him explode in anger. Watching his Hunnuli prance in agitation, she wondered worriedly what he might do. If Athlone had his way, the Khulinin could sweep down on the Geldring and begin a war before Medb arrived. Savaric might even decide to turn the caravan around and leave the gathering in a fit of honor. Lord Branth's move was a grave insult, but there were more important problems brewing at the gathering that required the Khulinin's presence.

Gabria pulled her hat low over her forehead and urged Nara up the slope. A short way behind the warriors, she slipped off the Hunnuli and ran the last few yards into the crowd of milling riders. The chieftain, Athlone, the Wylfling emissary, and the guards were all watching the encampments below, where warriors were suddenly swarming at the sight of the Khulinin. With a cautious look at the emissary, Gabria squeezed among the horses and heard Athlone's disgusted voice.

"If that conniving snake thinks he can do this . . ."

"Obviously, he already has," the emissary interrupted, trying to hide his amusement.

Athlone drew his sword and crowded near the Wylfling. "One more word, and I will relieve you of your duties as the Mouth of Medb."

The emissary shrank away from the sword poised near his throat and glared fearfully at the wer-tain. "My master will hear of this."

Savaric glanced down at the brooch on his cloak. "He probably already has," he said resignedly.

The emissary froze. His eyes narrowed to slashes, and his face seemed to shrink around his skull as he analyzed the meaning of Savaric's remark. He was shaken, but he rearranged his demeanor and hoped he had misunderstood the chieftain. "I am sure word has already reached my master of Lord Branth's petty attempt at insult. However, it appears it is too late to do anything but accept the situation. The council must convene."

Athlone slammed his sword back into its scabbard. "I will see Branth dead before he gets away with this."

Savaric shook his head. His initial wrath was cooling and tempering into a more devious anger. "He will not get away with anything. But now we have to move carefully. He is testing us. Somehow, we need to draw his teeth without drawing our swords."

Gabria smiled to herself. She had misjudged Savaric. She knew that she should stay behind the men and out of sight, but she was curious to see the camps. She wriggled past a guard's horse and stood by Athlone's heel, where Boreas's bulk hid her from the emissary.

Gabria looked down at the two rivers, where the tents of the four clans lay stretched out like dark birds. To the north of the island, in a wide, quiet bend of the Isin, was the ground where her clan would settle. The area was far from the bazaar and the council tent, and rather isolated from the rest of the encampments, but the Corin had always used it, preferring the convenience of water and pasture. Now it was empty, and Gabria

knew that the other clans would avoid it like a curse. If the Khulinin took it, they would pay an honor to the dead clan as well as irritate Medb's faction. She grinned at her idea.

The Khulinin men were deep in consideration of their next move. No one knew she was there. "You could camp on the Corin's land," Gabria suggested into the tense quiet.

Athlone turned furiously, taken by surprise. "Get back to the caravan. Now!" The emissary was looking curiously over his shoulder so Athlone nudged Boreas into his way.

"What did you say, boy?" Savaric was more startled by her suggestion than her presence.

"Why don't you camp in the Corin's place?" Gabria repeated.

A slow, devious smile curled Savaric's mouth, and he chuckled appreciatively at the thought of the other chiefs' reactions. He said, as if to himself, "Dathlar would be pleased."

The wer-tain leaned over and hissed at Gabria, "Get out of sight, you fool!" She ducked behind a guard's horse just as the emissary pushed around Boreas.

"Who was that boy?" the agent asked suspiciously.

Savaric replied blandly, "My brother's son. He sometimes forgets his place. Athlone, what do you think of his suggestion?"

"It has merit," the wer-tain said, studiously ignoring the emissary's frown.

"I agree." Savaric turned to his men. "Jorlan, we will camp by the Isin where the Corin once camped." The chieftain disregarded the astonished looks of the riders and added, "There will be no reprisals against the Geldring. We will behave as if nothing has happened. Is that understood?"

Jorlan and the warriors saluted. They were appalled at the whole notion, but their lord's word was law. Jorlan, who was filling in as second wer-tain, gave the necessary orders, and the caravan began to move reluctantly down the hill. Gabria ran back to Nara and returned to the end of the procession. It had been foolish to risk exposing herself to the emissary, but it had been worth it. She released Nara to run with the other horses and went to hide in Piers's wagon until the clan was settled.

The outriders moved the herds to the distant pastures while

the wagons rumbled down the hill. A few shouts of welcome met the caravan, and clansmen rode out to escort them. Yet few of the greeters showed their usual excitement. They were waiting nervously to witness the Khulinin's reply to the Geldring's insolence. A few Geldring, too, were watching from the edge of their camp; the rest were out of sight.

Then the clansmen stilled and gazed at the Khulinin, astounded at what they were seeing. The wagons turned off the main path and crossed the Isin, coming to a stop at the wide, grassy bend everyone had hitherto fearfully ignored. The other clans had expected anything but this. Savaric, as he watched the carts unloaded and the tents lovingly constructed, smiled to himself. He wished that he could see the look on Medb's face when the Wylfling saw the Khulinin camp on the Corin's land.

10

he Shadedron and the Ferganan clans arrived that evening amid shouts of welcome and a flurry of speculations. The clansmen were stunned by Savaric's move to the Corin's ground. The Khulinin were intentionally reminding the other clans of the massacre and were honoring the dead clan at the same time. The Wylfling had not yet come, and the chieftains wondered how Medb would react to Savaric's taunt. They were also taken aback by the Khulinin's disregard of the Geldring's insult.

Normally such a flagrant offense would precipitate a challenge or a violent protest at the very least. But the Khulinin merely set up their tents by the river and mingled with the other people, blatantly ignoring the Geldring. No one could decide if Savaric was bowing to Branth, and therefore Medb's superiority, or if he just felt that Branth was beneath his notice. Savaric gave no indication of his feelings.

Intrigue and gossip spread like wildfire through the camps. Rumors blossomed everywhere. The chieftains, when they were not puzzling over the Khulinin, studied each other warily, guessing who supported Medb. Branth strutted through the bazaar like a mating grouse in full feather, secure in his coming authority and power. Tensions, worries, and whispers spread through the encampments like smoke.

When the clanspeople discovered the Khulinin had a second Hunnuli, the smoke thickened. They tried every means to discover the rider, but no one could find the mysterious man who had tamed the spectacular mare, and the Khulinin were surprisingly tight-lipped about the horse and her rider. The black mare remained grazing with Athlone's stallion, unconcerned by the people who came to stare at her and the conjectures that crowded around her. Meanwhile, her rider stayed out of sight in the healer's tent.

Late that evening, three chiefs came to give Savaric the customary welcome, then declined his hospitality and quickly left, for they were uncomfortable on the Corin land. Lord Branth avoided Savaric altogether. Only Lord Koshyn, chieftain of Clan Dangari, stayed to share a cup of wine.

The young chief wore his light hair short in the manner of his clan and had a pattern of blue dots tattooed on his forehead. His eyes matched the indigo of his cloak.

Koshyn smiled infectiously and made himself comfortable on the cushions. "You certainly know how to make an impression." He accepted the cup Tungoli handed him and saluted his companion.

Savaric returned his toast. He liked the younger man and hoped the Dangari would not accept Medb's bribes. "Dathlar was my friend," he said simply.

"Yes. I think Branth was secretly relieved to find that you did not make an issue of his choice of camping places."

"I doubt it was his idea."

Koshyn stared out the open tent flap for a while, tasting his wine. "Care to make a wager?" he asked, his face crinkling in humor.

"What sort of wager?"

"I'd bet five mares that Medb leaves this gathering with the council in his complete control."

"Cynical, aren't you?" Savaric replied.

"I was offered a rich prize if I aided his bid for power. I am not the only one."

"I know. But what will be stronger: greed, fear, or independence?" Savaric paused. "All right, I accept." He looked frankly at the Dangari. "Are you going to ally with the Wylfling?"

Koshyn laughed. "That might give away the wager." He drained his cup, held it up for more, and gave Savaric a long look while the Khulinin refilled the cup. "Was there any truth to the rumor that someone survived the Corin massacre?"

Savaric only lifted an eyebrow and repeated, "That might give away the wager."

* * * * *

By the next afternoon, three other clans, the Reidhar, the Murjik, and the Bahedin from the north, had set up their camps along the rivers. The gathering went into full swing, and everyone tried to pretend this year was like every other. But the atmosphere among the camps was electric. Although the clansmen tried to appear casual, details, barely noticeable, gave away every person's true feelings. Hands stayed close to dagger or sword, faces strained into smiles, and chieftains were quick to break up arguments. The women, who knew everything despite the men's efforts to keep the problems quiet, remained closer to their tents. Even the merchants were nervous and kept most of their goods packed. Two days had passed and the Wylfling still had not arrived. They were the last. Every eye surreptitiously watched the south for any sign of the late clan.

Medb, it seemed, was delaying his arrival to let the clans stew. When the huge caravan of the Wylfling was finally spotted early that evening, every man ran or rode out to witness Medb's coming. It was exactly what he wanted. The Wylfling were the largest and wealthiest clan; they claimed the best land at the gathering for their camp and the richest pasture for their herds. When his caravan rolled into the valley, Medb arrayed his people to remind the clans of his power and might.

Wearing his long, brown cloak to hide his crippled legs and the rope that held him in the saddle, Medb rode at the head of his werod like a monarch. The warriors, over fifteen hundred strong, rode with their lances pointed to the sky and the chain mail of their long-coats polished to a bronze gleam. Their brown hoods covered their leather helmets, and the long, tasseled ends draped over their shoulders. Behind them were the wagons. Countless carts, wagons, animals, and people moved in an orderly procession toward encampments. Another troop of warriors followed, and a vast herd of horses and livestock took up the rear.

The clans greeted the Wylfling with none of their usual enthusiasm. They watched warily as each cart rolled by, and they silently counted each warrior. In a short year's time, Medb's clan had ceased to be a part of the whole. It was now a threatening force that loomed over them all and foreboded changes that few welcomed.

Savaric and Athlone stood at the edge of the encampment and nodded civilly when Medb rode by.

"Medb has had a most prosperous year," Koshyn said, coming up beside them.

Savaric nodded, his face bleak. "The Wylfling women have been most prolific. His werod has increased by several hundreds in a mere winter."

"The sun must be hotter in the south this summer, too. Did you observe a few of his outriders?" Athlone remarked.

"Even dust and distance cannot hide dark skins," Koshyn said.

Athlone shaded his eyes against the sinking sun and watched the riders maneuver the Wylfling herds to pastures across the Goldrine. "Turic mercenaries. I've seen one of them before."

Savaric followed his son's gaze and studied the distant horsemen. "Interesting."

"Care to increase the wager?" Koshyn suggested.

"Seven mares," Savaric replied.

Koshyn grinned. "Savaric, I believe you are hiding something."

The Khulinin chief tried to look astonished. "What have I got to hide?" he asked.

"How about a rider for that Hunnuli mare?"

"Oh, him," Savaric said casually, scratching his head. "He's ill."

Koshyn did not believe him for a moment. "How sad. May he recover soon."

"He will."

"I'm sure. Well, whoever he is, this unknown man cannot be the rumored Corin survivor. None of them had a Hunnuli. If there was a survivor, he was probably lost in that spring blizzard."

"Probably," Athlone said blandly. He was finding it difficult to keep his expression innocent.

Koshyn shot him a quick look, then shrugged. "Seven mares it is. I'll be interested to see who wins. Medb is going to move fast, so if you're going to pull the rug out from under him, you had better start soon." He walked off.

"Seven mares?" Athlone asked.

Savaric clapped the wer-tain on the shoulder. "The Dangari have the swiftest horses in the clans. Our stock needs new blood."

"What if you lose?"

The chief smiled, a slow lift of his mouth that belied the sadness in his eyes. "If I lose, I doubt I will live long enough to regret my debt."

Athlone chose not to comment on that. Instead he said, "I had heard recently that Medb was injured by a Hunnuli. Did you notice he was tied to his saddle?"

"Hmmm. Medb's injuries must have been crippling," Savaric noted. "That puts a different slant on things."

"I was glad to see it."

The chief knew what his son meant. "Yes. Gabran's duel becomes impossible now."

They walked back toward their own camp, keeping their heads close and their voices low.

"Why hasn't Medb tried to heal himself?" Athlone asked. "I thought sorcery could change anything."

"I doubt he has reached his full strength yet, so he may not want to reveal his power." Savaric slapped his scabbard. "And that, my boy, is our hope. Most of the clansmen do not know for certain that Medb has resurrected sorcery. This is his one chance to gain control of the council, so we must stop him while we can."

"But even with the mercenaries and the Geldring, he does not have enough men to overpower the rest of us."

Savaric jabbed a finger in the air. "He does as long as we stay separated."

"You mean unite the clans?" Athlone was skeptical. "Has it ever been done?"

"Not to my knowledge."

"How are you going to pull them together? It would take nothing short of a cataclysm to make these chiefs unite against Medb."

"How about the truth?" Savaric said mildly. "An irrefutable revelation of Medb's sorcery? In front of all the chiefs."

Athlone stopped dead. He immediately understood what his father was suggesting. "No! You cannot do it."

"It is the only way the chiefs will recognize their danger." Savaric stopped, too.

"They will recognize it well enough! They'll see you goad Medb's power and die in a blast of arcane fire, then they will run screaming back to their holdings, where Medb will be able to take them at his leisure." Athlone started walking again, his hands working in agitation. "Father, be reasonable. If you try to force Medb to reveal his sorcery, he'll kill you. You are the only one who could possibly hold these clans together against him."

Savaric caught up with his son and took Athlone's arm. The chief's eyes burned. "I have to try this. You said 'nothing short of a cataclysm.'"

Athlone stared at the chieftain for a long moment. He knew the determination that showed on Savaric's face would not be shaken. They had no real proof that Medb was a sorcerer, nothing tangible to show the council. Now Savaric wanted to provide the council with proof at the risk of his own life. Athlone doubted it would serve to unite the clans. They had been independent too long to see the sense of standing together, even in the face of the resurrection of sorcery. But maybe one or two would join the Khulinin to fight Medb.

"Will you at least talk to the others first?" Athlone asked, although he knew that talking would probably be useless.

Savaric's eyes softened. "Of course. I do not relish incurring Medb's wrath."

"We'll do that anyway," Athlone said, "when he finds out I have no intention of bringing the Khulinin to his heel."

Savaric suddenly laughed. "Then we have nothing to lose."

* * * * *

With the eleven clans together at last, the priests crossed to the island that evening and, from a secret cavern, brought out the gigantic council tent. In a large space on the bank of the Goldrine, under a few trees that grew by the water, the tent was raised with the help of men from every clan. Ten supporting poles on each side stretched the tan material over enough space to accommodate fifty men. Rich carpets were spread over the ground, and a fire pit was unearthed. Sections of the wall were rolled up to allow the breeze off the rivers to cool the interior. Cushions and stools were brought for the men's comfort.

Early the next morning, the banners of the eleven clans were hung outside the council tent. Dark gold, blue, green, brown, gray, black, purple, yellow, orange, dark blue, and maroon, they unfurled in the wind like flames. Only the scarlet of Clan Corin was missing. Everyone tried to disregard the banners around the tent, but the scene was strange and foreboding without the familiar splash of red. Time and again, men caught their glance wandering to the poles of the huge tent.

At noon the horns were blown, calling the chieftains to council. Forty-four men—eleven chieftains with their sons, wer-tains, elders, and priests—gathered within the cool, breezy tent. Women passed around flagons of wine and ale, and set bowls of fruit within reach, then they silently withdrew, for no woman was permitted to attend the council. Malech, chief of the Shadedron, called the men to order and the high priest blessed the gathering. The council began.

The first day the men only discussed minor problems. Savaric asked for information about Pazric's disappearance but received no news. Lord Branth was welcomed into the council, and the damage caused by the spring rains was discussed. Every man avoided looking at Medb, who sat ominously quiet with seven of his men. Few outside the Wylfling clan had known the extent of Medb's crippling injuries and no man dared comment. Crippled or no, it was obvious that Medb still had full control of his clan and his power.

Nor did anyone mention the issues that were uppermost on

every man's mind: the Corin massacre, Medb's unlawful bribes to the chiefs, the banding of the exiles, and the rumors of Medb's heretical practice of sorcery. The men were not ready yet to broach those explosive subjects. Instead, they talked of everyday events and watched each other, waiting for someone else to make the first move.

Medb said nothing. He sat on his litter within the half-circle of his most trusted guards and watched the chiefs with hooded eyes, like a lion eyeing his prey. They had nowhere else to go but down his path and they knew it. Let them leap and feint away. In the end they would come to him. Then his crippled legs would make no difference; when he unleashed the full power of his magic, every man would fall to the earth and worship him—or die.

When the council ended for the day, the men thankfully quit the tent to go to their own camps. After a night of feasting and dancing, in which the Wylfling took no part, the council reconvened the following morning.

The meeting was the same as the day before. Yearly business was transacted, a few major punishments were meted out, and several grievances were smoothed over. Again Medb sat in his place and said little. The tensions mounted like a tightly lidded pot set too near the fire.

Savaric wore his star brooch to the council on both days, although he said nothing to Medb about an alliance, and he covertly watched the responses of his companions. The stone drew many looks and comments, some envious, some admiring, but it was obvious where the stone had originated and many men wondered what Savaric had done to earn it.

Yet the Khulinin chief said little to anyone at the council. He watched and waited with the rest of the chiefs. Savaric was biding his time. He was waiting for the right moment, when the tensions were at their highest, before he made his move.

When the second day's council was over, Savaric nodded to Athlone. "Tomorrow," the chief said. "Tell the boy."

"What boy?" Lord Koshyn asked as he stepped up beside the Khulinin. He grinned at Savaric and Athlone. "Is your mystery man finally going to make an appearance?"

Savaric picked up his cloak from the cushion he had been sitting on. "The Hunnuli's rider has recovered from his illness," he replied.

Just then, Lord Sha Umar, chief of Clan Jehanan, strode over to join the three men. The frustration was plain on his handsome face. "Savaric," he said with annoyance, "the council cannot go on avoiding Medb's criminal behavior. Someone has to prod these chiefs into action."

Koshyn nodded. "We were just discussing that. I believe the Khulinin have a plan under their cloaks."

Sha Umar looked relieved. "I don't mind telling you, Savaric, Medb scares me. He is a menace to us all."

The Khulinin chief looked at the Jehanan thoughtfully. "Are you thinking of allying with him?"

Sha Umar snorted. "I am frightened, but I'm not stupid. I would rather have my clan die as the Corin did than live under his rule." He glanced at the entrance where Medb's men were carrying the chief's litter out of the tent. The three other men followed his gaze.

"We have to deal with him," Savaric said quietly. "Before he grows too strong."

"I'm glad to hear you say that. You can count on me to help." Sha Umar nodded to the men and left with his warriors.

"Do you want to change your wager?" Savaric asked Koshyn.

The younger man shook his head. "It would be worth seven mares just to be wrong. I will be looking forward to tomorrow." He, too, left the tent.

Savaric and Athlone, and their accompanying guards, walked back to the Khulinin camp. Neither man had much to say, for their thoughts were on the coming morning. When they reached the camp, Savaric retired to his tent and Athlone went to talk to Gabria.

During the two days of council meetings, Gabria had been fretting in Piers's tent. The waiting was interminable. Savaric had ordered the girl to remain out of sight, and Gabria knew that his plans would be destroyed if she were recognized prematurely. But this did little to alleviate her frustration. That hard-won, longed for moment, when she could confront Medb and fling his crimes in his face, was so close. Soon, she would see him broken and bleeding, dying in pain—as her family had at the treld.

Gabria savored the image. Oh, she might die in the attempt, but now death had no fear for her. She would be victorious and her clan would live forever in the glorious tales that would be told about her. Nothing would stop her. Gabria might wait now and cooperate with the chief's plan, but when the time came, she would fight Medb with every weapon she had. Not even the council would be able to stop her. The weirgeld *would* be paid.

Gabria's moods shifted restlessly from boundless rage to nervousness to irritation and impatience. She could not stand still. Her hands fretted at everything, and her body flinched at sudden noises. To make matters worse, Cor had taken to lounging outside the tent. When he was not working or eating, he was lolling in the shade of a tree near the healer's tent, making crude comments about Gabria to anyone who would listen, or taunting her through the felt walls. Gabria didn't know what Cor would do if she stormed out and confronted him, but both of them knew Savaric had forbidden her to leave the tent. Cor was making the most of it.

Piers tried time and again to force him to leave, but Cor kept returning to sit under the tree and taunt the Corin. Gabria tried to ignore Cor, for his disembodied voice sounded eerie in the dim interior and his insults only added to her agitation. In the brief silences when he was gone, she tried to calm her taut nerves. But very little helped. Cor's voice would soon abruptly cut through the quiet of the tent and send her clawing at the walls.

By sunset of the second day, Gabria was nearly out of her wits with tension and frustration. When Athlone strode in to talk to her, he startled her. She grabbed a knife and nearly stabbed him before she recognized him in the half-light of evening.

"I'm sorry," she said shakily. "I thought you were Cor."

Athlone took the knife out of her hands and set it on Piers's medicine chest. "He is elsewhere. I apologize to you. I should have dealt with Cor sooner." He watched as she paced back and forth on the rugs. "Father plans to take you to the council tomorrow," he said at last.

Gabria glanced up and her lips curled in a feral smile. "I will be ready."

"Gabria, don't get your hopes up," Athlone tried to explain. "There are too many things you do not know about."

The girl shook her head. "Do not worry about me, Wertain. I am fine."

Athlone watched her and knew she was not, but there was nothing more he could do then. No one had had the heart, or the courage, to tell Gabria that Medb was too crippled to fight a personal duel. No one knew how she would react or if she would even accept the truth. Athlone started to tell her, then he decided not to. In her frame of mind, she would never believe him.

The warrior bid her good-night and went outside. Piers met him near the tent. The healer was carrying a full wine skin and a blanket.

Piers held up the skin and shook the contents. "Would you believe it's water?" he asked. "I don't think I will sleep well tonight. Would you care to join me?"

Athlone agreed and the two men made themselves comfortable under the nearby tree. Together, they sat guard on the tent and its seething occupant through the night. Cor stayed well away.

Gabria slept badly that night. The shadows that haunted her after the massacre returned in strength and hovered around her as she drifted in and out of sleep. Her frustration from the two days of waiting boiled in her stomach, and her throat was tight with unshed tears. Tomorrow it will be over, she kept reminding herself. In the morning, she was going to the council with Savaric and, by sunset, the ordeal would be ended. As if to mock her ignorance, her dreams crowded in and the circling phantoms laughed at her with the voices of her brothers. Soundlessly, she cried out to them.

Then, from the void of ghosts and memories, came a dream as clear as the vision she had seen in the fire that night in the

Khulinin hall. Corin Treld. Gabria saw herself standing on a hill, looking down at the remains of the once busy camp. The sun was high and warm, and grass grew thick in the empty pastures. Weeds sprawled over the moldering ashes and covered the wreckage with a green coverlet. A large mound encircled with spears lay to one side, its new dirt just now sprouting grass. The darkness of her grief receded a little when she saw the burial mound. Someone had cared and had shown their respect by burying the clan with honor. It was an act she had been unable to do, and she gave her thanks to whomever had buried the Corin.

All at once the dream vanished and Gabria came awake. She lay on her pallet, staring at the darkness and wondering if the dream had been a true vision or merely her own wishful imagination. Then again, the source of the dream did not really matter. The image of the burial mound gave her peace and remained with her through the darkest hours of the night, helping to ease her terrible tension.

By the time the light of dawn leaked through the tent, Gabria was composed. The shadowy phantoms were gone; her nervousness had passed. The tension had drained from her mind and body. There was nothing left but a single, clear flame of resolution. Only the memory of the burial mound remained to remind her of her duty.

Gabria straightened her clothes and drew on her boots. Her weapons, now a part of her, were gently laid aside for the time they would be needed. The sword was already honed to a killing edge and her father's dagger glistened from constant rubbing. She folded her gold cloak and surprised herself by running a regretful finger over the light linen. She had grown comfortable with the Khulinin. It would be hard if, for some reason, she had to leave them, too.

Turning her back on the gold cloak, Gabria drew her scarlet cloak out of a leather chest and shook out the folds. The red wool cascaded to the ground. Such a true color, she mused, clear and pure like a gemstone; not muddied like blood. She swung the cloak over her shoulders and pinned it in place with the brooch her mother had given her. She smiled to herself.

Medb was in for a surprise.

Piers watched her worriedly as she finished dressing. He wanted to say something to ease his own tension, but he could find no words. The healer recognized the look of intensity that altered Gabria's face. Her eyes glowed with an untarnished light, and the dark circles that ringed her eyes made them look enormous. Her skin was flushed, and her movements were brief, as if she were preserving all her strength. Piers wanted to tell her, to warn her that her hopes of fighting Medb were in vain, but when he looked into her face, he could not find his voice. The girl was too withdrawn to listen. Only the sight of Medb and his crippled legs would convince her that her challenge for a duel was impossible.

Piers hoped that the realization would not break her. Gabria had survived so much and planned for so long to destroy the Wylfling lord in a duel that it might be difficult for her to see other possibilities for revenge.

When Gabria was ready, she sat silently with Piers and waited. The council was to begin at midday, so she had some time before Savaric came for her. She could not eat and she tried not to think, so she detached herself from everything except her resolution. Piers respected her solitude and simply sat with her in wordless support.

Earlier that morning, Savaric and Athlone had risen before the dawn. A messenger found them as the moon was setting and he bid them follow. To their astonishment, he carried a thin, long whip with a silver death's head crowning the butt. Only one small group of men bore such strange weapons and they had not come to the gathering for untold years.

Bridling their curiosity, the two Khulinin belted on their swords and walked soundlessly past the guards, toward the two rivers and the sacred island. The flow of the rivers made the only sound in the cool night, and a short breeze tugged at their clothes. The messenger stopped them at the water's edge and whistled softly. Three figures detached themselves from the shadows of the standing stones and waded across the rapids. Each wore no cloak, only a simple tunic and an ankle-length robe belted with leather. They carried no visible weapons except for whips, which hung curled at their waists. Behind them, the dark gray stones waited like sentinels, watching but not listening. Athlone shivered under their gaze.

One of the men came to Savaric and held up his hand in a gesture of peace. "Good hunting, Brother," he said. He was the same height as the Khulinin, and they eyed each other for several minutes.

Savaric tilted his head to one side. A slow smile spread across his face. "Seth. You are most welcome."

The strangers with the newcomer seemed to relax. They remained as stiff as statues, but they tucked their hands into the sleeves of their robes and moved back to give the chief and his brother more room.

Seth nodded imperceptibly. "I am glad to hear you say that. Does your hospitality extend to us all?"

The chieftain's glance swept over the four men, then returned to his brother's face. "Are all of you here?"

"No. Only the four of us. We need your help."

Savaric's eyebrows lifted. "Since when do the men of the lash need help?"

"Since the clans named us Oathbreakers. We wish to attend the council."

"What?" Athlone gasped.

Seth raised an eyebrow much like his brother. "What is the matter, Nephew? Has the council passed a law forbidding us entry to the gathering?"

Savaric put his hand on Athlone's shoulder. He shared his son's surprise. The men of the religious cult of the goddess, Krath, had shunned the gatherings for generations. Savaric wondered why, of all times, the men of the lash chose this year to come. Then he remembered that they were in sight of the guards and the camps, and he gestured to his brother. "Perhaps it would be better if we talked in my tent."

Seth agreed. He said something in a low voice to his companions and they disappeared into the darkness.

Savaric, Athlone, and Seth skirted the encampment and slipped into the chieftain's tent unseen. Tungoli was waiting for her husband and she nodded politely, barely hiding her surprise, as Seth entered. She fetched wine before retreating behind the sleeping curtain. The three men squatted by a small lamp and watched each other thoughtfully. In the dim light, Athlone recognized a strong resemblance between the two brothers.

The Oathbreaker was younger than the chieftain, but years of rigorous training, self-denial, and life in wild lands had aged him. His skin was dark beneath his thick beard. His eyes were carefully deadpan. It was said the followers of Krath could look into men's hearts and reveal the hidden evils that lurked there; they pried into secrets and opened guarded hatreds that were buried beneath facades. Because of this, few men dared to look an Oathbreaker in the eye and they themselves kept their eyelids half-closed as if to contain the horrors they had seen.

Savaric was the first to break the silence. "Maybe now you will tell us why you have come."

Seth leaned back on his heels and wrapped his robe carefully around his knee. "Medb."

"I did not realize he took an interest in Krath's cult," Savaric said.

"He has the *Book of Matrah*."

Athlone and Savaric were badly shaken. The wer-tain paled. He looked at his father, for the first time showing real fear.

"We suspected that he was reviving the black arts, but we never imagined he had such help." The chieftain stared into the flame of the lamp, his face grim.

"He asked us to translate passages for him," Seth continued. "The library in the Citadel of Krath contains the only sources available for such an undertaking."

"What was your answer?" Athlone's voice was harsh.

A glint of irritation escaped Seth's eyes and his mouth tightened. "We said no."

Savaric looked up. "I'm surprised. I thought Krath would have appreciated Lord Medb's methods."

"Our ways may be different from the men of horses and iron, but we do not sit lightly by when threatened by the likes of a miserable *chieftain*."

Savaric ignored the insult. Despite his blood kinship to an Oathbreaker, he could not understand what turned a man from the ways of the clans to the dark secrets of a bloodthirsty goddess. Seth was beyond his comprehension, and, because of that, Savaric took a perverse pleasure in cracking his brother's shell whenever possible. "You're skittish tonight, Seth," he retorted.

The Oathbreaker's expression went deadpan again. Even after years of training, he still could not maintain complete control before his brother. "We need you to take us to the council. Clan sentiment has never been with us and, without your endorsement, we would not be permitted to enter the council," he said in strict formality.

Athlone slammed his wine cup down. "You still haven't told us why."

"Medb promised to destroy our citadel if we do not help him."

"And you want our help defending that nest of assassins?" Athlone cried.

Seth stiffened. The mask in his eyes slipped slightly and, for a moment, Athlone fancied he saw the glow of a raging inferno in the depths of those black orbs. The wer-tain tore his gaze away and stared at the floor.

"You would do well to learn tact, Athlone. You are stirring embers that are best left alone." Seth paused. "We came to warn the council of Medb's book and his growing powers—and to ensure that he does not threaten us again."

Savaric nodded. Only the men of Krath's cult knew what was in the library of their citadel, but if the Oathbreakers wanted to break their self-imposed exile to warn the clans, it would be best if someone listened. "You may come." He paused and smiled at Athlone. "We will have several surprises for Medb in the morning."

"I hope he has none for us," Athlone muttered. "Father, you are not going to go through with your plan after hearing this."

"We will see. Perhaps, with the right bait, Medb will trap himself."

Seth drained his wine and said, "Only fools believe in an easy road."

11

t midmorning, Nara appeared by Piers's tent to fetch Gabria. Savaric decided for appearance as well as safety to let her ride the Hunnuli. The effect would be worth a thousand words when they came to the council.

When Gabria walked out with the healer, she saw Savaric, Athlone, several of the hearthguard warriors, and the four Oathbreakers already waiting for her. She was surprised by the presence of the men of the lash, but she only gave Seth and his companions a cursory glance. Seth, on the other hand, exchanged looks with his men, and, when Nara pranced to Gabria's side, he gave his brother an appreciative shake of his head.

Athlone helped the girl mount Nara's broad back. He looked into her drawn face and recognized the fires burning her within. He squeezed her knee. When she glanced down at him, her eyes were bright and distant.

"Keep a guard on your tongue. Do not do anything to risk the lives of this party. Do you hear me?" Athlone demanded.

His emphatic tone drew her back to the present. She nodded with some surprise.

The Hunnuli nudged her thoughts. *He is right, Gabria. Do not challenge the man yet. You are not ready.*

Gabria was watching Athlone talk to his father. "I am more than ready. My sword thirsts for his blood," she snapped.

I do not mean swordplay.

Gabria was jolted. "What do you mean?"

But the mare said nothing more, for Savaric was gesturing at them to lead the group. Gabria did not pursue the answer. Her mind was already set on her course of action and she did not want Nara dissuading her for any reason.

The Hunnuli tilted her nose down, arching her neck into curved ebony. She snorted.

"Are you ready, Gabran? It is time," Savaric said.

In answer for her rider, Nara threw her head high and neighed a challenge that reverberated through the camps. Boreas answered her from a distant meadow, and other horses neighed in return until the meadow echoed. The mare pranced forward, and the men fell in behind her. Gabria straightened her back. The girl flipped the edges of her cloak back until it lay neatly over the Hunnuli's haunches and flowed in a crimson tide to her boots. Behind her, the men walked, silently admiring the horse and her rider. Clan Khulinin gathered to watch them leave.

Gabria knew the effect the red cloak would have on people who did not know a Corin still existed, but she was not prepared for the impact her arrival made on the volatile atmosphere of the gathering. Nara's neigh had stirred the camps like a stick in a wasp nest. Hundreds of people were crowding the riverbank, staring toward the Khulinin tents. The chieftains, who were waiting for Savaric at the council tent, went outside as word of the Corin's coming spread through the gathering.

When the Hunnuli and her escort crossed the Isin, a babble of voices broke out. A wall of clansmen stood on the riverbank, blocking the way to the council tent. For a moment, Gabria wondered if they would let her pass. Confusion, fear, and amazement were on every face. The crowd shifted and grew. There were many people she recognized, but they seemed like strangers to her. Several people shouted at her; a few cursed her. Everyone now realized one Corin still remained, and they were bitterly reminded of their own negligence in honoring the memory of Clan Corin. Gabria ignored them all and raised her eyes to the banners flying above the council tent.

They reached the edge of the crowd. For the space of a breath, no one moved. Then Nara neighed again, imperiously. Immediately, the mob's attention focused on the mare, and a sigh drifted through the press. They moved aside, forming a

corridor. Nara pranced forward, just as a short gust of wind unfurled Gabria's scarlet cloak like a chieftain's banner. Every eye
followed the horse and her rider. Few noticed the Khulinin
chieftain behind the Hunnuli, or the Oathbreakers who
walked beside him. When Nara came to the council tent,
Gabria dismounted. The chieftains met her at the entrance.
Only Medb remained inside.

"My lords." She bowed to the other nine chiefs as Savaric
joined her. "You may not remember me: I am Gabran of the
Clan Corin. I would like permission to attend the council."

The nine looked at one another uneasily. Koshyn caught
Savaric's eye and smiled with a twist of irony.

Malech, the Shadedron chief, said dubiously, "No uninitiated warrior is permitted to enter without his chieftain."

"I am the son of Dathlar and the only Corin, so by rights of
survival, I *am* chieftain," Gabria said coolly.

Athlone choked at her audacity and looked away. The lords
talked among themselves for a moment, and Savaric held back
to allow the chiefs to make their own choice. Around the tent,
men from every clan watched and waited and held their own
council.

Finally, Malech nodded and gestured to the tent. "You may
join us, Gabran."

Before anyone moved, Savaric stepped forward. "Lords, I
have given permission for a high priest and three members of
the Cult of the Lash to attend the council as my guests. They
have several important matters to discuss with us."

The chieftains suddenly noticed the four strangers with the
Khulinin. Noise broke out anew as the men presented themselves. Several chiefs blanched and every clansman seemed to
move back, away from the hated black whips.

"Treacherous filth," Caurus, the red-haired chieftain of the
Reidhar, snapped. "Leave this gathering at once."

The others murmured in agreement. The members of the
cult had forsaken their vows of fealty to the clans and the
chiefs, rightly earning the title "Oathbreakers." They were not
specifically banned from the gathering, but they were certainly
not welcome.

A dark cloak of fear hung on the Oathbreakers' shoulders, a fear born of whispered rumors and stories of heinous deeds. Few men knew the secrets of Krath's followers because few survived who broached the confines of the Citadel of Krath. Only the Oathbreakers' reputation as highly trained killers and their aversion to metal were known to all. Because they used no metal, their only weapons were their bodies, their whips, and their finely crafted killing instruments of leather or stone. It was said an Oathbreaker could snap a man's neck with bare hands or remove a head with a flick of a vicious black whip. Their religious goal was to perform the perfect kill in the service of their demanding mistress.

But it was not the cult's bloodlust the clansmen despised, it was the subterfuge its members practiced. The stealth in the dark night, the garrot in the throat, the subtle poisons, and the furtive killings were incomprehensible to a clansman. No one knew when an Oathbreaker would strike. There was never any warning.

And now they wanted to join the council.

Lord Branth pushed his way forward and stared down at Seth. "How dare you return here."

Seth's cold eyes shriveled Branth's brashness to dust. "Medb dared us," he said in a voice sharpened with malice.

Branth fell back a step, and the other chiefs looked upset. Medb's involvement with the Cult of the Lash was something they had not considered. The tension built like a storm.

"You have my word that my brother and his men will not disrupt the council. They are here under my protection," Savaric said soothingly.

Malech's mouth tightened. "They must leave their weapons outside and may only speak on the matter that brought them here."

Seth agreed, and the four men piled their whips by the entrance, knowing no man would dare touch them. The chiefs and their men filed into the council tent.

Nara nudged Gabria. *Remember.*

The girl nodded and moved numbly after Savaric. Inside, Medb was waiting for her. Her determination burned whiter;

her fingers itched for the feel of a sword. She tried not to crowd Savaric through the entrance, but craned over his shoulder for her first glimpse of the Wylfling lord. Gabria had never seen him before, and her imagination had created many faces and forms for the man she knew only by reputation.

As the men sorted themselves and found their places, Gabria stared wildly about, trying to spot the murderer. He had to be there! Yet there was no one that fit her perception of an evil sorcerer. The only Wylfling she saw were sitting together near the head of the tent, and one she noticed with surprise, was seated on a litter with a brown blanket wrapped around his legs. She sat down by Athlone, her heart hammering. Maybe Medb was waiting to make an appearance. She clenched her hands and tried to still her trembling.

Lord Malech stood, his broad face sweating profusely, and held up his hand to quiet the talking. "Lord Medb, we have several strangers who have requested to join the council."

Gabria froze. Her eyes raked the assembled Wylfling to find the chief who responded. On the litter, the man with the brown blanket idly waved away a fly and inclined his head.

"So I heard." He turned to Gabria. "On behalf of the council, may I express our delight and relief in the survival of a son of Dathlar. Your father's death was a blow to us all."

Gabria's mouth dropped open. She stared and stared until her head swam and the fury began to boil in her stomach. She had been cheated! The days of humiliation and grief and sweat had gone for nothing! She wanted to shriek at the injustice of it. The last, bitter, blood-soaked laugh had gone to Medb, for now her clan's honor would have to be sacrificed to a cripple. She started to stand, not knowing what she would do, but Athlone slammed her down and gripped her arm like a vise.

"Don't move," he hissed. "Don't say a word."

Gabria could not have spoken if she wanted to. Her breath seemed to be strangling her.

The chieftains looked at her curiously, expecting a response. When she said nothing, Malech cleared his throat nervously and said, "The Corin massacre is a subject we have been avoiding . . . to our shame. Now we discover a Corin has survived.

We cannot sidestep this hideous crime any longer. Boy, will you tell us what happened at your treld?'' Malech averted his eyes from Medb and waved at Gabria to stand.

Athlone released the girl's arm with a warning squeeze, and she slowly climbed to her feet. Over the heads of the men, she could see Medb clearly, and her hatred fumed. No one had told her the truth. They had let her run wildly into a trap where the only escape was to retreat. She could not duel with a crippled man in any way; there was no other avenue of revenge that would satisfy her weir-geld. She could hire the Oathbreakers to assassinate him, if they would, or she could attack him herself one dark night, but both thoughts were repugnant and would not honorably settle the debt of vengeance.

Gabria could think of nothing else to do. Perhaps, if she convinced the council that Medb was responsible for the heinous crime, they would discipline him. Unfortunately, she doubted the chieftains would do much. It was obvious, even in the first few minutes she had been with them, that the chiefs were afraid.

The realization startled her. As Gabria looked about her and saw the men's grim mouths and tense postures, a small feeling of pride began to grow in her mind. These men who boasted so loudly around the fires at night quailed before a single chief, a man of their own standing, while she, a woman, was a rider of a great Hunnuli and had survived the worst doom a clansman could inflict on another. If she could survive that, she could endure this hideous disappointment.

Keeping her voice low and level, Gabria told the council everything she had told the Khulinin, as well as her vision of the massacre. She disregarded the growing agitation of the men and kept her eyes pinned on Lord Medb as she talked. Her gaze did not waver when she detailed her evidence of his guilt. The Wylfling chief sat motionless through the telling, returning her silent challenge with his gray eyes narrowed like a wolf's. Still, Gabria could see the angry glints in the gray of Medb's eyes and a tic in the muscles of his rigid neck.

Despite his shattered legs, Medb was still a powerful, vibrant man. His energy pulsed in every muscle and made him look

younger than his forty winters. He was very different from anything Gabria had imagined and, in other circumstances, she
would have thought him handsome. His features were chiseled
on a broad face and were framed by a short beard and curly
brown hair. It was a face meant to be open and friendly, not
twisted into a mask that hid malice and unconscionable deceit.

When Gabria finished speaking, an uproar erupted from
the council. The men shouted and gestured angrily. Several
leaped to their feet. In the deafening outbursts, it was difficult
to understand their arguments. Lord Malech tried to quiet
them, but his efforts were wasted in the chaos.

Savaric stood up. "Silence!" he bellowed, and the racket
died down. "The Corin have been dead for four months. Why
do you show your outrage only now?"

The men slowly quieted.

"Why do you just now bring forth this survivor?" Lord
Branth asked, adding a sneer of disbelief to his last word.

"To guard against his untimely demise. He is, after all, the
last of the Corin. Now that we all are witness to his existence, we
cannot ignore the reasons for the annihilation of his entire clan."

"The evidence I have heard condemns the greed and bloodlust in a few exiles who unlawfully banded together to harry
our clans," Branth retorted.

Shouts of agreement met Branth's statement, and Lord
Caurus of the Reidhar slammed a horn cup on the ground.
"Ten of my best mares were stolen by that pack of jackals and
thirty sheep were slaughtered and left to rot."

Lord Ferron of Clan Amnok said immediately, "This has
never happened in the memory of our clans. We must deal with
these marauders swiftly before they massacre another clan."

"The Corin were not massacred for simple greed," Savaric
said.

Branth snorted. "Then why? Because the exiles did not like
the color of their cloaks?"

"I should think that would be clear, especially to you,
Branth, whose holdings lie next to Dathlar's. And to all of you
who have listened to Medb's promises of wealth and power.
There is only so much power to go around."

Lord Jol, oldest of the chieftains, said fiercely, "I received no offer from Lord Medb. What is this?"

"Empire building, Jol," Koshyn said.

The chief barked a laugh. "Absurd. No one man can rule the clans; they are too far apart. Mine is almost in the northern forests."

Savaric turned to Medb. "But it is true, isn't it, Medb? Why didn't you negotiate with Jol's Murjik? Are they too distant to be of use . . . or were they next for the sword?"

Jol paled, and the warriors began arguing heatedly about the exiles, Savaric's accusations, Gabria's evidence, suspicions of others—everything but Lord Medb's complicity. Some wanted to believe Savaric was right. Despite Medb's offers, most of the chieftains were appalled by the idea of the clans in the chains of an overlord. They knew in their hearts why Clan Corin had died, but they did not know what to do about it. One of their own had never turned on them in this manner.

Even if Medb did confess to ordering the exile band to massacre the clan, the chieftains were fearful of punishing him. His strength had grown beyond any imagining and, with his mercenaries, he outnumbered every individual clan. The chiefs were also afraid of knowing the truth about his sorcery. If Medb truly had reconstructed the ancient spells, the clans were doomed. There was no one left who could fight him.

But Savaric would not let the chieftains evade the truth forever. He strode to the center of the tent and glared at Medb. "My blood brother died at Lord Medb's order. I cannot challenge him to a duel, but I demand the council take action to punish this most hideous crime."

For the first time since his greeting to Gabria, Medb spoke. "Fools," he hissed quietly. He held out his hand, palm up, and began to speak. His voice was gently compelling, as if he were speaking to a group of rebellious children.

Gabria looked at Medb in surprise as the noise ended abruptly and every man turned to listen. Their faces were blank and their eyes seemed to yearn toward him. The girl looked at Athlone and he, too, was staring at Medb with rapt attention. Even Medb's own men were craning over his shoulder to hear what he would say next.

"Are you weak-kneed girls who must hang on every word mumbled by a simple boy? For reasons I cannot fathom, I am being unjustly charged with a crime that is most foul. I had no cause to slaughter the Corin. They were fellow clansmen, horsemen like myself. Would I cut off my own fingers?" He sounded aggrieved. "And to what purpose? Their lands lie far beyond the farthest hoofprints of my outriders. It is absurd." He settled back on his litter and curled his lip in a smile. "Yet I can understand how you could be deceived by this boy's fable. You are blinded by the red cloak and an earnest air. The boy was coached well by Savaric, was he not?"

The men murmured to themselves, their eyes still pinned on Medb. His words made sense to them. Gabria's and Savaric's arguments began to melt away like ice in the warmth of the sun. Medb's voice was so pleasant, so logical. He could not have harmed the Corin; it had to have been the exiles acting on their own. Athlone, too, looked puzzled and wondered if maybe his father were wrong.

Gabria felt confused. She knew that Medb was lying, but his words were sensible and his tone was so sincere that she wanted to believe him. Something strange was happening in her mind, and she struggled to find the cause.

"I cannot help but wonder why Lord Savaric is trying to lay the blame at my feet. I have done nothing to him." Medb paused as if in thought, letting the warriors feel his wounded innocence. "And yet if I were to be deposed by this illustrious council, who would care for the interest of my clan? I have no son. Would my considerate neighbor thus feel charitable and watch the Wylfling's holdings while a new chief is chosen?"

Savaric struggled to utter a word, but his voice seemed to be lost. Furiously he stepped toward the Wylfling. Medb lifted his hand and the Khulinin stopped abruptly, as if walking into a wall.

Medb came to his point with slow relish. "I am not the only one who is threatened by Lord Savaric's greed. Even the Turic may fall to his guile. Already he is making plans to overthrow the tribes and steal the southern foothills of the Darkhorns, lands that border mine!''

Suddenly, Gabria laughed. This man, perched on his litter, bloated with his own monstrous arrogance, was daring to sully another man with accusations of deceit and greed? And these warriors, taken in by Medb's spells, were sitting like enchanted frogs, taking in every word. It was more than Gabria's battered self-control could tolerate. The effects of Medb's spell evaporated in Gabria's mind, and she stared around her and laughed again.

The sound of her mockery was bare of humor and sharp with frustration, and it sliced through the clansmen's stupor like a scythe. They started in surprise and looked at each other guiltily. Savaric's body jerked as the spell broke and he nearly fell. Seth reached out and caught him by the arm.

Medb's face tightened unpleasantly. He shot a considering look at Gabria. He gestured to two of his guards, whispered an order, and turned back to the chiefs to continue the thread of thought he had spun in their minds. This time, he set aside his spells and fanned the flames that he hoped would bring the council to his feet. His two guards slipped out of the tent.

"Corin," Medb addressed Gabria. "There were valid reasons for forbidding uninitiated boys into the council; your outburst is one of them. Please contain yourself."

"So, you do recognize my blood," she replied, holding her cloak up in her fist. "And I shall soon know yours." With the sorcerer beyond her reach, her obsession for revenge burned in her head. It warped her common sense into a blind carelessness.

Malech glanced apologetically at Savaric, missing the imperceptible movement of Medb's hands. But Seth noticed it, and he recognized the forming of an arcane spell. He quickly leaned over to Gabria.

"Take this," he whispered and thrust a small ball into her hand. "Keep it with you."

Gabria opened her hand and found a white stone ball, intricately carved. Within its hollow core were three other balls of graduating sizes, one inside the other. It took a moment before she recognized the object and then she nearly dropped it. The Oathbreaker had given her an arcane ward. But when she raised her eyes, she too saw the strange movement of Medb's hand.

The air hummed briefly in the tent; one warrior slapped at an imagined fly, and Gabria felt a slight pressure in her head. Then it passed and she sighed in relief. She should have known better than to tamper with the anger of a sorcerer. Her carelessness had almost cost her. Gabria hid the arcane ward in her tunic and threw Medb a look of pure hatred.

Medb caught her look and pursed his lips in annoyance. He had seen Seth pass something to the boy, and now he knew what it was. He was not surprised the Oathbreakers still had a few of the relics left by the old sorcerers, but he was irritated to see that the priest had given one to an outsider—and that the ward operated so well for the boy. There was something very curious here. The fact that the boy was alive was strange. The exiles had sworn they had killed Dathlar and all of his sons. Obviously they had been careless.

Malech interrupted his musings. "Savaric, keep the boy quiet or he'll have to leave."

The men were still considering Medb's words, and Koshyn asked angrily, "Do you have proof of your ridiculous accusations against Savaric?"

Savaric crossed his arms. "Your arrogance astounds me, Medb."

"Only when the cloak fits," Medb replied. "Perhaps this will convince you."

Suddenly there was a commotion outside the tent and Medb's two guards came in, dragging a young warrior dressed in a tattered, filthy robe that had once been Turic. Athlone uttered an exclamation and jumped to his father's side as the warrior was dumped unceremoniously at Malech's feet. The other men strained to see who the man was. Only Medb watched Savaric to witness his reaction. The young man moved feebly on the carpets, his body twitching as if he were trying to avoid imaginary blows, his hands clenching spasmodically. Moaning, he rolled over and stared wildly at the roof of the tent.

"Pazric," Savaric whispered sadly.

The warrior's face was caked with dried blood and was bruised and haggard; his skin seemed shriveled around his bones. Athlone knelt by his side and tried to lift him to a sitting position. Pazric flinched in terror from the wer-tain's touch and tried to scramble away, but his battered body failed him and he curled up, gibbering, by the fire pit.

Athlone stood up. "What have you done to him?"

"I?" Medb looked insulted. "My men found him like this, crawling in the desert and near death. The Turic left him to die."

"And this is your proof?" Lord Ferron said. The Amnok's face was as gray as his cloak. "This wreck you salvaged from the wasteland? Haven't you a healer in the Wylfling?"

Medb shrugged off the last question. "Don't you recognize him? This is the inestimable Pazric, second wer-tain of the Khulinin. Look at his neck. That is what they do to treacherous filth who are not worth the clean cut of a sword."

Pazric raised his head for a moment and every man looked. A bloodied discoloration encircled his neck like a collar. Purplish flesh puffed out around the edges of the marking and oozing gouges covered his throat like claw marks.

"A leather strap soaked in water," Medb said conversationally. "As the sun dries it, it slowly strangles its victims."

"This proves nothing," said Lord Koshyn.

Medb clapped his hands. "Dog! What was your mission with the Turic?"

Pazric cringed. His eyes bugged and rolled with terror. He forced his voice out of his ravaged throat. "To offer them a treaty."

"What treaty?" Medb demanded.

The other warriors moved nervously, helplessly, and watched Medb, Savaric, and Pazric. The four Oathbreakers glanced at each other knowingly.

"To trade land," Pazric croaked. He hid his head under his arms and cried with the effort of answering.

"What land?" Medb pushed relentlessly.

"Their holy land . . . southern foothills . . . for the Altai Basin."

"That's impossible." Lord Quamar shouted. His clan knew the Turic well, for the Ferganan's treld was in the south by the Altai River. "They would never accept a treaty like that."

"The Altai Basin is Wylfling land," Medb reminded them, knowing they were well aware of it. "Yet Savaric feels it is, or will be, open land for his unencumbered use."

Savaric disregarded Medb's insulting accusations and the growing dissension around him. Instead, he studied Pazric's huddled body. The wer-tain would sooner die than intentionally lie about his honor, his lord, or his mission. It was true that he had been sent to deal with the Turic tribesmen, but only to arrange a mutually acceptable meeting place for livestock exchange, and Savaric doubted that the tribesmen had perpetrated any of the brutal injuries on Pazric. They had dealt with him before and respected his integrity. But Medb, also aware of Pazric's honesty, must have captured him on his way home and warped his mind into a cringing mass of lies to sway the council. Looking at Pazric's face, Savaric debated how much of the second wer-tain's mind had been destroyed. The warrior's sunken eyes seemed turned to an inner agony that was controlling his every word, an agony that almost certainly came from Medb.

Savaric swallowed. No man doubted the chieftain's courage in battle, but sorcery was a fearsome mystery he had never faced. He shuddered at the recklessness of his idea to goad Medb, and he hated to use Pazric in his ruse, for there was an excellent chance that forcing Medb to expose his powers would result in someone's death. Unfortunately, it was the only chance he saw to terrify the chiefs into uniting against Medb.

"Lord Savaric, did you send this man to the Turic with a treaty offer?" Lord Malech asked unhappily. He was rapidly losing control of the council and he knew it.

Giving his son a warning look, Savaric answered. "Certainly. It is no secret we deal with the Turic."

"For livestock, but what about land?" Ferron asked.

Savaric shook his head. "The southern hills are not fit for a lizard, let alone a horse."

"Yet they have the Altai River and the sparse grass is excellent pasturage for goats like yours," Branth pointed out. "You have not answered the charge. Did you offer to exchange the Altai Basin for the Turic's land?"

"What does it matter if I had?" Savaric said with heavy scorn. He strode to Medb, ignoring the Wylfling guards, and pointed dramatically at the seated man. "Look at him. He is a useless hulk. If he lives to the next wintering, it will be an act of the gods. He cannot move without a litter or survive without aid. He is only a burden to his clan. And he is a chieftain! He must see to the welfare of the herds, the training of the werod, and the survival of his clan. No able-bodied warrior in his clan will tolerate his weakness for long, and before many days, there will be strife in his ranks. If he were truly concerned for the interests of his clan, he would step down and have a new chieftain chosen by the council."

Several men loudly agreed, and Branth blew his nose with scornful rudeness. Patches of color flamed on Medb's pale cheeks and his hands twitched on his lap.

Savaric pushed harder. Medb had been injured within the year, and Savaric sensed the mental wounds had not yet healed. Fighting down his anxiety, he rubbed the salt deeper. "Step down, Medb," he sneered. "You're a legless parasite on your clan. Not even the exiles want you."

Athlone, watching Pazric, abruptly stepped back in alarm. The younger warrior's eyes were filling with hate and his face contorted into bestial rage. He snarled, the sound bubbling and ragged. Savaric heard the warning and knew his ploy was working. Medb's mental control on the man was slipping.

"Admit it, Medb. Give up your clan. They don't want you. You're not fit to rule a feeble clan like the Wylflings, let alone an empire."

Savaric's last word ignited the explosive atmosphere. The clansmen burst out into a tumult of violent shouting, abusive curses, and vehement repudiation.

Medb sat upright in his litter, his dark eyes boring into the Khulinin chieftain. Despite his crippled legs, he seemed to dominate the huge tent as he swept his arms in a command to his guards. Gabria and the Oathbreakers jumped to their feet to defend Savaric, and Athlone, reaching for his sword, leaped in front of his father.

Medb laughed in scorn. "You poor whining fools. You snap

at my heels and never see the truth. I am tired . . ."

Medb got no farther. A maniacal scream rose above the
noise. Pazric stumbled upright. His swollen lips were pulled
back over his teeth; his robe swayed madly around his bruised
limbs. With unbelievable speed, he clambered over the fire pit
and sprang for Medb.

Athlone grabbed for him. "Pazric, no!" But Pazric's tattered robe fell apart in the wer-tain's hands. The young warrior
broke free and snatched at Medb's throat.

Without warning, a brilliant blue light flared in the tent; it
smashed into Pazric and slammed him to the floor. Gabria
cried with dreadful recognition, for Medb had used the Trymian Force. Everything else came to a horrified stop.

Medb slowly leaned forward and spoke a strange command.
A pale, coppery force field began to form around him.

"Now you all know your fate," he said. "The clans will be
mine or I will unleash the power of the arcane and destroy
every man, woman, and child that bears the name of a clan."

"Gods," Koshyn whispered.

"How?" Malech asked, his voice shaking.

Seth answered, speaking for the first time. It was too late to
warn them now. It had been too late the moment they walked
into the council tent. "He has the *Book of Matrah*."

Medb turned his dark gaze on the Oathbreakers. "And despite your inconvenient refusal to translate the sections I requested, I have mastered more sorcery than your feeble minds
can comprehend. And beware, whip lovers, soon I will have all
your books in my possession and your citadel will be rubble."

The translucent dome around the sorcerer was almost finished, and Medb pointed to Pazric's body. "Take your dog,
Savaric. He served us both well. Then count your days. By the
next gathering, I will be ruler of the clans. This council is over."
Medb gestured to his guards and four of them picked up the
litter. The dome hovered around his body.

Imperiously, Medb ran his gaze over each man, as if pro-
nouncing his fate with a single look. He gave a negligible nod
to Branth. To Athlone and the Oathbreakers, he showed only
contempt. At Medb's order the bearers carried him toward the

entrance. When he passed Gabria, he snarled, "You're the last of the Corin, boy. Do not hope to continue the line."

The Wylfling left the tent, and the council disintegrated. Lord Ferron left before anyone could stop him. Everyone else rushed to their feet.

"Is Medb serious?" Malech asked weakly.

Koshyn threw out his arms. "Gods, man. You saw him."

Seth said without emotion, "He has gained control of the arcane. What do you think a man like that will do with that kind of power?"

Athlone knelt by Pazric and gently pressed his fingers beneath the fallen man's jaw. "He's dead," he said dully.

Savaric shook his head. "He was already dead when Medb brought him in."

Gabria removed her cloak and laid it over Pazric's body. She was shaking badly, and the scarlet wool quivered in her hands when it settled over Pazric's battered face. The memory of the blue flame burned in her mind. Before, the Trymian Force had only been a word on Piers's lips and a nagging bad dream. Now she had seen it. It was a reality, a force that killed at a man's calling.

Gabria paused. A tiny thought nudged into her despair. It was a wild, frightening grain of an idea, yet it stirred her dead hopes. Perhaps revenge was not totally beyond her grasp.

"You were right, Gabran, weren't you?" Lord Jol said with bitterness. He appeared to have aged rapidly in that short afternoon. "Medb ordered the massacre of the Corin."

Gabria nodded. The clansmen were suddenly subdued, as if they did not want to share each other's despair.

"Yes, he did!" Savaric stated, turning to face them. "To make an example to all of us and to weaken our resolve. If he has succeeded in doing that, then the Corin died in dishonor."

"What do you expect us to do? Fight the monster?" Lord Caurus demanded, his face as red as his hair.

"Yes!" Sha Umar shouted. He was chief of Clan Jehanan and he intended it to remain that way. He stood by Savaric and shook his fist at the other chiefs. "Our survival depends on it. Medb has not gathered his full strength yet. Now is the time to attack—before he marshals his forces."

Branth laughed. "Attack? With what? Lord Medb would destroy you before the first bow was drawn. The only way the clans will survive is to swear fealty to him."

"I will never allow a broken-kneed, murdering *sorcerer* to rule my clan!" Caurus threw his wine cup into the fire pit.

"Then we must join together. We must unite our werods to fight him or we are lost." Savaric felt the chiefs' unspoken resistance, and he fought down a rising sense of despair.

Branth curled his thin lips in a sneer. "And who will command this united rabble? You, Savaric? And after you have disposed of Medb, will you pick up his sword and take his place?"

The Shadedron chief stepped forward. "And what about that band of exiles? We don't dare leave our clans undefended," Lord Malech said.

Caurus agreed. "We do not have a chance against Medb here. I say we'd be safer defending our own holdings."

"Better than putting ourselves between two greedy chieftains," Lord Babur of the Bahedin said with a glare at Savaric. Babur was ill and had said very little at the council meetings.

"I still think it is impossible for him to succeed," Jol said stubbornly. "The clans are too far apart."

"This is getting us nowhere. The council is over." Malech stalked out of the tent, trying not to hurry, followed by his wertain and advisors.

The remaining chiefs looked at each other unhappily. Branth strutted to the entrance. "If any of you wish to talk to me, I will be in my tent. Everyone knows where that is." He, too, left with his men.

Koshyn sighed and pulled his hood over his head. "There is little point staying here to argue with the wind, Savaric. The clans will never unite."

"But he wants us to bolt for our holes so he can take us one by one. We must try to work together," Savaric implored.

"Maybe. Maybe not. Good-bye, Corin. Take care of your Hunnuli." Koshyn and his warriors filed out.

Without another word to each other, the remaining men left the council, propelled by shame and shock. They had not yet recovered from witnessing the blatant and heretical use of sor-

cery in the sanctuary of the council tent. After two hundred
years of ingrained prejudice and hatred, they had seen the object of their scorn resurrected before their eyes. For the first
time, they were witnessing the bitter folly of their ancestors.
The men were also recoiling from the truth of the Corin massacre and Medb's shocking declaration of his intention to rule the
clans as overlord. The frightening possibilities of the arcane
and the logic of Savaric's arguments were lost in the morass of
the chieftains' fears for their clans.

In moments the tent was empty, save for the Oathbreakers
and the Khulinin. Savaric stared at the entrance as though trying to draw the others back. His eyes were bleak and his lean
body sagged with dismay. Gabria and Athlone carefully lifted
Pazric's body and carried it outside, where Nara consented to
bear it back to the encampment. Savaric and the four cultists
followed behind and stepped out into the hot afternoon sun.

Seth picked up his whip, coiling it carefully in his hands. "Our
journey was for nought. It was too late to warn the council."

"I thank you for trying," Savaric replied. "Will your citadel
be able to withstand Medb's attack?"

"For a while. Some of the old wards still operate, but our
numbers are dwindling. In the end, it will be the same for us as
for you, and Medb will have free rein in the archives."

"You could burn the books."

Seth shook his head. "It is difficult to destroy a sorcerer's
tome, and we would not do it. Someone else may have need of
them one day."

"Then defend them well." Savaric watched the people moving through the camps. Some word of the events of that afternoon had already spread, for no women were in sight and the
men moved with nervous haste.

Seth spoke to his companions briefly and turned to his
brother. "Take care of the Corin. And yourself."

The brothers clasped hands, then the Oathbreakers gathered their whips and disappeared among the tents.

The Khulinin and the Hunnuli silently bore Pazric back to
camp.

12

ime confirmed Savaric's worst fears, for the gathering did not survive the night. He argued desperately with every chief except Branth that evening, trying to weld them together against Lord Medb. Unfortunately, the traditions of generations and the stubborn individuality of every clansman were too ingrained. Most of the chieftains turned deaf ears to Savaric's pleas. The lords vacillated through the night while their clans seethed with emotions. The truth of the Corin massacre and Medb's sorcery was told and retold, and the stories grew with every telling until fact and rumor were tangled in knots. Fear ran rampant through the camps. By dawn, Lord Jol pulled the purple banner from the council tent and moved Clan Murjik north toward home.

Lord Medb watched them go with pleasure. He was angry at himself for losing his temper and revealing his power so early. He had planned to rope the council into his control first, then wait to unmask his sorcery when the manuscripts from the Citadel of Krath were in his hands. Not that it really mattered. There was no man who could dispute his rise to overlord now, and if the clans chose to return to their own holdings rather than fight together, then so be it. It would take longer to crush them, but in the long run it would mean a more final collapse. Each clan would be brought to its knees in its own treld and each chief would have to capitulate alone.

Of the twelve clans, only seven presented problems for Medb. The sorcerer counted the clans mentally: he had regained control of the Wylfling after his accident six months ago with the combined weapons of sorcery and fear; the Corin were

exterminated; the Geldring were his thanks to the treachery of
Branth; Quamar had given him the Ferganan that afternoon;
and Ferron would soon come crawling with the Amnok. That
left only the Shadedron, Murjik, Reidhar, Dangari, Jehanan,
Bahedin, and, of course, the Khulinin. If all went smoothly,
the Oathbreakers would soon be eliminated and, by spring,
the council of chiefs would cease to exist.

Of course, several of the chieftains were exceedingly stubborn. Lord Caurus of the Reidhar was a temperamental hot-
head, as well as a ferocious fighter and a man intensely devoted
to his clan. And while Koshyn of the Dangari was young, he
could not be treated lightly. No, what was needed was a demonstration that would break their spirits and bring the chiefs to
heel, a demonstration that would also salve Medb's pride and
give him intense satisfaction: the destruction of the Khulinin.
With Savaric dead and the powerful Khulinin weeded down to
more manageable numbers, the other chiefs would soon realize their deadly mistake.

Defeating the Khulinin would also enable Medb to finish
the destruction of the Corin. That boy, Gabran, was a nuisance
and a loose end. Medb did not like loose ends. He planned to
have a word about that with the exile leader as soon as they arrived. Such carelessness was unforgivable.

*   *   *   *   *

The next morning, the merchants read the signs of war in
the clansmen's faces, packed their goods, and quickly left.
That afternoon, the Shadedron gathered their herds to depart.

Lord Malech's shoulders slumped as he brought down his
black banner, and he glanced apologetically at Savaric. Without a word or gesture of farewell, he mounted his horse and led
the Shadedron south. Lord Ferron only waited until dark before slipping fearfully into the Wylfling encampment and
kneeling before Medb, giving the oath of fealty for the Amnok
clan.

By dawn of the second day after the splintering of the council, the remaining clans had separated into armed camps, bris-

tling with suspicion and anger. The Khulinin remained isolated on the far bank of the Isin. Only Athlone and Savaric crossed the river to talk with the other clansmen. They tried desperately to convince Caurus, Sha Umar, Babur, and Koshyn to ally with them, for with the addition of clan Amnok, Medb's forces were overwhelming. Already there were rumors that Medb was bringing more men to his camp, including the band of exiles.

But Caurus was secretly jealous of Savaric's wealth and authority. He did not trust the Khulinin to lead the combined forces, nor did he want the responsibility himself. Medb's magic terrified Caurus more than he cared to admit. Eventually he, too, gathered his caravan, and the Reidhar clan sought the familiarity of their own holdings near the inland Sea of Tannis.

Koshyn refused to commit himself one way or the other. He had only recently become chief, and he could not decide what was best for his clan. He listened and watched and waited for the final lines to be drawn.

Lord Babur, too, vacillated between Savaric's pleas and Medb's threats. His illness had grown worse, and he knew he didn't have the strength to fight a long war. But that night he died, some said by his own hand. His young son, Ryne, immediately threw Medb's emissary out of his tent and went to join the Khulinin. Sha Umar, a long-time friend of the Bahedin chieftains, came with Ryne and pledged the aid of the Jehanan to Savaric.

Even with the promised help of two clans, the days were long and bitter for Savaric and Athlone, and the stress began to tell on the whole clan. Pazric was sent to the Hall of the Dead on a funeral pyre, which Savaric lit at night to ensure the entire gathering would witness it. After a violent argument with Athlone about his negligence in telling her about Lord Medb's crippled legs, Gabria spent most of her time sitting on the banks of the Isin River.

Cor, on the other hand, thrived on the tense atmosphere of the camp, and his verbal attacks on Gabria grew vicious and more cunning. Only Nara kept him at bay, and Gabria wondered how long it would be before he gathered enough courage to change his weapon from his tongue to a sword. It would not be difficult to kill her in the night and blame it on an agent of Medb. She kept her dagger close to her side and stayed within Piers's tent after dark.

During the day, Gabria had little to do, and time dragged interminably. She lay for hours on the grassy bank of the river in the hot sun and tried to order her thoughts. The shock and disappointment of losing her chance to duel Medb had not diminished, and Gabria found herself examining more and more the possibilities of sorcery. Half a year ago, she would have been aghast at the mere suggestion of the arcane, but in that short time she had lost her clan and been exposed to more sorcery than she ever dreamed possible. It had gone a long way to changing her views of magic—as evidenced by her willingness to even consider it.

Still, whether or not she had a real talent for sorcery was inconclusive in her mind. Piers had his theories and Gabria had been lucky in guessing the truth of the brooch, but nothing had given her absolute proof. And if she did have a talent, what could she do about it? There was no one to teach her and she did not have the knowledge to use the *Book of Matrah* or the manuscripts in the archives of Krath's citadel. She might have an inherent ability, but if it could not be honed it was useless. Piers could not help her—he knew too little—and Nara was untrained in the rules of sorcery and could only protect her from others. The problem was like a sword in the hands of a woman. Gabria laughed at that analogy: she could handle a sword quite well.

Gabria was still debating the dilemma when she and Nara walked back to the camp for the evening meal. Cor had disappeared, and Gabria was happy for the reprieve as she trudged toward the tents. The camp was unnaturally quiet that evening, and people seemed to move with one eye over their shoulders. Smoke from the cooking fires rose sluggishly and hung overhead in the breathless air. Dogs lay in the tents' shadows and panted.

To the east, in the distance, two massive thunderheads piled

against the hills and rose like twin battlements before a wall of
steel-gray cloud. The setting sun etched the snowy heads of the
thunderclouds with gold crowns and mantles of rose, pearl,
and lavender. Deep in the clouds' cores, lightning flickered
endlessly, warning of the violence of the coming storm.

Extra outriders were posted that evening, and the herds were
moved closer to the shelter of the valley ridges. Other men
tightened tent ropes and checked the stakes. After the evening
meal, the fires were put out. As the dusk deepened, the storm
front moved closer and the lightning became visible in brilliant flashes or wicked streaks that cracked like an
Oathbreaker's whip.

Gabria sat restlessly on the ground before Piers's tent and
watched the approaching storm. Piers was in another part of
camp, helping a woman in labor; Savaric was with Koshyn;
and Athlone rode with the outriders. Gabria wished that she
were out there with the men rather than sitting in camp. Anything would be better than her edgy, frustrating loneliness.
The wind sprang fitfully and tugged at her hair. Abruptly, the
breeze died.

Before long, the thunder became audible. By the time night
was full, the explosions were incessant. Lightning flared endlessly through the massive sky, pursued by the incessant rum-
ble. Just then, lightning struck an ancient cottonwood tree by
the river, splitting it to the ground. Thunder shattered the
night, and the first drops of rain spattered in the dust. Gabria
fled for the tent.

She sat in the darkness and listened to the tent heave in the
wind, struggling against its ropes, and to the sounds of the
storm just beyond the thick material. Usually she loved storms
and reveled in the wildness of their passing. Tonight, though,
she huddled on a stool, feeling a strange sense of dread.

The fury of the storm made her nervous. She jumped at
every clap of thunder and stared wildly around when lightning
illuminated the tent's interior. Finally, she crawled onto her
pallet, pulled a blanket up to her chin, and lay shivering as she
tried to sleep.

Some time later, Gabria woke with a start of terror. Lying

motionless and trying to control her gasping breath, she strained every sense to catch what had frightened her: a faint sound or movement or smell that was out of place. She realized that she had been asleep for a while, because the storm had settled down to a steady rainfall and the thunder was more subdued.

Then, in the corner of her vision she saw the half-drawn curtain move, as if nudged from behind. She gently eased her hand toward her dagger, her heart hammering madly in her throat. But before her fingers found the blade, a dark shape sprang from behind the curtain, just as lightning flashed outside. In the instant illumination, Gabria saw a man lunge at her and she caught the flash of steel in his upraised hand. Her immediate thought was of Medb. He was trying to fulfill his promise with an assassin.

"No!" she screamed in fury and tried to roll off the pallet, but she was hindered by her blanket. The knife missed its mark and slashed down her right side, skittering off her ribs. The man grunted in anger and furiously pulled his weapon back for another blow. Gabria felt the wound like a firebrand as she struggled with the blanket and her tangled clothes, and her rage increased with the pain. Medb would not dispose of her this easily. She yanked off the blanket, threw it at the dark figure, and scrabbled for her dagger. The man cursed as the blanket tangled his aim, then he threw it aside.

"I'll get you, you little coward," he snarled and grabbed her shoulder.

Cor. It was Cor, not an agent of Medb. Gabria was so surprised, she missed her dagger and knocked it aside. The warrior dropped his weapon and yanked her around to face him. She fell with her dagger underneath her back. Gabria stopped struggling and stared at Cor's blurred face in the darkness. The whites of his eyes glimmered and his teeth showed in a grimace of hate.

He shook her. "I knew you were a coward deep down; you won't even fight to save your worthless skin. Well, I've waited a long time to do this. You thought you were so smart, turning me into half a man, useless for everything!" He leaned over her, his breath reeking of strong wine.

Gabria squirmed, trying to keep her dagger hidden behind her back. The guilt and pity she had felt for Cor died completely, and she stared back at him, matching his loathing. Cor pulled Gabria to her knees and forced her head back to expose her throat.

"I've been watching you and waiting. Now there's no one to save your neck." He pulled her head farther over his bent knee, until her spine creaked and her neck screamed in protest. "You see, with one quick snap, I could break your back and leave you dead, or better yet, just like that Wylfling."

Before Gabria could react, Cor jerked her up and punched her in the face. His fist exploded into her eye and she fell back on the pallet in a daze of pain and surprise. She closed her eyes and swallowed convulsively. Her dagger lay beneath her buttocks.

Cor slapped her. "Look at me, you pig-faced coward. I want to see you plead before I break you."

Gabria tossed her head up, her pain forgotten in a surge of rage and disgust at the madman who had beaten, ridiculed, insulted, and threatened her once too often. Her green eyes ignited and her hand curled over the dagger's hilt. "Go crawl in a hole, eunuch."

Cor snarled. His dark shape swayed, then savagely he grabbed Gabria's throat with both hands, his dagger forgotten in the urge to kill the Corin with his bare hands. His fingers dug into her windpipe and his nails tore her skin. Gabria felt her breath burning in her lungs as she tried to wriggle her dagger out from under their thrashing bodies.

Moaning incoherently, Cor squeezed harder and grinned maliciously. Gabria tore at his iron grip with one hand. But Cor didn't see her other hand. With desperation and fury, she lifted the blade and rammed it into his stomach. This time, there was no doubt of the presence or the origin of the blue flare.

In the darkness, Gabria saw the aura build in her arm and flow up the dagger into Cor's body. He jerked violently and clutched at the knife, his face a mask of hate and disbelief. His eyes rolled and he sagged on top of her. Gabria gasped and fainted.

* * * * *

The first thing Gabria became aware of was light. A small globe of yellow light intruded through her partly open lids into her darkness and drew her from unconsciousness. The second thing she noticed was pain. Then the pain rushed into her head and down her neck and side, until every bruised muscle and laceration throbbed madly. The heaviness she remembered across her chest was gone, and she heard someone moving around her. Gabria tensed, thinking it was Cor, but someone gently raised her head and a cup was pressed to her lips. She smelled the sweetness of Piers's own wine and relaxed. The wine warmed her bruised throat and settled gently in her stomach, where it spread with a healing heat through her body.

Gabria slowly opened her eyes—or eye since one was so swollen she could barely crack the lid. The orb of light wavered for a moment and settled into focus, revealing a small lamp hanging on its pole. She squinted at the light and looked higher into Piers's face. The healer appeared strangely upset, and Gabria smiled weakly at him. Outside, the wind had died and the rain was falling in a steady drizzle.

Piers let the girl finish her wine and then helped her lie down on the pallet before he spoke. "The evil fortune that fell to your clan does not seem to include you."

"Where is Cor?" she mumbled.

Piers glanced behind him. "He's dead." There was no condemnation in his voice, only sadness and regret that she had been forced to act.

The light and the effort of keeping her eye open was too much for Gabria, and her lids settled shut. She sighed deeply, wondering what Piers was thinking. After sharing his tent for so long, Gabria had come to like the healer and she hoped that the affection was mutual. Her hand groped for his. "I saw it, Piers. This time I saw it. As blue as Medb's bolt that killed Pazric."

Piers's hand caught hers and gripped it tightly. He looked down at the girl's battered face unhappily. She looked so young, too young to bear such burdens. The healer stood up and fetched his supplies from the wooden chest, poured more wine, and carried the things back to Gabria's pallet. Piers carefully moved her tunic and examined the long, ragged tear down her side.

Gabria held the wine cup and listened as he worked. She was puzzled that he said nothing. Maybe this time his disapproval outweighed his acceptance of her, and he had decided not to risk his life to protect her. Gabria would not blame Piers if he exposed her: sorcery was a serious crime to conceal.

Strangely, however, Gabria did not feel horrified any more by the reality of her ability. Now that it was confirmed by her own eyes, she faced it like some incurable disease that had to be accepted if her sanity were to be preserved. A small part of her quaked in terror at the truth of being a sorceress, but she imprisoned that part behind a wall of desire for self-preservation. Gabria found it difficult to believe that she could be so callous about such a heretical ability, but perhaps the months of secret fear and debate had strengthened her for the final acceptance.

"You're not saying much," Gabria finally said to Piers.

He was cleaning her wound and trying to work gently. "It is one thing to suspect sorcery; it is another for you to face it."

She sighed again and said, "I am not certain I want to. I seem to be like Medb. Does this mean I'll be twisted by the powers of magic into something cruel and depraved? Am I going to become an evil queen at Medb's side?"

"Magic is not an evil unto itself. It is only as good or as wicked as its wielder," Piers replied softly.

"That's not what my father's priest delighted in telling us. He used to recite countless incidents of the corruption of magic."

"Magic can be corrupting. It is a tempting power," Piers said, trying to be casual. "My daughter was tortured and killed for allegedly killing the fon of Pra Desh with sorcery."

Gabria gasped, "Why?"

Piers looked away into the distance. "My daughter married the fon's youngest son, against my wishes. The fon was the ruler of Pra Desh, but his family was a vicious, backstabbing pack of thieves. About a year after the marriage, the fon's wife poisoned him and needed a scapegoat when he died. Her youngest daughter-in-law was available, so the wife fabricated some evidence and accused my daughter of killing the fon with sorcery."

Piers explained his daughter's fate quietly, but Gabria could hear the undying rage still in his heart. "You said I reminded you of her. Was she a sorceress?"

"No." He spat the denial vehemently.

"But I am."

"So it would seem." Piers said nothing more and finished bandaging her side. She watched him worriedly.

Just then, Athlone burst into the tent, shaking off rain and splattering mud from his caked boots. "What's the problem, Piers?" he asked. He unwrapped his soaked cloak and did not seem to notice Cor's body lying to one side of the tent. Then he looked up. "Oh, gods. What happened now?"

Piers tossed a curved dagger to him. He caught it and turned it over in his hands. A wolf's head was carved on the butt of the handle.

"Cor was trying for a little revenge of his own," the healer said.

"Neat. Kill the last Corin and blame it on the Wylfling. Is she hurt?"

"Not seriously."

Gabria smiled painfully at the wer-tain. "They can't get rid of me that easily."

"What about Cor?" Athlone asked.

Piers nodded to the body on the floor and Athlone moved to examine it. He checked the wound, then rocked back on his heels and stared thoughtfully at the dead man. "Your dagger must carry quite a punch," he remarked.

Gabria tensed. She wondered if Athlone suspected anything. He could accept her wielding a sword and wearing a boy's disguise, but she knew he would never condone sorcery.

"I'm sure it did. So would yours if you were being strangled," Piers said.

"If I were being strangled," Athlone returned, "I would make damn sure of a killing stroke. This underhanded pin-prick wouldn't have killed a goat."

Piers looked irritated. "It punctured his stomach, Wer-tain. It is a slower way to kill, but it's just as effective as a slit throat."

Athlone met the healer's gaze skeptically and was about to reply when he saw Gabria wince and noticed for the first time the extent of her injuries. He changed his mind and nodded before standing up. It had not occurred to the wer-tain until that moment just how close Gabria had come to death. The realization shook him more than he believed possible. Athlone looked away. "I will tell Father what happened," he muttered and hurried out of the tent.

Piers began to wrap hot cloths soaked in salt water around Gabria's neck.

"My dagger did not pierce his stomach," Gabria whispered.

"Athlone would not be pleased to hear the truth."

"Neither would Savaric."

"Then we won't bother them with the truth." Piers tilted his head back and took a deep breath. "Sorcery is a thing little understood in this age, and, despite the clans' efforts to forget it, it will keep cropping up at the most inopportune times to wreak havoc. I believe the time has come to change that."

Gabria's green eyes opened wide. "Are you appointing me?"

"I am merely giving you a chance to do as you see fit." For the first time, Piers relaxed and looked at Gabria fondly. "I don't think you have the makings of an evil queen."

"Thank you," she said, grateful as much for his compliment as his protection.

"Thank my daughter. In a roundabout way, you are my revenge on the stupidity of her judges."

A short time later, Athlone returned with Savaric from the Dangari camp, where the chieftain had been arguing fruitlessly with Koshyn. Savaric's look was grim and his eyes, burning like dark coals, seemed to gaze elsewhere as his mind roved many paths. He glanced at Cor's body and Gabria's injuries and shook his head regretfully, his thoughts obviously already passing on to something else. He gestured to his son and left.

Athlone paused by the entrance and, for a moment, his eyes met Gabria's. To his relief, her gaze was as clear as spring water;

the awful brilliance he had seen in them the morning of the council was gone. But her face looked so sad. There was something in the unspoken pain in her eyes that pierced the wertain to the heart. Unhappily, he said good-night and closed the tent flap behind him.

*   *   *   *   *

After the storm, the morning came on fresh winds from the north. The sky was cloudless and clean, and the rivers flowed high between their banks. The ground was muddy after the rain. Before long, the hot sun dried the foliage and the tents, and the reddish soil returned to dust. The clanspeople recovered their herds from the shelter of the hills and set about repairing the damage caused by the storm.

Savaric made no attempt to return to the other camps. Instead, he stayed in the background and unobtrusively watched the happenings across the river. He judged the wind and eyed the far skyline and kept his own counsel. Cor was quickly buried beneath a cairn of rocks with none of the honor or grief that accompanied Pazric to his grave.

Savaric passed a quiet order that the Khulinin should pack to move under the guise of mending and cleaning. They did so, hiding most of their gear in the covered carts and keeping the pack animals close at hand. They would be ready to leave at a moment's notice.

Across the river, Sha Umar and the Bahedin's new chief, Lord Ryne, quietly prepared their clans to move. Koshyn still kept his clan isolated, while Branth readied his werod for war and Ferron quailed at the terms of his "alliance" with Medb.

Lord Medb, meanwhile, awaited his approaching reinforcements, kept track of the fleeing clans, and counted the days until Savaric's mangled corpse would lie at his feet. He learned of Cor's death from a spy in the Khulinin camp. No one seemed to know how the man died, but it was well known he had intended to kill the Corin. Medb considered this information carefully and filed it away. The boy was becoming more fascinating every day. Maybe he would wait a while before killing the brat. It might prove more interesting to study him.

Overall, Medb thought that events were proceeding well.
The only ugly incident that marred his pleasure was the betrayal of the bard, Cantrell. The old singer had lived with the
Wylfling for a year and brought status and honor to the clan
with his skills. Many chiefs had tried to lure Cantrell away, but
he seemed content to remain with the Wylfling.

Medb knew of Cantrell's ability to read men's fortunes; it
was a talent the bard little enjoyed and tried to avoid. But after
Lord Ferron had come to capitulate, Medb had felt invincible.
The night of the storm, he had called for Cantrell to foretell his
doom. The bard had reluctantly agreed, and for his pains had
been properly punished and cast out. It was regrettable, but no
man could threaten Medb with impunity. Not even a master
bard.

Later that day, just after noon, the Khulinin were still packing and cleaning their camp. Gabria had slept most of the
morning and, after a light meal, she went outside for a breath
of fresh air. Her side hurt abominably, despite Piers's medicines, and her throat and head felt worse. To avoid attention,
she wore her hat pulled low over her eyes and stayed in the
shadows of Piers's tent. She could see Nara standing in the
Isin's rapids, pawing playfully at the water. Boreas stood
nearby, watching her. For a moment, Gabria thought of calling
Nara, then changed her mind. The Hunnuli were enjoying
each other too much for Gabria to consider interrupting them.

Besides, Gabria didn't really want company. All morning
she had mulled over the tragedy of the night before. She could
hardly believe that she had killed a man with an arcane power
that she knew nothing about. It was a terrifying truth to face.
She could deal with her family's murders, her exile, and her
unlawful acceptance into Savaric's werod, because those things
were external. Sorcery was far different. It affected her being
and nothing short of death would ever change her or take away
this heretical talent. Dispiritedly, she pulled her hat lower over
her face and wondered what she should do. Medb was so far
beyond her reach.

Something caught Gabria's attention just as Nara neighed.

She looked toward the other camps and saw an old man working his way hesitantly through the ford in the river toward the Khulinin camp. He almost fell in the water. She walked curiously toward the river bank, thinking the man might be drunk. His head was down, almost as if he were having trouble seeing where he was going, and he leaned heavily on a staff.

Gabria stopped a few paces from the water and called, "Do you need help?"

Startled, the old man raised his head, and Gabria gasped in dismay. A bloody bandage was wrapped around the man's face, covering his eyes, and on either side of his nose, dried blood was caked in patches and matted in his beard. Horrified, Gabria clambered down the bank into the water and caught the old man's arm. He gratefully leaned on her and followed her guidance toward the tents. Several guards came running to help. They led the wounded man into Piers's tent, where he sank thankfully onto a stool.

"Get the healer quickly," Gabria whispered to one of the guards. He nodded, his mouth tight with anger. They all recognized the bard and were stricken by his hideous injury. The warrior dashed out and the other guard stepped outside to watch the tent's entrance.

"Thank you," the bard murmured. "I was beginning to think I would never cross the river."

Gabria looked at the bard unhappily. He was a distinguished man, and he wore a dark blue robe cut in an ornate pattern popular among the Wylfling. He wore no cloak and had no weapons. His hands were long and supple. He carried himself well despite the agony of his wound, but she saw that his skin was gray beneath the dried blood, and he gripped his knees with the effort of hiding his pain.

"Why did you come here?" she asked, kneeling by his feet.

"I was not welcome elsewhere." He pointed to his crude bandage. "I also hope to see your healer."

"Of course. He's on his way." Gabria leaped up to see if Piers was coming.

"Wait. Sit a minute. He will be here soon enough." The old man felt for Gabria's arm and pulled her gently to the ground by his side. "I am Cantrell."

"I know," she mumbled. Although Clan Corin had not been able to afford a bard, Gabria had heard this man many times at past gatherings and had loved his soaring tales and sweeping music. "You were with the Wylfling."

"Until recently. Medb took offense to one of my riddles," he replied calmly.

"Medb did this to you?"

He nodded. "And you are the Corin who tongues are wagging about?"

"Yes. How did you know?"

"By the inflection in your voice. The Corin always rolled their R's as if they appreciated the sound." He cocked his head in puzzlement. "But you are a woman. That is interesting."

Gabria bolted upright and stared at him. "How—?"

"Don't worry. I know you are trying to pass as a boy, but you cannot hide the telltale characteristics of your voice from a trained bard." He smiled wanly. "I'm sorry. I couldn't help showing off a little."

Gabria moved stiffly away from the old bard, her heart in her throat.

But Cantrell reached out for her. His hand found the girl's shoulder and groped down her arm to take her hand. His skin was cold and clammy, but his grip was strong. "Do not fear for your secret," he said gently. "I have heard a great deal about you at this gathering. I simply had no idea you were a woman. It makes your survival more intriguing. I—"

Without warning, the bard straightened. He gripped Gabria's hand tighter, and his ravaged face grew still. He sat for a long time, quietly rubbing her palm with his thumb, lost in deep concentration. Gabria watched him curiously; Cantrell sighed and his chin sank to his chest. She waited for him to speak. After a while he dropped her hand.

"I was right. You are intriguing. Seek the Woman of the Marsh, child. Only she will be able to help you."

"Who is she?"

But Cantrell shook his head slightly, and, at that moment, Piers and Savaric came into the tent. Puzzled, Gabria moved to the rear of the tent to keep out of the way while Piers unwound the blood-stained bandages. When the dirty material fell away, revealing the slashed, oozing remains of the bard's eyes, Gabria looked away. Savaric blanched at the sight and his face paled under his tan. With gentle hands, Piers tended to the hideous wound.

Cantrell sat like a statue during the operation, as if his face were carved of wood. Only when the healer finished wrapping new bandages around the bard's head did Cantrell allow his shoulders to sag and the breath to escape his lungs in a ragged sigh. The men remained quiet while Cantrell drank a cup of wine laced with a mild dose of poppy.

The bard was the first to speak. He felt for the table by his side and laid the cup down. "Thank you, Piers. You have well earned your reputation as the gentlest of the clan healers."

Piers glanced questioningly at Savaric, then replied, "You are welcome, Bard. You should have come to us sooner."

Cantrell leaned toward the chieftain. "There were many interesting things to hear in Medb's camp. Unfortunately, he wanted to listen to me as well, and he did not like what I told him."

"Which was what?" Savaric asked.

"A riddle."

"Oh?"

The bard tilted his head. "You keep your curiosity in check. That's good because I doubt you will understand the riddle any more than I did. My riddles, like most prophecies, are very confusing. If they were clear to us, they would negate the future they were created for. All I can do is give a man a riddle to accept as he wishes. Medb did not accept his."

Gabria turned her head and stared at the old man's face, engrossed in his words.

Cantrell said softly:

> "No man will kill thee,
> No war will destroy thee,
> No friend will betray thee,
> But beware thy life,
> When the buttercup bears a sword."

"And for that Medb blinded you," Piers said in disgust.

"He took offense at the implications."

Savaric smiled ruefully. "Is there a meaning in that riddle that holds anything for us?"

Piers said, "I don't like that part about no man will kill him."

"And no war will destroy him," Savaric added. He moved to the tent flap. "Medb has heard his doom and we are well aware of ours. Flower or no, we will have to fight."

Cantrell reached carefully for his staff. "Lord, it would be wise to move soon. Lord Medb is bringing in more mercenaries, and the exile band has been called. He plans to destroy the Khulinin first."

The chieftain and Piers exchanged glances, then Savaric said, "I was afraid of that." He called to the guard outside by the tent entrance. "Tell Athlone, Jorlan, and the elders that I want to see them in my tent. And send for Lord Ryne and Sha Umar. Now." The guard dashed away. "Cantrell, do you feel up to attending me a very short while longer?"

The bard nodded. "I am grateful for your hospitality."

"We are the ones who are grateful. Piers, we will be leaving tonight." With the bard leaning on his arm, Savaric walked out. The healer sat down and stared morosely at the pile of filthy bandages and the bowl of blood-stained water. Gabria came to stand beside him.

"Piers, who is the Woman of the Marsh?"

The healer started out of his musings and said, "What? Oh, a fable, I guess. She was supposed to live in the marshes of the Goldrine a long time ago."

"Is the woman still alive?"

"Still? I doubt she ever was." He looked at her strangely. "Why?"

"Cantrell told me a riddle, too." She stared at the leather chest where her scarlet cloak had been neatly packed away and thought of the gold brooch that her mother had given her many years ago: a golden buttercup, the flower that was her namesake.

13

ate in the night, when the air was chilled and the stars blazed across the sky, the Khulinin, the Jehanan, and the Bahedin gathered their caravans together and struck out southwest, following the Goldrine to the mountains. It was impossible to keep their leavetaking a secret, for the caravans were too massive and the animals were restless in the cool hours before dawn. Still, Savaric hoped to gain an element of surprise by slipping out without warning. A sleepy crowd gathered on the banks of the river to watch the clans leave. By sunrise, the caravans were miles away.

Medb anticipated their flight and immediately sent trackers to follow the clans' trail. It would be several days before his reinforcements arrived and, by the time he marched, it would be too late to catch the fleeing clans on the plains. But eventually they would go to ground, and when they did, Medb knew that he could crush them all.

For three days the clans followed the Goldrine River west toward Khulinin Treld. They traveled quickly, making few stops during the day and walking late into the night. The chiefs knew their time was limited and pushed their people hard. It could have been a difficult trip with three chiefs commanding the huge train, but the leadership seemed to fall naturally on Savaric. Lord Ryne was inexperienced in his new position as chieftain and leaned heavily on Savaric's advice. Sha Umar also bowed to the Khulinin's authority—he was smart enough to know Savaric was the better leader in a drastic situation like this.

So Savaric, almost instinctively, was leading them toward the safety of Khulinin Treld. Yet, as the miles stretched out behind the caravans, he began to have second thoughts. Khulinin Treld was the natural place for them to go; Medb would expect it and plan for battle in that terrain. However, the treld promised no real defense for a large group that contained many women and children. They could be starved out of the hall in a matter of days, and there was no good place for defensive stands. The treld was also close to Wylfling Treld. Too close for comfort.

However, Savaric knew of no other alternatives. They did not dare fight Medb on open ground: the three clans would be massacred in the first rush. There were no natural defensive positions near any of their holdings and no other clan that would give them aid. The Dangari had been Savaric's last hope, but Koshyn was still vacillating when the clans left. The Khulinin, the Bahedin, and the Jehanan were alone, with no hope for more aid, no hope for mercy, and no place to make a stand before Medb's larger, more formidable army. Savaric racked his brains for a solution. The responsibility of the clans weighed heavily, and, though he rode his stallion to a lather and wore himself into exhaustion keeping the caravans moving, Savaric came no closer to an answer.

The fourth night out of the gathering, the waning moon rose late beyond the grasslands to waken the wolves. The night was breathlessly uncomfortable. The moisture from the recent storm had quickly dried in the arid air, and the heat soared with every passing day. Now, even the nights gave scant relief. There was little wind to keep the mosquitoes at bay, and the dust settled slowly about the wagons. After setting the watch and posting the outriders, the camp fell into an uneasy rest. Savaric, weary of his own thoughts, gathered Ryne and Sha Umar and went to find Piers and Cantrell.

The bard had collapsed with a fever soon after coming to the clan and had been under Piers's care during the trek. To everyone's relief, he was beginning to recover. Savaric hoped he had regained enough strength to give advice. Cantrell was the repository of nearly every song and tale told by the clans for generations. Somewhere in that vast store of clan history and tradition, Savaric hoped to find the key to their survival.

They found Piers and Cantrell in the healer's tent, finishing
a light meal. The tent had only been partially raised over several poles and the wagon to give the occupants shelter. The
flaps were wide open to catch the fitful evening breeze. Piers
had not lit a cooking fire; only a small brass lamp glowed in the
dark interior. Even so, the tent was stuffy and hot. Cantrell lay
on a pallet near the entrance. His skin was gray with exhaustion, but he had eaten well and his wounds were healing.

Piers welcomed his guests and offered cups of wine. The
chiefs accepted and sat down around the bard.

Cantrell's face was unreadable beneath the bandages, but
his mouth lifted in a smile as he greeted the men. "Khulinin
Treld is far tonight, my lord," he said to Savaric.

"I am weary, Bard," Savaric chided. "We had hoped to hear
a song that might help us face the leagues still to go. Not an
observation on the distance to the treld."

"My voice lacks its strength and my hands lack an instrument. Would you settle for a tale?"

"I shall listen to your wisdom, master," Savaric said quietly.

Cantrell was still for a moment. He was well aware of the
deadly peril that faced them. For years he had traveled among
the clans—from the northernmost Murjik Treld on the fringes
of the great forest, to the deserts and the towers of the Turic
tribesmen. He had seen Khulinin Treld and knew its advantages and its weaknesses, and he had watched the buildup of
the massive Wylfling forces. He also knew Medb. The sorcerer
would hunt the Khulinin to the grave unless the clan found a
way to destroy him.

Cantrell had pondered for many hours what he might tell
Savaric if the chief asked his counsel. Advice was a two-edged
sword the bard did not like to wield lightly, particularly when
his prophetic riddles clouded the issue. Yet, during the long,
painful hours of riding in the wagon, he had remembered an
ancient tale that had survived the wars and invasions of countless years to be written on a scrap of vellum and buried in the
vast library of the Citadel of Krath. A long time ago, he had
been allowed to study some of the priceless manuscripts there
and had found that tale. It came to his mind now, and in its

substance he saw a glimmer of hope.

"Many years ago," Cantrell began, "before Valorian led the clans over the mountains to the vastness of the Ramtharin Plains, other peoples held this land. Short, dark-haired sons of the Eagle, they came from the west, beyond the Darkhorn Mountains, and joined the plains to their vast empire. Greedy for slaves, horses, and the riches of the grasslands, they subjugated the simple tribes that lived here and built their roads with the bones of the fallen. They built many fortresses to guard their mighty domain and garrisoned their armies within. From these walls of adamant, the invaders pinned their conquered realm in a grip of steel. Four of these strongholds were built to guard the steppes. One was located on the eastern flank of the Himachal Mountains, by the Defile of Tor Wrath."

Sha Umar looked startled. "Do you mean those old ruins on the spur of the ridge?"

Cantrell barely nodded, for his wounds still ached.

"I remember that vaguely," Lord Ryne said. His dark blue eyes shifted from one man to another. He was still nervous in such illustrious company, but his self-confidence was growing. "There was another fort near Bahedin Treld, along the Calah River. But that one was razed by the men of Pra Desh years ago."

"That's true," Cantrell replied. "But this fortress still stands. It has withstood many attacks. I believe there are wards set in the gates to protect it from arcane assault."

Sha Umar nodded and the other men looked both interested and apprehensive.

Cantrell continued. "When the western empire began to crumble, the strongholds along the frontiers were abandoned to bring the armies closer to home. After that, the fortress was used by other tribes and a self-proclaimed king or two. In the past years, its only enemy has been time." He stopped for a moment, then his voice began a slow chant.

> "Stone and timber, brick and mortar,
> Blood for fastness, bones for strength,
> Iron and steel and tears of mourning
> Built the walls of Ab-Chakan.

Guardian of the Savon River
Fair it stood upon the mount.
Bearer of the Eagle standard
Watcher of the Dark Horse Plains.

Seven towers wrought of darkness
Bound with gold and spells of might.
Swords of steel held fast the ramparts
Strength of heart kept safe the gates.

Distant horns called home the warriors
Empty now lie halls of stone.
Eyeless shadows watch from towers
Only wind walks on the walls."

Cantrell fell silent, letting the images of the song play
through the listeners' thoughts. "It's rather archaic," he said after a time. "But that is a fragment of a song I found long ago."

Savaric stared thoughtfully into his cup. Unlike the other
men, he had not traveled the eastern slopes of the Himachal
Mountains and was not familiar with the ruins or the defile
Cantrell mentioned. He was reluctant to remove his clan to
lands he did not know, and he had only the bard's reputation
to give any value to the consideration of the fortress. "This
place—Ab-Chakan—what is it now?"

"Well, the clans never had any use for a fortified garrison, so
it has been abandoned for years. But the walls still stand and
the defile has many caves that bore deep into the mountains."
Cantrell paused, his face turned toward the chiefs around him.
"For men with a little ingenuity, it could be an answer to a
prayer."

Sha Umar smiled slightly. "The werods will not like it.
Fighting within walls goes against the grain."

"So does dying needlessly at the hand of a paid mercenary,"
Savaric said dryly.

The Jehanan chieftain laughed. "I shall remember to tell
them that."

"Lord," said Cantrell. "I do not know if this is sound advice.
Ab-Chakan may be useless to your needs, but if it fails, the

defile can be defended for months by a mere handful. And Medb would not anticipate such a move. It might give you a little more time."

Savaric looked past the open tent flaps into the distance. "How far is this place?"

Cantrell pondered. "Several days journey north of Dangari Treld . . . perhaps thirty leagues from here."

"I hope that Koshyn doesn't try to get in our way," Lord Ryne spoke up. "We have few enough men as it is."

"I doubt he will," Sha Umar replied. His lean, aquiline face broke into a smile, and he gestured to Savaric with his wine cup. "Koshyn respects you even if he does try to straddle two horses at once. It's that band of exiles I'm worried about."

"Yes. They were called forth five days ago. If they find us before we reach shelter, there will be much blood spilled," Cantrell noted.

"Then we must move fast," Savaric said, suddenly reaching his decision. He felt more hopeful than he had in days. At last there was an objective to reach for that offered a semblance of success. "Are we agreed?" he asked the others. The men nodded. "Then we will turn north and go to this fortress." He paused and added, "Cantrell, if you wish to leave, I will provide a guide, horses, and supplies. Unfortunately, I can ill-afford to send an escort."

Cantrell waved off the suggestion. "I knew what I was walking into when I came for help. I have read the Khulinin's riddle of doom, my lord. Now I want to understand the answer."

Savaric's mouth curled up in a weary smile. "I hope you do not regret your curiosity."

*   *   *   *   *

Beyond the rim of firelight, where the herds dozed in the warm darkness, the outriders passed in silent vigil. They rode around the livestock, humming a soft song or stopping to exchange a quiet word with the sentinels around the camp.

On a low knoll near where the horse herd lay, Nara stood, darker than the night itself. Only her large eyes sparkled with faint starlight. Occasionally she swung her head to sniff the breeze or swished her tail at a mosquito. Except for these brief movements, she remained still. On the mare's back, Gabria shoved her bow aside, leaned on Nara's rump, and tried uselessly not to fidget. She was bored with the inactivity of guard duty and too anxious to sit still.

Time and again she remembered Cantrell's strange reaction to her—and his advice to seek the Woman of the Marsh. Gabria had tried to ask him to explain what he'd meant, but the days had been too hectic and at night he was too ill and tired to answer. Piers could not help her, and she didn't know who else to ask.

The marshes, as well as Gabria could remember, were southeast of the Tir Samod, where the Goldrine River, swollen with the waters of numerous tributaries, flowed down into a low, half-drowned land of reed-choked channels, pools, and treacherous mires before filtering into the Sea of Tannis. She had never heard of a woman living in the marshes. If there was such a woman, why was she important? Why would Cantrell tell her to seek this woman? Gabria wondered if the bard sensed her inherent ability for sorcery. Perhaps that was why his response was so odd. Maybe this Woman of the Marsh had something to do with magic.

For the past few days, Gabria had been able to put aside the realization of her power in the frantic departure and the hurried march of the caravan. It was easy to ignore Piers's thoughtful looks and Cor's absence, and it had been simple to keep the truth from Nara. But here, in the darkness, the shadows and distractions were dispelled and Gabria was forced to come face to face with a self she did not know. The girl she once had been, the girl who happily kept a tent for her father and brothers and who ran laughing through the days, had somehow become this short-haired stranger who wielded an unknown power and set herself above clan law. She had tamed a Hunnuli, ridden with a werod, and killed a man with the Trymian Force. Gabria did not recognize herself any longer, and what she found instead was frightening.

It did not matter how Nara might reassure her or Piers might protect her; she could not shake off seventeen years of in-grained distrust of sorcery. To her, magic was a power that corrupted any soul it touched and caused nothing but grief. Lord Medb was exactly what she expected a sorcerer to be: ruthless, deceitful, murderous, lusting for more power. If she were a true clanswoman, she would immediately turn herself over to Savaric and suffer the proper punishment before she became like Medb and threatened the welfare of the clans.

But the sense of survival that had sent Gabria walking out of Corin Treld refused to consider the notion. She would have to find a way to control her talent so she would never use it inadvertently again. Perhaps Cantrell had told her to seek the Woman of the Marsh because he knew this woman could help her deal with this unwanted ability. If only she knew how to find her.

Nara shifted and raised her head. Her ears swiveled forward. *Boreas and his rider are coming,* she informed Gabria.

The girl sat up quickly. She stiffened her shoulders and watched the black figure of Boreas materialize out of the darkness. Noiselessly, the huge stallion stepped up beside them and nickered softly in greeting.

The wer-tain sat silently, watching the dozing horses nearby. Gabria saw the dim sparkle of polished mail under the robe that covered him to his knees, but the glimmer of his helm was hidden beneath the hood of his cloak. She could not see the wer-tain's face in the shadows of his hood, and she hoped he could not see hers.

"Nothing stirs tonight," Athlone said quietly.

"No." Gabria had not spoken to him since Cor's death and she was not certain she wanted to now. She was horribly afraid that Athlone would probe into her actions and discover her power. The old threat she had once thought forgotten reared its ugly head between them.

"My father tells me we are going north."

"North," Gabria said testily. "Are we going to skulk in the mountains like thieves?"

He sighed, trying to be patient. "This caravan is too big to 'skulk.' We're going to an old stronghold called Ab-Chakan."

"I suppose that will be better than running over the plains like frightened rabbits."

Athlone turned his head and she could feel his cold glance. "If you had a better suggestion, you should have informed Savaric."

"I do not interfere with the councils of the wise," Gabria said huffily. She wished he would go away.

"Fine words for a woman who claims herself chieftain, disrupts an entire gathering, and threatens a sorcerer."

"And what was it worth? You let me delude myself with hopes of vengeance, then sat back and watched me make a fool of myself in front of the lords of the clans."

Athlone shook his head. "This is an old argument. I did not know he was injured so badly until I saw him the first day."

She was silent for a long while. The Hunnuli stood motionless, their ears cocked back to listen, their ebony eyes catching the light of the old moon as it thrust its horn above the hills. Athlone waited. His face was still shrouded in night, and his fingers picked restlessly at the folds of his robe.

Finally, Gabria slammed her fist on her knees. "What do I do now, Athlone? I've waited months to challenge Lord Medb. Now I have no satisfaction to quiet the voices of my brothers or wash away the memories of that day. Medb has slipped out of my grasp."

"There are other ways to gain vengeance. Some more subtle than others," he said.

Gabria whipped her head around and her heart began to pound. She could not see his face to read his expression.

"There are other ways," he added, his voice level. "Some more fitting than others, to seek your revenge against a man like Medb. Sorcerer or no, he is still a man with his own weaknesses. Seek those out. Learn his greatest fears and use them against him."

"How?" she asked sarcastically. "Do I stop him in the middle of a battle and ask a few questions, or do I visit his tent at nightfall?"

"Use your wits, Corin. None of us know how the coming days will unfold. Perhaps, if you're clever, you will have weapons at hand that will be sharper than any sword."

Gabria stared at the wer-tain. Just how much did he know about her? Had he talked to Piers or was he making his own deductions? Or was he simply offering his best advice? "All right, I'll watch. But I doubt it will do much good."

Athlone rubbed his hand down Boreas's neck. "We never know. Wars are terribly unpredictable." He stopped, then said, "I did not tell you, but I was very glad to see you alive the other night. If Cor had succeeded, I would have personally flayed him alive."

"I'm glad you didn't have the opportunity," Gabria replied, surprised and pleased by his remark.

"How long will you continue this charade?" he asked suddenly. "You cannot pretend to be a boy forever."

Gabria shrugged. "I hadn't thought that far ahead. I guess until Savaric finds out or Medb kills me."

Athlone's hand unconsciously gripped his sword hilt. "Medb will not kill you if I have anything to do with it," he muttered under his breath.

"What did you say?"

"Nothing. Tomorrow, you will join the outriders to search for Ab-Chakan."

She saluted. "Yes, Wer-tain." He turned to go, but she held out her hand and stopped him. "Athlone, do you know of the Woman of the Marsh?"

Athlone stiffened. Boreas snorted as his rider leaned forward. "Where did you hear of that?"

"From Cantrell."

"Well, forget it immediately. That woman is evil and dangerous. You have no business with her. I forbid you to mention her again." He kneed Boreas, and they vanished in the dark."

"That was strange," Gabria said, astonished by his vehement reaction.

Nara nickered softly. *The man does not understand yet. He thinks as you once did about magic.*

"Once did?"

Your beliefs have traveled far since you felled Cor the first time with magic.

"The first time," Gabria repeated weakly.

Surely you did not think I did not know. Hunnuli are most comfortable with magic-wielders. We can sense many things about our riders that men overlook.

"Then you know I killed him."

Of course. And now you know the truth.

"That I am a sorceress." Gabria sounded disgusted.

You are not a sorceress yet. Your powers are untrained, but you have much natural talent. That should not be wasted. Especially now.

"Well, what can I do about it?" she demanded, trying to keep her voice down. "Lord Medb would never teach me, and who else knows the forbidden arts?"

Follow the bard's counsel, Nara answered.

"The Woman of the Marsh? I don't even know if she exists!" Gabria said.

The woman is there. In the great marshes. She will help you if she feels your desires are strong enough.

Gabria was stunned. She knew that Nara was telling the truth, and the possibilities of what the Hunnuli was saying were incredible. She sat lost in thought for some time before she broke her silence. When at last she spoke, her voice was filled with sadness.

"Oh, Nara, these are strange days. Legends spring to life, clan fights clan, and our fates hang on the thread of a sorcerer's spell. Now I have a power I was taught to despise and I don't know what to do with it. All I can think about is Medb and magic and the look of death on my father's face." Her words failed, and she leaned despondently on Nara's neck.

The Hunnuli nickered in sympathy. *I cannot always understand men's feelings, but I, too, have felt loss and loneliness. When that happens, you must look for new strengths and the new pastures.*

Gabria listened to the gentle words in her mind. She slipped her arms around Nara's neck. "Will the marshes do?"

That will do very well. I have felt the need for a long run.

* * * * *

Two hours after dawn, Athlone sent his outriders forth as
scouts. Riding northeast, they spread out to find the fastest
road to the Himachal Mountains and the fortress of Ab-
Chakan. Gabria and Nara rode with them. They galloped for
leagues over the grassy, level end of the valley of the
Hornguard. Gradually the terrain rolled upward and the hills
surged toward the feet of the mountains. Ahead, the dark,
smoky smudge marking the mountains sharpened into individual peaks.

The Himachal Mountains were not mountains in the rugged, glorious form of the Darkhorns. They were mere van-
guards to the mighty range, and their crowns rose only to a
modest height above the plains. Yet, despite their shorter,
rounder tops, their slopes were steep and difficult and thick
with heavy underbrush and timber.

At the southernmost end of the mountains, where a wide valley led a stream out of the forests to meet the Isin River, Clan
Dangari had built their treld and ran their studs year round.
They were the most sedentary of the clans and were trading their
nomadic instincts for the pleasures of horse breeding.

Athlone's scouts cautiously bypassed Dangari Treld and continued north, seeking only the defile and the fortress. There
was still no word of Koshyn's movements and nothing had
been seen of the band of exiles. The Oathbreakers sent word to
Savaric that the army of hired mercenaries had arrived at
Medb's camp and the combined forces of the four clans and
the hired soldiers were marching after the Khulinin. Medb had
also followed through with his threat to the cultists and had
sent a large force to besiege the Citadel of Krath.

Time was running out. Savaric turned the clans north after
the scouts, and the race began.

The three clans had a five-day lead on the Wylfling and they
would need every hour of it to find the fortress in time. The
caravans moved much slower than an armed host and had
many leagues to travel. It would be close, but Savaric hoped
that the clans would make it to Ab-Chakan with a day or two to
spare. That hope was a real possibility—as long as the Dangari
or the exiled marauders did not slow them down.

The next four days were miserable, but Savaric's pride in his people grew tenfold. With the host of the sorcerer on their heels, the three clans drew together and fled for the mountains. Excess baggage, broken wagons, and sick or weak animals were left behind. They made no stops during the day and at night they only stopped long enough to rest the horses, water the livestock, and eat a cold meal. The clans lit no fires, and the tents remained packed; the people collapsed in the shelter of their wagons and waited for dawn. On the trail, the sun burned on their heads and the dust rose to choke them. Before long, the grueling pace began to tell, particularly on the children and the foals, but the caravan pushed on, knowing it would mean certain death if they were caught on the open plains.

Late on the second day of the journey north, several scouts, including Gabria, returned to tell Savaric that the walls of Ab-Chakan still stood and the caves in the defile were empty. Two men had been left to watch the fortress, and others waited along the way. Dangari Treld was quiet and no news was known of the exiles.

Savaric sighed with relief when he heard the scouts' reports, and he sent several more trackers out to follow the advance of Medb's forces. In secret, he wondered where Koshyn and the Dangari were.

On the tenth day of the trek from the gathering, Savaric got his answer.

14

ootsore and weary, the three clans swung east to avoid Dangari Treld and then north again to follow the Isin River. The Himachals lay on their left hand and the vast, wind-walked plains of Ramtharin lay on their right. Savaric was relieved they had traveled almost thirty leagues in the four days since leaving the Goldrine River—an unheard-of pace for a caravan so large—but the clans were exhausted. Men, women, children, and animals were pushed to the limits of their strength. Only the Hunnuli showed no signs of fatigue as the caravan trudged the last leagues toward the defile.

Along the mountains' foothills, the Isin River flowed south, following the lay of the terrain. Like a boundary line, it separated the rugged hills on the west side from the smoother grasslands that rolled east to the sea. After some debate, the chieftains decided to stay on the east bank of the river. There was very little cover to shield them from hunters and few places where they could easily defend themselves if caught, but their passage would be easier and faster.

The decision proved a wise one. As the caravan traveled farther north, the mountains tumbled down into rough hills, gullies, and sharp-backed ridges that would have been impossible for the wagons. On the east bank, the slopes were gentler and the patchy growths of scrub were easier to avoid. The clans moved faster, hoping that they were almost to the fortress and safety. Only the openness, something they usually loved, made them feel strangely insecure. No one knew when the exile band or Medb's host would sweep down on the slow-moving caravan, so people waited and watched and constantly looked over their shoulders.

Then, just after midday of the fifth day, one of the out-riders, scouting to the south of the caravan, wheeled his horse and galloped back to the line. Instantly, the werods herded the wagons together and drew a tight ring around them; swords glittered in the sun and a deadly shield of spears pointed out-ward from the ring. The outriders galloped in and all the mounted men filled the gaps behind the warriors.

The three chiefs drew their swords and waited as the scout reined to a stop. Savaric's face was stern. Gabria and Athlone waited side by side on their Hunnuli just behind him. The clans were quiet while they waited for the news.

"Lord," the Khulinin said to Savaric. "The Dangari are be-hind us. They ride swiftly without herds or wagons."

An excited murmur rushed through the listening clans. Their worst fears seemed to be realized.

"We should move back to the river and the shelter of the trees," Lord Ryne suggested.

Savaric shook his head and slammed his sword back into its scabbard. "No. We have no time. We will wait."

No one else moved. They watched warily as a large troop of mounted, mail-clad men swept toward them along the skirts of the hills. The riders carried their painted shields on their arms and in their hands were tall spears of ash. A blue banner floated at their head.

Suddenly they swerved toward the waiting caravan and gal-loped up with a noise like thunder. The three clans instinc-tively moved closer together, and the warriors' hands tightened on their swords. A horn cried out, clear and keen, and the company came to a halt not far from Savaric. The two groups eyed each other silently. Then, a lone man rode for-ward, leading a string of seven mares. A white horsetail flowed from his helm. His blue cloak was thrown back over his shoul-ders, and his fair face grinned in relief.

"Savaric, you are a hard man to track down."

"Koshyn, what in Surgart's name are you doing here?" Sha Umar yelled suspiciously.

"I could ask you the same, for you are on my holdings,"

Koshyn replied, ignoring the hostile looks of the clansmen. "But I've come to pay my debt. Seven mares, remember?"

"You choose a strange time to do so," Savaric said.

"The situation demanded it. The exile band is not far behind me."

Athlone, his eyes smoldering, urged Boreas forward. "And you led them directly to us!"

Koshyn's face darkened as though a cloud of rage had passed over him. "They attacked my treld last night and butchered five of our prized stallions and a score of mares before we could drive them off. They're licking their wounds now, but they will return."

Voices burst out in anger and surprise from the watching clanspeople. The warriors kept their spears raised, but their hands relaxed. Every person there understood the Dangari's grief and rage at the loss of their beloved horses.

"Why did the marauders attack your clan?" Savaric asked.

"Because I refused to join Medb. We left the gathering after you. Medb was furious. I think he diverted the exiles from you to take his revenge on us."

"I see. Thank you for the warning and the mares. We must go." Savaric wheeled his stallion and raised his hand to motion to the caravan. Although he desperately wanted the help of the Dangari, he would not beg for aid now—not after days of frantic flight and worry.

Koshyn rode forward and stopped him. The young chief's eyes were bright with anger, and the tattoos on his face faded into a dark flush. "We're going with you, Lord Savaric," he said. "I have been justly punished for my sluggardly courage and now I ask your leave to join you."

Savaric paused and looked at his fellow chieftains. Sha Umar shrugged; Ryne nodded firmly. Savaric stared at the Dangari's face for a full minute and weighed the fury and sincerity he saw in Koshyn's blue eyes. Then he nodded abruptly. "Your help is most welcome, but we must move fast if the marauders are following. Where is the rest of your clan?"

"They are coming. We're driving the herds to secret pastures in the mountains, and the women are gathering supplies. I came to find you and learn your counsel."

"Listen, then. We are going to Ab-Chakan at the Defile of Tor Wrath. Join us there as quickly as possible."

Koshyn stared. "That pile of rock? What for?"

"Piles of rock are easier to defend," Savaric replied curtly.

The younger chief looked over the weary clans and back to Savaric. He still couldn't believe the caravan had traveled this far so fast. When his scouts had told him the location of the clans, he wouldn't believe them until he saw the trail for himself. His respect for Savaric had doubled.

"We will be there," Koshyn said. He handed the lead line of the seven mares to Savaric, spurred his horse around, and cantered back to his men. With a ringing shout, they galloped back toward their treld.

Sha Umar grinned. "Now we will only be *very* outnumbered instead of *desperately* outnumbered."

Savaric leaned on his saddle horn and said, "If only the other clans could be so easily persuaded." He waved to the caravan, and the werod and wagons fell in behind him.

Nara waited a moment and watched the dust settle behind the vanishing company of horsemen. *We will have to go soon. Before it is too late.*

"Yes, tonight, I suppose. I hope we will find the clans still alive when we return," said Gabria.

Since she had made the decision to search for the Woman of the Marsh, a strange reluctance to leave the Khulinin had hindered Gabria. She kept putting off their departure, waiting for a better moment. Gabria realized that the days were pressing close, but every time she considered leaving, a thought like a stinging fly buzzed in her mind: it had happened once; it could happen again. She could return to find nothing left but blood and smoke and rotting corpses. The image terrified her, more, she told herself, than the fear of her power or an uncertain meeting with an odd woman of legends. If she stayed with the Khulinin, she would not have to face the agony again and she could live or die with them.

Nara understood her reluctance. She pawed the ground and snorted. *They will survive for a while behind the wall of that fortress. They do not need you yet.*

Gabria shivered slightly. "Can you promise me they will be alive when we return?"

I can promise you nothing. Just have faith in them.

She rubbed the mare's neck, feeling the rock-hard muscle beneath the velvet hair. "You are always honest, Nara. You give me heart."

The mare looked at Gabria sideways from beneath her long forelock. *That is why I am with you. Pack ample food; I do not know how long we will be gone.*

*   *   *   *   *

The afternoon slowly passed into evening. The sky was barred with high clouds and the sun faded to copper as it fell. It was nearly dusk when the scouts found the remains of an ancient road in the tumbled shrubs and weeds of the Isin's valley.

Built long before the horsemen rode the plains, the road had served the fortress of Ab-Chakan as a supply route to other cities and strongholds, places that had fallen to ruin after the demise of the empire. Now, only crumpled patches of paving stone showed through the grass and dirt.

As the clans traveled farther north, the road became more obvious. Its straight flight and level course were clearly seen on the flanks of the hills where it followed the river. Although the grasses and vines clambered over the stone, the road was still passable and the caravan thankfully used it. Even in the dim twilight, the clans could see the skillful handiwork of the men of old in the cut and lay of the stones.

Several hours after nightfall, the clans halted by the river. Savaric spread the word that they were five leagues from the fortress and would reach it the next day. Breathing prayers of thanks to their gods, everyone prepared for the night. Soon the camp sank into the silence of exhausted sleep. Only the sentinels and outriders moved beyond the edges of the encampment. The night was quite black, since the moon would not rise until much later and no fires or lamps were lit. A mild wind hummed over the grass, and the stars reflected on the river's surface like jewels on a black mirror.

Gabria waited until all was still, then she stealthily collected her gear. She took only a bag of food and her dagger. Piers would care for her things until she returned. After a moment's thought, however, she fished out the arcane stone ward and wrapped it carefully in her cloak. She dressed in a dark blue tunic and pants, folded her cloak into the bag, and shoved her dagger into her belt.

Piers and Cantrell were sleeping beside the wagon. She carefully picked up her bag and a water skin, and slid over to the bard. She gently shook him. He woke immediately.

Gabria could not see Cantrell's face, but she felt his body stiffen. "It's all right," she whispered. "It's only Gabria."

He lay still for a moment, listening, then he murmured in understanding, "You are leaving."

"Yes. Please tell Athlone not to worry. I will be back."

He chuckled softly. "The wer-tain will be very busy for the next few days, but I will tell him. Please be careful. My advice is not always commendable."

"The Hunnuli will see to my safety. Farewell." She slipped away.

Piers rolled over. "So she is leaving at last."

"Yes. I only pray it does more good than harm."

"Bard, she had no choice."

Cantrell sighed. "I know. But the Woman of the Marsh can be dangerous, and she may not accept another pupil."

"It is more dangerous to have an untrained magic-wielder in our midst."

The bard relaxed into his blankets. "We will see soon enough," he said sadly.

Piers lay back and looked up at the stars. "The gods give you speed, Gabria," he murmured to himself.

Nara was waiting for Gabria on the edge of camp. As silently as wind-blown shadows, they glided past the guards and disappeared into the darkness. For a short distance, the Hunnuli cantered south along the path the clan had followed, then she veered east and stretched out into a gallop. Like a cloud scudding across the night sky, she swept over the leagues of grass,

her legs thrusting forward in an endless rhythm. She ran effort-
lessly, and the air trembled as she passed. Astride the mare's
back, Gabria held fast to Nara's mane and marveled at the
speed the Hunnuli held. The girl leaned forward. The wind
whipped the mare's black mane into her face.

Nara felt her rider's joy and in answer, she leaped forward
ever faster. Her nostrils flared, her ears tucked back, and her
muscles flowed beneath her black hide. The immeasurable
plains opened before them. Far ahead, a thunderstorm etched
the horizon with lightning. Flinging her head high, the mare
raced to meet the storm.

They swung wide to the east to avoid running afoul of
Medb's army, eventually bending their way south toward the
Sea of Tannis and the marshes of the Goldrine. The storm was
left behind. After a while, Gabria was lulled by the rocking of
Nara's gait and she dozed on the mare's neck, watching
through half-closed lids as the land flowed away beneath them
in a blur. Imperceptibly the blur began to lighten and tinge
with color. Once, Gabria started awake and looked up to see
the sun poised on the rim of the world.

The hills flattened somewhat, rising in a slow, easy swell,
and their treeless slopes soon were covered with thick grasses
that formed a springy cushion under Nara's hooves.

The day quickly grew hot and the wind faded. Above, a
hawk circled in the brilliant blue sky, but it was the only living
thing that Gabria saw all day. Either the animals were lying low
to escape the heat or had fled at the sight of the running Hunnuli. By noon, shimmering heat mirages wavered in the distance. Gabria was stiff and thirsty, and, at last, she could feel
Nara beginning to tire.

The Hunnuli found a water hole in a depression between
several hills, and horse and rider rested in the shade of a small
copse of trees. Gabria and Nara left again a few hours later and
the mare galloped south with the wind. At dusk, they came to
the edges of the Goldrine Marshes.

* * * * *

It was late in the morning before Athlone knew that Gabria was gone. The realization that he had not seen the girl or the Hunnuli for hours came gradually as he led a company of the werod ahead of the caravan. When he questioned Boreas, he learned that Gabria had left in the night, but where she was going the stallion would not say. Blazing with fury, the wertain galloped Boreas back to the caravan. There were only two men who might know where the Corin went, and Athlone intended to find out what they knew.

Piers, walking by the side of his wagon, saw the wer-tain bearing down on him and spoke a soft warning to Cantrell, who was seated on the loaded bundles. The healer clucked to his old mare and began whistling nonchalantly.

"Where is that wretch of a Corin?" Athlone demanded as Boreas skidded to a halt. The clansmen around them stared curiously; Piers tried to look innocent.

"The boy will be back soon, Wer-tain," Cantrell answered.

Athlone's face was livid. "Where is he?" he shouted, almost forgetting to use the masculine term before the interested onlookers. Boreas pranced sideways under his rider's agitation.

The bard shrugged. His bandaged face showed no expression; his voice was calm and reasonable. "His cause was urgent and he will return. Let us leave it at that."

"I will not leave it at that. That boy is under my care and . . . stop that infernal whistling," he snapped at Piers. The healer gave him an aggrieved look, which Athlone ignored. "Gabran had no just reason to leave alone at this time! It's far too dangerous." His eyes suddenly narrowed. "Unless . . . he's been under Medb's sway all this time!"

"Athlone, read your heart," Cantrell said. "You know that is not true."

"Then why did he leave? And why did you let him go?" Athlone shouted at both men.

"We had no say in Gabran's decision," Piers replied. "But we would not have stopped him."

Boreas spoke gently in Athlone's mind, *Nara went with Gabria, Athlone. They will return soon.*

The wer-tain calmed down a fraction. "I hope to the gods

that boy does return," he said with feeling. "Because if Medb or the marauders don't kill him, I just might." Boreas spun around and galloped off, leaving Piers and Cantrell relieved.

"Have you noticed," Piers said, "that the wer-tain appears to care for the Corin more than he realizes?"

Cantrell nodded. "Interesting, isn't it? But the tragic paradox is if she kills Medb to save the Khulinin, clan law will order her death for using magic. Athlone, as wer-tain of her adopted clan, will have to fulfill that edict."

"Is that her doom?" Piers asked sadly.

"Only if she can find the answer to Medb's riddle."

"And if she does not . . ."

Cantrell finished the sentence for him. "None of us need worry about difficulties with clan law."

High, hazy clouds drifted in during the afternoon and obscured the sun with a half-hearted veil. Word passed down through the ranks that the fortress was only a few miles distant, and those with sharp eyes could already discern the black towers like tiny teeth against the reddish bluffs. The caravan was heartened by the news. Forcing their weary legs to move faster, they pushed on, hoping to reach the stronghold by dusk.

Suddenly there was a commotion at the rear of the caravan. It spread up the line like wildfire as a Khulinin, a crude, bloodied bandage on his shoulder, galloped by on a lathered horse. Two outriders rode at his side. Voices raised in consternation, for the Khulinin recognized him as one of the trackers sent to observe Medb's forces. The clanspeople watched as he halted before the chiefs at the head of the caravan. Many heads turned to look behind them, expecting to see the sorcerer's army bearing down on them. Many hands reached for weapons.

The tracker leaned wearily on his saddle and saluted his chieftain. His face was grimy with dust and sweat, and his brow was creased with pain. "They are close, Lord," he said, trying to keep his voice steady. "Three days at the most."

The men broke out in exclamations. Savaric cut them off. "Where?"

"They were moving toward Khulinin Treld, but they turned after us several days ago."

"I see. Have you seen the band of exiles?"

The tracker nodded angrily. "They chased us for a while. An arrow killed the other scout, Dorlan."

Savaric cursed under his breath. "Where are they now?"

"Harassing the Dangari. The blue cloaks are coming behind us, too."

Savaric's smile was dry. "I wonder who will reach us first."

*   *   *   *   *

Built during the reign of the eighth Tarn Emperor, the fortress, Ab-Chakan, was the culmination of one architect's dreams and skills. The builder had chosen his site midway in the Himachal Mountains, where the valley of the Isin opened out onto the plains. At the head of the valley, the hills closed in, forming a deep defile that wound inward to the heart of the mountains, where the cliffs rose in impregnable buttresses and the river sprang from the lightless roots of the mountains.

At the mouth of the gorge, where the river flowed out into the valley, the slopes ended abruptly in high bluffs. There, the emperor's architect had built Ab-Chakan on a small ridge of rock that thrust out from the southern cliffs and partially blocked the entrance to the defile.

The builder had constructed an octagonal fortress with black towers at each corner. Walls thirty feet high and so thick two horses could walk abreast along the top united the towers. The battlements had overhanging parapets and crenelations through which archers could shoot. The great stones of the wall were set with such skill that no wedge could be driven between their joints.

Realizing the value of the defile behind the fortress, the men of old also constructed a thick wall from the corner of Ab-Chakan over to the northern cliff, barring the entrance to the gorge. The Isin passed beneath the wall through a culvert. The river's current was too strong to swim or dam, and as it curled around the foot of the fortress, the Isin itself provided another natural defense for Ab-Chakan.

It was nearly dark when the wagons finally reached the cross-

roads, where a wide, well-paved road intersected their road
and went up to the main gates of the fortress. The caravan
halted and every eye turned to the hulking, dark mass above
them. Its blank walls and windowless towers were eerie and
seemed to loom over the clans in the twilight.

Even Athlone was reluctant to broach the hidden secrets of
the fortress at night, so the clans decided to spend the night in
the relative safety of the defile. Another road led to a crumbled
gateway in the river wall. The travelers carefully picked their
way over the remains of the road and into the gorge. The noise
of the tumbling river seemed horribly loud in the canyon, and
the wind-haunted walls of rock reared over them like prison
towers. The floor of the defile was uneven and rocky. The meager path was often blocked with stony debris, but the clans
pushed on deeper into the gorge, until they found a wide,
grassy area free of broken boulders. There they set up camp
and waited anxiously for morning.

Light came slowly in the deep gorge, but the chiefs and their
clans set to work long before the sun rode over the river wall.
They found caves near the mouth of the river, and they hid
their wagons and supplies. The herds were left under such
guard as could be spared. The women went to work gathering
what food could be found, baking unleavened bread, filling
the water skins, and gathering wood. The armorers set up their
small forges to repair weapons and make arrows and spear
points. The children were sent to cut fodder for the animals.

Savaric, meanwhile, put the men to work on the river wall.
It had stood for centuries, but floods and time had taken their
toll. The warriors put aside their horses and swords to carry
stone and shift earth. They spent the day strengthening the
gate and filling in the ruinous gaps in the stones.

Athlone was still angered at Gabria's disappearance, so he
threw himself into the unfamiliar labor. His men watched him
and wondered, but they were heartened by his tireless strength
and they worked long into the night without complaint or
slacking. Above them, the massive shape of Ab-Chakan sat in
forbidding vigilance.

When night came, the three clans were pleased with their

progress. The women and children had gathered a large store of food, water, and firewood. The river wall was patched and the gate was shored up against attack. Few expected the wall to survive a prolonged siege, particularly if the guardian fortress fell. But while its stones stood and defenders survived, the wall would help protect the herds and act as a last defense if the clans had to retreat into the defile.

The clanspeople went back to their camp bone-tired and, although they had done a major task, they all knew that the primary work had to be done tomorrow on the fortress. So the clanspeople treated their blisters with salves, rubbed their weary muscles, and prayed for more time—time to strengthen Ab-Chakan and to learn its secrets, time for the Dangari to arrive.

Savaric knew that Koshyn would keep his promise to come, but somewhere between Dangari Treld and Ab-Chakan was the band of marauders, and behind the Dangari was Medb's army. If anything went wrong, Koshyn's clan would be slaughtered. Savaric considered sending messengers to the Dangari to urge them on; instead, he settled for posting watchers on the bluffs. It would do no good to tell Koshyn something he already knew.

Nevertheless, Savaric could not keep his eyes from wandering to the south, where he hoped to see the dust of an approaching clan. Or of a Hunnuli. Athlone had told him of Gabran's disappearance and, although he was distressed at the boy's danger, he sensed Gabran had an important reason for leaving. If the gods allowed, the boy would soon return.

The next day, the clansmen broached the fortress. The three chiefs, along with Cantrell, Athlone, and a picked force of warriors, trod the ancient road to the main gates. The stone road that began in the valley crossed the river on a crumbling bridge and climbed the face of the short hill.

When the men reached the top of the hill, they stood on a broad, smooth ramp that led through the wall into the fortress. On either side were two of the eight towers, and, at their base, the walls molded into the natural rock and fell away to the valley floor. Before the men, the main gate stood partially open.

Two bronze doors, now weathered to a dingy brown, hung
in the huge archway of the front entrance. Fifteen feet tall or
more, they rose above the men's heads to a curved lintel carved
with strange beasts and letters. On each door a bronze lion's
head glared down at the interlopers. The lions, guardians of
the gate, were worn and grimy, but their topaz eyes still glittered fiercely in the rising sun.

Within the gate, the men glimpsed another wall and red-
colored buildings, dark doorways and patches of thick weeds.
The abandoned walls towered above them, and the wind
moaned in the empty towers. The men paused at the entrance
and stared nervously inside. The huge, echoing fortress held
only shadows, but the enclosed, lifeless confines were almost
more frightening to the free-roaming clansmen than all the
armies of Medb's host. Warriors with gleaming swords were a
tangible danger. These strange, old ruins were beyond their
knowledge. Still, the clans' survival depended upon this
stronghold and upon learning how to exploit its advantages.

Athlone boldly stepped forward and pulled on one of the
doors. Several men jumped to help him. They expected the
doors to be heavy, but the massive bronze gates had been clev-
erly hung so only one man was needed to open them. To the
warriors' surprise, the doors swung back and slammed into the
stone with a resounding boom. The men started like nervous
hounds as the sound reverberated through the courts and battlements. A flock of crows leaped out of a tower and flew overhead, cawing harshly.

Cantrell leaned on his guide's shoulder and laughed softly.
"If anyone is here, we have certainly made our presence
known."

The men glanced at the bard sharply, and Ryne said, "Who
could be here?" His voice was uneasy.

"Only the dead and their memories," the bard replied.
"These are only stones, Lord Ryne, hewn by men as mortal as
yourself. There is nothing within to be wary of."

Ryne was not convinced, but he did not want the others to
see his dread. He stepped through the gateway. Athlone and
the others fell in behind him. Before them, the road passed

through another, smaller wall and into the fortress proper. At one time, the area between the two walls was kept clear and free of debris, its wide space a vital part of the fortress's defenses. However, years of wind-blown dirt and wild growth had accumulated, and weeds grew profusely among the moldering trash, tumbled rock, and the rotting remains of a few wooden shacks put up by later occupants. While the main wall had only one gate, the secondary wall was pierced with eight, one at each tower and one at the road. Single bronze doors with small lions' heads guarded the gateways.

The clansmen walked into the fortress and gazed about with wonder. Despite the military function of the stronghold, its center was similar to a wealthy city. Inside the eight gates circling the inner wall were the decayed ruins of wooden barracks, stables, kitchens, and servants' quarters. But beyond those were luxurious houses and courts, broad paved paths, verdant gardens now overgrown and wild, and fountains—all built or decorated with skillfully carved granite or local red stone. Only the eight towers were built of ebony marble, a stone that glistened like black ice and was prized by the old invaders.

Savaric and the warriors slowly paced up the main road past the empty houses, toward the center of the stronghold. The clansmen were stunned by the sheer size of the fortress and the work that had gone into its creation. The men had never seen anything like it.

In the light of early morning, the shade among the buildings was still heavy and a chill lurked in the silent stones. There was no sound except for the men's footfalls. Athlone caught himself staring and listening for a voice in the halls, or a footstep on the side streets, or a face in the embrasures. Instead, all he saw were barred or broken doors, rotting roofs—many of which had fallen in—and eroding masonry with weeds and grass growing in every chink that could hold earth. Year by year, Ab-Chakan was falling into ruin, yet it surprised him how many walls still stood.

The warriors passed out of the buildings' shadows and saw in front of them, in the center of the fortress, the graceful rooms and terraces of the palace built for Ab-Chakan's general. A wide courtyard curved away on either side of the palace. In its center stood a fountain with a carved horse of black marble. Stained and pitted, the statue reared elegantly over a dried pool. Athlone strode to the horse's side and put his hand on the raised hoof.

"I'm beginning to admire these strange people," he said. "They certainly knew horses."

"And knew how to build," Savaric replied. His face was creased with worry, and he inspected everything closely. He was certain he had made the right decision to bring the clans here, but he was overwhelmed by the immensity of the fortress they had chosen to defend. No one in their group had any experience in this kind of warfare, while Medb would possibly have several advisors in his mercenaries who knew how to plan a siege.

"Now it is time for work," Savaric continued. "Ryne, you worked well on the river wall yesterday. Would you bring the werods and examine the walls and towers? Be sure there are no breaches or weak places."

The young Bahedin nodded, pleased to have such an important task.

"Jorlan," Savaric said to his new second wer-tain, "I want you to take two men and find the wells. If the water is bad, we will have to bring some from the river."

Sha Umar looked down the road to the great walls. "We'll need plenty of food. I'll start bringing in the supplies."

Savaric agreed. "Cull out the livestock, too. We'll leave the breeding stock and the horses in the defile."

The men left for their tasks. Cantrell and his guide, Athlone, and Savaric were left alone.

"I would like to see this hall," Savaric said, "before we become too busy."

The men walked across the court to the entrance of the great hall that formed the front of the palace. Seven arches graced the front of the building. Behind the middle arch was a smaller replica of the magnificent bronze gate. Athlone gingerly pushed it open, and the doors swung gently aside. The Khulinin looked into the hall.

It was lit by deep embrasures set just below the roofline, and the light of the morning sun poured through. Two rows of tall pillars supported the vaulted roof, which was still in good condition. On the floor, faint traces of gold still gleamed through the thick layer of dust, debris, and bird droppings. No hangings, trophies, or anything of wood or fabric remained. But on every wall were murals of ancient battles and generals long forgotten. The colors had dulled with time and the walls were scarred and filthy, but the figures were still clear and detailed.

Savaric and Athlone were staring, fascinated, at the walls when Cantrell suddenly raised his head. "There are horns blowing at the front gate," he said urgently to Savaric. "Leave me. We will find our own way out."

The two warriors bolted for the door and ran across the courtyard. As they raced down the road toward the main gates, they, too, heard the horns of the Khulinin outriders blowing frantically from the valley below. Other warriors were crowded around the gate and clustered on the walls. Savaric and Athlone charged up the stone stairs, pushed through the men, and stopped on the brink of the parapet.

There, a mile distant from the crossroads, a small company of horsemen was galloping from the south. A blue banner streamed at their head. Behind the troop, a cluster of wagons was following at full speed and a larger group of riders was fighting a running battle in the rear with an unidentifiable company of warriors. The attackers wore no cloaks and were less disciplined than the fleeing warriors, but they kept up a deadly barrage of arrows at the larger force and cut down anyone who fell behind.

Clan Dangari gained rapidly on the fortress, its attackers close on its heels. It appeared to the watching men that the pursuers did not realize the other clans were nearby.

Savaric and his men leaned over the wall to see the chase.

"Come on, Koshyn!" Athlone shouted. "Ride!"

Suddenly a score of horsemen led by Sha Umar left the shelter of the river wall and galloped toward the approaching clan, their horns blowing a welcome. The horsemen and wagons pivoted around the foot of the fortress and hurried toward the river wall. The attackers took one look at the approaching warriors and the clansmen gathered on the walls, then wheeled about and cantered off to the shelter of the woods on the other side of the valley. The weary clansmen rode gratefully into the defile to the sound of horns blaring wildly.

The Dangari had come.

15

ara stepped carefully onto a sand bar and snorted when she sunk up to her knees in quaking mud. *I am sorry, Gabria. I can go no farther.*

Gabria glared at the river in frustration, but she understood Nara's predicament. The giant mare was coated with mud and had already been mired once, and they were barely into the fringes of the great delta. Since daybreak they had been following the Goldrine as its banks eroded away to mud bars and beds of reeds. The river had quickly sunk into a morass of shallow channels, quicksand, and insecure little islands.

When Gabria and Nara arrived at the river the night before, they had camped in lowlands thick with thorns, brambles, and grasses. But in the morning, as the Hunnuli had traveled deeper into the wetlands, patches of rushes and giant marsh grass with silvery tassels crowded out the thickets. Just a little farther ahead, Gabria had been able to see where the pale gray of the tassels turned to a solid mass of tossing green. Sadly, the illusion of solidity was quite treacherous, for the grass was a shifting quagmire where no Hunnuli or horse of any kind could go.

Nara heaved her front legs out of the silt and lunged to a more solid bank. Her head down, she stood breathing heavily, her massive strength already drained by the leeching marsh.

Gabria slid off the mare unwillingly. She had hoped the Hunnuli would be with her when she faced the Woman of the Marsh, and she had relied on Nara's wisdom to seek a path through the dangerous mires. But it was obvious Nara could not go on.

She sighed. "How do I find this woman?"

The woman will find you.

The girl yanked her hat off and thrust it in her bag, then she crossed her arms, feeling very disgruntled. "And how can I be sure she'll help?"

She will help you. She is a magic-wielder. Like you.

Gabria looked away. Until that moment, no one had told her the woman was a sorceress. But her intuition had already informed her of that possibility long ago.

Nara's eyes glittered like black crystal. She nudged the girl gently. *I will wait nearby.*

Without another word, Gabria fastened the food bag to her belt, gritted her teeth, and stepped out bravely. The mud oozed to her ankles and water seeped into her boots, but she did not sink like the Hunnuli. She heard Nara plunging away behind her and, for a moment, her resolve almost crumbled. She faltered in midstep and thought of running after the horse. Then her foot slipped and she fell headlong into the river.

The water was warm and brackish and smelled of rotting vegetation, yet it cleared her head. Sputtering, Gabria stood up and looked down at herself ruefully. She was muddy from head to toe and smelled like a swamp; the sleeves of her tunic were black with mud and her bag was soaked. It serves me right, she thought irritably. I've come too far to panic now at the idea of facing my dreads alone.

Her jaw set, Gabria struggled downstream toward the heart of the marshes. The morning sun turned hot, and a smell of moldering vegetation began to rise from the river. Gnats and mosquitoes plagued her. The water spread relentlessly over the land and the ocean of marsh grass loomed closer. She soon found that what looked like one vast fen of grass was really an endless network of pools, quaking mires, and winding, half-strangled channels. Through these a cunning eye and foot could find a wandering, unsteady course over patches of mud, tiny islands, and sand bars. However, as the hours passed and Gabria floundered deeper into the marsh, she began to despair of her cunning.

The journey grew very tiresome. Great reed beds often
blocked her path, forcing her to wade or swim in deep,
scummy brown water. Thickets of grass towered over her and
shut her into a green rustling world. She knew the wind was
blowing above, for the tassels rippled in sun-drenched waves,
yet nothing stirred the water's surface but the swirl of a fish or
the leap of a frog. Soon, Gabria was perspiring heavily, which
only drew more fascinated insects.

The day dragged on as Gabria floundered south into the
marsh. She looked for anything that would help her find the
woman: a path, a hut, even a footprint or a small item dropped
in passing. But the marshes hid their secrets well. She found no
sign of any other human being, only water and reeds and
herons that watched her with jaundiced eyes.

At last, filthy and exhausted, the girl came to a long, dark
mere, where the water was deep and obscure and barred her
way on either hand. She stared at the water for a while and
wondered if Athlone would laugh if he saw her like this: more
mud than sense. It would hardly matter if he did, Gabria decided. She was too tired to care or to swim the mere. Weary and
numb, she crawled onto a dry-looking tussock and curled up in
the middle of the grass. Her food was ruined, so she drank a
few swallows of water, laid her head on the bag, and tried to
rest.

Darkness came and with it the noises of the marsh increased
to an uproar. Frogs croaked everywhere. Mosquitos hummed.
Thousands of creatures that sounded like rusted crickets
squeaked incessantly until Gabria was in a frenzy. The biting
insects were out in force, too, and they covered every part of
her exposed skin. She swatted and squirmed, but nothing
would keep them away. She was cold, wet, miserable, and very
lonely.

At last she decided she would have to move or go mad. But
just as she was about to sit up, Gabria heard a distant noise in
the mere. She froze and held her breath.

The noise came again—a soft splash like a creature paddling
in the water—or a snake hunting. She had heard of the huge
carnivorous snakes that inhabited the marshes, and although

they rarely reached sizes capable of devouring a human, she had no desire to meet one. Silently, Gabria's hand crept to her dagger. The moon, an old shaving, had not yet risen and the night seemed utterly lightless. Her eyes strained through the black to see, her ears listened fearfully.

Suddenly a small, lithe animal popped out of the water by her feet. Gabria leaped back like a stung cat and whipped out her dagger. The animal churred and bobbed its head. She stared at it in amazement. It was shaped rather like a short, fat snake with a blunt nose and tapering tail. However, it also had four webbed feet and a whiskered nose. Its round eyes glittered in the starlight. It chirped again in obvious inquiry, and Gabria eased her dagger back into her belt. It was only an otter.

"Hello," she said tentatively.

The otter chittered.

Gabria suddenly felt foolish. It was bad enough to be startled out of her wits by a small, harmless animal, but to talk to it in the middle of the night? She squatted down and shook her head. The marsh was wearing her to rags.

All at once, the otter snapped alert and, before Gabria could blink, it dove into the water and vanished.

Gabria sighed. She leaned back and stared at the stars beyond the walls of grass. The Khulinin would be watching those same stars, and she wondered if they saw them from the walls of Ab-Chakan. She had only been gone three nights and it seemed like years stretched between her and the clan. They were far beyond her reach and time was slipping fast.

A splash interrupted Gabria's thoughts and, to her surprise, the otter bounded back onto her island. It was holding something in its mouth, and it contentedly crunched through its meal before it washed its face and paws and chirped again at Gabria.

"I'm hungry, too," she muttered.

The otter glided to her side, tugged at her pants, and bounced to the edge of the grass. Gabria watched with growing curiosity. It called demandingly and came back to pull at her. Hesitant, she stood up.

The otter ran to the edge of the grass tussock.

A suspicion grew in Gabria's mind; she stepped forward. The otter squeaked happily and moved on. Gabria's suspicion changed to a certainty, and she bent over and followed the animal into the thick growth. It was difficult to see the dark-furred animal, for it seemed to blend into every shadow and shade. The going was exceedingly slow for Gabria, but the otter moved unhurriedly, keeping close in front of her as it chose its way unerringly through the treacherous paths of the marsh.

For hours, Gabria stumbled after the creature, through reeds and fens, around meres and beds of marsh grass, until she was bone weary and sick to death of the smell of stagnant water.

Still, the otter led her on, even when she was floundering in waist-deep water or struggling through grasping mud that sucked at her legs. Occasionally the animal turned around and chirped at her encouragingly before it plunged deeper into the marshes, along paths only it could see.

After a while, the water imperceptibly changed from black to dark pewter to pale gray, and the shapeless masses of night silently regained their form and hue. Gabria blearily glanced toward the east and saw the red rim of the sun ignite as it touched the edge of the sky. The otter saw it, too, and chittered at Gabria.

The girl staggered to a stop. Panting and exhausted, she held up her hand. "I'm sorry, but I've got to rest. I . . ."

Before she could say more, the otter bobbed its head, whisked into the reeds, and disappeared.

"No, wait!" Gabria yelled frantically. But the otter was gone and she was too tired to follow. She sank down on the driest patch of reed and mud she could find and put her head in her hands. She could only hope that the otter would come back. Gabria was not certain the animal was leading her to the marsh woman, but it had a definite purpose, and it was the only guide she had in this dangerous place.

Fortunately, she did not have long to wait. The sun was barely up above the horizon when the otter returned. The animal was swimming down a narrow channel, tugging at a rope floating in the water. Gabria staggered over to help. She pulled the rope and a small, slim boat floated out of the tall grass. The

craft was light, flat-bottomed, and the color of a faded reed.
The otter climbed into the boat and chattered at Gabria.

"Are you serious?" she asked, horrified. Plowing through
the mud was bad enough, but she had never been in a boat
and didn't want to try one now.

The otter squealed and patted a long pole lying on the bottom of the craft. Gabria looked aghast, but she climbed gingerly into the boat and sat down. A slow current pulled the
craft into deeper water. After a short time, when the boat
didn't show signs of immediately tipping her into the water,
Gabria relaxed a little. She stood up very carefully, grasped the
pole, and pushed it into the water. The pole hit the muddy
bottom of the channel and the boat moved forward. Gabria
grinned at the otter and pushed the pole in again. Very slowly,
they moved down the channel.

"Where to now, little one?" Gabria asked the otter.

As if in response, the animal dove off the gunnel into the
water. Its small brown head bobbed up in front of the boat.
Gabria followed in the otter's wake.

The sun was well up by that time, and the marshes glowed
green and gold in the morning light. The day grew hot. Gabria
was tired and her head was heavy with sleep, but she could not
relax. Her stomach was twisted into knots of tension and her
thoughts kept returning to the look on Athlone's face when
she had asked about the Woman of the Marsh. His reaction was
born of an ingrained fear of magic-wielders, but Gabria wondered what he would think of *her* when he knew the full truth
of her powers. She stared at the water. She wondered, too,
what her family would have thought if they had known of her
heretical talent. Would they have understood that her obsession for vengeance was leading her to a sorceress to learn the
ways of magic?

Gabria felt the tears in her eyes and forced them back.
Gabran would have understood. Her brother had loved her
unconditionally, and she knew that he would have supported
her decision to seek the Woman of the Marsh. Piers and Cantrell supported her, too. She realized now that the bard had
sent her to this woman to learn to use her natural talent, not to

subdue it. And Gabria finally decided that it was the right choice. Whatever the consequences, she wanted to learn every strength and weakness of sorcery, to find a way to destroy Medb.

The otter chittered.

Gabria started out of her thoughts and glanced ahead. A line of trees blocked her way and, as she followed the otter closer, the line became a dark, heavy wall of mangrove. The strange trees grew close together, their prop roots pushing into the stagnant water. Under their branches, the air was stuffy, and very little light forced its way through the dense foliage.

Gabria poled her boat with care through the tangled roots of the mangroves, following a twisted path only the otter could see. The trees grew close together, and open spaces of water became fewer and farther apart. The air was stifling and fetid.

At last, the otter crawled onto something solid and came to a stop. Gabria glanced up in surprise. They were at the foot of a huge framework of roots. In the center, the prop roots merged into a mangrove unlike any other. It was tremendous; its roots delved deep into the waters of the river. Its branches spread out in a vast, gloomy canopy.

The otter waved a paw at the tree and chirped.

"There?" Gabria asked in disbelief.

Reluctantly, the girl climbed out of the boat and teetered on the slippery roots. Before she could protest, the otter whisked away into the water and vanished. Gabria was left alone. She looked around. There were no insects or birds or frogs, and the gloomy swamp around her was completely silent. Gabria shivered. She would have given anything to be safe and dry in Piers's tent, instead of wet, filthy, and clinging like a snail to a slimy mangrove root in the heart of a sorceress's domain.

Gabria gathered her courage and clambered over the roots to the main trunk. The tree was incredibly wide; compared to other trees, its trunk was a massive column in a forest of sticks.

Where would a sorceress live in a thing like this? Gabria looked up into the branches, around the roots, even into the water, but there was no sign of any life, human or otherwise. The girl was beginning to think the otter had deceived her, when she saw a narrow, horizontal crack in the side of the tree. It was barely wider than a handspan and ran several lengths above her head. Gabria peered in. Although it was completely dark within the tree, she sensed it hid a cavity large enough to enter.

There was no other possibility. Gabria squeezed through the crack into pitch darkness. The air was stifling. It seemed quiet within the tree, but as Gabria's senses sharpened in the darkness, she became aware of a soft rasping and, even softer, a creaking rustle like tiny whispers. Gabria waited—for what she was not sure.

After several moments, a single shaft of red light struck down from somewhere above and illuminated the sorceress. The old woman sat on a chair, which in turn rested on a platform that hung from an unseen ceiling. She was more like a corpse than a woman, hunched and wizened and incredibly pallid. Her unblinking eyes shone red in the light. She had a beautiful, mad-looking face, and she stared down at Gabria with a triumphant sneer.

"So, you have come at last," she said, her voice harsh from disuse. "I have waited too long for a magic-bearer to find me."

"I—," Gabria started to say.

The woman cut her off. "You have come to learn. I know who you are . . . but I do not know if you are ready to pay my price."

Gabria stared up in fascination. She was both horrified and awed by the feverish power that blazed in the woman's red eyes.

The sorceress met Gabria's gaze, and her face contorted into rage. "I know what you're thinking," she cried. "You think I am only an old hag hiding in a swamp, tripping through my ancient skills and feeding on old grudges. Well, I was a powerful sorceress once, a Shape-Changer. My power brought men to their knees. Behold!"

She threw her arms wide and sang a chant in a strange tongue that reverberated to the rootlets and twigs of the great tree. Gabria pressed back against the wood. The interior began to waver and fade; the air hummed like a harp string. The woman's voice rose to a cry of triumph as a vision formed in the chamber. To Gabria's gaze, the tree was transformed to a palace where gold gleamed on mirrors, water sprang from a thousand fountains, and the walls shimmered with the silk banners of a noble house. Before Gabria stood a woman, a sorceress as she had always imagined one to be: fair yet dangerous, lovely and fell, clothed in gowns of velvet and bejeweled like a queen.

But as quickly as the vision formed, it dissipated to a thin mist and vanished in a puff. The woman, diminished to an ancient crone, sagged back in her chair with a groan of exhaustion. "My strength is almost gone," she whispered.

Gabria stared about bemused, half expecting to see the dark-haired woman still standing nearby. But the vision, whether the truth of the past or the dream of an aging hermit, was gone. The girl leaned back slowly and tried to keep her face expressionless. It was obvious the woman was a sorceress, and though she had lost the strength to wield her powers, she still had knowledge.

"It takes more wisdom than strength to use magic," Gabria said, trying to placate the old woman.

The sorceress glared at her irritably. "Foolish. What do you know of sorcery? I have watched you since the massacre of the Corin. All I saw were your paltry attempts to discourage a few overenthusiastic men."

"Discourage!" Gabria cried. "I killed a man."

"You see? Discouragement would have been better. But you bungled it. You know nothing of magic."

Gabria forced her anger back and said, "That is why I came to you."

"I take no more neophytes."

"Not even for a price?" asked Gabria after a moment's hesitation.

The woman looked down at her. "What price are you willing to pay?"

"Whatever you ask that is within my means."

"Your means. That is limited indeed." The sorceress waved her hand through the red light and her platform descended slowly to the floor of the tree chamber. Her hand, spiderlike, crept over Gabria's wrist and pulled her down to sit on the platform beside the chair. Gabria flinched at the dry, dusty touch, but she did not withdraw her hand.

"What is it you seek from sorcery, clanswoman? You know the practice is forbidden on pain of death."

Gabria could feel her blood pulse beneath the woman's grip. She knew without question that it would not avail her to hide the truth. "I seek vengeance for the murder of my father, my brothers, and my clan."

"Ah, yes. Is that your only reason?" Her eyes pierced Gabria's like needles, dissecting every layer of thought. "Vengeance is a dangerous motive for sorcery; it can warp your will and turn on you like a snake." The woman turned her nose up and her eyes slid sideways to watch the girl. "But it can also precipitate one's learning." She paused. "This Medb you wish to destroy, he has grown powerful of late and will require much cunning and will to overcome."

"He is also overconfident. He thinks he is the only sorcerer in the clans."

The woman nodded in agreement. She had studied Gabria for some time and was pleased with what she saw. "At the moment, he is. But the man is a savage. It is because of sorcerers like him that the people rose up against us and purged magic from the plains. Now, only I remember the bright days of grandeur and wisdom, when magic was a glory and its wielders were worshiped with honor." Her voice began to rise in fury. "But, now . . . Now, I hide my power from the eyes of men in the reek and mire of this foul swamp."

The woman's face twisted with rage, and her words screeched in her throat. Suddenly she began to laugh—a rude, maniacal sound that terrified Gabria. "A just punishment he shall have for doing this to me. We will topple this self-satisfied malefactor into the muck."

Gabria straightened and asked breathlessly, "You will help me?"

"Did I not just say that?"

The girl nodded, uncertain whether she was pleased or frightened. "Thank you."

"Do not thank me yet." She released Gabria's hand and sat back, her rage still embedded in her ancient face. She studied the girl for a moment and a sharp gleam, like a hungry rat, lurked in the sorceress's red eyes. Oh, yes, she would teach the girl the secrets of using magic. She would give Gabria enough knowledge to defeat that upstart, Medb. Then, if all went well, the girl would pay the price of her training. The Woman of the Marsh smiled, a slow, wicked twist of her lips, and cackled with anticipation.

16

thlone stood on the graying walls of the river gate and watched the exiles' guard fires burning like a fiery noose in the field before the fortress. In the gathering gloom, he could barely see the marauders clustered around their fires. The exiles thought they had little to fear. The trapped clans would not waste the time or the men to chase down an enemy that would scatter and flee at the first sign of strength.

It tested Athlone's tolerance to see the outcasts taunt and posture beyond arrow range, but he could do nothing about them. Savaric had ordered no shots fired or sorties made—yet. Let the exiles think the four clans were cowering in the depths of the defile.

Since the arrival of the Dangari that morning, Savaric and the other chiefs had made plans to bring the four clans out of the defile to the fortress under cover of night. One of Jorlan's men had found a hidden stairway leading from a storage room in the back of the fortress, down the back of the ridge, and into the gorge behind the river wall.

The stairs made it easy for Savaric and the others to slip down to the defile, but the way was too narrow and steep for a large group with pack animals. The clans could only enter the fortress by the front gates. However, a move like that was too dangerous during the day, for the exile band could wreak havoc on the women, the children, and the wagons of supplies. At night, the clans could slip into the stronghold in relative safety. Particularly if the marauders were busy elsewhere.

Athlone grinned to himself. He would not have to wai

much longer. The wer-tain sensed someone come up beside him, and he turned to see Koshyn lean against the parapet.

The young chieftain's face was unreadable in the deepening twilight, and his tattoos were almost invisible. "For men who are dead to our eyes, they are making a nuisance of themselves."

Athlone made a sound deep in his throat. He shifted restlessly. "They think we can only sit here on our pretty wall and show our teeth."

Koshyn glanced over his shoulder and studied the fading light in the west. "Let them be ignorant a little while longer. It will be dark soon, and we'll be able to ride." He turned around and stared up at the black, hulking mass of Ab-Chakan. The walls and towers of the old fortress rose above them in a massive silence, its stones hiding secrets and echoing with memories that were beyond the knowledge of the clansmen.

"I feel like a mouse scurrying around some unholy monolith," Koshyn said softly, as if afraid the stones would hear. "What are we doing here?"

Athlone's strong face twisted in a grimace. He, too, felt the weight of the old walls. "Trying to survive."

"In an inhospitable place that was never meant for us. We aren't used to stone beneath our feet and walls before our eyes. We fight with muscle, bone, and steel." He gestured to the fortress. "Not with crumbling, old masonry."

"Would you prefer to face Medb's fury on the plains below? It would be a glorious way to die."

The Dangari grinned and shook his head. "And fruitless. No, Athlone, I am not stupid—only afraid."

Athlone lifted his gaze to the west, half-hoping to see a Hunnuli mare galloping out of the night. But only the wind rode the grass; only the muted hooves of the horses waiting in the defile echoed in the night. "We all are," he muttered.

Abruptly Koshyn pushed himself away from the parapet and slapped the sword at his hip. "We are too gloomy, Wertain. While there are weapons at hand and an enemy to fight, let us ride as warriors are meant to."

Athlone smiled grimly. "You're right, my friend. We will be in paradise before this fortress falls. Come, we'll show the exiles our teeth."

They linked arms and strode down the stone steps to the gate, where Savaric and a large group of mounted warriors were waiting for full darkness. Behind the riders, in the depths of the gorge, stood the massed ranks of the four clans. The men, carrying packs on their backs, looked uncomfortable and edgy. The women and children stood in a large group in the center of the ranks, their arms full of bundles and their eyes downcast to hide their fear. Loaded pack animals, oxen and cattle that could be eaten later, waited patiently among the lines. Not a torch flickered or a fire burned. It was almost totally dark in the defile. Athlone could feel the anxiety of every person about him.

A shiver charged the wer-tain's nerves like the touch of a ghost. He had seen Ab-Chakan in the daylight and even then its empty chambers and ancient silences had unsettled him. He knew what his people were feeling now as they waited to enter the fortress in the depths of the night.

Another group of warriors taken from all four clans stood along the wall, watching Savaric. They were the volunteers who would remain behind to guard the river wall and the herds that had been driven deep into the defile. Athlone frowned. There were so pitifully few men to guard the crumbling, old wall. There was little choice, however; the remainder of the fighting men, nearly three thousand, were needed to protect the fortress.

The light of the sunset had died and night was upon the clans. The roar of the river seemed unnaturally loud in the quiet, crowded gorge. Despite the breeze from the rushing water, the air was sluggish and heavy with a damp chill.

Athlone pulled his cloak tighter around his shoulders as he and Koshyn went to greet the mounted warriors. Boreas came to join the wer-tain. In the darkness, the black horse was almost invisible. Only his eyes, glowing like moons behind a thin cloud, and his white mark of lightning could be seen. Eagerly he snorted and butted his nose on Athlone's chest. The wer-tain vaulted to his back.

Savaric came to the Hunnuli's side and looked up at his son.

The chief's hood was drawn over his nose, hiding his sharp features, but Athlone's gaze reached through the darkness to touch his father's in a wordless moment of understanding and sadness. In a passing breath, their thoughts and concerns became one and each gave to the other the strength that they would need for the coming days. Savaric nodded once. He squeezed his son's knee, joined his hearthguard, and in a low voice gave the warriors his last-minute instructions.

"Ride safely, Athlone," Jorlan said, coming up beside the Hunnuli.

Athlone greeted the other man. "I'll see you soon in the fortress."

"Hmmm," said the second wer-tain. "I can hardly wait to hole up in that monstrosity of stone."

"Think of the pleasure Lord Medb will have when he fully realizes the size of the nut we are giving him to crack. He will be quite surprised."

Jorlan's face broke into a malicious grin. "That's an image worth savoring."

"Athlone," Savaric called. "It's time."

The chieftain's command was passed down the lines of clansmen, and the tension immediately intensified in the defile. The ranks of men shifted forward in a press of armor, swords, and packs; the women drew closer together. At the end of the lines, Sha Umar and the rearguard waited impatiently to go.

Jorlan saluted Athlone as the mounted men moved to the river wall. Koshyn joined Athlone and the gate was eased open.

"Remember," Savaric whispered loudly, "we need time!"

On soundless hooves, Boreas passed out of the defile, and the company of riders fell in behind him. All were mounted on black or dark brown horses, and in the thick night, Athlone doubted the marauders would see them until they were on top of the fires. He urged Boreas forward until they reached the foot of the ridge beneath Ab-Chakan, where the river curved south. In the defile, the main ranks of the clans waited breathlessly, tight with tension, with only a long walk to a cold, dark ruin before them. But Athlone and the warriors with him could ride like clansmen were born to: with horns blowing, swords in their hands, and an enemy to fight face to face.

Athlone could wait no longer. An excitement and fury roared within him that was fired by days of frustration and running. He drew his sword. Koshyn caught his feeling and cried to the horn bearer with them. "Now, let them hear the song of the hunt."

The horn burst in the quiet night like a thunderclap. It rebounded through the hills, ringing clear with the victory of a quarry sighted and the joy of the coming kill. Before the last note left the horn, Boreas reared and neighed a challenge that blended with the horn's music and forged a song of deadly peril. In unison, the other men drew their weapons with a shout and spurred their eager mounts into a gallop toward the fires.

The exiles were taken by surprise. As the riders swept down on them, the outcasts broke out of their stunned lethargy and frantically ran for their horses. The Hunnuli burst among the largest group. Two men fell to Athlone's sword and one to Boreas's hooves. The rest scattered in all directions, the clansmen on their heels.

A few exiles were caught by the riders and immediately put to death. The remainder fled to the sanctuary of the rough hills, where they could easily lose their pursuers. Thus it was that the marauders did not see the files of heavily laden people and animals toil up the road to Ab-Chakan, nor did they hear the thud as the massive gates were closed.

At dawn, the horn bearer again sounded his instrument to welcome the sun and to gather the riders. Exhausted, their fury spent, the warriors rode back, pleased with their labors. They had suffered only a few minor wounds while nine of the exiles had been killed. The troop rode to the gates of the fortress, and the men who greeted them and took their lathered horses were relieved to have the riders back. The big bronze gates closed behind them with a thud of finality.

It was not long before the exiles edged back to their cold fires and took up their watch of the fortress.

As soon as it was light and the women were settled in the palace and surrounding houses, guards were placed in the tow-

ers to watch the plains for signs of Medb's army, and the chiefs
and their men set out to explore every cranny of the stronghold. The men spent all morning poking and digging and
opening things that had not been opened in generations. By
the time they returned to the palace's hall to confer, even
Koshyn was admiring the handiwork of the men of old and the
most reluctant clansman was realizing the capabilities of the
fortification.

The outer walls and the towers were still in very good condition. The inner walls were crumbling but defensible, and
many of the stone buildings in the fortress's center were sturdy
enough to shelter the clanspeople and the livestock. The cis-
terns, buried deep in the rock, were full, since the water was
constantly refreshed by seasonal rains.

As soon as the chiefs had planned their defense of the
stronghold, everyone set to work to prepare the old fortress for
what it had not seen in centuries: war. The walls were patched,
the trash and rubble were cleared out of the space between the
two walls, and the gate was secured with logs and chains. Wer-
tains and children alike began to grow confident in their new
refuge. It would take more than Medb and a few clans to rout
them out of this hill of stone.

The clanspeople were still working desperately when a horn
blew wildly from one of the towers. The people looked up at
the sinking sun in surprise. It was too early for the sunset horn.
Then the realization dawned on them all, and the chiefs came
running to the wall from every part of the fortress. The men
close by the main wall crowded up onto the parapet.

There in the valley, the exiles were galloping their horses
about and the vanguard of the sorcerer's army was riding up
the old road.

As planned, horns blew from all the towers and five
banners—one gold, one blue, one maroon, one orange, and
one dark red—were unfurled above the main gate.

Savaric's hands gripped the stone. "Medb is here," he called
to the people crowded into the bailey below him. "You all
know your duties."

Silently, the warriors dispersed to seek their weapons and

take their places along the battlements. Athlone ran up the stone steps to join the chiefs, and without a word, Lord Ryne pointed down to the valley.

Once again Medb timed his arrival to create the greatest impression. The sun was already behind the crown of the mountains when the sorcerer's army arrived at the Defile of Tor Wrath and the valley was sinking into twilight. A sharp wind blew the grass flat and swirled about the foot of Ab-Chakan.

Heralded by the wind and cloaked by the approaching night, the sorcerer's vanguard crossed the bridge and stopped at the foot of the hill just below the fortress. They waited in ominous silence.

Behind them, the main army marched to the command of drums. They came endlessly, countless numbers obscured by the dim twilight that hid their true form. They came until the valley was filled and the army spread out along the mountain flanks. There were no torches or lamps or voices or neighs of horses to break the monotony of the terrifying black flood. There was only the sound of the drums and the remorseless tread of feet.

The clansmen watched the coming host in dismay and disbelief. Never had they imagined anything like this. The force that marched relentlessly toward the defile was no longer Wylfling or Geldring or Amnok or foreigner lured by gold. It had become a faceless, mindless mass driven by the single will of one evil man.

The wind eased and all movement died in the valley. The night-shrouded army gathered its breath and waited for its master's signal. But the sorcerer held them firm. He let the troops wait, allowing them to see their goal and the clansmen to see their doom. In the fortress above, Savaric and the clans looked on with dread. Still Medb held back his army. The tension burned until it became almost unendurable.

Then a lone horseman rode out of the vanguard and up to the gates of the fortress. He was cloaked in brown and a helm hid his face, but nothing could hide the snide, contemptuous tone of his voice.

"Khulinin, Dangari, Bahedin, and Jehanan. The rabble of

the clans." He snorted rudely. "My master has decided to be merciful to you this once. You have seen the invincibility of his arcane power and now you see the might of his host. Look upon this army. Weigh your advantages. You will not survive long if you choose to oppose Lord Medb. There are still other choices: surrender to him and he will be lenient."

Savaric struggled to find his voice. Furiously, he shoved his hands over the edge of the stone wall and gripped it tightly for support. "Branth, I see you have lost your cloak." His voice was harsh with derision.

The Geldring made a broad sweep with his arm to indicate the army behind him. "Brown is such a strong color, fertile with opportunities."

"So is dung, but I wouldn't trade my clan for it. How do the Geldring feel about forsaking the green?"

Branth's words were clipped with anger. "My clan obeys."

"*Your* clan!" Savaric forced a rude laugh. "No longer, Branth. Your clan is Medb's and it is he they obey. The Geldring no longer exist. Go away from here, traitor."

Branth sneered. Behind him, in the valley, the army shifted restlessly. "Bravely spoken, chieftain. Soon, you, too, will see the wisdom of wearing brown. Only do not take long to decide. The army has already smelled blood." With a harsh cry, Branth spurred his horse back down the road.

Medb, in his enclosed wagon, nodded to himself in satisfaction. He forced his restive army back, away from the fortress. Anticipation would put a keen edge on the fear he had honed in the stronghold; when at last he released the attack, the clansmen would not survive for long.

Their fates were sealed as surely as Medb's victory was assured. The Khulinin and the others would cease to exist; their chieftains would soon be destroyed. Even if Savaric and his allies did surrender, Medb certainly did not plan to be lenient.

* * * * *

The first attack came before dawn, in the cold hours when reactions are slowest and muscles are chilled. It was only a probe to test the strength of the defenders and the clansmen easily beat back the attack. Still, the men found it was a relief to fight. After the long, interminable hours of waiting through the night, the screaming horde of mercenaries that swarmed up the road to the wall was a blessing. The chiefs knew it was only a test, and they quickly repaired their defenses to meet the next onslaught.

This time they had a long wait. After the mercenaries fell back beyond the river, the army's encampment was quiet for a few hours. Savaric posted guards and allowed the rest of the defenders to stand down, but few of the warriors left the parapets. They watched and waited to see what Medb was going to do next.

Around noon, the activity in the huge camp suddenly increased. Wagons were seen moving to the hills and returning with stacks of cut logs. Hundreds of men clustered together and appeared to be working on several large things the clansmen could not identify. The noises of wood being cut and hammered sounded long after dark.

In the fortress, Savaric and the clansmen continued their vigilance through another long, unbearable night.

At dawn the next day, the labors of Medb's army became clear. Three large objects were wheeled out of the encampment, across the old bridge, and set up at the base of the hill, out of arrow range but as close to Ab-Chakan as possible. The clansmen were in position on the fortress walls, and those in the front ranks watched curiously as the strange wooden devices were prepared.

"What are those?" Lord Ryne asked, voicing everyone's curiosity.

Savaric called to one of his men. "Bring Cantrell here."

The bard was quickly brought and carefully escorted up the stone steps to where the chiefs were standing on the parapet. "I hear Medb has been busy," Cantrell said after his greeting.

"There are three wooden things just below the fortress," Savaric answered. "They're heavy, wheeled platforms with long poles on top. The poles are attached at one end of the platform and have what looks like large bowls fastened to the other end."

"Look at that," Sha Umar added. "The men put a rock in that one device and they're pulling down on one end."

Cantrell's face went grim. "Catapults."

As if in response to his word, the device below snapped loose and a large rock sailed up and crashed into the wall just below the parapet. The defenders instinctively ducked.

"Good gods!" Savaric exclaimed. The men peered over the walls just as another rock was flung at the fortress. The missile hit the bronze gates with a thundering boom. The clansmen were relieved to see there was no damage to the wall or the gate, but as the morning passed, the men on the catapults found their range and the heavy stones began to rain down within the front walls of the fortress. Several clansmen were killed when a huge rock landed in their midst, and the old parapet sustained some damage. The other men were thrown into confusion as the boulders continued to crash down around them.

Then, just before noon, Athlone glanced over the wall and saw the army forming across the river. "Here they come!" he shouted. A horn bearer in the tower by the gate blew the signal to warn the defenders along the walls.

In the valley below, men rushed forward and set up make-shift bridges over the Isin River, and the sorcerer's army launched its full fury at Ab-Chakan. Under the cover of a deluge of missiles and arrows, the first ranks of soldiers with ropes and ladders charged up the road and the sides of the hill to the front walls. All the while, the army's drums pounded relentlessly and a roar of fury echoed through the fortress.

In the first frantic minutes, Athlone was too busy to appreciate the strategic advantages of his position, but as his men fought off the attackers, it dawned on him that the old stronghold was easy to defend. Not only did the swift river prevent a large attack force from crossing all at once, but the ridge's steep slopes slowed down the advance of the enemy and left them open to the deadly fire from the battlements. The clansmen cheered when the first wave fell back, and a glimmer of hope returned to their hearts.

The second wave came, more enraged than the first, and nearly reached the top of the walls before they were repulsed. Attack after attack was thrown at the walls and each was pushed back, foot by bitter foot, until the ground was heavy with dead and wounded, and the surviving defenders were shaking with exhaustion.

It doesn't matter, Athlone thought grimly as he threw away his empty quiver, how easy it is to hold this fortress. Medb has the greater numbers and the advantage of time. Eventually the fortress will collapse from the lack of men to defend it.

In mocking reply to Athlone's thoughts, the enemy's horns bayed again and a new attack stormed to the wall. This time the onslaught scaled the defenses. The clansmen drew their swords and daggers and fought hand to hand as the fighting swayed frantically over the battlements. Blood stained the old rock, and yells and screams of fury echoed around the towers. Time and again Savaric rallied the men and fought off the wild-eyed attackers from the parapet, only to face more of them with fewer men at his side. Desperately, he brought the men on the back walls around to the front and prayed the river wall and its defenders were enough to protect Ab-Chakan's back.

The clansmen lost all sense of time. The battle raged through the afternoon in a seemingly endless cycle of attacks and repulses. Sha Umar went down with an arrow in his shoulder. Jorlan was slain defending Savaric's side. The catapults continued to hurl missiles over the wall and at the gate, damaging the fortress and distracting the defenders. All the while, the drums pounded incessantly in the valley.

Then, without warning, the enemy withdrew. They fell back to their encampment and an eerie silence fell over the valley. In the tower by the gate, the horn bearer sounded the call for sunset.

The clansmen looked around in surprise as darkness settled down around them. They had won the day. But as the chiefs began to count their dead and wounded, they wondered if they would be so fortunate tomorrow.

Across the valley, in Medb's tent, the sorcerer's rage burned hot. His powers had doubled since leaving the Tir Samod, and he had healed his crippled legs. However, there were no spells to bolster his energy and he was near collapse from sustaining his army's rage during the long battle. He had suffered heavy losses. Finally, Medb realized he had underestimated Savaric. The four clans were backed into a stone burrow from which only something unexpected could flush them. There was nothing left to do but hold off further attacks until new plans could be made.

The sorcerer allowed his army to return to its encampment, and he went into seclusion to rest and ponder. Ab-Chakan would fall if he had to crumble it with his bare hands.

* * * * *

Shortly after midnight, Athlone mounted Boreas and joined a small troop of volunteer riders waiting by the front gate. Several men carried torches and bags of oil.

Savaric was waiting for Athlone and came to stand beside the big Hunnuli. The chief's face was deeply worried. "I don't like this, Athlone," he said forcefully. "It would be better to forget those catapults. They're too heavily guarded."

The wer-tain's eyes met his father's and he nodded. "I know. But those machines are wreaking havoc on us. Besides, it would do the clans some good to see those things burn."

"But if you get trapped outside the gates, we might not be able to help you."

"It's not too far, Father," Athlone replied. "We'll burn those things and get back as fast as we can."

Savaric sighed. He hated the danger his son was riding into, but he, too, wanted those catapults destroyed. Finally, he nodded reluctantly.

The wer-tain saluted him. Then, without warning or reason, a deadly chill touched Athlone's mind and a shade seemed to pass over his father's face. Alarmed, Athlone sat back on Boreas and rubbed his hand over his chin. The feeling of malaise was gone as quickly as it came, leaving in its place a dull, aching hollow and a newly planted seed of fear. He shook his head slightly and wondered what was wrong.

Savaric did not seem to notice. He bid farewell to his son and stood back out of the way. The bronze gates were opened.

The first inkling of disaster came with a flare of torches at the fortress gates, then a storm of horses' hooves thundered down the road and swept with gale force into the midst of the guard around the catapults. Led by a rider on a flame-eyed Hunnuli stallion, the horsemen surged into the stunned enemy. The riders' weapons ran red with blood, and their eyes gleamed in the joy of battle.

While Athlone and his men pushed the enemy back, the men with the torches rode to the catapults. They doused the devices with oil and threw their torches onto the wooden platforms. The catapults burst into flames and the riders began their retreat.

But Lord Branth was expecting a possible attack on the siege weapons, so he was waiting with his men in the encampment. At the first sign of attack, he charged across the bridge to meet Athlone's men, before the riders could escape.

The clansmen on the walls of the fortress watched in horror as Athlone and his riders were surrounded and the fighting grew bitter. Savaric shouted frantically for more warriors to ride out and rescue the men, but he knew that it was already too late.

Inexorably, the Wylfling and Geldring pulled down the riders. Athlone and his men were forced into a tighter and tighter circle. They fought back ferociously, anxious now only to survive.

Then, without warning, a spear was hurled over the warriors' heads into Boreas's chest. The great Hunnuli bellowed in pain and fury. He reared and his hooves slashed the air. He tried to leap over the fighters and carry his rider to safety, but the spear was buried too deep. The stallion's heart burst, and his ebony body crashed to the earth.

Athlone felt his friend's dying agony in every muscle of his body; his mind reeled in shock. He held on blindly when Boreas reared and sprang, but as the Hunnuli fell, he was too overwhelmed to jump off. The horse's heavy body collapsed beneath him. Athlone saw the ground rushing toward him just as unconsciousness dimmed his searing grief.

A triumphant shout roared from the attackers. They pressed forward and quickly slew the last surviving Khulinin who tried in vain to defend Athlone's body. Lord Branth shoved his way through the crowd to the corpse of the Hunnuli. He gleefully grabbed Athlone's helm, wrenched it off, and raised his sword to cut off the wer-tain's head.

"Hold!" The command stilled the chief's arm. Furiously he looked up and saw Lord Medb standing by the bridge, his face illuminated by the burning catapults. A second spear was in his hand. Branth quaked.

"I want him alive," Medb said. "I have a use for the son of the mighty Savaric."

On the wall of the fortress, Savaric watched as his son and the big Hunnuli fell. He saw the enemy swarm over their bodies and he saw Lord Medb standing straight and strong on the river's bridge. The chief's eyes closed. Slowly his body sagged against the stone wall and he gave in to his grief and despair.

17

abria lost track of time. The hours she spent with the Woman of the Marsh seemed to spring from an eternal wellhead and flow endlessly beyond her memory. The girl and the sorceress had descended to a large, round chamber that lay beneath the tree. They sat together around a small wooden table, the woman hunched over her words and gestures like a jealous priestess and the girl watching with a pale face and a fascinated light in her eyes. Slowly, as the uncounted hours passed and the rasping voice muttered unceasingly in her ear, Gabria began to understand the depths of her power.

"Will is at the center of sorcery," the woman said time and again. "You have no time to learn the complexities, the difficult spells or gestures that govern the proper use of magic, so beware. You are attempting to impose your will on the fabric of our world. Magic is a natural force that is in everything: every creature, stone, or plant. When you alter that force, with even the smallest spell, you must be strong enough to control the effect and the consequences."

Gabria stared into the sorceress's remorseless black eyes and shivered.

The woman's dark gaze fastened on her. "Yes! Be afraid. Sorcery is not a game for half-wits or dabblers. It is a deadly serious art. As a magic-wielder, you must use your power wisely or it will destroy you. The gods are not free with the gift and they begrudge any careless use of it."

"But can anyone use this magic?" Gabria asked.

"Of course not," the woman said irritably. "People are born

with the ability. That was the reason for the downfall of the sorcerers so long ago. A few magic-wielders abused their powers and those people without the talent grew jealous and resentful." The woman coughed and shifted in her seat. "But that time is past. As for you, your potential for sorcery is . . . good. Your will to survive is a facet of your strength. And that strength of will is the most essential trait of a magic-wielder."

Gabria nodded. "I understand."

The sorceress's face twisted into a mass of wrinkles. "You understand nothing! You have no conception of what it is to be a sorceress. You are a child. Do you know yourself at all? You must know every measure and degree of your own soul or you will not recognize when your sorcery has begun to leech strength from your being."

The woman sighed and leaned back in her chair. "Not that it matters. You will not have the time to learn, if you wish to defeat that worm-ridden Wylfling any time soon."

"Then what am I supposed to do?" Gabria shouted in frustration. "If I cannot learn my own abilities, how in Amara's name am I supposed to control this power?" Gabria discovered that she was shaking. She clamped her hands together and stared at the table.

The woman laughed, a cackle edged with arrogance. "You do not need superhuman knowledge or control for this task, only desire and concentration. The critical ingredient in any spell, no matter how simple, complex, or bizarre, is the will and strength of the wielder. Those, at least, you have plenty of. I am merely warning you, should you overextend yourself— particularly in an arcane duel." She paused and her eyes lit with a strange, greedy light. "I do want you to succeed."

The girl was puzzled by the odd look in the old sorceress's face, but before she could think about it, the woman hurried on.

"You need to know what you have become a part of, so listen." She jabbed her finger at Gabria. "The other trait you need for spells is imagination. Not all spells are rigidly defined. It is often better to create your own. On this we will proceed."

The old woman stood up and fetched a stub of a candle. She set it down in front of Gabria. "The reason you need to use spells is to formulate your intent. The words elucidate the purpose in your mind and help you focus your power on the magic.

"When you used the Trymian Force before, it came as an unconscious reaction to your will to survive, and so it was very weak and uncontrolled. But if you had used a spell, you could have changed the intensity of the force and used it at will."

"But how do I learn these spells?" Gabria asked.

"Sorcerers experimented with spells for years. They worked out many spells that were formulated for the greatest clarity and efficiency. But you do not always need to use them. Magic spells can be worded any way you wish." The woman suddenly snapped a foreign word and the candle in front of Gabria popped into flame. The girl started back, her eyes wide with surprise.

The sorceress snuffed out the flame. "You try. Concentrate on your purpose and speak a command."

Gabria gazed at the candle. She tried to picture a flame in her mind, then she said, "Light, candle."

A tiny flame puffed and died out.

"Concentrate!" the sorceress ordered. "Focus your will on that candle."

The girl tried again. She closed her eyes and demanded, "Light, candle." This time the candle's wick flickered once and lit in a gentle, yellow flame. Gabria opened her eyes and smiled.

"Good," stated the sorceress. "You are beginning to understand. You must know *exactly* what you are trying to do or the magic will go awry. That is why we use spells." She snapped another strange word and the candle's flame went out. "Now," the woman continued. "It is possible to do almost anything you desire with magic. But it is vital to know exactly what you want to do before you begin."

Gabria nodded, fascinated by the old woman's teaching. "What are some things you cannot do with magic?"

"You cannot create something out of empty space. You have to use something that is already there. See." With a brief word, the sorceress changed the candle to an apple. "You can alter form or change an appearance, but you cannot create."

"But what about the Trymian Force?"

"The Trymian Force, like a protective shield or any kind of visible force, is formed from the magic within you. That is why it is important to know your limits; you must not weaken yourself so much that you cannot control your spells. Remember that if you duel Medb."

The old sorceress brought other small items to the table and had Gabria practice basic spells: changing the object's form and altering its image, even moving it around the chamber.

As Gabria's confidence grew, her skill developed in leaps and bounds. She learned how to form the intent of a spell into the words that would trigger the magic and how to dismantle a spell before it went awry.

The sorceress, surprised by Gabria's rapid progress, taught her other spells of healing and shape-changing, and the rituals for the arcane duels. She also taught the girl the best spells to control the Trymian Force, call it at will, and most important, to defend herself against it with protective shields.

At last, the old woman nodded in satisfaction, and her wrinkled face creased in a smile. "You have learned all that I can teach you. Now you must teach yourself. Practice what I have told you, learn your limits and your strengths. Remember the dangers if you lose control of the magic." She went to an old battered chest by the wall, pulled out a small silk bag, and brought it to Gabria. "Go back to the clans. When you are ready, open this bag. Inside is the last item you need to become a full sorceress. The item will help intensify your powers and mark you as a true magic-wielder."

The old sorceress sank into her chair and was silent. Gabria leaned back feeling numb. The girl looked about her, amazed, for the time with the sorceress seemed so unreal. She wondered how long they had been in the chamber.

Gabria began to stand up, but immediately her exhaustion caught up with her. Her body sagged, and she caught the chair to keep from falling. She took a weak step toward the stairs that led up to the entrance. What day was it? How long had she been there?

"I must go," she mumbled.

The sorceress raised her hand and a spell caught the girl before she fell. Gently, she laid Gabria down on the floor. The girl was already asleep. For a moment, the woman stared down at her with glee in her heart. Never had she known an ability so strong. This girl had strength, will, and talent, and if she did not lose her wits, she had a good chance of defeating Medb. The old woman rubbed her hands together and cackled with pleasure. Once Medb was dead, Gabria could return to the marsh and pay her price, a price the girl did not need to know about. The sorceress's hands moved over the girl and she muttered a spell, one of the few complex incantations she still remembered.

She was stunned when the spell failed. She knew that her powers were weak, but the girl's natural defenses were not that strong. There had to be something else. The woman quickly searched Gabria's clothes until she found the small stone ward. Her eyes flew wide when she recognized it, for she thought all those wards had been destroyed. She shrugged, pocketed it, and recreated the spell; this time it worked perfectly. Chuckling to herself, she went to rest. It had taken the last remnants of her strength to force the spell on the girl, but it would ensure the payment was made if Gabria had to crawl from the edge of the grave to deliver it.

*   *   *   *   *

Gabria came awake and sat up in confusion. She was lying on a pallet in the chamber beneath the mangrove and there was no sign of the sorceress. Daylight glimmered through the hatch that led up to the tree trunk.

"Oh, gods," she whispered. "What day is it?" She jumped up in frantic haste and gathered her belongings. Her cloak and food bag were lying nearby, already replenished, and her water bag was full.

Something scratched at the wood outside, and the otter peered down through the hatch. It chirped when it saw Gabria was already awake.

Gabria flung her cloak over her shoulders. "I have to go," she muttered to herself. "I have been here too long." She climbed the steps, crawled through the hatch into the tree trunk, and peered through the crack in the tree. She remembered that it had been sunny when she arrived at the mangrove, and now the rain was falling in sheets and the clouds were low and heavy above the trees.

Gabria grasped her bag and followed the otter down the tangled roots to the small boat that bobbed on the tugging tide. The wind whirled past her head and yanked at her cloak, but she ignored it just as she ignored the rain. Only one thought prayed on her mind: How long had she been gone?

The journey back through the marshes was long and tedious. Gabria poled the boat with quiet desperation while the otter led her through the labyrinth of reeds and channels. Unerringly the animal found the river's main current and followed it laboriously upstream. The rain fell incessantly; the clouds moved sluggishly inland, pushing the tide ahead.

Fortunately, the otter had taken a shorter route through the marshes to find solid ground. Gabria had approached the marshes from the north, where the delta encroached farther inland. By following one of the main channels west, the otter cut off many miles of their journey.

A few hours after sunset, the rain stopped, and, for the first time, Gabria saw an end to the rushes and marsh grass. The river had swung away from her to the north in a great loop that eventually turned west again. Not far from Gabria, the marshes ended abruptly in a bold scarp of arid hills that were the last bastion before the great plains.

Gabria poled the boat ashore near the fringes of the reeds. The channels had dried to shallow pools and stagnant meres, making it difficult to travel by boat. The girl tugged the craft up onto the bank and stood gratefully on solid ground.

The otter glided to her feet and sat up, its round eyes glistening. It chirped and waved a paw at her. Then, with a flick of its tail, it dove into the water and was gone.

"Wait!" Gabria lunged after it, but the otter had vanished. The girl slid to a stop before she fell in the water and looked dolefully at the marsh. She had hoped the sorceress's guide would lead her back to Nara.

Water dripped into Gabria's eyes as she scanned the marshes to find her bearings. Although the rain had stopped, the impenetrably inky clouds were a solid, sinking roof. She was cold, wet, and miserable. Gabria knew vaguely where she was, for the hills that began near her feet stopped the southern encroachment of the delta. However, she had to go north. Nara waited for her on the northern edge of the marshes; now, between them, lay the silt-laden Goldrine River.

Gabria started walking. It was very difficult going; since she could only see a few paces in front of her, she could not choose the best path through the heavy brush and boggy ground. Several times, Gabria tripped over unseen roots or fell into a sink where the mud stank and the water was slimy. She struggled on for hours until her muscles were limp and her nostrils were deadened to the rank smells.

Finally Gabria stopped. It was still quite dark and she bleakly looked around and admitted to herself that she was totally lost. She had no idea which way to go and precious time was being wasted. She needed Nara.

The Hunnuli had told her once to whistle if help was needed. Gabria knew that it was impossible for the mare to hear her, and yet, she thought that, maybe if she used her new powers, she could reach the mare with her need. A slim chance at best. Gabria decided to try it. There was nothing to lose by whistling in the dark. She closed her mind to everything but Nara, inhaled deeply, and whistled, bending her will to the mare with all the urgency she could muster.

The night was silent for a long moment, then, astonishingly, Gabria heard a horse neigh, as if from many miles away. She whistled a second time and hoped desperately she had not heard amiss. The call came again, joyfully and much closer this time.

"Nara!" she shouted. The Hunnuli was coming. Gabria turned to face the direction from which she heard the sound of hoofbeats, and the giant black horse burst out of the darkness. The mare skidded to a halt in front of the girl and reared, her head thrown back and her mane flying.

Gabria gasped, "Nara."

The mare settled down and her breath steamed in a snort. *Truly you have learned your art well.*

The girl's mind whirled in happiness, confusion, and wonder. "How did you come so fast?" she blurted.

The sorceress sent a message to tell me to come south, but your call led me here.

"How long have I been gone?"

The sun has set four times since we parted.

Gabria mentally counted the days. That did not seem right. If Nara was correct, she had only spent two days with the marsh woman. It seemed like years. She leaned gratefully against Nara's warm shoulders and ran her hand down the livid white streak.

"Let's go home," Gabria said.

With the girl on her back, Nara trotted westward through the failing edges of the marsh, toward the hills where the ground was firmer for a horse's hooves. Once on the dry slopes, she ran with the speed of the wind. Behind them, an orange glow fired the east as the clouds broke before the rising sun.

* * * * *

Gabria and Nara came to Ab-Chakan before sunset, riding in from the south along the flanks of the foothills, in the shelter of the trees. Nara eased silently through the undergrowth to the edge of the broad valley. In the thickening darkness they saw the fires and torches of Medb's army. Gabria's heart sank. She had seen the Wylfling werod in full array, but even the tales of added forces had not prepared her for the vast fields of tents, wagons, horses, and piles of supplies she saw. She would never make it through that camp to the fortress. Medb's forces were spread out in a semicircle at least a half-mile wide. Not even a Hunnuli could bolt through those ranks alone.

Gabria dropped her head. She was too late. It had not occurred to her that she might not be able to reach the Khulinin, and now that possibility was all too real.

Suddenly a horn sounded on the walls of the fortress. Clear and proud, its notes soared over the valley. Gabria stared at the fortress with pride and she felt her crumbling will revive. Behind those alien walls of stone, the four clans were still adhering to tradition with the horn call to sunset. She noticed angrily that the sorcerer's army had not bothered to reply. They had sunk so deeply into conquest that they had abandoned the traditions of the clans.

She was leaning over to say something to Nara when the mare's ears swiveled back and her nose turned to catch the breeze.

"What is it?" Gabria whispered. Her hand crept to her dagger. Without her other weapons, she felt ill at ease, and she wished that she had brought her sword.

Men are behind us. The whip carriers. They are seeking us.

Gabria drew her dagger and hid it in a fold of her cloak. If the Oathbreakers were seeking her, they would find her. When they did, no weapon—save, perhaps Nara—would save her if the men of Krath wanted her dead. But the cold, hard feel of the knife under her hand steadied Gabria as she waited quietly for the men to come.

Gabria wondered why the Oathbreakers were trailing Nara. The last she had heard, the cult was besieged in their towers by Medb's forces, and no man among them would desert his post. She shuddered. If the Citadel of Krath had fallen, Medb would have all the arcane tomes, manuscripts, spells, and artifacts in his grasp. He would be able to bring the clans to their knees in a matter of days.

Just then, out of the twilight, a shrouded figure on a dark horse rode into the trees. The figure raised his hand in a sign of peace as ten other riders rode up behind him. The man threw back his hood, revealing his thin, cruel face. He nodded and said, "Hail, Corin, and well met."

Gabria inhaled sharply. It was Savaric's brother, Seth. She stared at the bloodied gash on his forehead and at the weary, blood-stained men behind him.

Seth nodded, his fury barely contained. "Yes, we are all that is left. The citadel fell yesterday. Now we ride to the fortress. Do you wish to go?"

Gabria could only nod. Seth motioned for his men to dismount. "We will go at midnight," the Oathbreaker said curtly.

Then, without another word, he withdrew with his men and
sat down to wait.

It was an hour after midnight when Gabria and the
Oathbreakers started. Hundreds of campfires burned in a
broad swath across their path. Guards and squads of men pa-
trolled among the tents. Somewhere a drum beat endlessly, as
if marking the single heartbeat of the enemy camp. Medb had
not bothered to fortify his flanks, for he expected no attack
from behind.

Gabria and the men, leading their horses, were able to slip
past the sentries to the outskirts of the encampment unno-
ticed. They gathered behind several wagons near the old road
and waited for the path to clear.

They only had to wait a few minutes before Seth nodded to
his men. As they mounted their horses, Gabria shot a glance
down the road and saw that it was clear. She mounted Nara
and closed her mind to everything but the road ahead, the
road to safety and the clan.

Gabria's eyes began to gleam. She leaned forward over
Nara's mane and the Hunnuli instantly sprang forward. The
mare's ears were flattened and her head stretched out. Her
hooves rang on the stone. Behind them, Seth and the cultists
galloped in a tight group, their whips uncurled and the wrath
of their goddess revealed on their faces.

Horns suddenly bellowed around them; men began shouting and running toward the road. The stone path still lay
empty, but through the tents came soldiers to cut them off.
Nara screamed a challenge as a mass of dark-skinned Turic warriors surged toward her. Gabria answered with the Corin war
cry and hung on as the Hunnuli tore into them.

Snapping and kicking with hooves deadlier than any sword,
the horse plunged into the attackers with ferocious speed until
the men fell back in terror. The Oathbreakers followed the
mare closely, their whips cracking with killing force. Arrows
rained down among them, and one of Seth's men fell. Still
they raced on behind the fury of the Hunnuli.

Before Gabria realized it, they had passed the main camp
and reached the fields and front lines. Startled, enraged faces

turned toward the riders and the horns blared again. Then
Nara raced past the defenses and toward the old stone bridge.
Before the mare lay the dark, littered, bloody ridge and the
road to the fortress gate.

Gabria prayed fervently someone would open the gate. Already she could hear the sounds of hooves as enemy riders galloped in pursuit. The fortress remained ominously quiet. Nara
neighed imperiously as she ran over the bridge and up the
road, but the gate still remained closed. Gabria glanced back
and, seeing the pursuing riders, she closed her eyes and gritted
her teeth. Open the gates, her mind cried.

A war horn sounded from the tower. As the ancient wall
reared up in front of the riders, the gate was thrown open and
Nara and the Oathbreakers' horses galloped through. Shouts
of anger came from behind as the gate crashed shut and was
barred. Gradually the yells and hoofbeats dwindled away and
a tense quiet fell over those in the fortress. Gabria lay on Nara's
neck, panting. The Oathbreakers wearily dismounted.

From out of the black shadows by the wall, a figure walked
through the men to Nara's side. The Hunnuli nickered a greeting, and Gabria looked down into Savaric's face. She was
stunned by the haggard lines on the chief's face and the weariness that dulled his movements. She slid off the mare and
saluted.

"Lord, I beg your forgiveness for leaving without your permission. I only know I felt my reasons were important and that
I had little time."

Many of the other warriors were staring at Gabria; Koshyn
crossed his arms. Savaric remained quiet and deliberately examined her from head to foot, taking in her filthy, tattered
clothes, her thin body, and her lack of a sword. At last, he returned her salute. "I'm certainly glad to have you back," he
said, then his eyebrow arched in disapproval. "The next time
you decide to leave, tell me first."

"Yes, Lord." She was relieved to find that he was not angry
with her, but she still had to face Athlone. And Gabria knew
he would have a few things to say. She glanced around and
wondered where he was.

She and the men were standing by the front gate, in the bailey between the two walls. A few torches flickered on the parapets, casting a dim light on the exhausted faces of the defenders and on the battered walls of the old fortress. Everywhere Gabria looked were signs of a hard-won battle. Broken weapons littered the ground, huge rocks and fallen masonry lay between the walls, blood stains marred the parapets. Gabria suddenly shivered. Where was Athlone?

Seth and his men walked to Savaric's side, and the brothers greeted each other.

"Does your presence here mean the citadel has fallen?" Savaric asked.

"For now."

"What of your library?"

Seth shook his head. "We had time to hide the most important books where Medb will never find them. But—" Seth paused and pointed to his men. "We are all that are left."

Savaric glanced around. "There are not many left here, either. If Medb tries one more all-out assault, we'll not be able to hold the fortress. I'm afraid you picked a poor place for a sanctuary."

Seth shot a look at Gabria. "Not necessarily." He looked back at his brother and for the first time noticed something in the chieftain's face: the lines of crushing grief. Seth leaned forward and asked, "Where is Athlone?"

Gabria stiffened.

For a moment, Savaric stared into the night, his face frozen. "Athlone is dead," he finally answered. "He took some men out last night to burn the catapults and I did not stop him. Medb's men overwhelmed them."

Gabria stepped back as if struck by a blow. She started to shake and her heart caught in her throat. Without a sound, she turned and fled into the fortress.

18

n the heated darkness of his tent, Lord Medb stirred on his couch. His eyes slowly opened like a bird of prey disturbed by the movement of a coming victim. A cold smile creased his face. So, he thought with satisfaction, all the prizes are gathering in the same trap. It made things much easier. Medb was not surprised that a few rats from Krath's citadel had escaped; that warren was so full of bolt holes, even he would have had a difficult time finding them all.

What did surprise the Wylfling lord was the return of the Corin and his Hunnuli. He thought that the boy was long fled, cowering in some hole. Instead, the Corin had broken through his lines to the safety of the fortress. Medb chuckled to himself. He knew the outcome of this siege. While it was true he had been surprised by Savaric's move to the fortress, it would still not avail the fool. The fall of the clans was inevitable. He had let his mercenaries try their hand at cracking Ab-Chakan, and the ruin still stood. Now it was his turn. He would let the clans stew a little while longer, then he would attempt another method of breaking them that would be faster and more efficient.

A new, delightful possibility had fallen into Medb's lap and he was pleasantly contemplating his choices. He chuckled and glanced at his unconscious prisoner, bound hand and foot to the tent poles. Medb had in mind a simple trade, after which the clans could go free with their beloved Athlone returned. They would not realize until too late that the man was not the same independent, fiercely devoted leader he had been. But by then Athlone would be chieftain and the Khulinin would be solidly in a Wylfling grip. Of course, if the clans refused to barter, Medb would still have the pleasure of forcing them to watch as Athlone died a particularly nasty death. He leaned back on his couch and laughed.

*   *   *   *   *

Morning came quickly on the wings of a rising wind. The night chill fled and the heat of the sun seeped into the earth. The clansmen and the Oathbreakers stood behind the walls and watched the sun illuminate the sorcerer's camp. There was no sign of the bodies of Athlone, the Hunnuli, or any of the men who had gone with them. Throughout the fortress, the clansmen gripped their weapons and waited in the mounting heat and dust. They knew Medb would not hold off his attack much longer.

In the general's palace, Piers was attending the wounded in the great hall. He had heard of Gabria's return, but he had not seen her and was beginning to worry. By midmorning, there was still no sign of her and Lady Tungoli offered to go look for the Corin.

She found Nara first, in the shelter of a crumbling wall near the main road. Gabria was curled up asleep in the mare's shadow. Tungoli gently shook her.

"Gabran," the lady said gently. "Morning is almost gone. Piers is pacing the floor waiting for you."

Gabria stretched her stiff muscles and looked up at the lines of grief etched on Tungoli's face. Her own sadness tightened her throat and her heart ached. She stood up and the two of them walked slowly back toward the palace.

"I'm glad you're back," Tungoli said after a few steps. "Athlone was very fond of you. He was terribly upset when you left."

The girl felt her tears burning in the back of her eyes, and she fiercely fought them back. She could not weep yet. "I'm sorry," she said, not knowing what else to say.

A small smile touched Tungoli's face. "I may be a foolish, wishful mother, but I don't believe he's dead."

Gabria stared at the chieftain's wife.

"It's only an intuition, I guess," Tungoli went on. "But I feel he is still alive. For now." Her mouth trembled and tears sparkled on her eyelids. "I would give almost anything to have him safe."

A small seed of hope stirred in the girl's mind. "If you're right, Lady, I will do everything I can to save him."

Tungoli took her arm. "I believe you, Gabran. Thank you." They walked on in silence to the palace.

Piers was delighted when Gabria came into the great hall. He waited beside the warrior he was tending and watched gladly as the tall, sunburned girl strode through the crowd to him. She moved with a subtle grace and wore an air of self-assurance most clanswomen tried to hide.

Piers clasped her with honest warmth. "Welcome back, Gabran. Your journey was successful." His words were a statement, for he could see the truth in her eyes.

Gabria nodded, touched by the unspoken concern in Piers's gesture. "For what it's worth."

The healer understood much of what she did not say. "Choices are often hard," he said softly. "But don't you think yours was already made?"

"I guess there never was a choice. I ride the only way left open for me." She smiled a little weakly. "Sometimes though, it seems to me I am very unfit for this task. Why would the gods lay so careful a trail and spend so little time preparing the one who must follow it?"

"That is the paradox of some of our best tales, Corin," Cantrell said behind her.

Gabria turned and greeted the blind bard. "I doubt anyone will sing tales of my deeds. Everything I've done has been unlawful."

"It is the ending of the tale that often decides that," he replied.

Seth came through the palace doors and saw Gabria. He came to join them. "Corin, I need to see you. Are you done here?"

Piers looked at the cultist in obvious distaste. "Go ahead, Gabran. We'll talk later."

Seth strode out the doors, expecting Gabria to follow. She hesitated. Her eyes met Piers's, and she saw his unmistakable support
and affection. Comforted, she ran to catch up with Seth.

* * * * *

The silence was the first thing Gabria noticed when she and
Seth passed the last building and came into sight of the inner
wall. They slowed and Gabria stared around with a growing
suspicion that something was wrong. There was no one by the
inner wall, so they walked through the first gate to the bailey.

On the battlements above, Savaric, Koshyn, Ryne, and a
crowd of warriors were leaning against the stone parapets, staring down at the fields. No one moved. Beyond the fortress wall
everything was quiet. There was no sound or sense of movement in the valley below.

Following Seth, Gabria picked her way over the trampled dirt
and tumbled stone to the stairs. They joined the chiefs on the
parapet and looked over the wall to the fields. The sorcerer's
army was in full array; the men stood in stiff ranks in a large crescent around the mouth of the valley. Everything was totally still.

Lord Koshyn suddenly stirred and pointed. "Look."

A large wagon carrying a number of men and pulled by four
horses rolled out of the ranks of men toward the fortress. The
defenders watched in growing suspicion as it crossed the bridge
and stopped by the remains of the catapults. It turned ponderously around, and the men on board heaved off something
large and black. As the wagon pulled away, a gasp and a moan
of anger rose from the watching warriors. It was Boreas, the
spear still protruding from his chest.

Medb did not give the clans long to recover from their shock.
Horns suddenly blared from all corners of the field and four
horsemen, bearing the banners of stark white, trotted out of
camp. They halted by the dead Hunnuli. The horns continued
to sing until the fortress echoed with their music. A second
wagon rolled slowly down the road. Behind it came a procession of Wylfling warriors; in their midst rode the sorcerer on a
large white horse.

Gabria stared at the sorcerer in amazement, for she had not known he had healed his crippled legs.

Medb's brown cloak had been discarded for a long robe of white—the color of death, the color of magic-wielders. He raised his hand and the procession stopped. Medb motioned a second time. Three Wylfling soldiers dragged the stumbling body of a man from the wagon to Boreas's body. They stepped back and Athlone fell to his knees. The horns stopped.

The clansmen immediately recognized the wer-tain, and a cry of rage roared out of the fortress.

Lord Medb laughed and spurred his mount forward. A Wylfling warrior seized Athlone's head, yanked it back to expose his throat, and poised his dagger inches away from the jugular. The clans grew quiet and waited.

"Khulinin. Dangari. Bahedin. Jehanan. Hear me!" Medb shouted. "I wish to congratulate you on your success thus far. You have held off your defeat quite admirably. However, your luck will not carry you forever, and I am afraid that when you fall, I will not be able to control my men. They are growing impatient and very angry. Most of you will not survive. But I do not wish to lose four clans, so I have a proposal for your consideration. Is there any man who will listen?"

After an angry pause, Savaric, Koshyn, and Ryne climbed to the top of the parapet and stood side by side. With a blade at Athlone's throat, they had little choice.

Lord Medb leaned forward like a snake eyeing its prey. "The terms are simple. For the safe return of Athlone, I want the Hunnuli, the Corin boy, and the four chieftains turned over to me. If these hostages are given quickly, I will withdraw my army and allow your clans to go in peace."

The chiefs exchanged glances. "What if we refuse?" Koshyn shouted.

Medb snapped a word. The Wylfling stepped back from Athlone. At another word, an invisible force yanked Athlone to his feet and held him spread-eagle in the air. From out of the ground, pale flames of red and gold flared up and around his body. Athlone writhed in agony, but Medb's magic held him mercilessly fast.

"Athlone will die very slowly before your eyes. And then your clans will follow," the sorcerer replied.

For a heartbeat, Savaric wavered. He would give anything to save his son from death. He would gladly surrender himself to Medb if he thought that Athlone would live. Unfortunately, he was certain of only one thing: Lord Medb could not be trusted to keep his word. His treachery was as plain as his heresy. Without a twitch of remorse, the sorcerer would slay his hostages, massacre the clans, and destroy Athlone anyway. In a voice that belied the tearing grief in his heart, Savaric shouted, "Your terms are intolerable. We cannot accept them."

Lord Medb threw back his head and laughed. "Don't jump into your fate so fast, Savaric. Give yourself time to think. You have one hour. At the end of that time, you will surrender the fortress or die."

Without warning, Medb raised his hand and pointed to the great bronze gates of the fortress. A blue fire sprang from his fingers. It struck the gates in a brilliant flash, searing along the edges of the bronze doors and scorching the stone arches. The ancient arcane wards in the entrance held for a few moments, then they cracked under the tremendous power and the gates crashed to the ground.

The clansmen stared down in horror as the dust slowly settled around the broken gate.

"One hour," Medb called. "Then Athlone dies." He stopped the flames around the wer-tain and waited as the Wylfling planted a post and hung Athlone up by his wrists. Then Medb reined his horse around and rode back to his army.

Gabria watched Athlone. From where she was standing on the parapet, she could not see his face, only his body hanging limp on the pole. She felt someone move beside her and turned to see Savaric staring down at his son. The chief's hands clenched the edge of the stone wall as if he wanted to tear down the parapet.

"Are you going to do anything to save him?" Gabria asked, although she knew what his answer had to be.

The chieftain shook his head, not even looking at her. "There is nothing we can do. Medb will not free him and I will not sacrifice the clans."

The girl nodded in understanding. Silently, she left the parapet and walked up the road toward the palace. Nara was waiting for Gabria in the big courtyard and came to join the Corin as she sat on the rim of the fountain.

For a long time, Gabria ignored the people passing by and stared at the mare waiting patiently by her side. The glorious Hunnuli, Gabria thought, they are as intelligent as humans, telepathic, impervious to sorcery, stronger and swifter than any other creature, and totally devoted to those few humans lucky enough to befriend them. They were creations of magic.

Everything Gabria had learned in her life had taught her to reject magic in any form, yet the clans did not reject the Hunnuli. In fact, Gabria began to realize how much magic was still a part of clan life. The magic was hidden behind different names, but the power was everywhere. It seeped in the rituals and traditions of the priests and priestesses; it was guarded by the Oathbreakers; it was sung of by the bards; it was embodied by the Hunnuli; and the talent to wield magic was still passed on from generation to generation.

Yet the clans, in their fear and ignorance, turned a blind eye to the power in their midst. Even after two hundred years, their prejudices had not allowed them to see the truth. Magic was not an evil, corrupting power. It simply was a force that existed, a force that could be formed into something as lovely or as hideous as its wielder desired. For the first time in her life, Gabria recognized how foolish her people had been to ignore magic.

Just then, Nara turned her head and her ears pricked forward. Gabria followed the mare's gaze and saw Cantrell walk carefully down the steps of the palace. He had a bundle under his arm.

Nara neighed and the bard called, "Gabran, are you there?" Gabria walked over to him and took his arm.

"Come," he said. "Walk with me a moment." They walked slowly around the courtyard, out of earshot of any casual listeners. The Hunnuli stayed close behind.

Gabria finally spoke. "Will the clans never learn to accept magic for what it is?"

"Not as long as Medb lives," Cantrell replied.

She sighed. "Then perhaps they need to see magic as something positive as well."

The bard gripped Gabria's arm tightly. "I heard Medb's ultimatum. There is not much time left."

They came to the front of the palace again and Gabria stopped walking. She knew what she had to do to free Athlone and save the clans—the conflict had stood at the end of her path since the day she left Corin Treld. But the very idea terrified her. She was no match for Lord Medb and she knew the consequences of her failure. Unfortunately, there were no more alternatives.

Cantrell held out the bundle he had been carrying. "I thought you might need this."

She opened it and found her scarlet cloak with the buttercup brooch, and a long, pale green tunic.

"The tunic was the closest I could find to white," the bard joked with a faint smile. He embraced her quickly. "The gods go with you, Gabria." He turned and left her.

Gabria wound her fingers in Nara's mane, and they went back down the road toward the main gate. Behind a ruined wall, Gabria stripped off her clothes. The rags that bound her breasts, the filthy tunic, and the Khulinin cloak were tossed aside, though she hesitated taking the gold cloak off. The Corin kept only her leather hat, her boots, and her pants. She tucked her father's dagger into her boot, then pulled the green tunic over her head and belted it with her sash. She thought about using her power to change the tunic's color to white, but she changed her mind. It was time magic-wielders had a new color. Gabria laid her red cloak over her shoulder and sighed with relief. Never again would she have to play the boy. Soon the clans would know her for exactly what she was.

Gabria took a slow breath and opened the sorceress's bag. A long, needle-thin diamond splinter fell glittering into her hand. Gabria stared at it, puzzled. The sorceress had told her this thing was the sign of a true magic-wielder, but she had not said what Gabria was supposed to do with it.

"You will need an assistant to help you complete the rite,"

someone said behind her.

Gabria nearly jumped out of her skin. Nara snorted, but it sounded more like an agreement than a warning.

Seth walked around the wall and joined her. "It is too difficult to insert the splinter alone."

"How do you know?" she gasped.

"The men of my cult have guarded the knowledge of the magic-wielders for years in hopes someone would need it."

"But how did you find me?"

His eyebrows arched. "I followed you."

Gabria studied him for a long time before she gave him the diamond. Seth took her arms and extended them, palms up. His weathered face was impassive. He spoke the words of the ancient rite as if he had spoken them every day of his life, without hesitation or distaste. The words were still hanging in the air when he raised the diamond splinter to the sun to capture the heat and light. The sliver glittered in his hand. Then, with a skill as deft as a healer, he pierced Gabria's wrist and slid the splinter under her skin.

The pain lanced through Gabria's arm, and she could feel the heat of the diamond burning under her skin. Immediately the splinter began to pulse with the pounding of her heart. A tingling spread through her hand and up into every part of her body. The sensation was warm and invigorating. Gabria looked into Nara's wise eyes and smiled.

Seth turned her wrist to look at the splinter pulsing under her skin. "Use this wisely, Corin. You are the last and the first, and it would be best if you survived."

"Thank you, Seth."

He grunted. "Go."

The girl mounted the Hunnuli, and the horse trotted toward the main gate. The one-hour reprieve was over. Medb had returned.

The Wylfling lord rode arrogantly up to the fortress. His army was ready to attack; his face was alive with triumph. "What say you, clansmen?" he shouted to the defenders.

Lord Savaric, Koshyn, and Ryne leaned over the parapet. "We will not deal with you," Savaric called.

"But I will!" a strange voice shouted below him. Hoofbeats clattered over the stone road and the Hunnuli galloped forward. The mare reached the entrance and went up and over the fallen gates with a terrific heave of her hind legs. Gabria's scarlet cloak flared like wings. The horse landed lightly and cantered a few paces forward to a stop.

Savaric shouted, "Gabran! Come back here!"

Gabria ignored him and calmly faced Medb. Her hat and her cloak still disguised her femininity and the embedded splinter that pulsed in her wrist. "I will make you an offer, Lord Medb," she said coldly.

"I do not deal with mere boys," Medb sneered. He snapped a word and magic fire flared around Athlone. The wer-tain jerked in agony.

"Gabran!" Savaric cried.

Gabria was silent. With deliberate slowness, she raised her hand and the ruby light of the splinter gleamed on her tanned skin. The flames around Athlone snuffed out, the cords binding his wrists parted, and his body sank to the ground. The wer-tain shivered once and his eyes opened. A Wylfling warrior, his sword drawn, jumped toward the fallen man. A blue flare of Trymian Force surged from Gabria's hand to the warrior's chest, flinging him backward into a smoking, lifeless heap.

The silence on the field was absolute.

"Oh, my gods," Koshyn breathed.

Medb stared at the Corin thoughtfully. So that was the answer to those many, puzzling questions. He parted his thin lips in a twisted smile. "What is your offer, boy?"

"You may have me and the Hunnuli in exchange for Athlone's life. But you must fight me to win your prizes."

He shrugged. "A duel? That is impossible. A boy cannot fight a chieftain."

"I am chieftain of the Corin, thanks to you. But I do not wish to use swords in this duel."

"An arcane duel? Against you?" Medb laughed. "If that is what you want, I will humor you." The sorcerer knew his strength was low. He was not fully recovered from the battle two days before, and he had expended a great deal of energy shattering the fortress gates. Still, he thought it would take little effort to crush this upstart. Smiling, Medb ordered his warriors back. He dismounted on the level space by the fallen gates.

"You are a fool, boy. Did the bard not tell you the riddle of my doom?" the Wylfling asked.

Gabria looked down at Medb. Standing straight and tall, he was a powerful, handsome man. "It is a riddle no longer."

"Oh?" He fixed her with a cold stare.

"*I* am the answer to your riddle, Medb, for I am no boy and my name in the northern dialect means buttercup." Before her stunned audience, Gabria peeled off the leather hat and shook her head until the loose curls fluffed out and framed her face in gold. Then she unpinned the cloak and let it drop over Nara's black haunches. The wind molded the green tunic against her breasts and slender waist. The sun glittered in her eyes, as hard and as bright as any sword.

"Gabran is dead these many days. I am Gabria, his sister, and daughter of Lord Dathlar."

For the first time since his hands touched the *Book of Matrah*, Medb was deeply afraid. This girl had come out of nowhere with a knowledge of sorcery and the emblem of a magic-wielder burning in her wrist. Where had she gotten her knowledge? And the splinter. He had not been able to find one, but this girl had not only attained one but had it properly inserted. For a moment, Medb's heart quailed and the hairs rose on the back of his neck.

Then he steadied himself. She was a difficulty he had not anticipated, but he had not struggled this far to be overcome by a girl and a riddle. She might be the "buttercup," but she was not bearing a sword. With a silent curse, Medb swore he would end the riddle once and for all.

The girl slid off the Hunnuli and the mare backed away, leaving her alone. Gabria pushed away every doubt that might distract her, closed her eyes, and concentrated on the ancient spell the Woman of the Marsh had taught her. She lifted her right hand and pointed behind Medb. "I, Gabria, daughter of Dathlar, challenge you, Lord Medb, and by my challenge set the first wards."

Medb's voice purred. "I, Lord Medb, accept your challenge and, by my acceptance, set the second wards."

Gabria opened her eyes. The spell had worked. Four scarlet pillars of light stood equidistant from each other, forming a square that enclosed Gabria and Medb in an area only twenty paces wide. A pale mist glowed between the pillars and arched overhead. The two were now surrounded by a protective wall of power that shielded the spectators. Gabria could see the clansmen watching with horrified fascination from outside the wall.

"You have unwisely challenged me," the sorcerer sneered. "But the question is not who is stronger, but by what means I shall prove it to you."

Medb lifted his hand and launched a sphere of Trymian Force. It was only a test, and the Corin dodged it easily. The blue ball exploded on the ward shield. He fired more at her, faster and faster, and she swayed and dipped around the bright, deadly fires as if dancing with them. The girl did not try to retaliate; she only avoided his assault and waited for his next move.

At last, Medb grew weary of playing with her. He had to be careful, for his strength was waning and he did not know how great this girl's powers really were. He studied the Corin for a moment, then he spoke a command.

Suddenly Gabria felt a tug of wind at her feet. The strange little wind whipped abruptly into a whirlwind of vicious intensity and wrapped around Gabria in a swirling, shrieking maelstrom. Dirt and grit flailed through the dark wind, tearing at her hair, her skin, and her clothes. She tried frantically to escape the maelstrom, but the force of the whirlwind tossed and buffeted her, ripped the breath from her body, and wrenched every bone and muscle.

Then, as quickly as it had begin, the wind died away. Gabria fell to the ground, panting and crying with pain. Her tunic was shredded and her skin was raw and bleeding.

"See how easy it is?" Medb said. "Let me show you another. You have survived the tragedies in your life well, but do you really know the terrors of your mind?"

Before Gabria could defend herself from it, a paralyzing chill froze her. She threw her hands across her face. Images crowded into her mind: her brother falling, his skull crushed by a battle axe; her father hacked by a dozen swords; Nara torn alive by wolves; Athlone hanging by shredded ligaments from a bloody pole. From a dark gray patch of earth, the rotting corpses of Clan Corin staggered out of their graves and pointed accusing fingers at her. Gabria stumbled into a desert of searing thirst and unendurable loneliness. A scream tore at her throat. Desperately she tried to rise, only to pitch forward when her legs would not respond.

Beyond the shield, Athlone struggled to his feet. He leaned against the pole, his eyes on the girl. "Fight him, Gabria," he cried.

"Do you understand now?" Medb chuckled appreciatively. "You should have stayed at your place by the cooking fires and left the wars to those capable of handling them."

Gabria tried to stop the chaos in her mind and bring her thoughts back under her control. She realized the visions that plagued her were fears she had known before. There was nothing that she had not already faced. A little at a time, she forced the images out of her mind and finally broke Medb's spell. She tottered to her feet.

The Corin knew now that she could not defeat Lord Medb in a confrontation of expertise. He had been studying and conditioning his talent too long. She lacked the skill necessary to destroy him outright. Gabria had only one hope, a slim one at best: to catch him off guard. If she could survive just long enough to take him by surprise, perhaps her untried powers would be enough. Quickly she rapped a spell that exploded underneath the sorcerer's feet and threw him to the ground in a sprawling heap.

Medb jumped up, enraged. "Enough of this!" he shouted. The Wylfling decided to use a killing spell he had already perfected. He spread his arms wide, his lips formed the harsh words, and slowly he began to bring his hands together.

For a moment, Gabria stood warily. She began to feel a pressure on all sides. There was no pain or distress, only a mild discomfort, as if she were wrapped in a heavy fur. She braced herself and tried to fend it away, but the pressure increased. Her head began to throb and her chest hurt. She was having trouble breathing. Straining to escape the pressure, Gabria clenched her teeth and used her power to form a protective shell about her body. The arcane grip grew stronger. She fought to maintain her shield, but Medb's grip contracted with a jerk, once and then again. Her protective shield cracked and the pressure closed in around her. The pain worsened, and the Corin's bones began to creak under the stress. Gabria moaned and her hands tore at her head.

Medb pushed his hands closer together and struggled to break the girl's resistance. He could feel his strength beginning to ebb, but he disregarded his growing weakness in his effort to kill the last surviving Corin.

Unseen by Gabria and Medb, Athlone began to stagger toward the arcane shield. He knew he should be horrified by what Gabria was doing, but instead he was strangely drawn to the arcane duel and his only lucid thought was to help his friend. He could not bear to see her die.

Gabria cried as Lord Medb strained harder. The pain in her body was almost overwhelming and her consciousness began to close in around her. In desperation, the girl gathered her last shreds of strength and courage into one final core of resistance. She clung tenaciously to one thought: she would never submit. Her last awareness flickered and she screamed her defiance.

Lord Medb tried desperately, but he could not crush the girl's last opposition. Her defiance was fueled by fury and righteousness and by a will that Medb sensed was greater than his own. Surprise and a seed of doubt crept into his mind. He felt his power weakening rapidly.

All at once, Athlone shouted furiously, "Medb, no!" The wer-tain stood by the arcane shield, his face dark with rage and helplessness. He put his fist through the shield and, to Medb's horrified surprise, the arcane wards shattered. The shield abruptly disintegrated, slamming Athlone to the ground.

Gabria felt Medb's power fade, and in that moment, she remembered the last line of Cantrell's riddle. Summoning every

ounce of will, she wrenched loose of the sorcerer's arcane grip.
The blackness vanished and the pain eased. Her vision returned with startling clarity. She had just enough energy left.
Before Medb was aware of what she was doing, Gabria
snatched her father's dagger out of her boot and transformed it
into a silver sword. The splinter in her wrist flared red with her
blood as she hurled the sword at the sorcerer. It soared in a glittering arc across the space between them and plunged into
Medb's chest.

A great cry shook the fortress. Medb jerked, contorted by
pain, and his cruel mouth shaped one last curse. Then he collapsed backward, impaled by the silver sword.

Gabria shivered uncontrollably. The world fell away and she
sank to the ground. But as the edge of consciousness darkened,
a vision came of a hollow tree and an old woman who waited
for her. Before the pain finally drowned her, Gabria clawed the
air, trying to answer to the strange summons that beckoned her
to the marsh.

ord Savaric did not hesitate after the sorcerer fell. With a wild shout he called to his warriors and raced through the gates toward Medb's army, which stood in stunned silence in the fields. The Khulinin were fast on their chief's heels. Lord Koshyn, Lord Ryne, and the clansmen raised their voices into battle cries that shook the towers, and the four clans sprang after the enemy.

Clan Amnok broke immediately. They had wanted no part of Medb's treachery, but had been swept along by Lord Ferron, their cowed chieftain, and trapped by the sorcerer's tyranny. Now, without Medb's arcane goad to force them on, they turned and ran. The Geldring, too, were reluctant to fight; despite Branth's ravings, they fled with their wer-tain to the camp. The Ferganan simply threw down their weapons and refused to fight. Only the mercenaries, well paid and eager for battle, the exiles, and the Wylfling drew their swords and faced the charging clans.

The four clans roared joyfully. The sorcerer was dead, the enemy forces were cut in half, and Athlone had been saved. Now they were running to something they understood. As they charged across the fields, they beat their shields with their weapons and shouted their challenge across the plains. Their running feet raised clouds of dust, and, through the thick air, the sunlight glistened on their helms and their swords. With one will, both sides met in a deafening crash.

The tumult rattled through the fortress. Seth, from atop the wall, watched the battle for several minutes before walking down to the ground. His icy, remote eyes revealed no feelings

as he felt Athlone's wrist and laid the unconscious man in a
more comfortable position. Then he turned to Gabria. She was
lying in a heap, her face pale and her golden hair dirty with
sweat and dust. The Hunnuli stood over her.

"Tell her we still guard the most treasured books of the old
sorcerers. She may have need of them one day."

The Hunnuli did not answer, as he expected, but she flicked
her head in understanding. Gabria stirred as the noise of the
battle finally drew her awake. Seth put a skin of water to her
lips; she drank thirstily and struggled to her feet. He watched
her impassively.

The girl looked around at Medb's body, at the furious fighting that raged in the fields, and at Athlone lying nearby. For
just a second, her gaze softened as she looked at the wer-tain.
At last she met Seth's eyes.

He nodded to acknowledge her. "It was said in tales long ignored that sorcery would one day be found in the hands of a
woman."

Gabria didn't answer. She was tired beyond exhaustion, but
she could not rest. The strange image of the Woman of the
Marsh remained in her mind, compelling her to come. She
hauled herself up onto Nara's back and put on her cloak.

Seth kept his stare pinned on her. "You are leaving?"

"I have to," she said curtly.

At Gabria's command, Nara wheeled and cantered south
down the old road. The girl did not watch the fighting as they
passed or look back at the fortress. The noise of the battle
receded, and before long they were alone.

"Please take me back to the marshes, Nara," Gabria said,
her voice indistinct and empty.

Nara's thoughts were worried. *What have you left to say to
this woman?*

"Don't be concerned. I need to see her."

Nara asked Gabria nothing else, but a foreboding chilled her.
Her rider was so remote. The girl's unresponsiveness could not
be explained simply by weariness or distress. There was something different, an unnatural sense of urgency that precluded
everything else. The mare settled into a gallop. There was little

she could do but comply until they reached the marshes and she could learn the real purpose behind their journey.

*   *   *   *   *

Like a wild tide, the four clans swept through the remaining forces of the sorcerer's army, until the ground was littered with dead and the earth was stained with blood. The Wylfling and their mercenaries fought bravely, but by the close of day they were defeated. Most of the exiles were cut down, except for a few who escaped to the hills. The Geldring, Ferganan, and Amnok clans had already surrendered, preferring the punishment of the council to annihilation by the enraged, triumphant Khulinin, and they stood aside while Savaric tore down Medb's banner.

The fighting was still going on in the valley when Athlone regained consciousness. For a moment, he thought he had drunk too much, because his stomach was queasy and his thoughts were a jumble of bad dreams and unfamiliar pain. Then he opened his eyes and saw that he was lying beside several other wounded men by the gates of the fortress. Piers was tending a warrior close by. The memories flooded back with all their griefs and furies.

The wer-tain's moan brought Piers to his side. The healer helped him sit up, then forced a cup into his hands. Athlone stared numbly down the hill at the body of Boreas while he drank the liquid. Whatever Piers had given him burned in his stomach with revitalizing warmth, and, after a few minutes, he was able to stand. When he saw Medb's body, his jaw clenched.

"Why did she have to do that?" he groaned.

Piers said quietly, "Gabria had no choice, Wer-tain. She had to use the weapons at hand."

"The weapons at hand," Athlone repeated ironically. He could remember using the same words to Gabria. "Where is she?" he asked after a while.

Piers's face clouded with worry. "She and Nara went south. I think she is returning to the Woman of the Marsh."

"Returning!" Athlone cried. He threw the cup to the ground and ran for the nearest horse.

Piers yelled angrily, "Athlone! You'll never catch a Hunnuli on that."

The wer-tain ignored him, grabbed the bridle of an escaped mount and swung up in the saddle. He savagely reined the animal around and kicked it into a gallop.

*   *   *   *   *

A day later, Athlone's horse fell and did not rise again. No Harachan could catch a Hunnuli or even keep pace with one, yet Athlone, his heart sick with fear and confusion, had urged the horse on until it had dropped. Now he was on foot and farther from Gabria than ever. In the hours he had ridden like a madman, he had given no thought to anything but keeping to Nara's trail and finding Gabria. But that day, as he trudged southeast in the hot sun, he had too much time to think and his emotions twisted inside him.

Athlone could hardly believe Gabria had killed the sorcerer with magic. He guessed she had learned sorcery from the marsh woman, but why had the girl decided to use magic as her weapon against Medb? Gabria had never shown any sign of using sorcery . . . or had she? As Athlone jogged along, he began to remember things that had seemed odd to him: her fight with Cor and the man's strange illness; Cor's later death at her hand; and even the fight Gabria had had with him at the pool, when she had felled him with a mere shoulder wound. Athlone vaguely recalled how he had called her a sorceress, but how could he have known? She was nothing like what he expected a magic-wielder to be, nothing like Medb. Gabria rode a Hunnuli and she had saved the clans. She had saved him. Where was the evil in that?

Athlone groaned and ran faster. He had to find her before she was lost in the marshes. Suddenly, to his relief, he heard a Hunnuli neigh a strident greeting. Nara galloped down a long hill to meet the wer-tain. She was drenched with sweat and caked to the knees with dried mud. And alone.

Come. Gabria has met the Woman of the Marsh. She sent me away.

Athlone was nearly overwhelmed by the force of the mare's distress. Gabria would never have ordered Nara away if she were planning to return. He vaulted to the horse's back without hesitation and held on as Nara burst into a dead run back the way she had come.

It was early morning when the Hunnuli reached the western fringes of the marshes. Nara worked her way down the river as far as she could go before she was forced to stop and let Athlone slide off.

"How will I find her out there?" he demanded, glaring at the marshes around him. Weary, hungry, and feverish, he was starting to feel ill.

Nara neighed. *The marsh woman came to meet Gabria in a boat. They went downstream past that bend. Gabria is nearby. I can sense her.*

Athlone threw up his hands and plunged into the mud. Before moving off, he stopped and, without turning around, asked, "Nara, if Gabria is a sorceress, why do you stay with her?"

Nara snorted. *The Hunnuli were bred to be the guardians of the magic-wielders. It is only evil we cannot tolerate.*

Athlone nodded and trudged on. The full meaning of the Hunnuli's words did not come to the chief's son until much later.

*   *   *   *   *

At the same time Nara was racing away to find help, the Woman of the Marsh was leading Gabria ashore on a small, overgrown island, not far from where the girl had left the Hunnuli. The woman had thought about waiting for the girl in the tree, but when she had learned Gabria was coming, her anticipation grew too strong. The sorceress had brought her things in her boat and met the girl at the edges of the marsh.

The old woman clicked her tongue as she laid Gabria on a mat under a makeshift shelter and unpinned the red cloak.

The girl was in dreadful shape, but she had come and she was still alive—that was all that mattered. It would take a little more time to build up the girl's strength and tend to her most dangerous hurts, or neither one of them would survive the transference. Still, the sorceress gloated, after waiting two hundred years, another day will make little difference.

By nightfall, Gabria was sleeping heavily. She had been fed and drugged with poppy. While she slept, the sorceress pored over her musty manuscript to memorize the best possible incantation. The transference would have to be perfect and would require a great deal of strength and skill, but the results would be worth the effort.

The old woman cackled with glee. She would be young again! She could look in a mirror and see a beautiful, smooth-faced woman instead of an ugly shell. Best of all, she could return to the world. That fool, Medb, had accomplished that at least: he had broken the clans' centuries-old complacency and had opened the door to sorcery once more.

It was a shame the girl had to die, for she would make an excellent ally. She had incredible will and a natural talent. Nevertheless, the price had to be paid and the transfer of youth left little life in the donor. The woman laughed to herself and set aside her manuscript. She would not have to wait much longer.

Morning was streaming into the shelter when Gabria awoke. She roused slowly, heavily dragging herself through a drug-induced fog to awareness. When she finally opened her eyes, she wondered vaguely where she was, then she wished she could go back to the peace of sleep. Her body hurt abominably, and even more painful was the empty, aching loss in her heart. What had begun at Corin Treld had at last reached its completion, leaving her life in ashes. Medb was dead, Athlone was beyond her reach, Boreas dead, and Nara gone. And now, because of her duel with the sorcerer, she was condemned to death or exiled to a life of emptiness. There was nowhere she belonged but the grass-covered barrow at Corin Treld. Her clan was at peace now; perhaps they would welcome her.

When the sorceress came in, Gabria stared at her apathetically. "Oh, it's you."

The woman put on a smirk of false sympathy. "Come, my child. It is time to pay your debt."

"What debt?" Gabria mumbled. She tried to rise, but the crone pushed her down.

"Thanks to me, you have destroyed a powerful and dangerous sorcerer. But now there is no life left for you. You do not sacrifice anything by relinquishing your youth to me. It is a fair deal for us both." The sorceress held up a small, lighted oil lamp.

Gabria glanced at the lamp, wondering what the old hag was talking about. Before she realized what was happening, her gaze was captured by the light of the flame and the sorceress mesmerized her into a mild stupor.

The old woman sat beside Gabria on the mat. She set the oil lamp between them, took the girl's hand, and started the spell. The magic began to build around Gabria, and the Woman of the Marsh grew absorbed in her task.

Suddenly, without warning, a commotion on the edge of the little island disturbed the woman's chant. She looked up worriedly just as a large and angry warrior burst into the shelter. He was flushed with fever and his body trembled with rage.

The woman screeched, "Stay away! Your magic can't hurt me!" and jumped to her feet. She pulled Gabria's stone ward out of her pocket and thrust it in the man's face.

Athlone knocked the ward out of her hands. He took one look at Gabria and pounced on the sorceress. "What have you done?" he bellowed, shaking her like a rag.

"She must pay," the old woman screamed. She clawed at his fists, but it was like scratching steel.

Athlone dropped the old woman and leaned over her. "Pay what?"

The woman hesitated, reaching into her sleeve.

"Pay what!" he demanded again.

She snatched a slim dagger. "The price for my help," she cried. "Her youth is mine now!" She stabbed upward toward Athlone's stomach, a faint blue aura cloaking the blade.

The wer-tain saw the knife coming too late and tried to twist away. The knife struck his belt, slithered sideways, and sliced into his left ribs. The crone's feeble Trymian Force was doused. Athlone roared in pained fury, and the woman screeched in real terror. She tried another stab, but Athlone hit her with his fist and knocked her to the ground. He heard a sickening crunch as the woman's head struck a large rock. She jerked once and lay still.

Athlone stood for several breaths, staring at the hag's body on the ground as if he could not believe she were dead. Then he wiped the sweat off his forehead, and a grim smile spread over his face.

Gabria cried out. Athlone whirled around and stared at the girl in horror. The marsh woman's half-finished spell had ruptured and the forces of magic she had gathered and not used abruptly coalesced into livid red clouds that swirled around Gabria in a gathering tornado. The oil lamp spilled and flames spread around the Corin, setting her cloak on fire. Gabria screamed again over the rising shriek of the unspent power.

Athlone was filled with terror at losing her. Without thinking, he leaped at Gabria through the wild forces and ripped her cloak off. The magical aura engulfed him.

Even as the uncontrollable power raged around him, the wer-tain was stunned by the natural, familiar feel of the magic. In a brilliant flash, he realized that magic and sorcery were not a perversion or an evil threat, simply a natural power inherent in his world—a power that could be tapped only by those born with a talent. At that moment, he knew without a doubt that he, too, had that talent.

The revelation shook him to the core. He understood a part of what Gabria must have felt when she had learned of her power. It was a bitter lesson to realize he had been wrong about something so vital.

As quickly as his acceptance took shape, Athlone noticed Gabria was doing nothing to escape the maelstrom. His skin was tingling and his ears ached in the rising shriek of energy amplified to an explosive crescendo.

"Gabria!" he yelled, pulling her close to him.

The girl hung against the warrior. Her eyes were closed and her body was limp.

Athlone held her tighter. Oh, gods, he wondered, has she given up? "What do you truly want?" he shouted at her.

Gabria was still for so long that Athlone thought he had lost her, then she stirred. Her answer was nearly lost in the roar of the whirlwind, but he heard it.

"I want to be myself."

She wrapped her arms around Athlone and forced her will into the center of the whirling magical vortex. Then, to her everlasting joy, she felt Athlone's mind tentatively reach out to her and offer his strength. Together, they slowed the wild whirl of broken sorcery and spread the destructive force apart until it dissipated into a mist on the morning breeze. The angry red light faded and the fire died down.

Gabria gritted her teeth against a wrenching nausea as the remnants of the spell vanished and the day snapped back to familiarity. It was over. Then she saw the burning remains of her scarlet cloak and the pent-up tears of five months flooded her eyes. She leaned against Athlone and sobbed.

*   *   *   *   *

For five days, Gabria and Athlone camped in a hollow by the river, spending their days along the banks and their nights in the warmth of each other's arms. It was a time of healing for them both and, under Nara's watchful eye, they slept a great deal and talked very little. Neither of them wanted to broach the subject of sorcery or the future until the time was right. For now they were content to be together for as long as they were allowed.

On the afternoon of the sixth day, Nara neighed a greeting to a horseman who appeared on a far hill. Athlone and Gabria exchanged lingering looks and reluctantly walked to their camp to wait for the intruder.

The young clansman, wearing a Khulinin cloak, reined his sweating horse to a halt and slid to the ground. His gaze slid past Gabria, but he saluted Athlone in undisguised relief and pleasure. "My lord, we have been looking for you for days."

Athlone turned cold at the title. His nostrils flared and he took a step forward. "Why do you call me that, Rethe," he demanded.

Rethe bowed his head. "That's why we had to find you. Lord Savaric is dead."

"How?" Athlone demanded.

"He was stabbed from behind . . . just after the fight for the camp. We think Lord Branth is responsible."

"Where is Branth now?"

The warrior looked up unhappily. "We don't know. The book of that accursed sorcerer is missing, too. Lord Koshyn and the Geldring's wer-tain believe Branth took it after he murdered Lord Savaric."

Athlone felt his grief well up. "Thank you for the message. Please leave us."

Rethe nodded but he did not move. "My lord, Lord Koshyn has called for an immediate reconvening of the council. He asks that you bring Gabria to the council."

"Why?" Gabria asked.

The messenger glanced past her nervously.

"Answer her," Athlone said sharply.

Startled by Athlone's tone, Rethe involuntarily looked at her. Gabria smiled briefly, and he relaxed a little. He and the other Khulinin could not fathom the realities of Gabria's true sex or her ability as a sorceress. She had spent five months in close companionship with them and no one even suspected. The clan owed its life to her and everyone knew it. Unfortunately the debt would not erase her crimes. Rethe had no idea how the clans would react if Gabria returned with Athlone, but he doubted few people would be pleased.

"I don't know," Rethe answered. "I was only told to pass on the message."

Athlone and Gabria looked at one another for a long time, their eyes locked in understanding. Finally, Gabria nodded.

"We will come," Athlone said.

Rethe accepted the dismissal, saluted, and rode away. Athlone watched him go as Gabria slowly began to obliterate their camp and gather their meager belongings.

Athlone stood for a long while, his face blank and his back

sagging. He walked out of camp and disappeared into the hills. Gabria sighed. She knew the grief he was suffering and she, too, grieved for Savaric. Nara lay down, tucking her long legs underneath her and Gabria cuddled into the haven of the mare's warm sides.

Gabria was asleep when Athlone returned at dusk. He gently ran his finger along her jaw. His heart jumped when her eyes opened, filled with love and welcome.

The wer-tain's voice was harsh with grief, but his hands were warm and steady as he wrapped his golden cloak around her shoulders. "I have no horse worthy to give you as a betrothal gift, so I hope you will accept this instead."

Gabria sat for a long time, gently rubbing the gold fabric between her fingers and thinking about her family and her clan. Finally, she replied, "The Corin are dead. It is time to let them rest." She looked up at him and smiled radiantly. "I accept your gift."

Athlone was delighted. The smile she gave him was worth the uncertainty and difficulties of the days ahead. The warrior had no idea if the council would allow him to marry the girl, but now that he was chieftain of the Khulinin, the other lords would have to tread carefully.

"You don't mind being with a known heretic?" Gabria asked. It was the first time either of them had spoken of the subject, and, though she remembered the Khulinin's shocked recognition of his own talent, she was not certain how he was dealing with it.

Athlone smiled faintly. "Boreas did not mind."

Nara snorted and nudged the new chief.

"Did you know," Gabria asked as Athlone settled down beside her, "that Nara is carrying Boreas's foal?"

Athlone's smile grew as wide as the sky.

20

wo days later, just before noon, Nara paused on a high hill overlooking the valley of the Isin River. From the crest, Athlone and Gabria looked down on the army encampment spread out before the defile. Sections of the big camp had been destroyed in the battle, but other sections were teeming with people and three new camps had sprung up displaying the banners of the Murjik, the Shadedron, and the Reidhar clans. Even as Gabria and Athlone watched, an outrider galloped among the tents toward the fortress and clanspeople began to swarm to the edge of the camps.

"They seem to be expecting us," Athlone said dryly.

Gabria nodded. Athlone gently twisted her around to face him and looked into her eyes. "Are you certain you want to do this?"

She leaned against him. "I have nowhere else I want to go. I belong to the clans."

"Even if the council passes a death sentence?"

Gabria smiled nervously. "Then I may change my mind."

Nara trotted down the slope to the valley. By the time she came to the edge of the encampment, a huge crowd had gathered. The clanspeople were strangely silent, for they did not know how to deal with the heretical sorceress who had saved the clans. No one cursed or reviled Gabria, but no one welcomed her, either.

The Hunnuli stopped, her path barred by the throng. Koshyn, Ryne, and Jol of the Murjik walked through the crowd and came to stand in front of Nara.

"Greetings, Lord Athlone," Koshyn said. "I am glad to see you are safe. Greetings to you, Gabria."

Athlone dismounted and gave his hand to Gabria. She slid off the mare and faced the chieftains, her back straight and her eyes proud.

Athlone was about to return the greeting when Lady Tungoli came running through the clanspeople and past the chiefs. She hugged her son fiercely, laughing and crying in turn, then she turned to Gabria and without hesitation embraced the girl with the same joy and relief.

"You did everything you could to save my son," she said softly in Gabria's ear. "Now I will do what I can to save you."

Gabria hugged her with gratitude.

"Athlone," Koshyn said, "word of your coming has forewarned us. If you are willing, we are ready to convene the council in the palace."

"My lords," Tungoli's clear voice rang out. "A favor. Gabria's fate affects all the clans. I ask that this meeting be held in the open so all the clanspeople may attend."

Koshyn looked at Ryne and Jol, then Athlone. They all nodded. "So be it," the Dangari said. "We'll meet in the courtyard." A murmur of approval swept through the watching crowd.

With one hand resting on Nara's neck and the other hand on Athlone's arm, Gabria walked up the stone road to the fortress. The crowd parted before her and followed close behind, as the girl, the Hunnuli, and the chiefs went through the fortress and gathered in the wide courtyard before the general's palace.

The remaining chiefs had already arrived and were waiting on the palace steps. Lord Sha Umar leaned shakily against a pillar, his arm in a sling from his arrow wound. Lord Caurus of the Reidhar and Malech of the Shadedron stood side by side, looking ill at ease, but there was no sign of Medb's old allies, Ferron and Quamar.

Koshyn quickly explained the change of the council to the other lords, and they, too, agreed. Seats were brought for the chiefs and they made themselves comfortable at the top of the steps, under the arched portico.

Athlone held Gabria close for just a moment before he went

to join the lords. The girl stayed at the foot of the steps, her fingers twined in the Hunnuli's mane. Tungoli stayed with her. The other clanspeople crowded into the courtyard until the area was packed.

Lord Koshyn rose. As the oldest, healthiest surviving chieftain of the four triumphant clans, he had assumed some authority the past eight days. He stood now and took control of the council. "Lord Athlone, we welcome you. We are deeply stricken by the death of your father."

Athlone nodded his thanks, for he did not trust himself to speak at that moment. He was still not used to the title of 'lord' or the aching grief that filled him whenever he thought of his father.

Koshyn went on. "I will tell you now what has happened since you left." He gestured to the five other chiefs. "We are all that is left of the original council. Branth has fled, as you know. Lord Ferron killed himself shortly after the battle, and Lord Quamar of the Ferganan has already stepped down. Of the sorcerer's army, the exiles and the mercenaries are either dead or scattered. The Wylfling await the punishment of the council.

"As for the three clans that joined Medb, they did so at the instigation of their lords and they did not fight in the final battle. Only the werods came with the army, their families still wait at the Tir Samod for some word of their fate. If you agree, Athlone, we have decided to suspend their punishment. We believe it is the only way to begin reuniting the clans."

Athlone rose from his seat. "I agree with the council's decision. There has been enough hatred and bloodshed."

Koshyn nodded once, then he looked down at the young woman standing quietly beside her Hunnuli. He was dismayed by the closeness he had seen between Athlone and Gabria. He had no idea what this council would decide, but he did not want Athlone to be forced to kill someone he obviously loved.

"Now we have to face the most difficult decision of all. Gabria, you have saved our clans and our way of life from destruction. For that, we owe you endless gratitude. But in doing so, you used a heretical power that is forbidden on pain of death."

"You have thrown us into quite a quandary," Sha Umar spoke up. "If we follow our laws and put you to death, we bring dishonor on the clans for rejecting our debt of gratitude, but if we ignore our laws and allow you to live, we open the door for any magic-wielder who wants to practice sorcery."

"Perhaps it's time we did," a voice called from the palace. The crowd stirred and muttered among themselves, for everyone recognized the rich voice of Cantrell.

The blind bard walked out of the palace doors accompanied by Piers. Cantrell's step was firm and unhesitating as he came to stand beside Koshyn. "We have tried to ignore magic for two hundred years, and look where our fears took us. The clans were nearly destroyed by a man who abused the arts of sorcery. If our people had learned from their mistakes and regulated sorcery instead of turning their backs on it, this war with Medb would not have happened."

"But magic is a perversion!" a priest shouted from the crowd. He was supported by yells of agreement.

"That is what our ancestors wanted to believe, and they stuffed their lies down our throats in every tale, prayer, and law. But I tell you," Cantrell said as he rose to his full height and spread his hands out to include every person there, "magic is as natural as the air we breathe. It is only as dangerous as the person who wields it. If Medb had not had magic at his use, he would have simply used other weapons to conquer us." The bard pointed to Nara. "Look at the Hunnuli. We all believe in the inherent goodness of such horses. They were gifts to us from Valorian. A Hunnuli nearly killed Medb, yet another stands here beside Gabria. If magic were evil as we have been taught, would the Hunnuli stay with the girl?"

The large crowd began talking and arguing amongst themselves. They had never heard or seen anything like this.

Lord Jol stood up. The old chief was shaken by Cantrell's words, but he did not like change and stubbornly clung to the safety of the laws. "This girl broke clan law!" he shouted, "She impersonated a warrior, joined a werod, attended a council meeting, and claimed herself chieftain. For those crimes alone she should be put to death."

Athlone came to his feet, his face dark with anger. "Those crimes occurred while Gabria was with my clan. As her chieftain, it is *my* responsibility to deal with her punishment. This council need only concern itself with her use of sorcery."

Koshyn nodded in agreement and held up his hands to calm the two men. "Today we only need to decide what to do about Gabria's sorcery. We have to remember," he said with an ironic twist of his mouth, "if we have her put to death, we are killing the last of the Corin. Another great dishonor for our clans."

The lords were quiet for a time, some of them looking at Gabria, others looking anywhere else but at the girl. The onlookers continued debating loudly with each other. Gabria remained still, her stomach twisted in knots. She was terrified of this meeting, but she had known from the moment she broke the Woman of the Marsh's magic that she would have to face the council.

Cantrell took a deep breath and walked with Piers to the edge of the steps. "My lords," the bard said, his voice ringing through the courtyard, "if you kill the girl, Gabria, for using magic, then you shall have to put me to death, too, for I, also, have the talent to use magic."

The noise around the palace abruptly stopped as every person stared at the venerable bard in shock.

Cantrell cocked his head at the silence. "I try not to use my talent, but it inadvertently comes out in my riddles."

Piers looked at the stunned faces around him and said, "My lords, you will have to kill me as well. I, too, have used magic. I do not have the talent to wield it, but I have a stone of healing that works by a magic spell and has healed several people in my clan."

Athlone shook his head. He should have known Piers was mixed up somehow with Gabria and the sorcery. He glanced at the other lords. Lord Jol was slack-jawed and Malech of the Reidhar was looking distressed; Koshyn had a faint smile on his face. Sha Umar simply looked fascinated.

Slowly, Athlone stood up and his movement drew everyone's attention. He motioned toward Cantrell and Piers. "I seem to have a talent to wield magic, too. I have only known for a few days, but in that time I have learned a great deal." He went down a step and held out his hand to Gabria. Proudly she walked up to stand beside him.

"I believe it is time to change the laws," Athlone continued. "Not only to save Gabria, but to save ourselves. Even if we kill her and wash our hands of this incident, another person with the talent will come forward, perhaps to destroy us. For our own survival, we need to learn the ways of magic again and to regulate it. I beg you, lords, change the laws. I do not wish to die, but I will stand with Gabria."

The other six chieftains stared from Piers and Cantrell to Athlone and Gabria. Before they had time to really think, Koshyn drew the lords together and began talking heatedly to them. Lord Jol continually shook his head, and Lord Caurus looked doubtful, but at last they seemed to reach some sort of agreement.

Lord Koshyn stepped forward. He said to Gabria, "I suppose it is too much to demand that you never use your sorcery again."

Gabria held tightly to Athlone's arm, her heart pounding. "My lord, I cannot promise that," she replied, trying to keep her voice steady. "There may come a time when I will need my power. Lord Branth is still missing and the *Book of Matrah* with him. But I will promise this, I will never use magic in any way that will harm the clans. I swear on the honor of the Corin."

The Dangari chief glanced back at the other lords. They merely nodded.

"Then listen to our decision. The council frees you, Gabria, from the punishment of death in gratitude for your courageous rescue of our clans. But the law forbidding magic must stand until such time as the council can decide what to do about this issue. Lord Athlone, you are to be held personally responsible for your actions as well as those of Gabria, Piers, and Cantrell. If at any time they break the laws that are decided upon, they and you will be put to death. Is that acceptable?"

The watching crowd broke out in an uproar of mixed relief and anger. They had no choice but to accept the chieftains' decision, but many of the clanspeople, especially those who had not been involved in the battles with Medb, were not pleased.

But at that moment, Gabria did not care. Athlone swept her up in a joyous embrace and Tungoli ran to embrace them both.

Athlone went up the steps with Gabria and faced Koshyn. The younger chief grinned broadly at them both.

"We accept your decision," Athlone called to all the chiefs. To Koshyn, he said quietly, "Thank you, my friend."

Koshyn's blue eyes twinkled. "Just don't make me regret it." He turned to watch Gabria as she went to embrace Piers and Cantrell. "I can see now the laws must be changed, but it will take a great deal of time and persuasion."

"Thanks to you, we have the time."

"How will you handle Gabria's punishment with the Khulinin?" Koshyn asked curiously.

Athlone grinned. "I will make her marry me."

Koshyn burst out laughing. He clasped Athlone's arm, and the two men went to join the other lords.

*   *   *   *   *

The evening light lingered softly in the sky as Athlone and Gabria walked alone by the Isin River. They followed the grassy banks past the encampments to a place where a burial mound had been built on a small hill overlooking the fortress and the valley.

There had been many dead to mourn after the battle with Medb's army. The bodies of the exiles and mercenaries had been burned and buried without ceremony. Medb's body was burned and dumped in the river. The dead of the clans were buried in a large mound near the fortress. Savaric, though, had been sent to the Hall of the Dead with every honor. His body rested now in the large mound crowned with a ring of spears.

Athlone and Gabria stood by the mound as the quiet twilight dimmed. Overhead, a hawk soared in the cool evening breeze.

"Do you think he was terribly disappointed with me?" Gabria asked, looking up at the spears silhouetted against the sky.

"I doubt it. Surprised, maybe. But he would have been proud of your courage," Athlone replied.

She laid her head back on his shoulder. "Do you suppose he would have put me to death for joining his werod?"

Athlone chuckled. "Father would probably have considered marriage to me punishment enough."

"But what . . ."

He tilted her head up. "Enough questions." Then he gathered her close and kissed her.

High above them, the hawk cried once and swept away into the darkness.

A Short Glossary

THE CLANS	CHIEFTAIN	CLOAK COLOR
Corin	Dathlar	Red
Khulinin	Savaric	Gold
Geldring	Branth	Green
Wylfling	Medb	Brown
Dangari	Koshyn	Indigo
Shadedron	Malech	Black
Reidhar	Caurus	Yellow
Amnok	Ferron	Gray
Murjik	Jol	Purple
Bahedin	Babur/Ryne	Orange
Jahanan	Sha Umar	Maroon
Ferganan	Quamar	Light Blue

Hearthguard: The chieftain's personal bodyguards. These men are the elite warriors of the clan and are honored with this position for their bravery, skill, and loyalty.

Herd-master: The man responsible for the health, breeding, and well-being of the horse herds.

Holdings: Land granted to a clan for its use while in winter camp.

Outriders: Those werod riders who guard the herds and the camp or act as scouts.

Treld: A clan's permanent winter camp.

Weir-geld: Recompense paid to the family of a murdered person in the form of gold or livestock, or by death in a personal duel.

Werod: The fighting body of a clan. Although all men are required to learn the rudiments of fighting, only those who pass certain tests make up the werod.

Wer-tain: The commander of the werod. These men are second only to the chieftain in authority.

FORGOTTEN REALMS

FANTASY ADVENTURE

THE FINDER'S STONE
TRILOGY

Sequel to *Azure Bonds*!

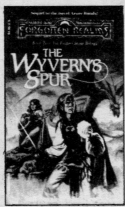

THE WYVERN'S SPUR

Kate Novak and Jeff Grubb

**The family heirloom of the Wyvernspur clan is missing. A
mysterious murderer stalks the streets of Immersea. It is up
to the youngest scion of the Wyvernspur family, Giogioni,
aided by the "famous" halfling bard, Olive Ruskettle, to
solve these mysteries. However, there are a few things in
their way. Giogioni is renowned for being a fool, and the
barely competent Olive has been turned into a burro! Available in March.**

DRAGONLANCE® *Preludes*

Darkness and Light
Paul Thompson and Tonya Carter

Darkness and Light tells of the time
Sturm and Kitiara spent traveling
together before the fated meeting at the
Inn of the Last Home. Accepting a ride
on a gnomish flying vessel, they end up
on Lunitari during a war. Eventually
escaping, the two separate over ethics.

Kendermore
Mary L. Kirchoff

A bounty hunter charges Tasslehoff
Burrfoot with violating the kender laws of
prearranged marriage. To ensure his
return, Kendermore's council has his
Uncle Trapspringer prisoner. Tas meets
the last woolly mammoth and an alche-
mist who pickles one of everything,
including kender!

Brothers Majere
Kevin Stein

Much to Raistlin's irritation, Caramon
accepts a job for both of them: they
must solve the mystery of a village's
missing cats. The search leads to
murder, a thief who is not all that he
appears, and a foe who is not what
Caramon and Raistlin expect.

DragonLance Saga

PRELUDES II

RIVERWIND, THE PLAINSMAN
Paul B. Thompson & Tonya R. Carter

To prove himself worthy of Goldmoon, Riverwind is sent on an impossible quest: Find evidence of the true gods. With an eccentric soothsayer Riverwind falls down a magical shaft--and alights in a world of slavery and rebellion. Available in March 1990.

FLINT, THE KING
Mary Kirchoff & Douglas Niles

Flint returns to his boyhood village and finds it a boomtown. He learns that the prosperity comes from a false alliance and is pushed to his death. Saved by gully dwarves and made their reluctant monarch, Flint unites them as his only chance to stop the agents of the Dark Queen. Available in July 1990.

TANIS, THE SHADOW YEARS
Barbara Siegel & Scott Siegel

Tanis Half-Elven once disappeared in the mountains near Solace. He returned changed, ennobled--and with a secret. Tanis becomes a traveler in a dying mage's memory, journeying into the past to fight a battle against time itself. Available in November 1990.

FORGOTTEN REALMS
FANTASY ADVENTURE

EMPIRES TRILOGY

HORSELORDS
David Cook

Between the western Realms and Kara-Tur lies a vast, unexplored domain. The "civilized" people of the Realms have given little notice to these nomadic barbarians. Now, a mighty leader has united these wild horsemen into an army powerful enough to challenge the world. First, they turn to Kara-Tur. Available in May.

DRAGONWALL
Troy Denning

The barbarian horsemen have breached the Dragonwall and now threaten the oriental lands of Kara-Tur. Shou Lung's only hope lies with a general descended from the barbarians, and whose wife must fight the imperial court if her husband is to retain his command. Available in August.

CRUSADE
James Lowder

The barbarian army has turned its sights on the western Realms. Only King Azoun has the strength to forge an army to challenge the horsemen. But Azoun had not reckoned that the price of saving the west might be the life of his beloved daughter. Available in January 1991.

FORGOTTEN REALMS

FANTASY ADVENTURE

THE MAZTICA TRILOGY

Douglas Niles

IRONHELM

A slave girl learns of a great destiny laid upon her by the gods themselves. And across the sea, a legion of skilled mercenaries sails west to discover a land of primitive savagery mixed with high culture. Under the banner of their vigilant god the legion claims these lands for itself. And only as Erix sees her land invaded is her destiny revealed. Available in April.

VIPERHAND

The God of War feasts upon chaos while the desperate lovers, Erix and Halloran, strive to escape the waves of catastrophe sweeping Maztica. Each is forced into a choice of historical proportion and deeply personal emotion. The destruction of the fabulously wealthy continent of Maztica looms on the horizon. Available in October.

COMING IN EARLY 1991!

FEATHERED DRAGON

The conclusion!

FORGOTTEN REALMS
FANTASY ADVENTURE

Pool of Radiance

James M. Ward
Jane Cooper Hong

A possessed dragon commands the undead armies of Valhingen Graveyard and the beasts from the ruins near Phlan. Desperate, a spellcaster, a ranger thief, and a cleric join forces to deliver Phlan and the entire Moonsea region from the dark possession of evil incarnate ...Tyranthraxus.

NOW AN AWARD-WINNING SSI COMPUTER GAME, TOO!